Thank you for choosing a D K Girl story.
I'd also like to offer you a free e-book, a dystopian novella set in a world where death is precious, and life is never-ending.

Scan the QR code to download your e-book copy of Ending Altered.

(Link will take you to StoryOrigin to download)

'A well written gay dystopian story! Something a bit different. Genetically evolved humans, the new top of the feeding chain. Good short read!'
- Goodreads review

'The author truly created a world that is unpredictable, intense and hauntingly human.' -Goodreads review

The Death Wish

Pitch & Sickle

Book Eight

D K GIRL

CHAPTER 1

Pendle Hill, with all its history and horror, lay a day, and one infuriating night, behind them. Pitch adjusted his seat on Lalassu's broad back, scowling over at Silas whose dull brown wool cape matched his equally dull, brown gelding. The horse was a stolen addition to their party, thanks to Tyvain who had willingly gone along with the ankou's ridiculous decision that it was safer for Pitch to ride alone upon Lalassu. Silas claimed some nonsense about being better able to notice an oncoming threat; though Pitch suspected part of the issue was more to do with how his arse rubbed against the ankou as they rode. Still, Silas would not hear a word of daemonic insistence that Pitch was capable of looking after himself. Silas insisted on playing sombre bodyguard.

So yesterday some poor bastard would have gone to set out for his afternoon ride only to himself without a mount, and a small pouch of coins in exchange for his troubles.

'I can definitely see a greater sway in that poor horse's back, with all the weight it carries, Silas.'

The ankou pulled from his thoughts with a smile. 'Is that so? I think he is doing most admirably.'

'Well you would, because you can't see how much shorter its legs have become since you mounted it.'

Silas laughed, but it was a heavy sound, as though he did not have the strength to shift his ribs. The cape that Isaac had given him certainly didn't do the ankou's complexion any favours, but its unflattering colour could not be entirely blamed for making him appear so drained. In the weakness of the morning light Silas was pale, and looked altogether as exhausted as Pitch himself felt. The night in a gods-forsaken barn had done neither of them any favours at all.

According to Jane, it had not been a barn, thank you very much, but a very simple country house with beds enough for all. Pitch was told to appreciate the fact no owners were about, so none of their tired party had to bother with any enchantments or sweet talk to secure accommodations. True, no one had the energy for such things, but that was not to say Pitch had forgone hope of a lazy tumble between silk sheets with Silas. No matter how badly his body ached—and gods it fucking ached with unpleasant pains—he was hungry for at least a minute alone with the ankou.

Evidently, one minute was far too much to ask.

The residence had been made for a family of Gilmore-esque dwellers, apparently. The beds were single and tiny, barely able to accommodate Silas by himself, let alone with company. They indulged in some heavy petting, a decent rub to tide them over, but Silas had not done well with knowing the rest of the group was just a paper-thin wall away. He'd preferred to keep to kisses, which Pitch agreed to endure. But, besides all that, Pitch had admitted to himself with great ire, that they were both too fucking exhausted for fucking.

From behind, a snort came from one of the black geldings pulling the carriage. Silas's attention darted there, that pained expression appearing on his face again.

'Jane will inform us if Sybilla needs anything,' Pitch said. 'We can't go much slower or we shall be at a halt.'

'I know…but she is being most stubborn in continuing on with us. I fear it is far too taxing on her.'

'And I fear you shall end up with a black eye, if you keep fussing over her as you do. Not everyone is as tolerant of your coddling as I am, you know.'

As Pitch had hoped, that shifted Silas's concerns from the angel, and delivered a more enthusiastic smile. 'You are indeed so very patient with me, my dearest.'

'Don't you forget it.'

The journey away from the cockaigne appeared meandering, taking a westward turn at first, then they kept north. Tyvain, Jane, Sybilla and the simurgh, with Scarlet playing attentive nursemaid as per Lucifer's instructions, all travelled in the carriage. Jane refused to allow much of a pace; citing Sybilla too poorly to manage a lot of jolting about. The journey was slow, but an hour ago Isaac informed them, in his grumpy way, that they had reached the outskirts of the Yorkshire Dales.

'Bloody rollin' hills. Enough to make a man seasick,' he'd mumbled into his scarves.

But of course, the ankou had a very different opinion.

'Isn't this countryside astounding, Pitch?' Silas said, his voice deep and growling. 'How I would love to see these hills in the springtime. I dare say they would challenge your eyes for beauty, with their hue of green.'

'Well, they could try, I suppose.' Pitch was trying very hard to be astonished at the lay of the land, at how breathtaking it all was, but in truth he was more enamoured by the new and stirring timbre of Silas's voice. Depths that made it rumble in his chest, and caused Pitch's nerves to thrill; and other parts of him to protest at how neglected they felt. 'I could do with some springtime right now. The temperature has plummeted, don't you think? Or perhaps I am simply noticing it more, now that I've been abandoned alone on horseback.'

Silas cast him an indulgent grin. 'I imagine that cloak is as warm and cosy as it looks, not to mention you are a fire daemon, my darling. And I know for certain your flames are warming you nicely. You were like a stovepipe to hold onto.'

Pitch touched at the rather sublime fuchsia cloak that Tyvain had won in a bet at the town they had stopped in to take some lunch the previous day. Well, she insisted it had been won, but Pitch suspected it too was the result of sticky fingers. Along with the soothsayer being sick and tired of hearing Pitch complain about his borrowed attire from Isaac. 'Is that why you are punishing that poor horse and not riding with me? If I was too hot for you, I can remedy that.'

Silas chuckled. 'It was not your flame's heat I found difficult to bear.'

Was he a little rosier in the cheeks? 'My good fellow, were you having trouble keeping your thoughts pure, as you rode up against me?'

Definitely rosier in the cheeks now. Pitch's suspicions about the motive behind separate horses had been spot on. 'You know I was. And it was inordinately uncomfortable for me. For you as well, I dare say. What with all the...with all the....'

Pitch grinned. 'With all the what, sweet Silas?'

'Stop it.'

'But I don't understand. With all the what?'

Silas's glare was only mildly threatening. 'Stiffness,' he hissed. 'The ruddy great pillar I had because you insisted on twisting about so.'

Oh, this was a delightful game. 'Did you grow hard? I did wonder at that poking in my back, I thought it felt a little bigger than your thumb.'

Silas shook his head, glancing back to where the carriage had drawn closer. 'Will you stop it. Isaac shall hear.'

'I can already bloody hear ya,' the coachman called, 'and I'll be havin' nightmares if ya don't damn well shut up.'

'Oh come now, don't pretend you won't think of this when you next fist yourself,' Pitch said. 'I know you shall picture me, pressed beneath this mammoth of a man, legs and arse wide open. Jealous, and rightly so.'

'Fucking tosser.' Isaac flicked the reins, urging the geldings into a faster walk. Silas and Pitch pulled aside quickly, lest they be run off the road.

Phillipa, who was perched on the roof of her beloved coach, nearly sputtered out her ghostly innards as she tried very hard not to laugh aloud.

'Ain't funny,' Isaac shouted.

'It is a little,' the spectre returned.

With the back of the carriage now in view, Silas heaved a great sigh.

'Pitch, you are atrocious. That was very unkind, and hugely embarrassing.' He scolded gently, and, great gods of Arcadia, Pitch nearly swooned right off the mare. The ankou's baritone was positively sinful. He had emerged from the wreckage of the cockaigne an absolute delight to listen to, with a commanding tenor in his voice that had been absent before.

'I promise I'll behave myself if you ride with me again.'

'I do not trust that promise in the slightest. Besides, a distraction, such as you are, my dear, is ill-advised. We need to keep our wits about us still, no matter how decisive our victories in the cockaigne.'

Pitch sobered at that. 'You do know how to ruin a mood.'

Silas edged his horse closer, reaching for Pitch. But he was no longer feeling quite so bawdy and jovial and tried to urge Lalassu away. Of course, the bloody Pale Horse betrayed him, shifting to where Silas was within reach. Enough so to run his hand up Pitch's back.

'That's not my intention, you know that. I am going a little out of my mind not being able to hold you. If you had any idea how wonderful you look in that magnificent cloak, what that colour does for your complexion...well, you'd know it is torturous not to be closer to you right now.'

Pitch was not the swooning type, not at all. But that voice...and the sickeningly sweet words, the sincerity they held–and being so damned tired he was ready to cry with exhaustion–had him clutching at Lalassu's mane, lest he fall off the damned horse. Silas's saddle creaked as he leaned in, and Pitch did likewise. They were but an inch from a kiss when the soothsayer ruined what pitiful closeness they could find.

'You're goin' too fast, ya bastard. What are we runnin' from?' she shouted, hanging her head out one of the carriage windows. She was a quick study, finding Pitch and Silas in their respective leans. 'Oh feck, forget I asked. Ride on.'

She slipped back inside. Silas kept on, regardless of the interruption, and brushed his lips against Pitch's. But his damned horse was no ally, discomforted at being so close to Lalassu, who was a decent few hands taller, and much wider of girth. The brown horse side-stepped, pulling Silas out of reach.

He groaned with dissatisfaction. 'When we stop for lunch,' he declared. 'You and I shall go off on our own, and continue this. I swear to you.' He nodded his head towards the Pale Horse. 'Do you hear that, Lalassu? And we shall take our time. Send word to Sanu that we may be a few hours later than planned.'

His attempt at lightheartedness fell short, and a look passed between them that Pitch understood well. They did not yet know where Lalassu guided them, but they knew this to be the final journey well enough.

Silas's gentle smile hurt to look at, and Pitch turned away, nudging at Lalassu's sides, sending the mare slightly ahead of Silas and his steed.

They rode on, keeping the horses at a walk behind the carriage. Lalassu showed no impetus to pass them, and considering she was the only one who knew their way, Pitch made no attempt to guide her. After a while Silas took up humming, a quiet contented melody that was almost as pleasing to listen to as his growling voice. It was lulling, and soothing; and gave Pitch a strange sense of being close to the ankou, which he sank into greedily.

He had no idea he'd dozed off until he was jerking awake, arms flailing, torn from a dream where he'd been drowning in pastel colours, and feathers. So many fucking feathers, choking him, filling his belly where the emptiness left a wide open space to fill. His arms had been leaden; raising them even fractionally was a mammoth effort, and when he finally managed it, all he saw was a great spanning wing of lavender and subtle peach.

He coughed, clutching at his throat.

'There now, you're safe, just a dream.' Silas rode right alongside him, with one hand braced to Pitch's shoulder. Lalassu's mane covered Pitch's legs and lap ensuring a fall had never been a concern. 'You fell asleep rather quickly.'

Another few coughs and Pitch got a handle on things. His throat loosened, and he blinked himself back into reality. 'Where is the simurgh?' he said, hoarsely.

'In the carriage, with Scarlet, and the others. It has not stirred.' It had not done so since leaving Newchurch, slumbering in a sort of hibernated state. 'Is there something wrong?'

Pitch shook his head, fully awake now, and feeling a bit of a ninny for the wild awakening. 'Keep on. It was a stupid dream, that's all. I've not slept in what feels like several decades, I suppose there are bound to be repercussions.'

'You can speak to me freely, you know that, don't you? If it helps to talk of what you've endured...'

Not so many months ago Pitch would have launched into whole-hearted ridicule and derision at that. Ranting about how he did not need anyone to lean upon. He still did not like the idea of using anyone as a crutch, but then, Silas was not just *anyone*.

'Perhaps in time,' he said, staring at the carriage, a few horse-lengths ahead of them still. 'But it truly was just a dream. I think it a remnant of being restrained for so long.'

'Very well, consider the offer always open.' Silas squeezed his shoulder gently, and let go.

'What I truly need, what we both need,' Pitch said, 'is a decent wash, and a visit to the finest tailor in the dales.'

'Oh, bloody hell, yes. And a dressmaker who can sew up a corset for you,' Silas added. 'Christ, what I would not do to see you caught up tight in whalebone and lace.' He made a small, irritated sound. 'Sorry. You have just spoken of being restrained and –'

'Gods, there is no comparison, take back that apology at once.' Pitch scowled. 'I would like nothing more than to have you bind me tight. But I think satin, rather than lace, what say you?'

'I say I'll be demanding we stop at the next damned town and taken straight to their seamstress.' Silas practically glowed with delight. 'What shade do you think? I'm partial to green of course.'

Pitch hiccoughed a laugh, his ribs protesting distantly. 'Of course. So I hope you shall not be disappointed if I say peach quite takes my fancy.'

They carried on in that vein a while, inane, silly talk that was like a balm to the soul. Both smiling, laughing, ignoring the bruises and cuts and hurt of the cockaigne. They spoke as though this quest was all but over, the worst of it left behind in the UnSeelie Court's realm. But Pitch knew Silas was likely doing just as he was; pretending each step they took through the scenic countryside was a mere joy ride, and not the blasted funerary procession it likely was.

Lalassu jolted him from his dangerously melancholic thoughts with a turn of foot, a sudden lurch into a trot on the widened road that brought them up alongside the carriage.

'Bloody horse,' Pitch cursed as he struggled to find his rhythm.

Isaac slowed the carriage. 'What's going on?'

'Buggered if I know,' Pitch grunted.

But the answer was quite obvious just a moment later.

The Pale Horse threw up her head, so much so that Pitch glimpsed the velvet tip of her nose before she lowered her snout once more. Her mane lifted, and the weaving began. The intricacies of the design spread themselves out, the fanciest he'd seen the mare create thus far; a narrow building, squat and rough in design, two storeys, that seemed to sit directly on top of the arch of a bridge.

'What is that supposed to be?' He frowned. 'Silas, decipher your horse, will you?'

But it was Isaac who spoke up first. 'I know that place.'

'You know what that tangle of horsehair and fleas shows us?'

Lalassu snorted, and Isaac scowled. 'That's Bridge House at Amble-side. We're headed for the Lake District.'

Pitch glanced back at Silas. 'It does not sound like your favourite kind of place, my dear.'

'I dare say I've visited far worse,' Silas said, giving Pitch a grim, tired smile. 'Isaac, how far, do you think?'

'I reckon we've got a couple of hours ahead, a little more perhaps. We will be there well before sundown.'

'Praise the feckin' saints,' Tyvain called out. And this time even Jane was relieved enough to join in.

'Now that is news to my ears.' The elemental leaned out the window. 'Sybilla really needs to be lying down, this bumping about is doing her no good.'

'Don't be using me as your excuse when it's your arse you're worrying about.'

'It's my boobies, if you must know. A lady can only take so much jiggling about.'

Sybilla laughed, and though it was weak, and every bit as exhausted as Pitch felt, he couldn't help but relish hearing the Valkyrie's amusement.

Her injuries—terrible burns—were a shocking sight to behold. The attack that Pitch had believed killed her, had done awful damage. It was an absolute miracle that she had survived the strike of Gabriel's halo. Silas had been oddly reluctant to speak of the circumstances in any detail, saying only that they'd talk of it when he was certain Sybilla was not in earshot. Regardless, it was clear that her efforts to save both he and Silas at the churchyard had taxed her terribly. Pitch's thoughts went to the Dullahan, too. Another who had gone to great lengths to rescue them.

Silas had been right in trusting him, so it turned out.

'Onward we go then, let's not tarry,' Phillipa declared, joining Isaac on the driver's seat, much to his teeth-grinding annoyance.

'Watch yourself, ghoul.'

'How dare you, sir. I am a spectre.'

'You're a boil on my arse. Good thing Ambleside's got a darn decent alehouse, is all's I'll say.'

Isaac clucked his tongue at the pair, and the horses leaned into their braces, working into a brisk walk that took them away, leaving Silas and Pitch to watch their progress.

Neither of them made move to follow.

Beneath the rumble and rattle of the carriage Silas said, 'Do you think Ambleside is where the Sanctuary is, so close to the cockaigne all this time?' He stopped short of asking Pitch if he recalled the place; a good thing, for the answer would have been curt, and sharp and unfairly hurtful.

Pitch shrugged, running his hand over Lalassu's waterfall of a mane, which was now returned to its long, uncomplicated lengths. 'If we do not believe anything is possible by now, Sickle, then more the fools we are. But it would certainly seem odd.'

Silas hummed his agreement, and still they remained unmoving. Just staring ahead, with the swish of the brown horse's tail all that disturbed the silence. The day was cool, as all tended to be in December; a fire would be welcome, as would a warm meal and a soft bed full of hardened ankou.

But still, the reins remained loose in his hands. 'Do you suppose we could walk a while?'

Silas did not falter. 'Of course. I'd relish the chance to stretch my legs. There is no great rush.'

Which was a lie, of course, and they both knew it, but they dismounted nonetheless, and walked along together; secluded between the horses, as the sun began its lazy winter rise.

CHAPTER 2

The village of Ambleside came into view precisely two hours and fifteen minutes later, as the day reached mid-morning and all the mist had vanished from distant hills.

They travelled along Stockghyll Lane, a narrow but neatly compacted roadway that eventually brought them alongside the River Rothay. Not so great or wide a river, but its waters sparkled with the coolness of the month, and the gurgling over smoothed rocks could be heard despite the clunk of carriage wheels. All geographical details were supplied by the grunting Isaac, whose clear resentment of them all was superseded by his unexpectedly prideful desire to enlighten them about their surrounds.

'Caught a decent trout or two in those waters.' Isaac spoke with the nearest Silas had heard to enthusiasm. 'And Beatrice cooked them up nicely and served them with an apple mash a man could grow well addicted to.'

Silas glanced at Tyvain who leaned out the carriage window. She gave him a look that told him she was equally bemused to hear the normally sullen Isaac divulging details of what amounted to a life beyond his carriage seat.

'Ya have a taste for Beatrice's mash then, eh?' Tyvain said. 'Ya sly dog, didn't think ya had it in ya.'

'You don't know anything about me, hag.'

And no one could argue with that.

Ambleside was a quaint village of mostly slate stone houses, interspersed with the distinctive white stucco and tarred beams of several Tudor homes. As they entered into the village proper they came upon the particularly curious structure that Lalassu had weaved in her mane. A small bridge spanned a narrow section of the river, and upon it sat a tiny, two storey building of stone, with a rather worse-for-wear roof.

'There's Bridge House, built over the water so as to avoid paying land taxes.' Isaac's grunt was approving. 'Been everything from an apple store, to counting rooms for the local mills, a weavers, and last time I was through here, a cobbler had set up shop there.'

Pitch jerked to attention. 'A cobbler? Lalassu, halt at once.'

He swung his leg over her neck, dismounting in one fluid movement.

'Whatever are you doing?' Silas said.

Pitch made a grand flourish towards his feet. 'Do you see those atrocities you all deign to call boots? A size too small and mouse-nibbled at the toe on the right? I'm going to bang on that man's door this instant and have him make me a brand new pair.'

Isaac had provided Silas and Pitch with coats, but he'd been unable to produce a pair of boots for Pitch's bare feet. That had involved sneaky work on Jane's part. Phillipa had scouted the village of Newchurch for sign of any boots left on doorsteps. With the morning being so early they'd been in luck, and the air elemental had used a brisk breeze to seconder a brown leather pair. Pitch had been unhappy instantly, of course, for the fit was tight and the colour not one he'd prefer, but the air was cold enough to redden everyone's noses and Silas had pressed him to wear them. Fire daemon, or no.

Now Pitch was striding off in those very same boots, putting on quite the exaggerated show of being in discomfort. He'd not limped this badly even when his troublesome hip was at its worst. Silas watched him with an exasperated smile.

'What makes you think we have time for a cobbler to make you a pair of boots?' Jane stood by the riverbank, her breeze stirring the pussywillow that grew there. 'That's a day's work.'

'What makes you think I want boots? I shall have the finest shoes, and we'll stay for as long as it will take him.' Pitch called over his shoulder, the glorious fuchsia cloak fluttering around him. 'The lake's been there for a long while, it can wait a day more.'

Jane looked to Silas, who shrugged. 'I have no intention of getting between him and a decent pair of shoes.' And the village looked pretty as a picture...indeed, *felt* lovely as one too. For the first time since they'd set out from Pendle Hill his prickling of unease had subdued itself enough to allow him to consider taking a proper rest. Silas would breathe easier once he'd seen Charlie's face again, but Lalassu, and indeed, the scythe passed on no sense of urgency. The mare was calm, the blades quiet. He dared listen to that inner sense that told him...they were safe here.

That this was a different type of Sanctuary than the one they sought, but a sanctuary nonetheless.

A reward, perhaps, for all they'd done to ensure the survival of the Cultivation? Silas clutched at the small hope as though it were the crown jewels. But he was not a fool. He could only pretend to be one, and that would suffice for now. The village was far too pleasant for darker thoughts.

'Does anyone have any coin?' Pitch had halted his stomp across the way, and began to backtrack. 'I'd rather not pay the man with bodily favours, I shouldn't think you'd like that much, would you, Sickle?'

Silas would muster every lost soul from miles around to terrify the cobbler, if he so much as laid a finger on the daemon. Outwardly though, he faked a yawn and flicked a hand. 'You are your own man, Mr Astaroth. I stake no exclusive claim to you.' But good god he'd like to. 'You are a free man with freedom of choice.' That much at least was no lie.

Pitch burst into a gale of laughter, one tinged with surprise as much as mirth. 'Truly? So what you're saying is you are done with me.' His pout should be outlawed.

'Of course I'm not saying that.'

'Could ya blame him if he was though, Astaroth?' Tyvain's chesty laughter rang out. 'You're a handful.'

'Rather more than a handful, I assure you.'

'No one wants ta hear it, ya great plod,' Tyvain retorted.

As they debated where to take accommodations, with Isaac insistent that there was but one suitable public house, the Golden Rule, with a stout to sell your mother for, Silas's thoughts drifted.

He was tired, gravely so. Drained to the very core. Which was concerning, and irritating. Now was not the time to be anything but Pitch's greatest protector. They were so near to the end.

'Silas?' Pitch's voice, close now, startled Silas. 'Is everything all right? Do you sense something untoward?'

Silas hadn't realised that his horse had stopped moving, or that he had dug his fingers into its mane, clutching at the strands. He looked down at Pitch, the prince's eyes the most astonishing shade of green with the winter afternoon light.

'Everything is fine,' he said, a little weakly.

'No teratisms about?'

'No, no. Nothing like that.' There was nothing upon the air to disturb his senses, certainly no Blight-ridden souls. The scythes were silent upon his finger. He ran the pad of his thumb over the metal. 'This is a quiet place. I think...I think we are safe here.'

'We are.' Pitch nodded, watching Isaac drive the carriage on. 'Everything is...quieter here. Is it not?'

'Very much so.'

Jane meandered along the riverside, the stirring of air amongst the pussy-willow billowing out behind her like an invisible gown. She was smiling, her hand lifted to where tiny sparrows fluttered about her, as though in some tittering conversation with the air elemental. Jane laughed, and Silas realised that was exactly what was happening.

Pitch stretched to lay his hand upon Silas's thigh. 'But you're still frowning a little. You're not truly worried about the cobbler now, are you?' The light seemed to brighten when Pitch smiled in that way, lop-sided, entirely charming.

Silas laughed, rather self-consciously. 'No, no. Besides, I meant what I said, I have no claim on you.'

Pitch's hand slid higher up Silas's thigh, fingertips delving at the crease of his hip. 'I think we both know that is not the case.' The blood roared in Silas's ears, and he knew his blush ferocious. 'Shall we carry on then? The shoes can wait, if I'm honest. I don't know about you but I'm desperate to get out of the horrid clothes that lie beneath this cloak.' He brushed his hand down the length of Silas's leg. 'Are you with me, Sickle?'

'I am.' Come what may.

'Good. Whatever time is to be had here, I dare say it will be short. Best we make the most of it.'

Silas's desirous haze quickly cleared. 'I wish it were not so.'

'As do I.' Pitch leaned his full weight against Silas's lower leg. He smiled again but it was more strained. 'But all things have an end, do they not? And unless the Hag has been regaling you with details of our future, neither of us know what that end shall look like.'

He stepped away, tilting his head down so that his hair covered his face, and whatever expression it held.

Silas hurried to dismount, his legs unsteady with the sudden grounding. 'Tyvain has told me nothing, and I would share it with you if she had.'

'Would you though?' Pitch studied him hard. 'If what she had to say was not pleasant, would you tell me?'

'Pitch, what is this about?'

He was aware of being watched, glances from passing villagers as he stood close to Pitch.

'I'm simply curious, that's all. We deliver the simurgh to the Sanctuary, then what?' As he spoke his hand lifted to his belly, where his fingers moved against the bright colour of his cloak. 'This godsforsaken task has been all-consuming, and seemed, quite frankly, impossible...until now. We have survived this far. I just wonder...' He darted his tongue over his lips. 'I wonder if, perhaps, that silly idea of yours about the cottage in a deep dark woods might need some further considerations?'

Silas's chest tightened to hear the fragile hope in Pitch's words.

'I'm not sure that...' Silas cleared his throat, and toyed with the loose reins. 'I'm not sure that I said dark woods...'

'You definitely said woods.'

'Yes, but not dark. Unless that's what you'd prefer?'

'Me? The one who was cast into an abaddon, the very definition of darkness?' A dim topic, but the prince was not sullen when he spoke, jesting with a lightness that had Silas breathing easier.

'Then we agree the woods shall not be dark in the slightest. In fact I think we shall build this cottage in a glade, somewhere the light always falls upon it.'

'Won't that be a tad annoying when it comes time to sleep?'

'It won't be light at night.'

'You said the light always falls –'

Silas sighed. 'During the day, of course.'

Pitch bit at the corner of his lip, his grin absolutely wicked. Silas swept an arm about his waist, pulling him in. 'You are truly sent to try me. I shall make you quite sorry for it later on.'

That, to his great satisfaction, drew a gasp from the daemon, emerald eyes widening. 'Mr Mercer, you scoundrel, do not tease me so. You had me all in a lather last night but then fell asleep with my blue balls in your hand.'

'A lie!' Silas leaned in very close, careful to share his words with Pitch alone. 'It was your cock in my hand. And those balls were quite empty, I assure you, though it makes sense you don't recall as I think you were asleep before you finished spilling over me.'

'That is a filthy mouth you have there, Mr Mercer.'

'Isn't it? I've had a wonderful teacher,' A part of Silas was dying a silent death at being so horrifyingly forward, but good god it was bracing, and wondrously arousing to see it cause Pitch's eyes to shine. 'I shall show you a few other things he taught me, once we are alone.'

Pitch's breath quickened, his chin tilting up, vibrant pink lips, with scant hint of old cuts and bruises, parting.

'We're alone enough here.'

Silas lowered his head, deciding the brown horse was shielding them well enough to seek out a very brazen kiss in the middle of the village thoroughfare. Lalassu nickered, and a small voice spoke up.

'That's the prettiest horse I ever did see, sirs. Can I pat her?'

With some confusion, and much regret, Silas lifted his head.

A thin chap with a dirty face and terrible scar upon his chin, along with an unfortunate cross-eyed gaze, stood nearby, with a tarnished pail in hand. He held his free hand lifted, fingers twitching, as though he fought an urge to touch at Lalassu before permission was received.

The mare took a step forward, a short burst of air from her nostrils coming before she nudged at the man's pail. Silas's horse pulled at the reins, seeking to join her, straining his muzzle towards the apparent treats. The man giggled, and it was such a childish sound that Silas found himself paying more attention to the chap. He was actually far younger than Silas had supposed, there under the grime on his cheeks.

'They can smell the apple cores I just gave to the pigs.' He dipped his hand into the pail, and pulled out the sorry remnants of what once might have been an apple. 'That's all I've got left. But if your master and his pretty friend want to take some rooms at my Pa's place, I can get you all the apples your heart desires.'

Pitch nudged Silas. 'Did you hear that? He says I am pretty. He's not as dull-headed as he looks.'

The boy sniffed, his nose wet and running once more. 'My name is Herbert, mister. And just cause you have beauty, don't mean you can be nasty to those of us who don't. My Pa says kindness don't cost nothin'.'

Pitch nearly choked on his own spittle, and it was all Silas could do to keep himself from laughing.

'Very wise words, young man,' Silas said, which earned him a vicious poke in the side, one he ignored. 'Your father has done well by you.'

'Will you come stay then?' Herbert was utterly unperturbed by the unhappy daemon, which Silas found both amusing, and quite courageous. 'I'm the best groom in the village, everyone will tell you. Your horses will gleam after I'm done with brushing them down. And we ain't half as expensive as the Rule.'

'Go away, Harry.' Pitch tried to reach for Lalassu's dangling reins but the mare tilted her head.

'It's Herbert.'

'I don't care.'

'Pitch.'

'Silas?'

'Be nice.' With Pitch glowering but holding his tongue, Silas turned his attention to the young man once more. Lalassu was enjoying a scratch behind her ear, her eyelid heavy, her head lowered so the youth could reach the spot. 'Thank you, Herbert, but our companions are likely already at the Golden Rule, arranging rooms.'

'You'd do better at my Pa's place. And he and my Uncle Samuel would be mighty happy to be hosting fellas just the same as them.'

'Like us? I doubt very much they are the same at all,' Pitch scowled. 'What the blazes are you on about?'

'It's all right, you two together. I think its fine, and really nice. Don't matter the shape our affectamations come in. That's what my pa says.'

'Do you mean affections?' Silas asked, amused.

The lad nodded vigorously. 'That's the word.'

'Oh good gods, this trite nonsense again,' Pitch groaned. 'The sooner you purebreds decide to just fuck whoever you like and make no bones about it, the better, I say.'

'Pitch,' Silas glared. 'He's a child.'

'Who knows exactly what I'm talking about, thanks to Pa and Uncle Samuel.'

'My name is Herbert, and Pa says it's best I don't be doing any forn-imications just yet, on account of being barely fifteen summers.'

'Your father is a monster,' Pitch exclaimed. 'It's called fornication, and you'd best get out there and get to it, boy. Dip that wick at once. To hell with Pappa.'

Silas grabbed Pitch's arm. 'Will you stop?' He sought to sound stern but saw how much Pitch was enjoying the tease, the way a food connoisseur enjoyed dining in a fine restaurant. His impish happiness was a delight.

'I'm trying to save Harold's life, Silas.'

'My name's Herbert. Do you really think I should be doing that, mister?' he asked, another wet sniff coming. 'The unholy things?'

'The more unholy the better.'

'Absolutely not, young man.' Silas decided the teasing must end.

The young fellow was simple, a true innocent, and Silas suspected his father was protecting him from the very things Pitch sought to encourage.

'Sheer cruelty,' Pitch huffed. 'Of the highest order, depriving Herman of bodily delights.'

'My name's Herbert.'

'I still do not care.'

'But I do. I like my name.' The boy's bravery had Silas's thoughts shifting to Charlie with a pang. 'And I'm real good with horses, and my Pa has the nicest inn you ever did see. It's called the Churchill. That's our name.'

'Herbert tells you the truth. Always does. The Churchill is a right welcoming place.' A comely woman with the most astonishing brunette curls called out from the steps of a nearby residence, where she'd seated herself with a half-woven basket, preparing to finish the task. 'But don't tell Paul at the Rule I'm taking any sides, there's no arguing his whisky is the cream of the crop in Ambleside.'

Pitch sucked in a breath. 'Fuck the inn, Silas.'

'Pitch, language.'

'He'll hear a lot worse than that if you keep me from a whisky a moment longer. The others are probably already halfway into their cups by now. Let's go.'

He reached for Lalassu's dangling reins again, but again the mare denied him, shifting her bulk so he ended up catching his fingers on her stirrup.

'Sodding bloody horse, do you wish to take a one way journey to the glue factory?' Lalassu stomped her foot, dangerously close to Pitch's boot. And the brown horse's flick of the tail was coincidentally near to his face.

The foul language flowed.

'Please sir, it's been a quiet winter round these parts for travellers.' Herbert rubbed at his cheek, smudging the dirt there, his uncertain eyes fixed on Silas.

'Silas, come on.' Pitch had given up trying to move Lalassu along, and was a few steps away. 'Which way is the Rule then?' he asked, of the basket-weaver.

'Keep on heading that way.' She gestured with a length of willow. 'Big fancy sign and all, can't miss it.'

But Silas still stood with Herbert. He took in the tattered state of the boy's trouser hems, the hole in the toe of his boot, and how both horses seemed to gravitate towards him, one either side, and quite at ease. He was ready to declare his preference for the inn, when Herbert said something quite miraculous.

'The Rule's cook can't cast a shadow on my Uncle Samuel's cookin'. Do you sirs like baked goods? No one makes a pastry like my Pa's Samuel.'

'Good gods, fuck the Golden Rule.' There was no damage done to Pitch's hearing at least. 'Why did you not say that to begin with, stupid boy?'

'Pitch,' Silas sighed, a wave of weariness striking him. 'Dear god. What is wrong with you?'

'I'm tired, filthy and bloody hungry, Silas. Why are we still standing here, talking with Henry when there are cakes to be had?'

'Herbert.' The boy certainly was not wanting for courage. 'My name's Herbert, mister.'

'It truly doesn't matter.'

The lad pulled back his shoulders, making the pail rattle with the earnestness of the move. He wiped a dirty hand against his threadbare trousers. 'But bakin' seems to matter a lot to you. And Uncle Samuel won't be in the mood for cookin' if he hears you've been terrible mean to me. I don't think I want you two coming to my place after all.'

Silas wished in that moment he had one of those fancy cameras that were about, so he could take a picture of the utter astonishment upon Pitch's face. The basket-maker was beside herself, laughing in such a way that reminded Silas of Tyvain's guttural chortle. The soothsayer would likely come searching for them soon enough, telling them to hurry the hell up, but as pleasing as the company of friends was, Silas was growing rather fond of the idea of greater privacy.

Pitch swallowed hard, glancing at Silas before he spoke. 'Herbert, my good fellow, we have had a rather piss-poor few days...months, really, and I am so tired I can barely see straight. We are dirty, rather battered, and well overdue a night on the cups. I apologise...for being such a bastard. But if you felt the way I do, you'd be a right cunt about things too.' Silas grimaced, but said nothing. Bawdy as it was, Pitch's explanation was not far wrong. 'Your father's inn sounds wonderful, and Samuel's baking near to divine, and I can already tell from the gleam in my large friend's eye here that he would very much like to take advantage of your offer. I hope you won't let the fact I am an arsehole prevent Mr Mercer from getting what he wants. He deserves good things.' In testament to his own exhaustion, Silas became teary, hearing Pitch speak so earnestly.

Herbert lips wobbled in an amusing show of consideration, his glance moving between Silas and Pitch. 'Suppose you ain't so bad then, not so bad as you try to be, anyways. And you do both look mighty tired.'

'Like you cannot imagine,' Pitch said. 'Herbert, will you be so kind as to show us the way to the Churchill, so we might find somewhere to try and put ourselves back together?'

Herbert gave Pitch a solemn nod, and without another word gathered the horses' reins, and led them on.

CHAPTER 3

The trip to the Churchill took them right by the Golden Rule, and Pitch was sorely tempted by the waft of ale that came from it. Silas spotted Tyvain before the soothsayer noticed them. She was seated inside near the window, pint in hand, slouched back in her seat, chatting to a fellow whose beard put Silas's to shame, nearly touching at his ample belly. They were locked in conversation, and Tyvain looked for all the world like she was a local. Jane's meandering walk had put her only just ahead of Pitch and Silas. She waited at the main doors as they approached. The sleeves of her shirt were dark with dampness, as were a few strands of her hair.

'Did you bathe in the river?' Pitch said. 'Does the Golden Rule have no basins?'

She smiled, and something shifted within her hair. One of the sparrows peaked from between the strands. Odd woman.

'Some of the asrai were rather exuberant when I chatted with them. The young ones tend to burst themselves when they are overly excited.'

Pitch felt Silas tense, and recalled something of the asrai being involved in distracting him in Sherwood Forest. He rubbed his hand over the ankou's arse by way of a very different distraction.

'What did they tell you of this place then?' Silas asked, not nearly distracted as he should be, Pitch decided.

'They are carefree, Silas. All is well.' She glanced at Herbert who was staring at her rather wide-eyed. 'Hello there.'

'You're beautiful,' the boy declared, not a hint of abashment about him as he stood dwarfed by Lalassu's powerful bulk.

Jane burst into an equally beautiful gale of laughter. 'Thank you. And you are very handsome.'

'Oh good gods,' Pitch growled. 'We'll be at the Churchill. There is cake.'

He tugged at Silas's awful heavy coat, but the ankou was unmoved.

'What of Sybilla?' Silas, ever the sensible one, enquired. 'Shall I help you settle her in, Jane?'

She shook her head, and two tiny finches darted from beneath her hair. 'We shall manage. Go on then. You know where we are if you need us. Enjoy, gentlemen.' She turned to enter the establishment, but paused. 'Tobias, what of the...' she glanced at Herbert. 'Your baggage? Would you prefer it stays with you?'

'No.' Pitch needed no time to consider. 'Leave it lie.'

'Are you sure?' Silas said, quietly.

'Very. I'd...I prefer...' Never to take in the simurgh again, to be the master of his own body once more. He'd prefer to pretend a while longer that he was free. 'Not yet. Leave the bag in the carriage. Have Phillipa and Scarlet remain with it.'

Jane nodded. 'Good care will be taken.'

'You are welcome to come to the inn, too.' Herbert was far too occupied with Jane's beauty for Pitch's liking. 'There's room for everyone.'

'Thank you so much, but we will let Pitch and Silas settle in on their own.' Pitch caught himself before he exhaled too loudly with relief. 'Perhaps we shall come for a drink later on? But best you show these fine gentlemen to their room now, they both look dead on their feet.' She winked at Silas but his smile barely lifted.

'Yes, miss.' The boy nearly danced himself out of his own shoes. 'Right away.'

The fool actually saluted her, before turning on his heels, a set of reins looped over each shoulder, waving Silas and Pitch onwards. 'Quick, this way. Come on.'

'Horatio! Damn you, I am not running in these fucking boots.'

Silas laughed, though there was not much energy about it.

Pitch brushed his hand against Silas's fingers. The ankou's skin was cool, and he allowed his flame to the surface. 'Are you sure everything is alright?'

'As you said to Herbert before, it's been quite the time.' He leaned toward Pitch. 'And I think the past week is catching up with me. I did not sleep well when you were gone.'

It really was nothing to be pleased about, but Pitch could not deny the warmth at hearing it said. To be missed...what a strange, quite lovely thing.

'Well, that was rather silly. I for one had the most wonderful slumber whilst packed into a glass tomb. Right as rain, I am.'

They both laughed, quietly, at the obvious untruth, and Pitch slipped a single finger into Silas's hand, who clasped it like a treasure.

Herbert guided them off the North Road, where the Rule sat, and onto the main street. They arrived ten minutes later, with Herbert declaring it loudly, pointing until they had both murmured their approval. The Churchill Inn was pretty, with its lower level pale rendered brick, whilst the upper levels were exposed slate and stone work. Three levels, with dormer windows on the roof, hinting at a usable attic space. Gold lettering across the inn's middle declared its name. The brown remains of ivy clung around the doorway, but winter had made a skeleton of the plant for now.

'I can't decide whether to wash or eat first,' Pitch said.

'You could do both, could you not? Sit in the bath and indulge in a tart? Now there's a sight I shall look forward to.' Silas's grin suddenly slipped and he grasped Pitch's finger tighter.

'What is it?' Fucking gods, what now? 'Is there danger?'

The ankou seemed to gather himself, his hold loosening. 'Sorry, no, nothing of concern. There was just a very strong waft of the graveyard, it caught me off guard. I just...' He seemed uncomfortable, furrows creasing his brow.

'You just what, my dear? Come on now, spill it. I need notice if we are to run again, these boots are torture, and I'm really not dressed for it.'

That smoothed out the big man's lines a little.

'Nothing like that. I may have to excuse myself later on and take a stroll.' He touched at his chest. 'I think I need...'

Up ahead, Hartford or whatever the blasted lad's name was, hollered for his father. 'Some fellows are here for a bed and tarts, pa.'

There was so much to be said about that particular sentence, but Pitch held back the urge.

'Go on, Silas.' This feeling of concern that came so readily where the oaf was concerned was bloody annoying. Life was far simpler when one did not give a damn.

'I need to spend some time there.' Silas glanced at him and Pitch felt a prick of unease. 'The graveyard, I mean. It will do me good, I think.'

Pitch stopped, pulling his fingers from the ankou's hold. 'Because you are not good now? Are you unwell?' His own stomach did unwelcome flips at saying it. 'Silas, don't fuck around. What is wrong? Out with it.'

'I am not unwell, but I am drained...' he paused, and after coming to a visible inward decision, continued on. 'I'll be honest and say I feel tired in a way I've not know before.' Pitch must have failed at hiding his concerns for Silas's expression fell. 'No, no, there's no need for concern, I assure you. A decent rest and I'll be fine. I don't suppose I can take on the likes of the Herlequin and a goddess, and expect to walk away with little more than a sore thumb.'

Pitch scowled. 'What is wrong with your thumb?'

There came that irresistible deep chortle again. 'Nothing, merely a turn of phrase. I'm just saying, it hardly seems surprising to be a little tired. We both need rest, I know you are the same.'

Pitch's lips parted with a denial, which was simply stupid. He was fucking exhausted.

'That's the front door there,' the boy called, pointing out the bleeding obvious before Pitch could press Silas further. 'Tell Pa that Herbert sent you, I'll take your horses around to the stables in the back.'

Pitch huffed. 'Half the world shall know we've arrived, with all that shouting.'

'Come on with me, pretty mare.' The boy patted at Lalassu's shoulder, then gave the brown horse an equal share of attention. 'And Mr Chocolate, you shall love our stables, plenty of fresh hay, and a dandy brush with your names on it. What do you think of that?' He turned suddenly. 'What *are* their names, sirs?'

'Lalassu is the pale horse,' Silas returned. 'And...well, you were right, that is Mr Chocolate, the brown.'

Herman's poorly directed eyes widened. 'Lalassu. That's the most wonderful name I've ever heard.'

Lalassu snorted and tossed her head, and with no more to-do the mare and gelding trotted off to follow the strange, slow young fellow whose laughter was every bit as childish as he. Childish but, Pitch must admit, endearing.

He turned his attention back to Silas. The ankou was not quick enough to cover the pinch of discomfort that lined his face, but he plastered a rather wolfish grin over whatever ailed him.

'Shall we?' He swept his hand towards the door: a simple entrance of smoothed brown wood, framed by the winter-slumbering trails of a climbing rose. Wood smoke scented the air, a thick trail coming from the bulky chimney at the far right of the building.

'We shall.' Pitch led the way inside.

'Welcome to the Churchill Inn, gentlemen. I see you've made my son's acquaintance.'

Hector's pa was a stocky man whose belly sought to escape his vest, making pearl buttons strain. His wide smile showed hint of a singular blackened tooth towards the side of his mouth, and his neck was impressively thick. There was an affable air about the man, a sense that he was every bit as jovial as he appeared. Stepping across the threshold into the warmth and murmur of afternoon drinking, Pitch found his knots undoing.

'Herbert is a credit to you, sir,' Silas said.

'He said your cook makes tarts.' Pitch knew himself blunt, but truly felt the past few days earned him every right to be.

The publican appeared taken aback for a moment before his expression cleared. 'Ah, you mean my partner Samuel? He is a master of the pastry, I have to say. A sight to behold in the kitchen.'

'I don't know about all that but does he have any strawberry tarts about?' He earned a displeased nudge from Silas.

'Excuse my companion, Mr...'

'Churchill.'

'Of course, Mr Churchill,' Silas said. 'We wondered if you might have any rooms available?'

'Just one, that's all we need.' Pitch was in no mood for the prejudices of humankind. He was not going to sneak about simply to pander to their bigotry. He wanted Silas in his bed, and he would have him there. 'Your boy told us this was a welcoming place for all types. We are all types, I assure you.'

The innkeeper gave him a look, and it was best described as appraising. There were all manner of calculations going on behind his plain brown eyes. Gentle considerations though, not conniving.

Silas inhaled, no doubt about to smooth over daemonic bad manners, and Pitch was readying to use some enchantment on the human man to hurry things along, when the innkeeper nodded. 'We pride ourselves on an open door here at the Churchill, my dear fellow. Let me show you to your room right away.'

'You didn't say about the tarts?' Pitch raised a brow, aware he was being quite the demanding tosser, but a little too tired of tight boots and appalling clothing to care.

The innkeeper's laughter made his jowls wobble. Far more pleasant jowls than those Iblis had designed for his Dr Severs. These were made for humour. 'I'm sure you know that strawberries are no friends of winter, but my Samuel is a master of creation. I have no doubt he can whip up something to suit your tastes. The sweeter the better, then?'

'Saccharine like you would not believe.' Silas too seemed to have shed some of his angst. Likely it was the clutter of potted plants in the small foyer that pleased him, enough of them to have Pitch thinking of the Crimson Bow, with its crowded but pleasant interior. His fingers went, unbidden, to where the puncture in his earlobe was a reminder of Tilly. Another blasted creature to worry over. 'He has the sweetest tooth I've ever known. It would be truly wonderful if something could be done by your fellow.'

Mr Churchill led them towards a narrow flight of carpeted stairs. 'He's the best with pastry this side of the Scottish border, so far as I'm concerned. You'll not wish to leave Ambleside again, once you've had a taste of his wares, I can promise you that.'

'I do hope you are not simply talking the talk because he has your balls in the palm of his hand.'

The innkeeper nearly missed a step, glancing over his shoulder. 'Pardon?'

'What?' Pitch shrugged. 'He's your lover, is he not?'

Silas hissed something low and urgent but Pitch waved him off. Mr Churchill's look of alarm slid away, replaced with wide-grinned amusement. 'You're a forward one, aren't you?'

'Also, like you would not believe.' Silas sighed, gesturing for Pitch to head up first. But the innkeeper had not yet moved on.

'You're not entirely correct.' The innkeeper pulled back his shoulders, his eyes bright. 'He's not just my lover, he is the love of my life.' He glanced between Silas and Pitch. 'Perhaps you already know that feeling, perhaps you'll come to know it, all I can say is there's nothing like it.' He nodded at some inner thought. 'There we are then, that's said, and to hell with worrying about it.'

Pitch glanced at Silas. The ankou watched the fellow with a wistful smile. 'Good for you, Mr Churchill. I think it perhaps the only feeling truly worth its salt. I'm glad you've known it.'

'And you?' The man said, gently, keeping his gaze very fixed on the ankou.

Pitch cleared his throat. He could not stand another moment of this discussion.

'Mr Mercer has had many lives, and no doubt many loves,' he said. 'And tells them all, I'm sure, that he's terribly in love. He falls very easily and unwisely.' He regretted the snide words the moment they spilled from his tongue. Silas was holding onto the banister like it were a ship's rail in a storm-tossed sea, the weight of his exhaustion tangible. 'Mr Churchill, would you please show us to our room, I think my man here is in need of a decent lie down.'

'Of course, of course.'

Ignoring Silas's mutterings about needless fussing, Pitch insisted the ankou go first. He did not trust that Silas wouldn't collapse there and then. He'd have offered his shoulder, but Silas's breadth took up most of the width of the stairs. Once they reached the corridor though, Pitch lifted Silas's arm and draped it over his shoulder.

'Here we are, make yourselves at home.' Mr Churchill opened the door to the very last room along the corridor. 'I'll have some hot water sent so you can wash, and then I'll get to the kitchen and have a word with Samuel.'

Pitch's pulse jumped. Gods he was hungry. 'If there are no strawberries, perhaps cherry?' He wrinkled his nose. 'Pear if there really is no other option.'

Pitch knew he was being unreasonable with his requests considering the time of year, but if one did not ask, one certainly did not receive.

'Will do my very best. I hope you are very comfortable, gentlemen. Is there any luggage you need brought up?'

'No,' Silas replied. 'We are travelling light.'

Churchill nodded, and left them alone, closing the door softly.

A generous lead-paned window drew Pitch's attention from the busy botanical wallpaper. Their second-floor level afforded a view over the tops of slate-roofed cottages and out towards the rolling green hills beyond. Despite it being early afternoon, the winter sun was waning, the light dulled with hint of evening's approach, but it made for a gorgeous landscape in the failing light.

'Quite attractive, this place,' Pitch said.

Silas groaned, and Pitch abandoned the view at once.

'What is it?'

But there was no need for the ankou to explain.

'Oh fuck,' Pitch breathed.

The mahogany bed, with its half-tester canopy and lace drapes, was set into a recess in the far wall. The flame mahogany footboard was so high Pitch could have hidden behind it; and the creme, buttoned headboard was barely visible behind an astonishing array of pillows.

Silas stepped up to one side of the bed; where a bedspread with dominating yellow florals lay without a crease out of place. He spread his arms wide, and declared, 'Thank bloody Christ.'

Silas toppled forward, a mighty oak falling, and landed face down. He groaned into the thick eiderdown, and patted at the empty space beside him.

'Come and join me, it is heaven.'

'Then don't dirty it with those blasted boots. Here...' Pitch lifted Silas's right foot and set about undoing the laces, tugging forcefully until he almost went arse-over-tit when the boot slipped loose. 'Curse these infernal ugly things.'

Silas merely laughed into his soft haven, his sound muffled. 'Oh bloody hell, I'm never moving again.'

'That had best be a lie.' Pitch grunted, bracing as the other boot came free. He tossed it towards its pair, over by an elegant, mirrored armoire dresser. He wrinkled his nose in disgust at his reflection.

'You might want to close your eyes while you fuck me, Silas. I'm as pretty as the arse end of a manticore at the moment.' He tried in vain to rearrange his hair into some semblance of order. 'Something reeks, too, and I'm not sure if it's me, or your feet.'

Silas laughed. 'I suspect both. And let it be said, you'll never be un-fuckable as far as I'm concerned, but perhaps we should wait until the wash basin arrives?' He'd not yet moved from his fallen scarecrow pose upon the bed. Pitch threw off his own boots, casting them as far across the substantial room as he could manage. They landed near to where a well-worn brown leather armchair took up the corner, in prime position beside a carved wood hearth, its fireplace laid out with kindling.

'Wait? I shall pretend I did not hear you say that.' Pitch unclasped the cloak, letting it pool around his feet in a flow of fuchsia. He shrugged off the bland coat beneath, and the smock beneath that, before he clambered onto the bed in dirty trousers and thin shirt, and straddled Silas. Pitch leaned down, nuzzling the back of the ankou's ear. 'The water might take an hour, could we not at least warm ourselves up a little?'

Now Silas's groan was all for him. Pitch shifted his hair and laid feathery kisses upon his exposed neck. Leaning down like this, so close to the tantalising softness of the mattress, he was torn between notions of fucking Silas mindless, or having an afternoon nap. But his incubus blood was singing out. For a decent bit of handwork at the very least.

'I'm so very filthy, Pitch.'

'And thank heavens for that.'

Silas's laugh bucked his hips. 'You know what I mean. I fear you'll chip a tooth on the grit if you keep kissing me that way.'

'Just roll over, I shall I'll take care of the rest if you aren't in the mood.'

'I beg your pardon?' Silas moved quickly, flipping himself over, nearly throwing Pitch off with the sudden roll. 'Come here.' He resettled Pitch over his middle, and took his hand, guiding it to where fabric bulged. 'There is not enough tiredness in the world to keep me from wanting you.'

Pitch rolled his eyes in a show of disdain for the sentiment, whilst inside his blood reached a new crescendo.

He moved his hips, teasing at the hard lump between his thighs. Silas gasped, and cupped a hand to the back of his neck, dragging him down, and claiming Pitch's lips in a forceful kiss. Their cocks were crushed against one another, both pleasurable and painful, and it drew moans all around. Pitch closed his eyes, which was actually a terrible idea.

Fatigue swept through the darkness to find him. He pressed a hand to the mattress to brace himself, and whilst he still nipped at Silas's bottom lip, he grabbed a handful of the ankou's bland coat and rolled to one side. Silas moved with him, letting himself be shifted onto his side so they lay now face to face. Pitch groaned anew with the relief.

'Wonderful bed, isn't it?' Silas kissed his chin, his hand tracing the undulations of Pitch's side.

'Surprisingly so.' He hooked his leg over the ankou's thigh, the reach spreading his arse cheeks, and straining the fabric of his trousers. Silas's hand drifted to find his buttons. And Pitch's eyes fluttered closed once more.

'We should get you out of these clothes.'

Their lips brushed, their noses glanced.

'Absolutely,' Pitch mumbled.

Neither of them made another move. Pitch peered through one narrowed eye. Silas had his eyes closed, too. Their kisses were airy, their foreheads touching. And though desire was hurting his balls, Pitch could not deny one very putrid truth.

'My gods, we stink.'

Silas nuzzled his nose against Pitch's cheek. 'We are positively awful. Why on Earth did no one mention it?'

'I suppose they weren't sure how to tell the lord of death he smells like a mortuary.'

'How dare you, sir.'

The ankou's fingers came back to life, forgoing undoing buttons and slipping down the front of Pitch's trousers to touch at dampness and rigid heat. He pinched the tip of Pitch's cock.

'Oh, gods.' He thrust his hips forward, pushing himself deeper into Silas's hold.

'Did you like that?'

The rumble of Silas's voice, the hunger there, drew a gasp from Pitch. 'Do it again, I'll let you know for sure.'

Silas shifted his hand, gaining greater purchase. His thick fingers crushed at hard flesh; starting a beautiful dance of pleasure and pain. Pitch arched his back, grasping at Silas's shoulder. 'Again.'

The ankou made a small, needy sound and obliged. This time using all his fingers, wrapping them about Pitch's cock, clenching hard, and being beautifully, perfectly mean about it.

'Bastard,' Pitch panted. 'Do it again.'

The growl that came from the ankou made Pitch's balls tighten harder. Which made the pain all the more delicious when Silas's fingers found them, took hold, and squeezed their denseness tight.

Pitch keened like a rabid animal, white flashes going off behind his closed lids.

'More?' Silas whispered.

'Yes, gods, yes.'

Silas balled his fist, crushing twin jewels with eye-watering ferocity. Pitch sailed into exquisite agony, alive to every end of every nerve. He rolled his head against the mattress, his incubus hunger maddened by the harsh play.

There'd been hint that Silas was capable of such roughness, but no sign he might enjoy it every bit as much as Pitch did.

The animalistic noises coming from the ankou, the possessive way his teeth teased at the lump at Pitch's throat whilst he so efficiently punished his balls, were a revelation.

'Such a good boy,' he murmured in Pitch's ear. And it was impossible not to shudder. Not to swell so hard it seemed impossible his skin would not break. 'Can you take more?'

Not if Silas kept talking like that. Pitch's head spun, and he was fairly sure he replied, but equally certain whatever he said was babble.

Silas relaxed his hold only a moment, to urge Pitch flat onto his back, and then drove his grip home again, pulling down as he did so this time; stretching the fine sack of skin around Pitch's balls until it could be dragged no further. Pitch's moan grew with the sweet torture, warmth spilling from the tip of his cock; pain balancing him upon a tipping point of sheer paradise.

'I want you to come for me.' Silas was an utter fiend. 'Will you do that for me?'

Yes. Yes. A simple word, one Pitch was incapable of speaking. Only a ridiculous gurgle escaped his constricted throat. The base of his spine began to burn; heralding the sheer ecstasy that would soon spill into his groin and erupt from his prick. He moaned like the very best harlot in the very best brothel.

The ankou shifted his mouth to Pitch's lips, breathing his command against them. 'Come for me now.'

He squeezed, mercilessly, at beleaguered balls, whilst also taking firm command of Pitch's straining cock; sliding his hand up and down with such fever, Pitch was sent soaring beyond all chance of control.

Pitch shouted to the gods: his back arched, his release unstoppable. He came with a violence that sucked the breath from his lungs, and had him digging his nails in where he clung to Silas. He bucked and stuttered and went a little mindless with it all; and if anyone had asked him his name there and then, he'd have had no fucking clue what it was.

His incubus blood was greedy, drawing in the sensual, crackling energy between them. Gorging itself on the heat and desire that emanated from Silas. The ankou was a great body of lust, a beaming sun of want that saturated Pitch in a way very near to overwhelming. Silas held nothing of himself back. He was open, available. Ready to give far too much.

Pitch winced, and reined in the ravenous hunger that consumed him, even as his body still twitched with the violence of his spend. An incubus could lose control.

And he'd sooner starve than harm this man.

Then it was over, save for the shudders. Silas moved in for another of his deep kisses. He rolled his hips forward, and his arousal was still painfully evident.

'Let me tend to that,' Pitch panted.

'Not yet.' Silas traced a fingertip along his hairline. 'You are glowing. Let me watch you enjoy your pleasure a while longer.'

Pitch smiled, tired and entirely sated. He slumped into the mattress, and Silas lay his head upon Pitch's damp chest.

'You are quite the scoundrel, Mr Mercer.' He twisted his fingers through Silas's dark hair. 'I did not think you'd care for more forceful indulgences.'

'Ah, there you see, we have much to learn of one another.' Silas ran his fingertip through dampness on Pitch's exposed belly, his shirt having ridden up as he contorted. 'I care for anything that makes you lose yourself like that. I could watch you spend all day.'

Pitch's eyes were determined to close. 'I am preternaturally talented in many ways, but alas, endless climax is not in my repertoire.'

'Very disappointing. Perhaps you should go bother the cobbler after all.'

Pitch flicked at his ear, eliciting a delightful whimper.

'Before I go, I have something to attend to.' Pitch wriggled from beneath Silas's leaning weight, pushing the ankou flat onto his back. 'Stay, do not move an inch. It is my turn for ordering about, now.'

Silas grinned, and lifted his arms, crossing his hands beneath his head. 'Very well, then. It's close enough to Christmas, I suppose gifts are in order.' His eyelids were heavy, the rings beneath his eyes growing more pronounced as the light weakened with the afternoon. Now there was not just the reek of travel and maltreatment permeating; but the cloying, glorious scent of fucking.

Pitch nudged Silas's legs apart and lay between them. This was likely the most putrid he'd ever been in his human form. They were both wretched, and moving like decrepit old men. Pitch was sticky, hollowed out with fatigue, and yet, despite it all, he'd never been so content.

'I'm not one for all this festive season malarky, myself.' He flicked at the buttons on Silas's trousers, and slipped the ankou's superb and rigid cock free. Pitch licked its reddened tip, and peered up through his lashes, the way he knew Silas liked. 'But I can deliver a very decent gift.'

CHAPTER 4

The gift-giving was almost complete when there was a knock at the door. Silas grabbed a pillow, shoving it over his face to stifle the cry of pleasure that could not be stopped; his cock driven deep into Pitch's mouth, every drop being taken with great enthusiasm.

The prince slowly drew his lips down Silas's length, a wet popping sound coming as he pulled off. He sat up, wiping at scandalously wet lips.

'Who is there?' he called, his fingers teasing at sensitive folds of skin.

'Stop it.' Silas gasped, swiping at Pitch with a boneless arm, his body still twitching.

'Sorry to disturb you, gentlemen,' an unfamiliar voice called out. 'My chap, Robert, said you were hoping for some sweet treats?'

Pitch's brows shot up. 'A perfect compliment to my meal,' he whispered.

They shared a brief kiss, which did err on the salty side, and then Pitch was up, adjusting his shirt where it had slipped over his shoulder. He padded over to the door as Silas tried to rise; feeling every inch of his oversized body in the struggle to sit upright. The room reeled and tilted. And there again, in fuller force, was that nagging itch. The one that bade him visit the graveyard, wherever it might be in this village.

He pressed his lips, determined not to worry Pitch again. He'd seen the daemon's reaction when Silas admitted his fatigue was extreme, and he regretted being so honest. Pitch deserved at least a few hours with nothing to bother about. Besides, it was not an alarming sensation, per se. The niggling did not foretell of danger. At least, not one that endangered the prince, or any of those in their party. Whatever this was, it was Silas's concern alone.

Pitch opened the door, and ushered in a handsome, older gentleman and a younger person with short golden hair, carrying a large wicker basket. A woman perhaps, given the slenderness of limbs and neck; but as they were dressed in blue overalls with rolled-up shirt sleeves and a kerchief tied around their neck–all the trappings normally reserved for a lad–Silas would make no presumptions. Something of their demeanour, purposeful and unaffected, reminded him of Charlie. Good god, he missed the lad.

'We come bringing hot water, and warm pie.' The gentleman was well turned out: greying hair swept back over his ears without a strand out of place, and his useful tweed jacket showing a hint of crisp white at the cuffs, while a pointed collar was held in place with clover leaf lapel pins. He held two generous-sized buckets: one in each hand, steam lifting from the water within. 'Billy be careful with that pie, so the crust doesn't break. And make sure you don't spill any of the cream.'

'I may 'ave done this a time or two before.' Billy, the holder of the wicker basket, countered in good nature. 'Don't you be worrying about these strangers disliking your food, Samuel. Never met a person who didn't think everything you make was divine.'

'Robert tends to extol my virtues too highly, I fear, though,' Samuel, the well-presented man, said. 'One day I shall meet my match, and fail to live up to the enormous reputation he builds for me.'

'He's proud of you,' Billy countered, neither of the newcomers batting an eye at the dishevelled men occupying the room, as though strange guests were commonplace.

'I wish he'd be quieter about it.' Samuel's laughter was quite lovely, but tinged with stress. 'Now, I'm so sorry to bother you both...'

'And evidently we are being a bother.' Billy set down his basket on the sole, small table in the room, and went to open a window. 'That's better.'

Pitch made a beeline for the unattended basket. 'What sort of pie is it?' But before he could pull back the gingham cloth covering it, Billy returned and slapped at his hand.

'Now, I thank you to wait just a moment, Mr...?'

'Mr Last Voice You'll Ever Hear, if you do that again.' Pitch returned.

Samuel chuckled where he stood pouring the water into the basins on the sideboard.

'Tobias is fine,' Silas said. 'And I'm Silas.'

He swung his legs over the side of the bed, glancing down to ensure he was decent. The world swum again, and he cursed quietly. He debated on how strange it would look for him not to get up at all, and decided that Pitch would spot it immediately and far too many questions would follow. He reached for the foot board, grateful for its exaggerated height, but Billy, who was not so food-focused as Pitch, had noticed something amiss. Silas gave them a look, and a small shake of the head, hoping they'd not ask if he was alright.

Billy frowned, but Silas was saved from any awkward conversation by an exclamation from Pitch.

'Fuck me dead.'

The daemon held up a finger covered in a sticky golden and pink chunk of pie. He groaned, not altogether unlike earlier, when Silas had his cock in hand.

'This is sinful, truly.' He stuck his finger deep into his mouth, earning a peculiar look from Billy, and a beaming one from Samuel.

'They are last season's peaches, and a fine crop it was.' He set down the empty buckets. 'But here, let me cut you a proper piece. There's clotted cream to go with it, if you'd like.'

'My gods man, if you seek to seduce me, consider me yours.' Pitch made another sound best kept to the bedroom. 'And I usually despise peaches. You are a god among men.'

Billy glanced at Silas. 'He enjoys a pie then?'

'Rather so.' Silas still held onto the end of the bed, unwilling to chance a step away.

'Silas, you must taste this.' Pitch spun about, holding a fresh cut of pie in a cloth in his hand. He had a dab of cream on his top lip, and his eyes were luminous. Unnaturally so.

Billy gasped.

Silas stepped forward, fighting off the lingering dizziness. 'Pitch, best you don't –'

'Here, you must try this.' Pitch saved Silas from having to stagger across the room, rushing towards him, smiling his cream-speckled smile, with an air of delight and happiness that stung Silas's eyes to see. Tiredness made his tears far too ready.

Pitch lifted the pie and its accompanying dollop of cream, towards Silas's mouth.

'Lean down, will you? You fucked me too tired to lift my arms any higher. I know you are not overly fond of sugar, but you'll try it for me, won't you?'

Silas obliged with parted lips and a stoop of his shoulders. The room shrunk till there seemed only the pair of them. Pitch licked his lips as he watched Silas eat.

'Wonderful?' he whispered.

'Wonderful.' In truth, he couldn't taste much at all, a hint of vanilla perhaps, but little more. It had been the same for some of the dried meat Tyvain had produced on the ride. Silas's sense of taste seemed as tired as he was.

There was movement around them: the slide of the pie tin as Samuel cut it into generous slices, the bustle of Billy as they gathered up Pitch's bright pink cloak and the dreary brown wool cape Isaac had passed to Silas.

Pitch was grinning, ready with another piece to share; their bodies touching, the daemon's heat strong enough that, if they weren't careful, the others in the room might notice.

'Well then,' Samuel cleared his throat. 'We shall leave you be. And you be sure to let me know if you'd like anything else from the kitchen. I've heard you are partial to a strawberry, and I'm certain I have preserves stashed in the cellar. I'll see if I can find them to make some tartlets.'

Silas grabbed at Pitch as he went into something of a swoon. 'Did you hear that, Silas?'

'I did,' he chuckled. 'You are a saint among men, Samuel.'

'Well, I don't know about that.' The man smiled, clearly pleased at the flattery. 'The hot water is ready for you, there's some cloths just over there. A bar of soap if you're that way inclined.'

Silas dragged his gaze from Pitch's face just long enough to give the man a thankful nod. 'Your hospitality is very much appreciated.'

'Leave a spoon with the pie if you will.' Pitch brushed the remaining morsel he held against Silas's lips. He had his back to Samuel and showed no sign of altering that, nestled in against Silas as he was.

Samuel's gaze softened as he lingered by the doorway. 'Seems you've been through some things, all of you. I hear tell the rest of your party is at the Golden Rule?'

'Clearly these gentlemen have far better taste, staying with us,' Billy re-entered the room, arms laden with clothes. 'But these were sent over from there about a half hour ago, I almost forgot.' They held a white shirt to their nose. 'The most pleasing scent of jasmine is upon all of them. Must ask the laundress at the Rule if she'll share her secret with us. The messenger said to send apologies to Mr Mercer for the fit but it's the best they can do until tomorrow, when the tailor opens his store again.' They exchanged a glance with Samuel. 'But I heard Roy was there for lunch today...settled in early...which doesn't bode well for him being up before noon tomorrow.'

'We'll get you sorted, don't you worry.' Samuel picked up the empty basket and beckoned Billy. 'Come on now, let's give them their space back. Good evening, gentlemen. Hope you enjoy your stay...' His gaze flicked to the discarded, mucky boots. 'And find some rest from whatever troubles ail you.'

Silas swallowed his mouthful of pie. 'Thank you. How is Herbert doing with both horses? They are not giving him any trouble, I hope?'

'Our boy has a way with the animals.' Samuel's pride lifted his shoulders. 'They couldn't be in better hands. He'll insist on staying with them all night now, and they so much as flick a tail in a manner he isn't happy with, he'll come running to get you. Don't you worry.'

The pair left them, Samuel closing the door with a quiet click.

Pitch had been unusually quiet during the exchange, and made no move to rustle through the clothes Billy had placed on the armchair.

'Everything all right, my love?'

Pitch leaned into him, stifling a yawn. 'Fine, fine.' He pressed a sticky finger against Silas's lips until he obliged and sucked it clean. 'But now I've had a taste of pie and drunk you dry, I can hardly keep my bloody eyes open. Which is infuriating, because I wouldn't mind another round with you between my legs.'

'Still famished then? I under-performed, it seems.' He led him to the dresser where one large washbasin sat alongside a smaller one: porcelains of white and delicate blue respectively, both a little chipped, clearly well used.

Another yawn came. 'I told you I would have room for more dessert, did I not?'

Silas pulled out the stool that had been set beside the dresser. 'Here, come and sit your arse down, please.'

'I'd prefer to have my arse up, where you can do your worst to it.' But he obliged, sighing as he seated himself. 'But my gods, I feel as though an elephant is draped over my shoulders.'

'It's not been an easy time. You need to rest.'

Pitch reached for Silas's trousers. 'I don't want to rest, I want you.'

No matter how tired, how dirty and dishevelled, and plagued by worries he was, Silas would never weary of hearing such a thing said.

'And I you. Always.' Silas picked up the bar of soap, one that smelled faintly of bergamot, and was quite sure his hand trembled. 'But I am appallingly filthy.' And, he had to say it but could not, he was too tired to undo his trousers, let alone use what lay beneath. The fatigue was leaden now. The clawing urge to wander among the graves almost unbearable.

'Far more filthy than I've known you. It's delightful.' The glint in Pitch's eye said they were not speaking about mud and blood. He did not protest as the prince undressed him, his flame hinting just beneath his skin, heating the air as layers were removed. 'Warm enough?' Pitch asked.

'Yes, thank you.' Silas dipped a cloth into the warmth of the water. There was a swirl of oil on the surface, and a hint of mint as he wrung the cloth. If nothing else, they'd both smell a hell of a lot better after this. 'Now your turn. Take off your clothes, Mr Astaroth.'

Pitch obliged in the blink of an eye, shrugging off the shirt and standing to wriggle out of his ruined trousers. His cock was at a lazy half-stand.

Silas set about cleaning him up, letting the water run from the cloth and chasing the droplets as they skirted down Pitch's body, slipping into the shallow v-shape that ran from his hip to his groin. Silas carefully steered clear of the royal prick, despite the huffs of protest from Pitch himself.

He took in the lingering bruises, the pink marks of scarring, upon Pitch's body. Silas did not realise he was frowning until Pitch cupped a hand to his face.

'It is no easier to look on your injuries, Sickle. But we are healing, both of us, and all shall be well soon enough. This ridiculous quest of ours is almost done. We are nearly there. It is almost over.'

A heavy silence fell between them. Silas would have bet the scythe itself that Pitch wondered just as he did. What did delivering the simurgh to the Sanctuary mean for them?

He forced a smile. 'It is almost over, indeed.'

He continued on, removing what remnants of the cockaigne he could with gentle swipes of the cloth, refreshing it with the warm water every few strokes. Pitch closed his eyes and was swaying into the press of Silas's hand as he worked his way around to Pitch's back.

'Is there anything left of it?' the prince said quietly. 'The pitchfork, I mean.'

Silas ran the cloth along the length of Pitch's spine. The daemon dropped his head, exhaling. If Silas narrowed his eyes, he could just make out a greater paleness on Pitch's skin, where the tattoo had made its mark.

'Very little.' He followed the markings over one shoulder blade, then the other. 'Just the ghost of it, I'm afraid.'

'Afraid? Would you rather it had stayed? Was it not ugly?'

Silas shook his head. 'It was not ugly. It delivered you from pain. Are you sure –'

'I told you I'm not in pain, not with the simurgh gone now.'

Silas had barely stopped to think about the Cultivation; a testament to how delirious his fatigue made him. But with Tyvain, Jane and Sybil-la–not to mention Scarlet, Phillipa and Isaac–watching over the crea-ture, chances were high it was doing fine without he and Pitch. And he'd not deny, there was a part of him that held hope the blasted thing would simply fly on to where it was meant to be. And their quest would be truly done.

Silas kissed between Pitch's shoulder blades, where his skin was mint-scented and radiantly warm. 'Just promise me, you will tell me if that changes.'

'You have my word.'

He dragged the cloth low, over the crease in Pitch's arse, squeezing so the water ran down the inside of his thighs, eliciting a weighty moan from the daemon.

'Gods, we need to get this clean up done with, or I shall simply need you to start all over again with that cloth.' He spun about, urging Silas onto the unoccupied stool, and straddled his legs, grabbing for the other cloth that waited by the small bowl of water, dousing it, and bringing it to Silas's chest in one, smoothly-executed manoeuvre.

The water that spilled through the curled licks of hair on Silas's chest was not so warm as that which he'd lavished on Pitch. He shuddered as the daemon worked him over. Pitch brightened as his fire pulsed hotter.

They interspersed the bathing with kisses, both their movements rather languid, both their pricks never quite reaching full attention, despite how Silas's heart thumped. Pitch even stifled another yawn at one point, whilst his hand moved between Silas's legs, ensuring no dirt dared linger on a deadman's taint.

When they were done, the basin water was a putrid murky brown. They stood face to face, entirely naked, and though his eyes were vibrant with want, Pitch was plagued by another yawn. He groaned and knocked his forehead against Silas's chest.

'They've cursed me,' he declared. 'Me and my cock both. That's all there is to it. The sorcerers have had the last laugh.'

'What ever do you mean?' Silas rested his hand over the nape of Pitch's neck, caressing him.

'I have you naked, two inches from me but do not have the energy to spread my legs for you. I'm too tired to fuck. This is truly the apocalypse.'

Silas burst out laughing. 'You are a fool.'

'A fool who cannot satisfy you. Go ahead, laugh at my predicament, I don't blame you. Nor shall I be surprised if you seek release elsewhere.' This time his yawn stretched his jaw so wide his eyes closed.

'Will you stop talking nonsense. I'm not going anywhere.' Silas scooped him up, cradling him against his chest, enjoying the heat of his body as much as its loveliness.

'You shall be most disappointed in claiming this prize, you savage, but use me if you must.' Pitch sighed dramatically. 'Don't say I did not warn you when I fall asleep as you plunder me.'

The daemon was being ridiculous, and their shared, exhausted delirium made him seem fantastically funny. Silas's ribs ached, tears squeezing from his eyes.

'Stop laughing, I am ashamed enough as it is. You are a nasty man, Mr Mercer. Mocking me so.' Pitch pulled at Silas's chest hair.

'Bloody hell.' He spluttered through laughter he could not make subside. Silas had not touched a drop but felt punch drunk with tiredness, and contentment.

He managed to stay steady enough to use his foot to nudge back the covers, and laid Pitch out on the bed, before climbing in to join him beneath fantastically heavy covers and a sea of pillows.

'I'm sorry,' Pitch mumbled. 'I'll just close my eyes a moment and then I'll satisfy you, I promise.'

'Hush, you know very well all I need is to have you close.' Silas patted at Pitch's hip, urging him to roll onto his side, and snuggled in against him. 'My beautiful little eunuch.'

Pitch's giggle was adorable. He wriggled in closer, and Silas settled in behind him, moulding himself to the prince's shape, draping an arm over him once they were nestled like peas in a warm, soft pod. Pitch clutched at his arm.

'Just a little snooze,' he slurred.

'There is no rush. Sleep well, my love.'

Pitch's reply came in the form of a soft snore. Silas closed his eyes, and joined him soon after in longed-for slumber.

CHAPTER 5

Silas stirred, eyes fluttering open to find that darkness had claimed the room. They both still lay in the exact same positions, and judging by the numbness of Silas's arm, and the tingle in his hip, neither had moved at all. The bed was sublimely warm with Pitch's natural heat. A welcome return of the strength of his flame.

Silas knew what it was that had woken him. That infernal niggle. The one that had him sitting up now, very carefully extricating himself from the warm, perfectly, perfect way he lay with Pitch.

The daemon mumbled, interrupting the gentle lilt of snoring he was prone to when he slept deeply.

'It's all right, back to sleep now.' Silas stopped short of saying he was heading off to relieve himself. Memory of the last time such words left him were still acrid and unpleasant. 'I'm right here.'

He'd not say again he was leaving. But this incessant scratching at the back of his head—the certainty of knowing he needed to see the graveyard— was too powerful to overcome. Even when it meant doing the very last thing he wished.

He considered having Pitch come with him, but he'd seen the exhaustion writ large upon his beautiful, still-bruised, face. The daemon deserved to rest.

And so did Silas, but he'd not find true quietude here. Sleep, lovely as it was, would not revive him fully.

He waited till Pitch resettled, and was relieved when he did so with very little protest. Silas slid from the bed, and sucked in his breath at the contrast in temperature. Though it was entirely unnecessary, he tucked the blankets in around Pitch until only a few glimpses of his gold-flecked hair were visible. The gold-blonde was all but dominating his head now, the softer browns near lost.

Silas searched around for his clothes, biting his lip at the merciless cold against his bare skin. The search was clumsy in the dim light. A kneecap was thumped against the dresser, and it took a few tries before he found anything to fit, clearly having grabbed hold of clothes intended for the slender, shorter daemon at first; but finally Silas was clad in trousers, which were fall-fronts, he realised, after a pointless search for a single button. Pitch would be most pleased at that. The shirt's thick material felt best suited to a lumberman working in the woods, and fit Silas as though sewn for him.

A coat would have been preferable in the midnight cold, but Silas was tired of searching. He drew on the seven-league boots. Well, the plain old boots now, for the cockaigne had taken a toll on them in all manner of ways. The magic imbued in the footwear had fled. What he wore now were plain old, sturdy, mud-encrusted boots. But at least they fit him just as readily as they had before, and their thick soles were useful against the cold.

Silas made his way out of the inn as quietly as he could. Pitch's was not the only–and certainly not the loudest–snore to be heard, as he crept downstairs and out of the building. The loudest came from a high-backed armchair in the bar, where the hearth held a few glowing embers still. The sleeper was evident only by their feet, crossed at the ankles, darned socks visible as Silas passed.

He drew in a breath as he stepped outside into a perfectly still evening and the powerful, enticing scent of grave dirt found him. He pressed a hand to the doorframe, the intoxicating smell leaving him dizzy, his heart thumping with anticipation. Once he was sure he wouldn't stumble, Silas made his way onto the street.

It was late, he surmised, by way of the utter stillness of the village. The niggling tugged him to the right, and he hurried on. Hints of the approach of Christmas time were evident. Aside from the weather, he spied several wreaths of holly upon doorways, and on passing the grocers, could make out the peaked silhouette of a Christmas tree deeper in the store. The sight of it struck at Silas with a pang of great melancholy but a fluttering of subdued happiness was there too. He'd enjoyed Christmastime in the past. He was quite sure of it.

If only he could remember such times. He suspected much happiness to be found.

The waft of dank earth and loam, gentler now after its first powerful burst, teased at his senses, luring him onwards. He passed by the store where the woman had sat with her basket, weaving. There was an oil lamp still flickering despite the emptiness of the shop. Another tree, much smaller than the last, sat on a small table just to the right of the window. The light was glorious against all the trinkets that hung upon the boughs of the tree, causing them to shine; candy canes, stars of silver tinsel, and astonishing blown glass baubles. Some were simple balls, others were distinct shapes: a dog there, a train engine, even a tennis racquet, of all things, but most superb of all, a parrot with gold and green foil that shone rich and lovely in the weak light.

Silas paused at the window, despite the irritating drag at his senses. The tree with its embellishments was so terribly pretty. Pitch would have adored it.

He carried on, wrapping his arms about himself as he went, regretting his decision not to find his coat, but distracted by thoughts of Arcadia. Did they have such celebrations as Christmas, he wondered? From what he knew, it did not seem such a place, but then, he knew so very little about Pitch's home. Maybe Pitch had experienced a Christmastime here...with Edward perhaps? Had it had been Christmas Eve when the lieutenant gifted Pitch the pendant watch? An exchange between lovers.

Silas's mood soured at the thought. Which was ridiculous. He should be pleased that Pitch had known pleasanter times, happiness in a different skin, with a different man. But Silas had never been able to banish from his mind that day at the Moon Inn, when he'd been an appalling voyeur, and watched Edward and Pitch in their most private moment.

There was a small part of Silas that resented Edward for having laid with Pitch, he'd not deny it. But such jealousy was astoundingly stupid, and the poor lieutenant did not deserve it. Considering all that had gone on since, Edward probably wished he'd never met Tobias Astaroth. And there was the fact that Pitch had likely bedded three quarters of the British Isles, perhaps the continent too, not to mention Arcadia. Silas would wear himself out if he chose to be jealous of all who'd shared the prince's bed. He knew all that. He knew his sense of possessiveness, when it came to the daemon, was terribly juvenile and ill-mannered. Silas was a sensible man. For the most part.

Just not the part where Pitch was involved.

So he'd enjoy the distraction of his own petty jealousies. They helped him to ignore the enormous, greater picture that faced them both.

The Sanctuary. The lake. The coming of an end.

Silas carried on, breathing deeper, letting the heady waft of the graves tickle at his senses, while he pictured Pitch as he'd been a few hours previously. Lost to pleasure. A pleasure that Silas bestowed, and no one else. A smile found his lips as he enjoyed the distraction of his own silliness, which in turn helped him ignore the biting cold, and the tiredness that was bone deep, despite hours spent sleeping. Lifting his feet was a chore, and his mind was foggy with the need to close his eyes.

The lure of the graveyard took him down a narrow alleyway between two thatched-roof cottages, and out to where a small church was now a visible hulking shadow further across the way.

The whispering began then.

The prickle at his skin that announced the presence of a soul. The very first sense he'd had of any deathly stirrings. The scythe remained ever silent though, unbothered by the ghost who watched them.

They watched from a distance, hidden in shadow, but not in the least threatening. Their excitement was palpable. He strode on, the gates of the cemetery now in sight, and the single whisper was joined by another. Then another.

Until Silas was walking along with a pack of lost souls in tow. They kept to the shadows, slinking alongside him, making the darkness stretch and slide with their movement.

He sighed. 'You really are not so well hidden as you think.'

That drew an excited murmur from his little crowd, some of delight, others sounding not so sure.

It's him. Definitely him, look at that beard.

The beard huh? Nothing to do with the way he's glowing like a bloody full moon, and sounds like a choir from heaven.

Oh lordy, what I wouldn't do to be able to touch things again. Namely his lovely beard.

Will you leave off about the beard, Matthew?

It's lovely.

I'm scared.

Me too, Claudia. Do you think it will hurt?

The chatter was incessant now. There were at least five souls that he could sense.

My word, he's handsome, isn't he? The tales don't do him justice.

Hush, you fool man. If that daemon hears you, you'll be tasting his fire.

And why the heck would I be worried about fire then? How would the daemon harm me? We're dead, he's very much not.

We're dead?

Very funny, Georgina. That joke got old about fifty years ago.

'Excuse me,' Silas rubbed at his arms. He swore the temperature had plummeted further. His breath was a ghostly plume, and the tip of his nose was numb. 'There seem an awful lot of you here.'

He spoke to us!

Did that already. Told you your hearing wasn't so good, Peter.

He talking to us?

'Yes, I'm talking to you. I've not seen a town with so many souls about...' It was not unease, not exactly, which was bothering him. The scythe was too quiet for that, but the situation was strange nonetheless. 'How have so many of you in this town avoided the goddess?'

He knew teratisms could move freely about, another misfortune of the Blight, but it should not be so for those who were simply lost. Their place of death anchored them, kept them within certain confines.

The low gate of the cemetery came into view, crooked on its hinges.

We are not all from here, Mr Death. The speaker was feminine, light of breath.

'Call me Silas, please.'

There were squeals and coughs of delight.

First name basis, you 'ear that?

Power in that name, don't you think?

I am Claudia.

The one who professed to being frightened.

'You said you were scared, Claudia. You should not fear me.'

I don't.

Not you we are shitting our britches over, Mr Death, sir.

'Silas.'

Lovely name for a lovely looking fellow. Doesn't he sound sweeter than honey?

'You hear my melody?' It was the first time he'd been told such a thing.

Right nice tune it is, too.

You can hear it, Peter? Thought you claimed to be deaf as a post.

Clear as day to me, when all you lot seem to have mouths full of marbles.

'What are you frightened of?' Silas would have liked to enquire as to what his naming melody sounded like, but that was indulgent and unnecessary.

The Gloaming, sir, Claudia said, in her airy way.

That's what them old ghosts call it...old-fashioned as they are.

Claudia's been haunting her child's last resting place for near on three hundred years, ain't you love?

But it was another who spoke up, the one Silas thought they had called Matthew. *The Blight, that's what we younger sprogs call it.*

Either name, it is the same. Claudia found her voice once more. *It has been dreadfully fierce around these parts of the country. I was frightened I'd succumb to it, but then a new melody started to play, not yours, though you are louder now than it ever was. It was just as comforting as you, though. And drew us towards this place...this haven.*

A murmur of agreement ran through the shadowy crowd. He was yet to see a single one of them, but he felt them all as surely as he did the cold, which was only becoming more intense.

'A haven?'

Somewhere the Blight wouldn't touch us. The melody promises us safety.

Like the Pied Piper, looking after them kids.

Christ, Matthew, that's a terrible comparison. That weren't no happy tale.

Well at least there are no rats about. Silas recognised Georgina's cheery voice.

Maybe it won't end well for us neither. Not like we've been good little dead people. Should have moved on ages ago, we all know it. Perhaps we deserve it, if this is all a ploy to lure us to our doom.

The Pale Horseman won't hurt us. His melody is wonderful. And I've heard he's kind.

Those folks that were made teratisms would disagree with that.

And there's that daemon, remember? Might burn us into the next life.

Hush! Don't rile the ankou, what the blazes is wrong with you Matthew?

'I'm not going to hurt anyone. Neither is Pitch,' Silas scowled. 'But I would appreciate it if you gave me a moment to think.'

He observed the churchyard.

For all intents and purposes, it was regular. Headstones in mostly straight rows, more so than many others he'd seen, with the usual weight of age causing some to tilt or lean. There were no mausoleums; nothing fancy at all. The church itself was stone, with a tiled, steepled roof and a circular stained-glass window over the dark wood doors. Silas swallowed, shoving his thoughts from where they strayed to the Dullahan. Caught in his glass prison.

Memory of those turbulent events buoyed his resolve, and stirred his ire.

The graveyard was *his* domain.

The fate of these ghosts was his responsibility.

He'd not be made anxious by the stillness here. He'd not question his desire to settle his feet into that damp earth.

The heavy scent of the grave ripened, coating his nostrils as he dragged it in.

What do we do, Silas? Claudia's fear stirred him. *'Should we be afraid?'*

'No. There is nothing to fear here.' He slipped loose the latch of the gate. 'We go on.'

CHAPTER 6

Ambleside's graveyard was quiet, but it was very, very far from empty.

It brimmed with lost souls. Their shadowy, indistinct outlines filled the yard.

They were perched on headstones, clustered on plinths in great groups, lying across the grass where there were not graves available, and huddled on the steps of the small church. He even spied some draped over the branches of the naked-limbed cherry trees, over by what appeared to be a gardener's shed.

And every single one of the souls was fast asleep.

'Christ, what is this?' he whispered.

His arrival pushed at the heavy air, like a sea breeze at a sail, and a hum moved through the prone ghosts as their ethereal forms shifted. That strange wave of motion came again, as the souls he guided moved into the graveyard immediately behind him.

There were gasps, soft cries and even a sob. But not a one of them was uttered in any distress.

Rather, they sounded in awe.

Oh Silas...it is beautiful. Claudia gasped.

Is it heaven?

Close enough, my friend, close enough.

A long drawn out sigh came, loud enough that it seemed more than one of the souls was involved in the sound.

Silas frowned, dragging his gaze from the carpet of slumbering souls. He turned; to find all but one of his curious gang of ghosts had fallen fast asleep.

Thank you, ankou.

He was not certain who it was that remained to address him. The robustness of their shadow suggested one of the men, but he had no time for questions. The soul sank to the ground, adding their darkness to the low mound of those who had already succumbed to the strange sleep that held the entire graveyard. Their forms were a pile in front of the open gate, taking up one of the last remaining spaces he could see in the entire yard.

A squeak drew his attention. Scuttling out from a hole down near the base of the church doors, the church grim made an appearance. A white form that darted so quickly he wasn't quite certain what the creature was, until it drew nearer. Despite having only three legs, the white ferret moved at quite the clip, slipping up and over the array of prone forms that separated it from where Silas stood. Its yew-berry-red eyes fixed on him.

He crouched to meet it, extending his arm to allow it to scamper up and find a place upon his shoulder. If he were not mistaken there was something of a relieved air about the creature.

'Have you been waiting for me?' He received the nuzzle of a wet, cold nose behind his ear in reply. 'What is going on here?'

He was expecting no reply from the ferret; even Forneus had never managed such a feat.

'We have gathered them for you.'

Silas whirled about, spinning so quickly his passenger hissed, digging in tiny claws.

Herbert stood by the central grave, the most elaborate in the yard. The headstone was shaped like a small temple, with a weeping angel upon its top, covered in so much lichen it looked as though the wings truly were feathered. Two lost souls lay together on the length of its stone base, clasped hands discernible, despite their blurry forms.

'Herbert? Gracious, what are you doing here at this hour?' The boy wore no coat, and to Silas's horror, no shoes either. 'Christ, you'll freeze if –'

'Do not concern yourself with that,' the boy said, in a voice entirely unlike his own. 'He feels none of it.'

Silas's eyes widened. 'Izanami?'

'Take your succour, ankou. You must replenish what was lost.'

'My succour? What is happening here? Was it you who summoned all these souls?'

'Against the law of things, yes.'

'Why? Do you wish me to send all of them on?'

'You overestimate yourself, ankou. The strength is not in you.'

Silas swallowed. 'No…it is not.' A terrible thought struck him. 'Is this my end too? Are you here for me?' He shook his head, and took a step back. 'I will not go, yet, Izanami. I will not leave him. It is not yet done, and we are so close.'

'Calm yourself. I do not take you from him yet.'

Silas balled his fists, the scythe vibrating in his curled fingers. He refused to think too deeply on that single word, yet. There was an abyss of sadness in its simple form. 'Then tell me what it is you seek here.'

'You two Horsemen are close indeed. Which makes the Blight grow ever stronger in defiance. Its reach stretches ever wider, and gathers those it taints in greater number. I have made an exception to my involvement here, and have gathered many of my lost children, so that you might be made exceptional.' Herbert lifted an arm, and swept it to indicate the entirety of the graveyard. There was darkness on his palms, dirt perhaps. 'You push at your boundaries, Silas Mercer.'

A new panic gripped him. 'I am tired, but I am not done for. I can see this through. I'm certain. What can you do for me?'

The question was bold, perhaps stupidly so. Who was he to demand anything from Death? But then, he'd done so once and come out victorious. Sybilla lived to prove it.

Herbert smiled, but it somehow held none of the vivacity of the boy himself. 'There will come a time when your stubbornness shall no longer amuse me. I am fickle that way.'

'So long as it is not today.' Silas's pulse thumped unkindly, sick with the notion he might have stepped into his own grave here.

'It is not today.'

'Then tell me what I must do.' Herbert shivered hard, and Silas knew that death had lied to him. 'The boy feels you there. He is in pain.'

'He is human. To feel pain is in their nature. You know that.'

'But his pain is not natural, nor necessary.'

'Neither is your daemon's. Shall you reprimand the one who made it so...as you reprimand your goddess?' Herbert's teeth rattled against one another. The boy's fingertips were dark in the gloom. Frozen black.

'Forgive me.' Silas moved closer, hands lifted in supplication, while his inner thoughts raged. He would throttle the angel who had confined Pitch to such a fate, if given half the chance. 'Tell me, quickly, I beg you. What must be done?'

Herbert tilted his head, and with the misalignment of his eyes it seemed as though he did not look at Silas at all. 'You take your fill.'

'Of what? I need you to speak plainly.'

Herbert turned, and walked through the headstones and sleeping souls, towards the shed by the cherry tree. Silas followed, trying not to tread upon the hordes of quiet dead, even though he doubted they'd feel it if he did so. Not a one of them moved as he passed by.

'Come. You will lie with the dead.'

On the far side of the cherry tree, hidden by the girth of its trunk until now, was an open grave. A shovel jutted from the pile of freshly dug earth, its pale handle marked in places with darker patches.

Herbert's hand raised once more, and Silas cursed beneath his breath, as understanding came in a horrid wave. That was not dirt there at all, darkening his palms. It was blood.

There on the handle of the shovel too. Skin broken by the laborious digging of this deep grave.

The revulsion was almost enough to sway Silas from thoughts of what had been said. *Lie with the dead.*

The ferret rubbed against his neck, impossibly soft, and strangely comforting. Giving him the courage he needed to speak his next question. 'I am to return to my grave?'

'And find renewed life among the dead.' Herbert's shoulders twitched, his head jerking to one side. 'The child falters.'

'Let him go. It is enough.'

'Get in the grave, then it will be enough.'

The hole made for him was wide but not deep. This was not designed for the bulk of a coffin, with a substantial depth for mourners to cast their fistfuls of dirt into. Silas stepped down into the hole. It was like stepping into a deep tub, his thighs level with the grass. He moved quickly, so his fears would not impede him. There was no time for them now, no place for them to grow. Silas sat down in his grave.

'What must I do? To be strong enough?'

Herbert was unsteady as the goddess squatted him down onto his haunches. 'Take off your clothes.'

'What?' Silas spluttered. 'That is not –'

'Let nothing come between you and this earth. Do as I say.'

'At least turn the boy away.' Silas rose, and pulled his shirt over his head.

'They own the same parts as you.'

'But they are his own. There is no need to traumatise the boy further.'

'Stop talking and shed your clothing. You grow tiresome. The boy will remember none of this.'

With a scowl Silas pulled off his trousers, regretting his decision not to hunt for a pair of drawers when he was dressing. Once his boots were removed he was utterly naked, but only Herbert's exposure to it concerned him. There was neither time nor place for bashfulness otherwise.

Silas sat down with knees raised, covering himself. Herbert crouched once more and picked up a handful of earth, letting it trickle onto Silas's toes.

'You will strengthen here, but does the vessel know what fortitude he shall require for his task?'

Silas's scowl returned. 'Pitch understands very well the burden he carries.'

'But can he shoulder it as he must? I am not obliged to send you, my Pale Horseman, to the Lady of the Lake. You are mine, first and foremost.' In all that had been said through the young man's mouth, this sounded least human of all; the infinite reach of death was there in the sombre, unnerving sound. 'And if Death is better served in keeping you here, where you can alleviate the imbalance caused by the Blight, then so I shall keep you.'

Silas ran cold with fury. The scythe sparked against his skin. He reached up and touched at Herbert's chin, gently so as not to harm the fragile human, but pointedly, so the inhuman presence within knew Silas unafraid.

'For all your might, my goddess, you and I are unable to restore the balance lost because of Blood Lake and its halo. We merely defend against it, whilst Pitch has the power to destroy that blasted thing entirely. The power and the ability.' Silas released the goddess-touched boy. 'I have served you well, and long. Do not think to keep me from him. Or must I remind you that I have brought about the downfall of one goddess, already?'

He'd gone too far with such a threat. But his fatigue, his fear, his utter sick and tiredness of being at the mercy of others was done with.

Silas held the goddess's gaze. There was a disquieting blueness at Herbert's lips when Izanami spoke at last.

'The centuries have not eroded your resilience, ankou. There was always so much humanity in you. Life makes such resolute creatures, defiant even in the face of utter certainty.' The boy's head turned, taking in the mass of slumbering souls. 'Let us hope your daemon is as stalwart as humankind.'

'There is no one more valiant.'

When Herbert turned back, his eyes were aglow, entirely silver.

'Time shall tell.'

Silas gestured to his discarded shirt. 'Please, cover the boy. It is too cold for him here.'

Silver eyes blinked. And Herbert reached for the shirt, shrugging himself into a measure of material that was far too big for him.

Silas laid down in the grave. It's length and width were generous. He had no sense of being enclosed. There was room to spread his arms out from his sides a little, though he preferred to continue to cover himself for the moment. He stared up at a sharply clear sky; stars were spread like scattered diamonds, with the pearly curve of the moon perched amongst them.

'Do you understand what it is that the Blight truly craves, my ankou?' Herbert spoke with a timbre no mere boy should possess. 'What it hungers for and does not have?'

Silas exhaled; a long bloom of white air. And he saw the answer right there, in the twist of his breath. 'Life. It has no life.'

'Clever man.' Herbert took another fistful of dirt and let it rain down upon Silas's belly. The warmth was luscious. Welcome. 'For death to have true power, there must be life. That is what the Blight seeks. But life is too strong for that dark power when she is ripe and full of youth. The Blight preys instead upon the shreds still to be found in lost souls. Those misguided among the dead who think they can ignore my call. Now you must take your fill of what little life remains with them, and use their great number to renew yourself.'

Silas tore his gaze from the jewelled sky. 'Will these souls suffer for it?'

'They shall not wake whilst you reap. And when it is done they shall have no choice but to follow me. This is their last day as a lost soul. As this is your last taste of life, Silas Mercer.'

He did not falter, did not look away. 'I understand.' He had one final concern upon his mind. 'Would you make sure that –'

'That the prince does not think himself alone?' Herbert leaned over the grave, and the goddess brushed her fingers against Silas's cheek. 'Your only fault these centuries past has been to retain far too much of your human heart. The vessel will be told that he is not abandoned. Now rest, Horseman. Drink of these fading lives, so that you might revive and see us through to restoring the balance lost.'

CHAPTER 7

It was a churn in Pitch's belly that had awoken him. The shift of something in the emptiness within, the space the simurgh had left. He had sat up, gasping for breath, his heart pounding.

To find a three-legged ferret at the end of their bed.

A bed empty of the wide spread of the ankou.

'Where is he?'

He'd pulled on his trousers and his cloak, and followed the creature.

To the graveyard. Of course. For where else would Silas prefer to be, when not in Pitch's bed?

But he'd not expected to find his ankou naked in a grave. Curled up on his side, like a child in the womb. Pitch's heart had stopped. He was sure of it. All the pulses in his body held still. He'd imagined, for a moment, that it was over. That all was lost, for everything lay in that grave.

He had no idea how bright his flame was burning until the boy told him to stifle it.

'Calm yourself. He is not gone.'

Herbert though, looked like he was on his way to being so. The boy was shivering so hard it was a wonder he could stay on his feet. The shirt he wore was clearly not his, trailing near his knees, dwarfing his shoulders. Silas's shirt. Any fool would know it. Especially this fool.

Pitch reshaped his fire, making it less injurious, and more useful to a child possessed.

'He is freezing. You are too much for that boy.' Pitch had little time for the goddess who had held him back in that gods-forsaken cave in the cockaigne.

'I am too much for everyone. That is entirely my point.'

'What is happening here?'

'What he needs. Your task takes much from my ankou. It will take more yet, should all things come to pass.'

Pitch resisted the urge to singe the boy's cheek. He'd only punish a child if he did so: not the goddess for her cruel reminder. 'He told me he was just tired.'

'As the winter is just cool.'

He shook off his irritation. Gods were cryptic, there was no changing that. 'He has been keeping something from me, I'm sure. Is it your doing?'

'The end is always my doing.'

'Fuck, will you just speak plainly?'

The glow of silver brightened. Herbert blinked slowly, and no longer shivered with Pitch's flame so close. 'I grow tired of that being demanded of me.'

'Then perhaps you should learn from it.'

'Careful, daemon. It is not you I favour.'

'I do not need your favour. You are not my goddess.' Other Celestials held greater sway over the children of Arcadia. 'What is happening to Silas?'

Pitch's flame crackled between them, burning in the quiet that held.

'You busy yourselves too much with one another. There will come a time when you must let him go. That time has always been forthcoming. It is the fate of all who live and die.'

'I know.' The ache that came with saying it reached into his bones, twisted around every vein. 'But this is not his time. You said yourself, he is not gone.'

He had a dreadful moment of imagining the goddess a trickster. A tormentor. Letting him stand over Silas's grave with false promise.

'He is not gone this day, but his days have always had a number upon them.'

Pitch nodded. 'And he knows that number, doesn't he? That is what he keeps from me.'

'You've grown wiser, daemon.'

If it was so, it did not bring any solace. Pitch went to his knees beside the great pile of soil dug from the grave. His cloak fluttered wide, shifting dirt, causing it to trickle down where Silas lay. 'Why did you summon me? What am I to do here?'

Pitch knew how to fight, to lash out at his enemies, to bring destruction. But there was not a flame, nor vestige, nor halo in all the known worlds that could help him here.

'It was he who summoned you. What you do here is no concern of mine. What you shall do, matters far more, Prince of Arcadia.'

Pitch studied Silas's lifeless form, hearing the goddess speak but caring little to return a reply. Silas lay like a great stone effigy of himself. Unmoving. Not breathing. Silas had summoned him here, but Pitch was clueless as to how to help him. 'How long will this last?'

'As long as it must.'

'What am I to do then? I don't know what he needs.'

'He summoned all that he needed.'

'I didn't bring anything...what is that supposed to mean?'

Pitch turned, and found himself alone, save for the ferret who had scampered up the length of the shovel and now balanced on its handle. A light frost had settled upon the graveyard; a dusting of white everywhere, except for the circle around Pitch, where his warmth had made it impossible.

Was that it then? A fire daemon was what Silas needed?

He shifted off his knees, unclasping the cloak and letting it fall away. He stepped down into the grave. Treading carefully, moving thoughtfully as he lay the cloak over Silas's body; the man he knew would be unhappy with such nakedness, no matter how magnificent a body he had. Silas was mighty, but he was also a prude. Satisfied with the tuck of the cloak, the hue of pink pleasing against the darkness of Silas's beard, Pitch settled behind the ankou and drew the remainder of the cloak over himself. He was just as cold as Pitch had imagined.

He settled his arm over Silas, just as the ankou did so often for him.

Pitch brought his flame forth, a heat beneath his skin that made the air beneath the cloak warm, the soil beneath them heated as a warming pan.

'Better?' He knew no answer would come. He did not need one. The heat was already there against Silas's skin.

Pitch nuzzled against Silas's hair, and breathed in all that made this man what he was. Perhaps there was a chance the ankou knew him here.

Pitch did not intend to sleep again. But then, he'd not intended to spend his night in an open grave. Nor to find it the only place in the world he could imagine being.

At some point, however unlikely, he slept.

Coughing woke him. He struggled to recall where he was; a hard surface beneath his hip, the scent of loam, the warmth of his flame, still bright beneath his skin.

The embrace reminded him.

'Silas?'

But the ankou remained deathly still.

'Sorry, did I wake you, Tobias?'

He moved swiftly, but with care not to disturb the immovable ankou, tucking in the cloak about his shoulders so the heat remained caught beneath. He rose, on his knees, to peer over the edge of their shallow pit.

'Sybilla? What are you doing here?'

The Valkyrie, clad in a thick, black coat with fur at the neck and cuffs, sat upon the ledger of the grave nearest to Silas's open plot. She rested her back against the headstone: eyes closed, and stroking the white ferret that was curled in her lap.

'The grim was very insistent I come here. It seemed it was in my best interest not to ignore the furry fellow.' Her voice was studiously flat, her true feelings about her predicament well hidden. 'Evidently Silas is not the only one who will benefit from time spent amongst all these dead. So here I am, at the behest of a church grim.'

'You know it a grim?'

'I do.'

'But Silas could not have told you.'

'He did not need to. I see it for what it is. I see all these souls, for what they are.'

Pitch peered around the yard. A mist hung about some of the headstones, the end of a row hidden in its pallor. 'I see an empty space.'

'It is very far from empty, though it does grow quieter as they leave us. You do not feel how they make the air spark?'

He turned back. Sybilla had opened one eye but closed it quickly now. 'No.'

Her reply was an indecipherable hum.

Pitch took in the terrible scarring left by the halo, and could not shake the guilt that came. If he'd not been so pathetic, if Seraphiel had not muzzled his flame so extensively, the angel need not have suffered so.

Suffered...and died? She'd gifted him her magick, but he'd not thought that possible without a Death Wish.

Pitch glanced down at Silas. The ankou had been furtive when pressed for details of the Valkyrie's miraculous survival. And it was indeed that. Miraculous. She had defied death.

It struck him then, with a firm hard blow to his senses.

'You died. Silas brought you back.' There was no question in Pitch's mind. He did not need to see the angel nod her head. But she did so.

'I was there upon death's threshold, but Silas would not let me cross over.' Sybilla's hand stilled over the snow white pelt. 'Is this my fault, Tobias? Did my return cost him too much?'

Pitch fingered the material of Silas's discarded trousers. 'So far as this fool is concerned, there's no cost too high for such things. And if anyone can be accused of taxing him beyond his limits, it is me. This fucking quest.'

'Don't let your mind darken so, Tobias. I see where your thoughts try to take you.'

'Then I truly pity you, for it is a fucking awful place to go.'

'You cannot leave him. If you go without him, he will find you. But he will suffer all the while until he does.'

Pitch ran his thumb over the dirty fabric. 'He does not suffer now though, does he? I doubt I'd have to ask the goddess twice to keep him. She could hold him here, as he is.'

If Silas's days were numbered, then let them be spent wandering aimlessly in a pretty garden, or foraging for wild mushrooms; whatever the hell he wanted, so long as it was peaceful.

'Tobias?' The firmness suggested it was not the first time the angel had called his name. 'Are you alright?'

Not in the slightest. The idea of leaving Silas behind might be noble, but what a pity Pitch was so far from being a nobleman. He folded the trousers and set them aside.

He was too selfish to let Silas go as easily.

'I'm fine.'

Sybilla urged the ferret from her lap, and pushed away from the headstone. Despite the silvery shadows Pitch saw her wince. 'Silas defied his goddess for me. I cannot imagine what greater lengths he would go to for you.' Sybilla glanced skyward, the whites of her eyes vibrant in the dim light. 'Nor you for him. I feel a trace of your affections in my returned magick.'

That was perhaps the most appalling thing Pitch had heard of late. And, not knowing how a decent fellow would handle the situation, he stayed true to his miserable self. 'Oh, please tell me you know we fucked about in that dream? I see now your magick was likely the reason we found each other at all. Were you aroused by what you saw? Could I perhaps entice you to dabble in a pillar or two?'

'Gods, you are a fool.'

'But a desirous one, no?'

'No.' A genuine smile found her punished lips. 'You have no idea how desperately my magick raced to me, when it knew I had survived. Anything to escape the tawdry existence it shared with you.'

Laughter drifted between them, here in the middle of a graveyard, surrounded by ghosts and grim and monsters.

'I'm glad you didn't die.' Pitch laid his smouldering hand on Silas's shoulder. The shimmer of heat made the drying strands of the ankou's hair shift.

The angel did not reply, her gaze fixed towards the centre of the yard, where the tallest of the headstones stood. An angel, of all things.

'But I did. My wings did not survive, nor my halo. I am grateful for this chance to make amends, of course, but I am not as I was, before.'

'Amends?'

The Valkyrie levelled her gaze at him. 'I should have been able to protect you, and I could not.'

Pitch found it too hard to hold her gaze. He looked away. 'Before you spend another moment flagellating yourself, may I suggest you redirect your whip towards another angel. If Seraphiel had not had Edward turn me into a useless suit of bones in this devastatingly gorgeous skin, I'd have been able to protect myself. Hastings would not have had to sacrifice themselves, you would still have your wings, I would not have spilled secrets like a fucking fountain, and Silas would not have become a carcass for Morrigan to pick to the bone.' He laid a hand to his belly, the movement out of Sybilla's line of sight. The angel waited. 'You could all be back at Holly Village by now. Or down at The Atlas perhaps. Silas would be stuffing his face with that awful Indian dish he adores.'

'Kedgeree? It's rather wonderful, actually. Despite the British dampening it down, and insisting it a breakfast dish.' Sybilla got to her feet with a grunt, using the headstone as a prop. 'He has very decent taste, for the most part.' She made a point of eyeing Pitch up and down. 'But on occasion Silas does go quite off the rails.'

Pitch's gesture was not polite at all. 'You must be feeling better. You have returned to imagining yourself remotely funny, but your humour is as dire as that bloody dish.'

'I thought her rather amusing.' The croaky, rough sound had Pitch's blood lighting up.

'Silas?'

'Welcome back, Mr Mercer.' Sybilla's chuckle was warm. 'You've been missed.'

Pitch stared down at the ankou, who was moving slowly, eyes fluttering. 'You bloody sod, how long have you been awake?'

'It is good to see you too, my heart.' Silas grunted, trying to push himself to his elbow but having no luck with it until Pitch set a hand beneath his shoulder.

'Here, be careful. Take your time.' He eased Silas to sitting, the cloak falling away to rest in the ankou's lap. Pitch clucked his tongue. 'Keep it on, you'll freeze out here, damn you.'

'Are you fussing over me?' Silas still had that rumble. And it still did odd things to the pit of Pitch's stomach.

'I am simply trying to speed up the process of getting back indoors. Where the civilised people are.'

'I think you are coddling.'

'I think you shall get a clout on your ear if you don't shut up.'

'I think it is time for me to leave,' Sybilla announced.

The ankou laughed. A choked, rather chesty sound, with an inhale that clearly took in more dirt than intended. Silas coughed and spluttered.

'You idiot.' Pitch banged at his back, in what he presumed to be a helpful move. He'd seen it done once or twice in various pubs. 'Stop making such a fuss.'

'Great gods, you are the worst nursemaid I've ever known.' Sybilla stood beside the grave, arms folded, looks disapproving. 'Stop hitting him.'

'I'm all right.' Silas coughed, though not as badly as before. The force of his fit though had made tears run. 'It's passed now. All is well.'

A sharp squeak came from the edge of the pit, the ferret peeking from beneath the length of Sybilla's dark coat.

'Hello there, pretty one. Thank you for bringing him to me.' The ankou brushed a thick-fingered hand down the animal's back. The scythe on Silas's finger was altered, changed from its duller pewter tone to a shining silver that was difficult to miss.

'Excuse me?' Pitch feigned indignation. 'I have been lying in the dirt for you, yet your thanks and attention goes to an elongated rat?' The ferret bared tiny fangs.

'Oh, Pitch? You're here?' Silas put on a show of his own, squeezing the bridge of his nose, and blinking groggily. 'I didn't notice you.'

'Utter bastard. Fine, I will leave.'

Silas moved much faster now, grabbing at Pitch's arm. 'Not a chance. Why are you barely undressed?'

Pitch made a weak play at trying to remove himself from the ankou's hold. He'd forgotten entirely he wore only trousers. 'I've been making my way through all the men of the village, whilst you snoozed with the dead.'

'Really?' Silas moved him easily, and though Pitch could have bested him with some effort, there was no mistaking the easy strength that came from him. Nor how Silas's brown eyes held specks of brightness in their depths now. 'Will you show me what they taught you?'

Sybilla heaved a loud sigh, and even the grim ferret made a noise of discontentment and jumped from the grave. 'Right, well that is my signal to leave, then. I'll let the others know you're up and about, and all is well.' She paused. 'All is well, I'm assuming, Silas? You seem...you look brighter, glowing more readily.'

Pitch frowned. He could not even make out Silas's usual dull aura, and the angel seemed too far away in the dim light to notice the change in Silas's eyes.

'I feel much better, thank you, Sybilla. All is definitely well.' Silas propped himself on his elbow, staring up at the angel. 'Bloody hell, you are...well, you have a decent glow yourself. I'm glad this has helped you too.'

'As am I. But I had best return before the others wake to find me gone. Mind you, I doubt Tyvain and Isaac shall rise before noon. They enjoyed the hospitality at the Rule last night a bit too much.'

Pitch's head snapped up at that. 'Who is looking after the simurgh?'

'I've covered much of the Golden Rule in runes, and my room is saturated with them. Little wonder I felt so bloody rotten. Jane is there, and Phillipa and Scarlet too, of course.' She picked at some leaf litter that had snagged in the fur cuff at her wrist. 'And the Cultivation is not without its own protection. The divine magick it contains is remarkable.' She looked to Pitch. 'As is anyone who could hold the likes of it, for so long.'

Silas's hand found the small of his back, but that only made the intolerably sweetness of the moment worse, and Pitch edged away.

'Not as though I've had much choice,' he muttered. 'I thought you were leaving?'

'And so I am.' The Valkyrie leaned down and offered her arm to the ferret. 'Come, leave them be, before you see a sight that shall scar you for all the afterlife you live.' The ferret scampered up the angel's arm, wriggling into place upon her shoulder. She turned away, but then reconsidered, and glanced over her shoulder. 'There is something else I must tell you both. Now seems as good a time as any.'

Silas pressed a kiss to Pitch's shoulder. 'Go on.'

'I've had word from the Lady Satine.' She touched her temple, as though that explained the messaging well enough, which in truth, it did.

'Though it is not with her usual aplomb. The message is most basic. But in short, many of our party have come to the end of their road. Ambleside shall be where we part ways.'

Pitch stared at her, caught off-guard by how her words quickened his pulse.

'I understand.' Silas said, though he did so very quietly. 'Very well then. Do they know?'

'No.' Sybilla pressed her lips. 'It only came to me when I sat here in long silence. And the message was so faint, if I'd not been surrounded by the quiet of the dead, I doubt I'd have heard at all.' She glanced at Silas. 'Perhaps the journey's end approaches for all involved.'

'You will leave us too?' Pitch worked very hard at sounding careless.

Did he sound too needy? Silas was watching him. Concerned again. Damn it.

'There was nothing said of me.' Sybilla shook her head. 'So I assume I continue on with you. But all the others shall remain.'

'Well, good luck getting that damned wisp away from the simurgh.' Pitch scoffed. 'You'll likely have to trap Scarlet in a witch bottle and hurl it out to sea to keep them from following us.'

Not in a thousand years would he admit he could not imagine saying goodbye to that infernal creature.

'I'll take my leave now gentlemen, and leave you to...well, whatever it is one does after one steps out of their grave.'

They bid their farewells, with vague promises to meet for a late break-fast. Sybilla strode away with firm posture and an easy gait; Silas was not the only one revitalised in this graveyard.

The ankou took up his caresses the moment he back was turned. 'It pains you to imagine leaving Scarlet behind.'

'I hardly care what they do, Silas.' Blast this man, could he read bloody minds now?

'Don't hide from me, my love.'

And curse all the taints of the Celestial, that drippy endearment was becoming less painful to hear, and Pitch found his tongue too easy to use around Silas. Ready to blurt the mortifying truth. So Pitch did the only reasonable thing he could do.

He punched at the ankou's shoulder. 'Stop with your syrupy non-sense. I'm just saying, they are a stubborn creature.'

'And they are not the only one I know.' Silas fended off Pitch's distracting attempts to fasten the cloak and wrapped him in an embrace so tight it really wasn't comfortable at all, but Pitch didn't go so far as to protest. 'Perhaps Scarlet shall just do what they please, and stay with us. Now, shall we get out of this grave? I had you brought here so you wouldn't worry, but I didn't expect you to lie here with me. I'm grateful for it though.' He traced the line of Pitch's jaw. 'And I thank you for your flame, I felt its warmth where I was.'

'What happened there?' Pitch tried to keep his expression smooth, though really he wanted to melt into the ankou, perhaps bring down more dirt upon them so they could hide away here.

'I was nourished...regained what was lost in the cockaigne. More perhaps.' Silas was thoughtful. 'The goddess returned my strength to me.' His glance took in the graveyard. 'But it came at the expense of others.'

'What others?'

'Those who had not yet chosen to let go.'

'Lost souls?'

The pained expression on his face was equally painful to see. 'Yes.'

Pitch took Silas's face between his palms, warming his skin, letting the fire dance against the new flecks of amber in his eyes. 'But they at rest now, are they not?'

'Yes.'

'And you are well.' He knew the answer already; it was plain to see. No more dark circles. The ankou was vigorous, grand and imposing in a way Pitch had not known before. He brushed his lips against Silas's, enjoying the shiver that came. 'You are very well.'

The ankou touched him, as he so loved to do, and the lines of concern fell away from his face. 'I feel wonderfully well. Shall I show you how much so? Let me take you back to our room, and I shall make you moan for me until you beg me to stop. Would you like that?'

If ever a pointless question had been asked.

'I suppose I might be agreeable.'

Silas's deliciously deep chuckle sounded again. He ankou shifted onto his knees, and the cloak fell away, leaving nothing to the imagination;

for which Pitch was eternally grateful. 'My trousers and boots should be here somewhere.'

Silas barely leaned on Pitch as they both stepped up and out of the grave. In fact, he was nimble; swift and graceful, despite his hefty size.

'Why bother with them?' Pitch was eager to see what else the ankou was newly swift and graceful with. 'I'm just going to remove them.'

Silas tugged him in close, and delivered a fast and breathless kiss. His tongue demanding entrance, his body seeking to melt into Pitch's. 'I warn you,' he mumbled. 'I am quite invigorated. I may wear you out.'

Pitch blinked, the blood thundering in his ears. 'Oh my dear, that is a challenge I was born to accept.'

The ankou handed Pitch the cloak as he took up his trousers. He nodded towards the shed.

'Do you remember the last time we visited a shed like that?' Silas's grin was positively evil as he bent over, taking a preposterous amount of time to cover the thick pillar that dangled between his legs.

Pitch could hardly forget the ramshackle place at the bottom of the garden where Silas had used his tongue in all manner of ways, in all manner of sublime places. But it was also the place where the ankou had first blurted out his deep affections. To think of that moment–of how dreadfully Pitch had handled the occasion– made his empty belly twist in unfamiliar ways.

'I do,' he said, with a sniff. 'But I've just slept in the dirt for you, I shall not be fucked in a dusty, spider-ridden old shack, amongst spades and rakes and smelly hessian sacks. I am a prince, I'll have you know.'

Silas bowed, deeply. 'Of course, your highness. Forgive me, I am simply overwhelmed by your breathtaking beauty. Best you cover up, before I can no longer contain my passion for your enchanting self, and seek to ravish you, right here upon this pile of dirt.'

'You would not dare.'

'I would dare anything for you.'

'Idiot.'

The ankou righted, and Pitch sucked in his breath. Silas shone. Not with any discernible light, save for that in his eyes, but he was luminous nonetheless. Pitch had not realised how downtrodden the ankou had become, until he was no longer weighted down. He was beautiful; with how alive he truly was.

'What? Do I have dirt on my face?' Silas buttoned up his trousers, then dragged on his boots, not bothering to tie the laces. 'My hair is likely a bird's nest.'

'You look dreadful.' And if they did not get to their room, there was every chance the pile of dirt would suffer for it after all. Pitch threw the cloak over his shoulders, busying himself with the clasp. 'You shall have to blindfold me before you stick your cock in me, otherwise I shall spend the whole time screaming in terror.'

Silas smiled; a sun breaking over the horizon. 'I do love you.'

Pitch could hardly blurt out an insipid *I rather like you too,* or a pitiful, *I won't survive if you are told to leave me, too, s*o he had no option but to point out the obvious. 'Your laces are undone.'

He turned, throwing up the hood of his cloak, and moving as briskly out of the graveyard as his feet would allow without breaking into a run. He had to maintain some level of decorum, after all.

'Wait, I want to check the shed for a coat. I'm half bloody naked.'

'I don't see the problem,' Pitch called back but did not wait.

There was a delay before he heard Silas following, at a run. His footfalls heavy and steady; their tempo somehow threatening and thrilling at the same time. Pitch threw glances over his shoulder, and nearly squealed at the blatant hunger in Silas's gaze. The ankou looked awful in the stained smock he'd found, the sooner he was rid of it the better.

Pitch jogged along, feeling as though he were being hunted down by an enormous wolf; and entirely approved of being eaten alive.

Day-break had barely done its breaking, but already the village folk were stirring. A woman stepped from her house, an overflowing basket of laundry at her hip, her eyes widening as she looked up the road behind him. 'Are you in some kind of trouble, sir?'

'I truly hope so.'

No sooner had he said it than the pounding of footsteps ceased.

'Oh, Pitch, wait! Do stop and look at this Christmas tree here in the dressmakers. I think you will adore all the glitter upon it.'

Pitch stopped dead, thinking himself caught in some kind of poor prank. 'A tree? You wish me to look at a godsdamned tree, right now, Silas?'

He was very aware his stern reprimand gathered many glances. But was the ankou mad?

'Sorry. No, we can return later.'

There he was, beneath all that brimming, sterling manhood and vigour; the dolt who apologised too much. Pitch smiled, but made sure Silas did not see it.

'Exactly. Come along.'

Pitch was close, so very close, to the Churchill Inn, when a figure stepped from the alleyway that led to the stables.

'Hello, Pitch.'

The heat in his veins cooled, and it was no small feat to offer up a smile.

'Hello, Charlie.'

CHAPTER 8

S ilas only ended the hugging under great duress; namely Pitch's threats to burn Silas's hair if he did not let Charlie have some room to breathe.

'You are stronger than a dozen oxen, Silas. Leave him be.'

But he'd refused to let go of Charlie's hand as they made their way inside, and could not take his eyes from the lad, which was causing poor Charlie some consternation.

'It is truly me, Silas. Do you not believe it?'

Waking in the cemetery, feeling as though he could take on any foe, any force, that awaited, and knowing the passing of all the lost souls had been so very peaceful, Silas had already been filled with happiness. But now...now he was strained at the seams with utter joy. 'I am so pleased to see you, Charlie.' His eyes stung, and he knew the onset of his tears obvious to all, but what did that matter?

'You're not going to start with the hugging again, are you?' Pitch sighed. 'You may want to sit elsewhere, Charlie, for your own good.'

The lad laughed and Silas thought he might just fly apart with contentment.

'Are you sure you are well?' Silas asked, for the third time.

After asking a housemaid where they might find some privacy she had directed them to this room; part formal dining room, part parlour, with a settee of faded sage velvet and deep mahogany fitted into the corner nearest the fireplace. With its larger size they were all afforded a seat without being atop one another, but that had not stopped Silas from sitting almost on top of Charlie so he could determine for himself the answer to the question.

'I am.'

The lad was certainly tired, but no more than a night out would have made him. There were no evident bruises, scratches, or damage. Charlie's choppy hair needed trimming, and he looked to have spent far too long in his clothing: his brown corduroy trousers, and yellow-creme jacket with its spotted waistcoat beneath, creased beyond measure.

Pitch finished with giving the maid instructions to make her way to the Golden Rule at once and wake their companions. He joined Silas and Charlie, dropping onto the vacant end of the settee with a sigh. His cloak puffed up like the top of a pink mushroom.

'How many times has Charlie told you he is fine?' he said. 'Would you have him strip to prove it to us? Is that your end game here?'

Silas frowned but Charlie burst out laughing, blue eyes sparkling. 'I worried you might have changed, after all you've been through, Tobias.'

Pitch's grin was there, but Silas was attuned to his subtler signs. The lad's remark was meant in kindness, but troubled Pitch nonetheless. As did Charlie's next remark.

'Edward will be ever so pleased to see you both. Sanu has showed us many things, a lot of which we could not understand without context to do so...but we knew you both were alive...and that was more than enough for us.'

'Has Edward's circumstance...changed?' Pitch was gruff, picking at his nails as though whatever the answer he cared very little.

Silas made yet another silent declaration to punch Seraphiel in the teeth, if that opportunity ever arose. Even if it were the mere spectre of the angel, Silas was equipped to show the ghost his displeasure.

'He's doing very well, truly, Tobias.' Charlie rose and pressed his hands towards the fire where it crackled cheerily in the bricked hearth. The light drew out the slivers of auburn in his hair. Of which there seemed far more than Silas recalled. 'He is a strong man, and endures his hardships with such a stoic temperament. I am terribly proud of him. And he assures me he feels no worse than he did since that day in the Fulbourn, when it all began.' It was clear the lad's feelings for the lieutenant had only grown since last Silas had watched them together at the country estate. 'But I will be honest with you both, and say I fear he is not being honest with me about his suffering. I hope this can all be over and done with, before too long.'

Silas rose and moved to stand behind the lad, placing his hands on his shoulders. Charlie was no slip of a thing, even if he was diminutive in height there had always been something steely about him, but when he reached his hand to find Silas's, and clung on tight, it was a timely reminder that he was young, and human, after all.

'Does he say anything of Seraphiel?' Pitch asked, and Silas knew the question would have burned its way up his throat.

Charlie took a moment to answer. 'Not specifically. Only that whatever lies inside Edward is restless. Impatient, I think, now that you are so close.'

'To the Sanctuary?' Silas asked.

But Charlie shrugged. 'To where you need to be. But if where we've been waiting is a Sanctuary...well, I dare say you'll be disappointed. And you won't like the journey there. It was a bastard of a walk on foot. I'm knackered.'

'Well, we are hardly stupid enough to walk. It shall be horses for us.' Pitch had forgone his nails and was punishing a lose thread on the settee.

'I didn't have that luxury. Sanu needed to remain with Edward, and the Priest's Hole is not exactly near to any stables, or even a paddock where I could have stolen a horse.'

'How did you find us, Charlie?' Silas took up another log to throw on the fire, as the lad rubbed his hands before the subtle flames.

'A cuckoo arrived, even though it is far too early for them in the season.' Charlie's grin was wry. 'But since when has anything made any sense of late? Sanu gave the bird a few strands of her tail, and that seemed to be all that was needed. I understood I was to follow it, and it led me...here.'

'Silas,' Pitch exclaimed, perching upon the very edge of the seat. 'That is hardly the question that needs asking. Sweet, holy Celestials, did you say you have been in a priest's hole, Charlie? You lucky thing. The pious ones are often the most lewd.'

'Pitch, truly?' Silas sighed as he dug the poker into the coals, stirring them.

'It's fine, Silas.' Charlie sighed. 'Edward and I have already placed bets on how long it would take for Tobias to make a crude remark about it.'

'What? Priest's holes are quite enjoyable. I've known a few in my time. How big is yours?'

'And you say you are four hundred years old?' Silas said, exasperated 'Are you certain you've not embellished that with several more centuries than it deserves?'

'Says the ancient old man whose crows' feet are showing.'

'You are idiots, amongst many other things.' Charlie grinned, sitting down once more, as Silas encouraged the fire. 'But it is so wonderful to see you in such good spirits.' He reached for Pitch, grabbing his hand and squeezing. 'I have missed you both, so terribly.'

'And you lad, have grown far more adept at a decent lie.' Pitch pulled his hand from Charlie's grip, but Silas's heart danced to see the slight pink in his cheeks. 'Tell me more of this priest and his hole.'

Charlie gave out a put-upon sigh. 'Must you make every turn of phrase salacious?'

'Yes.'

'Fair enough. But this is not the hole you are insinuating, and you know it. Where Sanu took us may once have been used as a hiding place for a persecuted man of the cloth, but it's not sheltered a priest from strife in a long while. Now his presence is a legend only.'

'If you say so.'

'And I do,' Charlie laughed, and it was truly a wonderful moment for Silas as he found his place on the settee. 'You may have known many a pious hole, Mr Astaroth, but I assure you, you haven't known this one, unless you are prone to rutting about in remote caves in the middle of the Lake District, which, honestly, I just cannot imagine.'

'But you say you have walked from this place, Charlie?' Silas said, before Pitch could strike again. 'How long has this journey taken you?'

'A full day's walk.'

Silas and Pitch exchanged a glance, and he felt he knew the daemon's mind. A day's walk was not so far. They were upon a brink from which there was no return.

'But we can do it in far less time on horseback, of course,' Charlie said, misunderstanding their quiet.

'I see no need to rush.' Pitch was sullen.

'Edward is alone, I cannot leave him –'

'It's alright, Charlie,' Silas said, laying a reassuring hand on the lad's knee. 'Of course we will go as soon as we've made preparations.' Perhaps those preparations could take a while, a day, a week. Silas shivered, despite the fire's substance.

'I was being very cautious. Too slow, I'm sure,' Charlie said. 'It has been a harrowing time, not knowing what has become of everyone.' He grew thoughtful. 'Sanu tried very hard to show us, but about the only thing we truly understood was the loss of Hastings. The mare grieves, I do not need her language to know that. I'm so sorry to hear the news.'

Pitch's gaze shifted to the window, his focus distant. 'Our enemies have paid their price. There is only one left to bother us still.' He shrugged. 'Perhaps two, if my dear Pappa changes his ever-shifting mind, again.'

'Your father seeks you harm?' Charlie glanced at Silas, his concerns clear. But Silas shook his head.

'He is no longer a concern, I'm certain,' he said. 'There was a misunderstanding, but all is well now.'

He expected a curt, vile rebuttal from Pitch, but none came. The prince was still worryingly lost in his own thoughts. He rubbed at his finger, as though he still wore the scythe there.

'Pitch? Everything alright?'

In answer he got to his feet, turning his back on them. 'Stop fussing, Silas. I'm going to bathe. I'm certainly not going to traipse about the countryside with dirt between my arse cheeks. '

'Oh, what a wonderful idea,' Charlie sighed.

'If you think to join me, best you clear it with Silas first.' Pitch was careless. 'We could have him watch, I suppose? In time, he may be convinced to join us.'

Charlie's eyes went wide. 'I don't want to bathe with you.'

'Oh, I suspect you do.'

'You are no detective then, I assure you,' Charlie coughed with laughter, chasing the bleakness from the room. 'I could not think of anything worse.'

Silas sighed, playing his part in the charade. But he kept a careful watch on his lover. Despite Pitch's return to vulgar form, Silas did not trust the honesty of his mood. The prince was not so carefree as he sought to appear.

'I need not go with you, if you'd like a moment alone?' Silas was struck by how rarely the daemon had such an opportunity. If Pitch were not in the hands of his captor, he was a prisoner of a different sort, with Silas unwilling to let him out of his sight for fear of losing him again. 'I shall not be insulted in the slightest if you'd like to be on your own for a while.'

Pitch stopped where he had paced halfway to the door. He stood, saying nothing for so long that Charlie tugged at Silas's sleeve, giving him a questioning look. He shrugged, uncertain the cause of this strange pregnant pause.

'What of you, Silas?' Pitch said, finally, in the hushed way he so rarely adopted. 'Do you wish to distance yourself from me?'

Silas frowned at the sudden frailty. 'You know the answer to that, Pitch.'

'But perhaps your goddess gives you no say in the matter. Perhaps, you are yet to tell me that you too have been instructed to end our journey here.'

There it was. The crux of the matter. Understanding the prince's darker thoughts nearly buckled Silas's knees.

'My goddess knows better than to waste her divine breath with such pitiful notions. No such instruction has come, and if it did, then heaven help the messenger, for they would have all manner of blasphemy to carry back to her.' He strode up to Pitch, who had not yet moved. To his relief he caught the subtle lift of a cautious smile on the daemon's lips. All the knots which had wound themselves, unravelled quickly, but he had one more point to make. 'Do not ever ask me again, if I am considering leaving your side.'

'Or what?' Pitch was returning to himself, the wickedness hinting in his eyes once more.

Silas ran his hand over Pitch's arse. 'Or, I shall take you to the Royal Botanical Gardens in London, and make you listen, as I list every single plant by their Latin name.'

Pitch's sharp intake of breath, the flutter of fingertips at his mouth, made Silas's blood warm. 'You are a monster.'

'You had best believe it.'

Charlie coughed. 'Gentlemen, the consensual torture shall have to wait, I'm afraid. We are about to be bombarded.'

CHAPTER 9

Tyvain was at the forefront, her voice booming through the entire inn. 'Where the bloody hell is he? Gonna tan his bloody hide.'

Silas moved to call to her, but the soothsayer had already found them.

Charlie leapt to his feet, dashing past Silas and Pitch to meet Tyvain halfway across the room. They collided in a messy hug that saw them falling onto a red velvet chaise by the wall just inside the doorway. The soothsayer gave the lad a loud telling off.

'Scared me half to death. If I had a switch, you'd be getting a beating right now.'

Charlie laughed off the berating with his usual good-nature. 'Well, I'll be grateful for small mercies then.'

'Look at the state of ya. Too skinny by half.' Tyvain adjusted the creased smock she wore. Her skirt, a plain navy blue, was equally as creased, and her hair even more haphazard than normal, Silas suspected she'd been sleeping fully clothed.

'I'm fine, Ty. And not undernourished at all, I assure you.'

'Well, ya too pale then. Freckles have multiplied.'

Jane swept into the room, her hair in the most delightful braid, with ribbons of white interwoven throughout, contrasting the creamier hue of her morning dress. She nudged the scrutinising soothsayer to one side, dropping a small basket she held, before helping Charlie up from the chaise to deliver her own hug. 'So very good to see you, my dear. We've all been worried.'

'How is Edward?' Sybilla was the last to arrive, and Silas could not help but marvel at how easily she moved, the grim suffering of before all but gone; only the scars remained. 'Is he holding up?'

Charlie's smile faded. 'He's strong, remarkably so, but I doubt...' She glanced to where Pitch stood at Silas's side. 'It is best we do not delay too long, that's all.'

'Fine, but no way in all the hells are we headin' off, without a moment for you ta catch ya breath, and get some food in that tiny belly 'a yours,' Tyvain declared.

'I am rather famished, I'll admit.'

The soothsayer clapped her hands, rubbing them together. 'That's sorted then. I'll see if we can't get some breakfast sorted, maybe there's stew left over from last night. Could smell bread bakin' when I was outside, sure to be a cook about somewhere. We need to be heading off on full stomachs anyways. Now how's about you lot who need washin' do somethin' about that? Charlie, Silas and Astaroth, that means you. I'll sort things with the kitchen.'

The Hag of Beara left the room, hollering her instructions to any poor attendant nearby, and Silas looked to Sybilla. 'You haven't told her?'

The angel, clad in a light coat of grey, with a darker hue in her trousers, lowered herself onto the settee. 'She was sleeping when I returned...and I'll admit, I'd decided to wait until we had a proper sign that the journey was to begin.' Sybilla gestured at Charlie. 'But now we happily have Charlie back with us, I'll let you tell her, Silas.'

He winced. 'Why me?'

'What's this about?' Jane frowned, and the curtains behind her fluttered with an impossible breeze.

'You're not coming with us,' Pitch replied. 'None of you. We are down to the privileged few, and only myself and Silas–and I presume that loathsome bird –are counted among them. Speaking of which...does the simurgh still remain? Or has it seen fit to fly off and take care of this debacle under its own steam?'

'I'd like to see it try. The wisp and the ghost make fine guards, and very serious ones at that,' Sybilla said, and lo and behold there was a twitch at her lips. The angel was amused, almost smiling. The Valkyrie was nearer to her old self than he'd known since the dreadful events after Sherwood Forest.

'Don't glare at me, Jane. I don't make the bloody rules,' declared Pitch. 'If I did, it would be compulsory that I stay in a suite in the Savoy in London, and be debauched by a deadman until I could not stand, which would necessitate him hand-feeding me cake and jellies. Sadly, I am here with you lot instead.'

Jane ignored his nonsense. 'I don't understand why we cannot go with you.'

'And it is not for us to understand,' Sybilla said. 'The Lady Satine was very short on explanation, but I know beyond anything else, that this is how it must be.'

Silas watched Jane, her complexion the palest he'd ever seen, making her wondrously large brown eyes seem like fathomless pools. 'It is for the best, Jane. You will all be safe.'

She turned on him. 'You won't be, though, will you? I hate this, Silas.'

'I know.' He moved to the air elemental who tried to shrink away from him, pressing herself up against a bookshelf.

'Don't try to placate me.' She scowled up at him. 'Don't tell me you shall be fine.'

'I shall do no such thing, for I have no idea. I truly hope so. I hope we shall deliver the simurgh to the Sanctuary and that it shall do what the angel intended, and end the travesty of Blood Lake, without any great disaster or violence.' He held her gaze, knowing that she thought as he did; such a tidy outcome was unlikely.

'Oh Silas,' she whispered. 'I am so sorry such a sweet man has been given such a bitter task. You come back to us. You hear me, Mr Mercer? You too, Tobias. Both of you had bloody well better drag your arses back to us, or there shall be hell to pay. Look after each other as you have done so well, and get back to Holly Village as soon as you can, for it shall be dreadfully quiet without you. And dull. Gods, so dull.'

'I doubt all in the village shall think so. Gilmore will savour knowing the drunken dandy who tossed him in the air has died a foul and final death,' Pitch's nonchalance made Silas sick to his very stomach. 'And I doubt he'll be the only one.'

Anger spilled beneath Silas's skin. 'Don't speak like that. Did you not hear Jane, and Tyvain, and Charlie? They are concerned for you. None of them shall farewell you with a happy heart.'

He would not, simply *would not*, listen to Pitch discount his own worth so easily.

The soothsayer had returned, and stood in the doorway glowering. Isaac was with her, adorned in his numerous layers. 'When was anybody gonna bother tellin' me that you're goin' on alone, then?'

Silas darted a glance at Sybilla. She lifted her shoulders in a subtle shrug, and a look that said this situation was his to bear.

But it was Pitch who did the talking. 'Fine. You're done with, hag, and your services are no longer required. There, happy now?'

Tyvain surprised Silas by laughing, a genuine belly laugh, her temper vanishing in an instant.

'Saints, you're a prick. And it's kinda a relief to see you're still the cunt we all know and despise, Astaroth. But I wish me cards 'adn't been so right. Don't much like the idea of stayin' behind.'

'What did your cards tell you, Tyvain?' Silas asked.

'That she's lousy at shuffling a pack,' Pitch said.

Tyvain sucked at her teeth. 'That she spent last night thinkin' she was just pissed, and readin' 'em wrong, when they kept sayin' this here town was the end 'a the road for most of us.'

Sybilla made a small sound. 'Truly? You said nothing of it.'

'The angel thought you'd throw an almighty tantrum to hear it,' Pitch declared. 'Left it up to Silas to tell you.'

Tyvain snorted, tugging at the generous folds of her smock. 'Oh I threw me tantrum alright. In the privacy of me own room. Then had to spend half an hour trying to find where all me feckin' cards had flown to. The floorboards in this place aren't close enough together for my liking.'

'I'll admit, I'm shocked at how well you've hidden it,' Jane said, gently. 'Did the cards have anything else important to say?'

'I'd 'ave told ya, wouldn't I?' There was a notable pause. 'Now 'ow's about ya go get yourselves sorted for breakfast then? Charlie, there's a room for ya, down the way here. Proprietor gave me the key, amenable bloke he is, said he'll get onto some food for us soon as ya like.' She turned to Isaac who'd not said a word, where he waited in the corridor. 'Got that key that bloke gave us?'

The coachman grunted, handing her a tarnished key. 'You gonna get out of the way if I give it to ya? Didn't follow you to stand here like a shag on a fucking rock.'

The key was handed over, Tyvain stood aside, and Isaac moved like a dark cloud across the room, ignoring Silas and Pitch entirely, to warm his hands at the fire.

'Right then,' Tyvain said. 'Let's meet back here in a half hour, shall we? Charlie, you come with me, and don't you boys be doin' any fuckin' around up there. And I mean that as it sounds. Ain't no time for that.'

'There is always time for –' Pitch began.

'We will see you back here on the half hour, Tyvain.' Silas planted his hands on Pitch's shoulders, giving them a gentle squeeze. 'You have my word.'

CHAPTER 10

It was just over an hour later when they returned downstairs, in a fairly decent state, and washed to a degree more reasonable than before. Silas thought the time frame quite reasonable, considering the dressing and quick wash had been done in a swift ten minutes, and the rest of the time had involved being on his knees, tending to all the tenderest of places on Pitch's body.

'Your buttons are askew, my dear.' Jane gestured to Pitch's linen shirt, visible beneath his unbuttoned jacket of deep bronze green: with silver buttons, and elaborate silver and pink embroidery at the collar and cuffs. The buttoning of his shirt was certainly misaligned, but he made no haste to sort them.

'Well, you are to blame for that, are you not? Bothering us so.'

She inclined her head. 'But was it not worth it for the clothing I'd found?' The small wicker basket she'd brought in on her arrival had held the jacket Pitch now wore, along with a most fetching pair of stovepipe trousers, a deep black satin that clung in all the right places.

'He looks marvellous, Jane. You did very well,' Silas said, his lips still humming from services rendered.

'I'm yet to see him in something he cannot wear to perfection,' Charlie added, his face pink with having been scrubbed clean, his hair slicked back with oil. 'It's extremely annoying.'

'But there's no corset vest. No waistcoat at all, for that matter,' Pitch returned. 'Which makes the interruption of Silas's carnal explorations of my body unforgivable.'

'For the love of all holy things, shut that mouth of yours, Astaroth.' Isaac was already seated at the dining table, a rectangle of polished mahogany that had been cleared of its decorative table runner, and most places set with beautiful Damask placemats, polished silver cutlery, and large Vaseline green wine glasses. 'I'm about to eat, and don't need to hear nothing about your body.'

He'd placed himself at the head of the table, nearest to where the fire snapped and cracked cheerily, and already had his fork in hand and a napkin tucked into the high collar of his, unsurprisingly, dark jacket. At least he'd seen fit to discard his scarves, and his overcoat. All of which were thrown haphazardly over the settee.

'You look very fine, too, Silas.' Charlie grinned. 'Blue has always suited you.'

The coat that Jane had secured for him was not quite the blue of his beloved Inverness; it was far duller–more a late evening sky than brilliant midday–but the cut was fine and the fit was only marginally too tight.

'Places, places, now.' Tyvain strode into the room, beaming. 'Mr Churchill is a right saint, don't know how he's done it so fast, but we are ready to feast, my friends. Sit down, sit down.'

Silas pulled out a chair for Pitch, who was the epitome of good grace as he bobbed in a grateful bow, inclining his head. Suave, until the moment he made a sly grab at Silas's trouser front and pinched.

'Stop it.' Silas knew himself entirely unconvincing as they took their places side by side. Charlie and Jane sat opposite, their places yet to be set, with Sybilla taking the other head of the table. A spare chair, for the soothsayer, remained beside Pitch.

'If there's a heaven, you're headed there, Mr Churchill.' Tyvain stepped aside to allow entrance of the inn's publican. He pushed a trolley ahead of him, laden with a plethora of bowls and plates and condiments. 'I dunno how you've accommodated us so darn fast.'

'I'm not entirely sure myself,' Robert laughed. 'But the kitchen was already bustling when you came to me with your request, which was an oddity in itself. Never known cook to surface before mid-morning, especially when it's been a busy night before.'

The waft of hot food, all manner of scents, had Silas salivating.

'Cook is your fella, then?' Tyvain hovered by the trolley, wringing her hands. 'Heard about his mastery with a decent pastry even over at the Golden Mile.'

'I can vouch he is deserved of all praise,' Pitch declared.

'Feckin' Christ, 'igh praise don't come 'igher than that.'

Robert beamed. 'My Samuel does indeed have the magic touch with sweets. But there is no way you'll see him out of bed at this hour. No, the cook is a different fellow.'

The onslaught of scents was mouth-watering. Silas breathed them in; baked bread, hints of cinnamon and cloves, the richness of meat dishes and the unmistakable crispness of baked potatoes. His stomach gurgled in anticipation, earning him an amused side-long look from Pitch.

Two serving girls entered the room, one carrying a tray that held the missing cutlery, wine glasses and napkins. She had a three-pronged candelabra tucked under her arm, whilst the other serving girl held a deep basket, with corked bottles peeking their head from within. A wreath of holly was looped over her arm, another adornment for the table.

'Forgoing the distinct lack of sweet treats,' Pitch folded a leg beneath him on the chair, to add the extra height needed to peer over the table towards the trolley, 'I must say this all smells divine.'

Silas nodded. Whoever this chap was in the kitchen, Silas had decided him far more a legend than Samuel...and he'd not yet taken a bite. His stomach let loose another eager growl. He was utterly famished, having only taken a few mouthfuls of pie last night, unwilling to deprive Pitch.

'Eat a decent meal, then you can 'ave your dessert.' Tyvain chided Pitch, moving to assist Robert in unloading the laden trolley while the young women whisked about setting the empty places, and laying out the meagre embellishments. The candelabra was set at the centre of the table, with the holly wreath around its base. Long slim candles were produced from deep pockets, and lit with deft strikes against flint-sided boxes.

'My god it smells incredible.' Charlie moaned.

'Let's get this last supper underway then, shall we?' Tyvain said, cheer-ily.

Silas winced at her choice of words. He glanced at Pitch. The daemon seemed not to have heard, or was covering it well. He still sat perched upright, watching the unloading. His eyes were bright, not with flame, but with a relaxed eagerness. A happiness, Silas dared think.

Charlie and Jane chattered excitedly between themselves about what they would try first, thanking the attendants who had set the table. Sybilla lounged back in her chair, a half-smile upon her wounded face, looking more comfortable than Silas had seen her in ages. A platter of Brussel sprouts was set in front of her, steam rising from their plump little bulges. A roasted chicken, ringed with baked tomatoes and with fresh parsley decorating the drumsticks, was placed alongside.

Everyone was, to Silas's utter delight, content and in fine mood.

'That fire's not decent enough,' Isaac grumbled. 'Too cold by half.'

Well, most were content.

'That's cause you ain't used to having less than a hundred layers on, you sulky bastard.' Tyvain was busy uncorking a bottle of wine.

Pitch rose from his chair, and went to the fireplace. The fire was actually fairly decent, but was waning. Within a moment of him lifting his hands, the flames were jumping, crackling fiercely in the hearth. Isaac tilted his head back, and sighed deeply.

'Suppose you're good for something then, Astaroth.' Isaac's lips twisted, and Silas wondered if the man was feeling ill, until he realised it was a smile. 'I thank you.'

Tyvain spilled some of the wine she was pouring into Sybilla's glass. 'Jesus wept.'

'Shut ya trap,' Isaac growled. 'I'm just being civil.'

'Since bloody when?'

'Ty, let him be.' Sybilla dabbed at the spill with her napkin, but one of the attendants was already reaching for the salt dish.

'Leave that to me, miss.' The girl, all rose-cheeked and dark-eyed, fussed around the angel, who gave her the sort of smile which put the lass into a bit of a tizz. Sybilla was definitely in a fine mood, if she found energy enough for some flirtation.

'Don't worry Isaac,' Pitch said. 'I know you're still a surly prick who shall be dancing a jig once I'm gone.'

Silas's contentment frayed on hearing the daemon's easy dismissal of himself once more. But he'd not allow either Pitch, or his own worries, to stain this moment.

'This is truly wonderful, Mr Churchill,' Silas said. 'You have gone to so much trouble for our sake' And had done so, seemingly at the drop of a hat.

'Well, it is a good practice run for Christmas, really. We've got five tables booked for a lunchtime gathering. It's the first year we've tried such a thing.'

'Oh, of course!' Jane cried. 'Christmas! We've had such trials, there's hardly been time to look at a calendar. How close is it? A week or so?'

Mr Churchill set down a serving plate heaped high with green beans. He seemed bemused by the question. 'Must have been quite the trials. It is five days away.'

'Then this shall be our Christmas dinner,' Jane said.

Charlie looked fit to dance out of his chair. 'Yes, yes, oh what a fabulous idea.'

'What a lot of fuss over nothin'.' Was Isaac's surly contribution.

'Mr Churchill, the holly wreath is lovely,' Jane grabbed onto her idea with both hands, 'but I don't suppose you have anything more for the season?'

The blushing attendant who stood by Sybilla, jumped in before her master could answer. 'I've been practising those paper hats for your Christmas Day opening, Mr Churchill, sir. Got a dozen of 'em at least in the cupboard up in the attic. Those paperchains, too. They ain't all the best, but would they do?'

'Yes, yes. Go on, Mary. Retrieve them if you will,' Robert smiled fondly. 'And whatever else you can find that might brighten the room for the occasion. Oh, and Mary,' the girl paused, already halfway to the door. 'Will you send someone to check in on Herbert in the stables? Let him know the bread is out of the oven.' He set down a covered dish, one with tiny brown flowers around the rim of the lid, and gave Pitch and Silas a look. 'He wouldn't hear a word of it when I said he should sleep in his bed and not the straw with your horses.'

Silas shifted, all degree of uncomfortable, recalling the goddess's use of the boy. He was appalled he'd not thought to check on the young'un himself. 'I hope he was warm enough...it was a cold night.' Though he himself had not felt a shiver since waking in the grave, renewed.

'He'll be fine. A resilient lad, our boy. And he'll adore the excuse to have an early Christmas celebration.' Mr Churchill set down the last of the dishes he'd brought in. A hexagonal butter dish with purple and gold trim. None of the dinnerware matched, but it only made the spread more tantalising to look at.

Charlie and Jane were animated, chatting about Christmas experiences. 'The tree, no doubt,' Charlie said, in answer to Jane's question about her favourite aspect of the season. 'You?'

'Gifts! Of course. And I do enjoy an eggnog.'

'What a lot of hoo-hah over nothing,' Pitch sighed.

Silas turned to him. 'You don't enjoy the season?'

'Rather irksome in all its sentimentality.' He played at a shiver. 'And I am terrible at gift-giving, for I am not interested at all in what others like. And who can be bothered with wrapping paper?'

Silas nudged his knee against Pitch's leg. 'You are getting quite slovenly in your ability to lie. That new Inverness coat you had made for me is the most wonderful present I've ever received.'

'Really? That must be why you didn't even bother putting it on to go and take a piss in Sherwood Forest,' Pitch said, and though his comment stirred memories that stung, the daemon's laughter was so frivolous and clearly without any hint of blame that Silas simply smiled. 'And let's be honest, you likely do not remember any other presents you've received, my dear.'

'Not a one, but I know I would like yours best.'

'Dolt.' Pitch's hand rested on his thigh, resting there with no sultry intent, just finding its place. 'Now, can we please eat?'

'First decent words you've spoken, mate,' Isaac growled. 'No point putting down a feast this good and not lettin' us stuff it in our gobs.'

'Touch it before I say so and lose a finger.' Tyvain swatted him over the ear, having just finished filling his glass.

'There's one more dish, but it will take a little longer.' Mr Churchill stood, hands on hips, surveying his efforts. 'Some fancy thing from India, that Cook insisted on. Powerful smell on it, too. And spicy, I'm told. Anyone fancy burning their tongues?'

Pitch nudged Silas. 'This fellow will adore it. He does enjoy having his tongue in hot places.'

'Astaroth,' Isaac growled a warning.

Tyvain saved the day by finally taking her place on Pitch's far side. She snatched up her glass so enthusiastically wine spilled onto her hand. 'Right then, a Merry Christmas, to my family. The most fecked up bunch of bastards I've ever known, or hope to know.' She chewed on her lip before continuing. 'And I love ya, all of ya.' Her pointed gaze went to Pitch. 'Even you, you fucking prick.'

'Oh sod off, hag.'

Charlie stood up, arm raised for another toast. 'Can I echo those sentiments? Yours Tyvain, not yours, Tobias. And just say that I have no idea how I ended up here, only that I know it is exactly where I was supposed to be...' His gaze moved to Silas. 'I think I've known, from that day in the forest, when our paths crossed, that there was no other place for me.'

'Paths far more than crossed, if I recall,' Pitch declared. With his hand still upon Silas's thigh it was easy enough to give him a decent pinch over the knuckles. 'What? Am I wrong?'

'Go on, Charlie.' Silas rested his hand over Pitch's; the wine smoothing a warm place in his empty belly. 'Finish your toast and pay him no mind.'

'Well, there's not much more to say about it,' Charlie shrugged. 'I echo Tyvain's sentiments...the part about family, and loving you, I mean.' The lad blushed. 'I've never been in so much peril in my entire life, and yet I've never felt so protected, so cared for, as I have with you all. So entirely seen.' His voice hitched, and a tremble in his hand rippled the wine in his glass. 'Christ, I've barely had two sips and I'm rambling.'

He slumped back into his seat.

'Not at all, Charlie. We love you, too.' Jane wrapped her arm about the lad, the hint of jasmine played between the heavier scents of the awaiting feast. 'I do not wish you in harm's way, but I'm so very glad you and Silas found each other, and us in return.'

Silas swallowed, far more overcome by the moment than he'd intended to allow himself. The notion of family struck hard at him. Especially here, at the end. When they must leave them all behind. Pitch entwined his fingers through Silas's, leaning in. 'Does that make us brothers then? If this is a family? I'm fairly sure fornication among siblings is frowned on in this dreary world. Shame. I did so enjoy rutting my big brother.'

Silas sputtered with laughter. He gave Pitch's hand a tight squeeze. 'Lucky I would break any law for you.'

'Lucky indeed.' Pitch grinned, taking another sip of his wine, a stain already darkening his pink lips.

Sybilla drew herself to standing, glaring away Tyvain's move to assist her. 'Don't you dare. I'm fine.' She raised her glass, which was already half-empty. 'One last toast, to those we have lost, and those we've found along the way.'

'To those lost, and those found along the way.' Everyone chimed in, glasses tinkling as they were knocked against their neighbours.

'See,' Pitch muttered. 'This is why I don't like this Christmas lark. It is both downcast and jovial at once. Very confusing. I have no clue whether I should be laughing riotously, or crying into my drink.'

'I think that is rather the whole point of the occasion,' Silas said. 'Wonderful, isn't it?'

'Fucking ludicrous, is what it is, and you absolutely love it, don't you? You gloriously odd man. I can just imagine you, searching days for the perfect tree to cut down, fussing over the number of branches, the right girth, the perfect pinnacle bow for the star. But then despairing over how many birds you might deprive of nests –'

'They wouldn't be nesting at this time of year, but it would be best to search the branches in case there are any old nests, or broken egg shells that might attract the ants. Wouldn't want them taking over the parlour.'

Pitch gave him a sidelong look, and Silas grinned. But darker thoughts had stirred; he wondered if he had shared this time of year with family, loved ones...or had he sat alone in a quiet house, no decorations on the mantle, no one to sit at the table with?

But Silas could not seem to find it in himself to wonder too deeply. His past life memories were every bit as lost as those they mourned.

What was not lost was right here, with him. Beside him. And it was a glorious place. His veins brimmed with vigour, his heart bulged at the seams with love. He lifted Pitch's hand, and kissed his knuckles.

'Now, please, enjoy, everyone,' Robert called from the doorway with his empty trolley. 'But keep some room for the kedgeree, you won't regret it.'

'Dunno what that is, just hope it don't stink like that feckin Cullen stinker you 'ad at 'Arvington 'All, Charlie.'

The lad laughed. 'It was called a Cullen skink, and I assure you it is a delicacy.'

'A Scottish delicacy,' Silas muttered, mostly to himself, something stirring in the faded recesses of his mind.

'You've tried it, Silas?' Charlie asked.

He nodded, frowning. 'I have…'

'And didn't think much of it apparently,' said Pitch.

'I don't know…I'm not sure what I thought of it. Only that I know it. Well.'

Blast these vague, half-baked memories. But no one pressed him further; far too busy with piling their plates. Their conversation moved on. All save for Pitch, who kept watching him.

'Didn't you say you thought that lake of yours to be a loch?' he asked. 'Now the foul Scottish food stirs you, and you've mentioned Edinburgh Castle as seeming familiar. Perhaps it's not just your death that occurred in the north, my fine fellow, but your life too.' Pitch dolloped an enormous serve of mashed potato onto his plate. 'A pity you did not retain the accent. I'd have no clue what you were saying most of the time, but good gods it would harden me to listen to you.'

The daemon's lewd wink lifted Silas from the melancholy that had found him.

'A pity indeed.'

He had far more than a hunch that he'd spent time in the north. Aside from his terrible visions of the loch where he'd drowned, there was Charlie's Scottish origins, with their residence a fancy Northern estate.

When Nemain chose to drown him at the greensward, Silas had learned that it was Charlie's ancestor who'd tried in vain to rescue him the day his brother killed him. He understood that the goddess had put her Blessing upon the meagre bandalore thrown to him in the rough waters, and made it her scythe. He *knew* that it found its way to someone of Charlie's bloodline during the times Silas was human, and returned to him when he was not so. But just like he *knew* of the dish, Cullen skink, he did not know any fine details.

But really, what did any of that matter now? The scythe was upon its last journey. As was Silas.

'Bon appetite, everyone.' Jane grabbed at a plate laden with smoked haddock.

'You mind your mouth there, girlie. Don't be swearin' at me with your fancy French.' Tyvain reached for a bowl of glistening green peas, where a dollop of yellow butter slowly melted in their heat.

There was spirited activity as everyone filled their plates, passing bowls, swapping condiments, and refilling wine glasses. Pitch leaned over the table, adding an astonishing array of extras to his mashed potatoes. Silas chose to sit back and wait until the way was clear to fill his own plate. He topped up his glass, and Pitch's too, enjoying the brimming of life in the room, the chatter and easy alliance.

'Here we are, then.' Mary had returned, arms laden once more, with the most unexpected cargo. The lass held a small spruce, planted in a wooden bucket. The slender branches of the young tree were drooping under the load of tinsel and shiny balls bestowed on it. 'Cook had this little wonder set away for our Christmas opening, but said it was better off in here, with you all.'

'It is beautiful!' Jane sighed.

'Looks pitiful small.' Isaac spoke through a mouthful of roast chicken.

'Remind ya of bits of yaself then, does it?' Tyvain goaded the coachman, who was too hungry to give her more than a dirty look.

Mary carried the tree near to the fireplace, setting it down where the flames could illuminate the tree's sparse decorations; causing them to sparkle, diamond-like, in the glow.

'There we are then.' A hessian bag hung from looped strings over her arm, and she dug into it's depths now. 'And here's your hats.' She moved around the table, handing out coloured paper hats, each cut roughly into the shape of crowns. 'A white one for you, my lady. Will suit you no end.'

Sybilla smiled widely at her over the top of her glass of wine. 'And green for you, sir. Them eyes of yours are wondrous.'

'Thank you,' Pitch was uncommonly gracious. 'I know.'

Silas huffed with amusement. 'Such humility. You are a gem.'

'And you adore it.'

'I do.'

His stomach ruined the moment with a growl. 'Gods, man, will you eat something?' Pitch jabbed his laden fork towards Silas's mouth. 'Try this. The salt to butter ratio is utter perfection in these potatoes.'

Silas leaned in, taking the mouthful, sliding his lips along the prongs of the fork with slow measure. Pitch bit at his bottom lip, watching Silas just as carefully as he was being watched.

'Fucking hell, just eat your own food, ya makin' me sick.' Tyvain jabbed her elbow into Pitch's side.

The fork clattered against Silas's teeth, and he very nearly choked on mashed potatoes. Pitch's crown slipped as he whirled to admonish the soothsayer, who merely sucked her teeth at him, before returning to her brussel sprouts.

Recovering quickly, Silas wasted no more time in filling his plate. He was the last to do so, but there was by no means a shortage of food. For some time there were only murmurings of conversation, comments as to the sublime nature of the meal; everyone too busy eating to chat much.

And then the kedgeree arrived.

Mr Churchill dispensed with the trolley this time, using two great padded mittens to carry a large, white porcelain terrine into the dining area. His jaw clenched as he bent to lower the heavy dish to the table. Sybilla shifted her chair to give him greater access.

'Righto! This has had our mouths watering in the kitchen, I assure you, but there's a fair few more hot spices in it than I've ever know in this dish.' He lifted the lid with a grand flourish, and at once they were bombarded by the richness of the seasoning.

Silas was struck with how familiar a waft it was.

He knew this dish. He'd eaten a huge bowl of it.

At The Atlas.

That meal came flooding back. Kaneko had been credited with its making then. But that was impossible now.

He glanced at the tiny Christmas tree, labouring under its laden boughs. A tree the cook just happened to have ready and prepared for this unexpected gathering.

The same cook who had managed to deliver a feast of preternatural proportions, at the drop of a hat.

Silas shoved back his chair, standing. He snatched his paper crown from his head and cast it beside his plate.

'No one touch the kedgeree. Sybilla, put down the ladle.'

The angel frowned. 'Silas? What is it?'

'Want it all ta yaself?' Tyvain chortled. 'Well, I ain't fightin' ya.'

'I will.' Jane sent a playful breeze whipping around Silas where he stood. But he ignored them all.

'Mr Churchill, take me to the kitchen at once.'

He was frightening the poor man, Silas saw it in the roundness of his eyes, the sudden uncertainty that gripped the normally assured fellow. 'Is something wrong?'

'Now, sir. Do not delay. I need to see this cook of yours.'

CHAPTER 11

The cook was waiting for them. Standing by the oven with a cloth over one shoulder, a smudge of black on one cheek of their familiar face. Silas stopped dead in the doorway, his pulses galloping.

'What are you doing here?' he demanded.

But before the man could answer, Pitch's voice rang out behind him.

'So brusque, Mr Mercer. Has your little ferret friend got into the corn?'

'Get back,' Silas hissed. 'I told you to stay at the table.'

Pitch shrugged. 'I didn't listen. Who are you talking to?' He rose on tiptoe to try to see past Silas, his paper crown slipping. 'Why are you ruining this Christmas hogwash with your dramatics?'

'Pitch, I said get back,' Silas shouted.

'What the fuck is wrong, Silas? Stand aside, now.'

'Gentlemen, there is no need for me to cause strife between you. I come with no ill-intent,' the cook said, gently.

'Fucking gods,' Pitch said. 'Is that Ahari?'

With a frustrated exhale, Silas stepped into the kitchen, moving out of the doorway.

'Hello, your highness.' Mr Ahari gave Pitch a short bow.

The kitsune wore a cook's garb; his apron blotched with orange stains from the kedgeree, sweat glistening on his brow from the kitchen's heat. The old man did not look well, thinner than last they'd met, and that had not been so long ago. His skin held a grey pallor that was not pleasing, and his hair was a stark white now, no peppered hints of grey remaining.

Pitch did not enter the room, nor allow his flame to rise, for which Silas was thankful. If Ahari had poisoned them all, they needed him alive to learn if an antidote were possible.

Was the old man truly that callous? Silas's reasonable mind begged the question, while his distrusting self screamed that he'd proved himself a traitor.

'No closer, Pitch. Do you feel alright? Not light-headed, sleepy perhaps?'

There were no sneers of indignation from the daemon, just a simple, understanding shake of his head. 'Merely annoyed at going back to cold potatoes.'

'It is good to see you so well, your highness.'

'The same can't be said for you. You look fucking awful, Ahari.'

'It's been a difficult time,' he said, solemn, his eyes filled with a sadness that might have made Silas a little gentler, were he not remembering how close Mr Ahari's actions had come to stealing Pitch from him forever.

'What have you done to the food, Ahari?' Silas drew on every note of his new, imposing quaver.

'Nothing, of course, nothing.' To Silas's surprise Mr Ahari went to his knees, head lowered. 'My Lord Death, I do not expect to ever gain your forgiveness for what I did.'

'Good. Then you'll never be disappointed.'

The kitsune's shoulders dropped. 'But I must tell you that I did it in good faith. I thought it for the best...for everyone...' He seemed even less convinced by his words than Silas.

'What did you do, Ahari?' Pitch said.

Silas had not yet had a conversation with him about the events at Cumberland House; about Mr Ahari siding with Lucifer to keep Silas from searching for a lost prince.

'I sought to keep safe as many of those I cared for as I could.' Mr Ahari leaned his hands to the black and white tiles. The rest of the kitchen staff continued with their business, as though neither Silas nor Pitch nor Ahari conversed at all.

'You thought to make us safe by keeping us prisoner in York?' Sybilla stepped up behind Pitch; another who had ignored Silas's order to stay seated. 'And Lucifer do as he pleased, even when you were aware it may include the death of the prince?'

Pitch watched Ahari intently. 'You stopped them from coming to my aid? You were happy to allow me to die?'

'Absolutely not.' Mr Ahari shook his head emphatically. 'No. No. Lucifer never threatened such a fate for you. I'd never have agreed to hold the others back otherwise.'

'Then what fate did you agree Pitch could face? The abaddon?' Silas asked. 'How bloody noble of you.' He'd been so afraid, so deathly afraid, and he had trusted the kitsune. That was hardest to forgive.

'I understand your anger. You have every right to it, but please try to understand...my choice was impossible.' Mr Ahari wavered, head still lowered. Pitch stepped up to him, keeping Silas back with a simple shake of the head.

'Have you done anything to the food, Ahari?' Pitch said, with a calm so unlike him. 'Do we have reason to doubt you, now?'

The kistune looked up, and in that sudden move there was hint of the fox beneath his skin, the sudden sharpening of features, the blackness of his eyes, the shimmering sway of a multitude of tails behind him.

'None, none, my boy. I swear to you. I want nothing more than to find some way to make amends.'

'With food?' Silas demanded. 'And a ridiculous tree? That was you, was it not?'

Ahari nodded. 'I saw how you looked at that tree on your way to the cemetery last night. I thought, you'd be pleased to have –'

'Last night?' Silas demanded, wishing Pitch would keep greater distance from the old man. 'You've been in Ambleside all this time, watching us?'

'Oh no, no, good sir. I've been watching you for longer than that. When I learned you were...' he hesitated.

'Alive?' Pitch said.

With a grimace, Ahari nodded. 'I begged Satine to allow me to help in whatever way I could, to see you through to the end of the journey. She was very, very displeased with me.'

'Rightly so.' Sybilla leaned against the doorway, arms crossed, no visible sign of discomfort. Silas blinked, thinking he'd caught hint of a shimmer around her.

'Yes. Rightly so.' Ahari, normally a ball of cheeriness and vague distraction, was glum. 'But she came to understand what obstacles I faced, and knew me no villain. She allowed me to follow you, keep watch over you.'

Silas glared. 'Do you expect us to trust a word from your mouth?'

'No. Not at all. But do you think Lalassu would not be aware of the fox lurking in the woods all that time, and not challenge it, if she saw fit? You trust your mare, Horseman.'

Silas folded his arms. 'She missed your treachery in York.'

'She expected it no more than I did. And it was not treachery, not at the heart of it.' Ahari rubbed at his rosy cheeks, sighing deeply. 'There was a choice to be made, and perhaps...I chose wrongly.'

Pitch grabbed a stool from beneath a set of high shelves, and set it beside Ahari. 'Here, sit down you old fool, before you fall down.'

The kitsune's shock was fit for the stage, his heavy-lidded eyes widening. 'You're too kind. Thank you, your highness.'

'Call me that again, and we shall truly have issues.' Pitch looked to Silas. 'We have no issues here. The kitsune is, as he says, no villain. But a bloody good cook, I have to say.'

Mr Ahari brightened. 'Well, thank you, your highness.' He touched his fingers to his lips, shrinking beneath the daemon's glare. 'Sorry.'

'Pitch, you were not there in York,' Silas began, still able to feel the sheer terror of that moment of betrayal. 'I cannot –'

'Ensure no one is too hard upon Mr Ahari when next you meet,' Pitch said, a steely look upon his face. 'The kitsune had no choice but to follow my instruction. Those were among the last words Lucifer spoke to me, before he left us at Newchurch. What did he threaten you with, exactly Mr Ahari?'

'The lives of all kitsune.' The old man grew pale with memory. 'That Weatherby's betrayal may signal a greater treachery amongst my kind, and an inquisition would be the only way to root out the guilty who sided with Elyssium. Many more would die as Weatherby had done.'

'There we are,' Pitch said, with the aplomb of one declaring a puzzle completed. 'Dear Pappa was his usual congenial and subtle self, to get his way. Mr Ahari has been used, and I am no stranger to how that feels. We should move on from this...before my potatoes are too icy to eat.'

'Gods, thank you.' The old man pulled the cloth from his shoulder and covered his face. He sobbed quietly.

Sybilla moved into the room, and with a nod towards Pitch she embraced Mr Ahari. 'Come, join us at the table.'

Silas watched on, the strings of bitterness untying themselves from where they had lodge fast around his heart. The man who had hauled him from the grave, who felt in some strange way like Silas's anchor between life and death, was no betrayer after all.

Sybilla helped Ahari to his feet, and the old man lowered the cloth from his face, his eyes sparkling with tears.

'It tore me apart to see your distress. Silas, I truly hope you believe me.' Mr Ahari looked positively pained. 'And I could not have been prouder to see you defy all who tried to stifle you. Even the King of Daemonkind could not stop you, could he?' His smile was tender but weak. 'You are both so very marvellous. Standing tall, when all others have fallen. I hope you can forgive me, in time.'

Silas gave him a subtle nod, feeling Pitch's gaze as well.

'Let's get you on a seat before you fall down,' Sybilla said, guiding the old man towards the door. 'You are hardly the only one who has made mistakes.'

Mr Ahari leaned into the angel. 'You are a benevolent creature, Sybilla.'

'No. I simply know what it is to carry guilt. Come.'

They left the kitchen at a slow shuffle, talking softly between themselves. Pitch waited quietly, amongst the bustle of the warm room, where pots bubbled and kitchen staff worked in a magickal daze, chopping and stirring, sweeping and washing, without regard for the two men who stood nearby.

'Everything all right, Sickle?'

'I'm not sure I can forgive him fully for keeping me from you.'

'Go easy, my dear. I doubt very much he shall ever forgive himself. But not everyone can defy a lord of Arcadia so readily as you.' He bobbed onto his tip-toes, landing a very unexpected kiss to the tip of Silas's nose.

Barely had Silas leaned towards him, searching for more, than Pitch was skipping out of reach with an impish grin.

'The rest of me is for dessert.' He extended his hand. 'Come along now, Mr Mercer, you cannot escape. If I must endure this half-baked Christmas cheer then you shall be by my side. No arguments.'

Silas had none to give.

CHAPTER 12

After a couple of hours spent indulging, drinking and stuffing themselves silly with all the delightful offerings, everyone was submerged in that pleasant restfulness that comes with big meals. Silas had only managed to eat one serve of the kedgeree, as it turned out that the others were not so averse to the dish after all. Isaac, in particular, had to be held back from picking up the terrine and licking it clean.

They slouched in their chairs, happily tipsy, the conversation fading to quieter chats between neighbours, rather than verbose arguments involving the whole table. Pitch had absolutely revelled in the discourse over which style of ballgown would best suit him. Silas won the conversation by declaring it was whichever one lay upon their bedroom floor. His cheeks had burned at the audacity, but to hell with propriety, he'd decided. Even Mr Ahari, still withdrawn amongst those he'd betrayed, had been overcome with deep belly laughs.

Pitch had turned his chair, and placed his legs over Silas's lap, despite Tyvain's admonishment.

'Bloody ruffian. At least kick ya boots off.'

Pitch had ignored her.

Silas rubbed his hand over the prince's trouser leg, tracing the contours of his knees; teasing at moving higher, only to retreat. Eliciting a wry smile from Pitch. Silas was about to suggest it was time to retire to their rooms, when Tyvain made a choked sound, and Charlie gasped softly.

The lad stared at the soothsayer with a brightness in their gaze Silas had not noted before. 'Tyvain, is there something wrong?'

'Well it ain't right, but you know that already, don't ya lad?' Tyvain pushed up her sleeve, scratching ferociously at her bare arm. Her skin was blotched with red welts. 'I see it in your face. Ya feel it too.'

'I wish I didn't, but yes.' Charlie nodded, and looked to Silas. 'It is time for us to go.'

Silas inhaled, trying to still the upheaval in his belly. 'I see.'

Jane sucked in a breath. 'Ty, is that what the marks tell you?'

The soothsayer screwed up her nose. 'Nah. These are from the Brussel sprouts.'

'No one's allergic to Brussel sprouts,' Isaac snorted. 'You daft woman.'

But Tyvain was intent on Silas and Pitch. She tapped at the side of her head. 'Wish I could tell this damned voice to feck off, but we all know that won't do much but stave off what's gotta 'appen anyway. They are wantin' us...to let ya go. It's time you left now, boys.' She swallowed, and glanced at Charlie. 'The party is over.'

Jane bowed her head, taking hold of Charlie's hand.

'Yes, it is,' the lad said, giving Silas an apologetic look.

Silas smiled, to soothe his friend's obvious distress. 'It's alright, Charlie. Edward has been alone too long as it is. And it is not as if we weren't expecting the need to carry on. Ambleside is lovely, but not our final destination.'

He wished he knew more of that place. Really all they understood of Blood Lake was that it was where they needed to go; as to what it looked like, what they should expect, he knew no more than the housemaids who had served their meal.

Pitch's low belch was delicate, hidden behind a raised hand. 'Could have at least let us digest our meals. Don't blame me Silas, if this meal comes up to say hello again, once we are trotting about.'

'There'll be a bit of time to catch your breath as we head up the Struggle,' Charlie said, clutching Jane's hand. 'We won't be making the horses go at a trot up there.'

'The Struggle?' Silas said. 'I'm not sure I like the sound of that.'

'It is the road out of town we must take. Rather a steep climb, and not easy on the horses. My legs certainly didn't enjoy it.' Charlie rubbed at his thighs. 'It just seems to go on forever.'

'Of course it fucking does.' Pitch stabbed at a cold piece of roast pumpkin on his plate. 'Up a mountainside and into a priest's hole. If ever there was proof needed that Seraphiel was a vindictive cunt, then let this be the pudding. Speaking of which, did you not say there would be dessert, Ahari? Best you sort out a few saddlebags worth of pastries and cake for me. Perhaps a slice of pie for Silas.'

Mr Ahari jumped to his feet. 'Of course, of course. I shall wake Samuel at once. I forgot I had him still sleeping, truth be known. I'll see to it right away.'

'Best you do, old man.' Pitch was as cool as winter's northern winds. 'Don't let me down in this, at least.'

Mr Ahari faltered, grabbing at the back of his dining chair. 'Tobias...I'm so –'

'I know. Go.'

The kitsune found a new vigour at that, and dashed from the room at an admirable pace.

Pitch downed the remainder of his wine in one gulp, and reached for the nearest bottle, pouring himself a messy refill, growling at Silas when he tried to assist.

'I'm not an invalid. Leave it, Silas.'

Pitch had had more than his fair share of the assorted wines. But Silas felt he understood the air of desperation in the daemon's regular reach for the bottle, the quick draining of his cup. He felt it himself: the strain of keeping his smile in place, the strain of keeping from ruining this precious moment with a breakdown of any sort.

The daemon suddenly stood, his chair rocking dangerously. 'I'm going to check on Scarlet and the bird.'

'Shall I come with you?' Silas asked, reaching to steady Pitch as he swayed.

'No,' he snapped, then deflated at once. 'I mean to say, no thank you. I'd prefer to go alone, if you don't mind?'

Pitch winced, as though imagining his words might cause pain. Silas had to gather himself before he replied. 'Of course, I don't mind, my love. Do what you must. I shall see to the horses.'

Silas was not sure if it was inebriation or something else, that gave Pitch an air of uncertainty. He chewed at his lip, appearing ready to say more.

'Good.' Was all he said in the end. 'I won't be long.'

Pitch made his way around the table, using the back of Sybilla's chair to steady himself. He struck his knee against Charlie's pushed-back chair, and swore with his usual eloquence. A familiar habit, which made Silas oddly content.

'The angel set more runes in her room than it has nails in the walls,' Isaac said, swirling the last of his own wine. 'The wisp and the bird are safer than houses, or we'd know about it. You're just tryin' to get out of doin' any work so far as packing is concerned.' He chuckled at his own assessment, every bit as drunk as anyone else at the table. Silas thought it was the first time he'd heard the man laugh at all.

'Fuck off back to where you came from, Isaac.' Pitch flicked his finger at the coachman as he reached the doorway. 'All of you, for that matter. I've no idea why you are here bothering us to begin with. Be good little naturals, and piss off...sooner rather than later.'

And with those congenial words, he was gone. Leaving everyone else in a subdued silence. One that was broken only by the clink of glass as Jane poured another wine.

'Well, I for one am glad 'e did that. I don't fancy goodbyes much either.' Tyvain worked at her teeth with a toothpick, jerking her free hand towards Silas. 'Would ya be insulted if I took my leave now, too? And if I don't say nothin' about how I reckon you're an all right kind of fella, brave as a saint, patient as one, too. Astaroth proves that. I won't mention neither, that ya ain't too hard on the eye, bloody good in a fight...and that ya deserve so much more than what ya got?' She jerked her chin towards the empty doorway. 'So does 'e. That lad ain't so bad, if I'm 'onest. And if he cares to know, I don't blame 'im for runnin' off, rather than sayin' goodbye.'

'Thank you, Tyvain.' Silas tilted his half-full glass her way, blinking at the sting behind his eyes. 'I too will hold my tongue and not say how much your braveness and vivacity has emboldened me in return. I'll not mention that you being so full of life, helped remind me what it is to be alive. Again. I shall certainly not tell you that your friendship is very precious to me and that I thank you for it, most deeply.'

A stifled sob came from Jane. 'This is awful,' she sniffed, wiping at her eyes. Charlie set a comforting hand upon her shoulder, his eyes also glistening.

'I think I almost preferred being set upon by the Hunt and having to flee,' he said softly. 'We had no time to think of anything but staying in one piece. Certainly not farewells.'

Isaac drew a white handkerchief from somewhere in his layers, passing it to Charlie, who in turn handed it to Jane. She accepted it with a nod, and blew her nose.

'That daemon prick has the right idea,' Isaac said, gruff as ever. 'Better we just all piss off now. No parting speeches or any of that poppycock.' He sounded a little husky to Silas's ear.

'I think we finally agree on something, Isaac.' Sybilla got to her feet, and Tyvain did not even attempt to assist her. 'I had best see to arranging a horse for Charlie, though I suppose he could ride your brown gelding if you and Tobias have Lalassu.'

Silas shrugged, pushing his plate away. He still wore his papercrown. He drew it off his head, no longer feeling the spirit of the season. 'Whatever you think is best...' But he frowned. 'Wait, are you sure you are up to riding? And what horse shall you use?'

The angel moved to the door, her steps resolute and unfaltering. She paused, pressing her hands to the doorframe. 'I am well and truly up to riding. Just not today.'

She walked on, leaving Silas staring at an empty space. He jumped to his feet, rushing to follow, leaving his papercrown fluttering in his wake.

'Sybilla,' he called. 'Wait. What are you saying?'

The Valkyrie did not slow down, and walked with a purposeful gait down the corridor. Which would have pleased him any other time, but now it was irksome. They passed through the main public area, much busier now as the clock ticked closer to midday. Silas dodged the customers who were in a far more relaxed mood than he.

'Wait, Sybilla. Stop, please.'

It was not until she was outside, standing on the pavement, that Sybilla halted. The late morning was filled with weak winter sunlight, but the frost still persisted on windowpanes untouched by the brightness. Silas shivered at the sudden decline in temperature, Pitch's daemonic-stoked fire had been far warmer than he'd realised.

'Let's not make a fuss over this, shall we?' Sybilla folded her arms, doing her best to look stern, and there it was again, the slight shimmer at her outline. 'Plans have changed.'

A strangled teasing began at the back of his mind, a far distant hint of melody.

'You aren't coming with us.'

'No. My journey alters from yours now. There is much else for me to do.'

Threads, tiny silver threads, wove out of the shimmer around her. Silas took a step back.

'No...it cannot be.'

'I am happy for it, Silas. Don't look so saddened.'

The glinting threads were fine as spiderweb, but there was no mistaking them.

Silas had only ever been able to see the aura of a natural once before. In Balthazar Crane.

'The goddess has made you ankou.' The words were sharp as they moved up his throat. 'But you are not dead, I saved you.'

Sybilla's gaze softened, and her notes were so whisper-thin that even the slightest sound upon the street vanished them. 'You delayed what is inevitable. Did Izanami not tell you that already?'

Of course she had. The goddess had made it patently clear when Silas had dug in his scythe and refused to let the angel go, that he was not overriding death, merely stalling its arrival.

'Yes, but I sought to keep you in the land of the living. Not that of the dead.'

Sybilla stepped closer, away from the ears of curious passersby. 'You kept me somewhere between them both. For which I am eternally grateful. But there is much strife in the realm of the dead, and you know it, Silas. The Blight touches far too many, but that is not your burden to bear, now. It is mine. I will do what I can, whilst you and Pitch do the rest. You removed one of the goddess's ankou in Sherwood Forest. There was a place among the guardians of the dead where Balthazar Crane once stood. A place that is now mine.'

'Oh, Christ...Sybilla, I'm so sorry –'

'For what?' He startled when the Valkyrie suddenly pressed her hand to his face. 'You foolish, lovely man. This is a blessing. My time was up, and then it was not, because of you. Every breath I take since that day, I owe to you. Every chance I have to see an end to the machinations of the Blight and the lake which feeds it, is a chance I have because of you. Before this...before you and Tobias, the Order was simply filling in the cracks. Patching up holes that could never be truly covered over. They would break open again–it was always just a matter of when–because Blood Lake still brought its pressures to bear. At least now we have a genuine chance to bring this saga to an end. If I do so not as a Valkyrie with her blade, but as a messenger of death with her poor imitation of your magnificent bandalore...then so be it.' Sybilla reached into her coat pocket, pulling forth a short length of stark, white bone. 'A witch's bone. My bandalore. My scythe. Their power helped me open the entranceway to the cockaigne –'

'That white staff you held.'

She nodded. 'Yes. The witches I wronged helped me save you. And now they shall be with me as I make recompense for the wrongs I did to them.' She stepped away. 'Do not be sad for me, Silas. Be glad. I see an end to this, to all this pain and bloodshed. Because of you and Tobias. Because of the strength you inspire in each other. And I am glad of it. And proud to walk in your footsteps, Pale Horseman.'

Silas stared after her, long after she'd left his sight, headed for the stables. The angel might see an end to this, and be glad of it, but he could not say the same.

Silas feared the price yet to be paid, when all was said and done.

CHAPTER 13

It was not simply the desire to avoid goodbyes that had Pitch hurrying from the dining room. There was necessity too.

The simurgh, or at least some part of the Cultivation, called to him. No, call was too gentle a word; the bastard thing was demanding Pitch pay heed. Leading him on.

He made his way quickly to the back entrance of the Churchill, stepping out into a narrow courtyard where an unlocked gate gave him access to the alleyway behind. He moved unhindered, passing by only two other living beings, one of which was a black cat that hissed and slunk back through a hole in the fence. The other was a chap carrying a barrel on his shoulder, which hid Pitch from his view for the most part, and spared the need for any enchantments. At one point there was no choice but to cross the main road, and then follow the North Road along a while, before he reached the rough white stucco and dark beams of the Golden Rule public house.

He stepped inside, struck at once by the staleness of hops, the rich scents of cooked meat and the low hum of the clientele. Pitch found his way upstairs, keeping his gaze fixed, showing pompous disregard for all who sought to catch his attention. His head was fuzzy with the drink. The only clarity was there in the ceaseless guiding whine of the simurgh.

Ignoring the bobbing housemaid in the hallway, her cheeks cherry red with a blush, and breathless with offer of assistance, Pitch stepped into Sybilla's room. His temper had swayed far to the nasty side of reasonable.

'Stop.' He slammed the door shut. 'You are giving me a headache. I'm here, damn you.'

He turned around and was promptly assaulted.

A squeaking blot of vibrant yellow and blue, hurtled at him at a rate of knots. Scarlet flattened themselves against his cheek. The wisp kissed him, butterfly wings touching at his skin, before darting into his hair, and wriggling about like a mad thing.

They had taken to this ridiculous behaviour on the ride from the cockaigne. Leaving their guarding duties alongside the simurgh to make a further tangle of Pitch's hair, and pepper him with those weightless kisses. He'd grumbled and cursed and shook his head of course, hoping that no one took any notice of the smile he sought to wipe from his lips. He was certain Silas had noticed–of course the blasted ankou would have done–but he had said nothing of it.

'Scarlet, that's enough.'

The wisp settled a little, but remained in his hair. Pitch strode over to the bed, where the curtains had been closed around the four-poster. Each pillar was utterly covered with runework. He swept the curtains back, and the simurgh lifted its head, dusk-pink crest rising, golden beak raised and topaz eyes watchful, but not alarmed. The creature's colours had a greater vibrancy now, far more so than on the journey, where their dullness had concerned him. That dullness remained upon the damaged feathers though, with no visible improvement there; those upon the wing and the creature's neck, which had been stripped of their vivacity by Gabriel's meddling. The Cultivation was not self-repairing, Pitch's hopes to the contrary were all but faded now.

The simurgh's intense gaze had Pitch's meal stirring unpleasantly in his belly. Or perhaps it was the wine. He'd drunk far too much. But he'd hoped to dull himself for more than just goodbye.

'So, you wish to return to me.'

The simurgh said nothing, of course, it neither could, nor needed to. Pitch knew the purpose of his summons. His overfull stomach roiled.

'You could have fucking well given me greater warning. I would have left that last potato.' He made light of a situation that was anything but.

Scarlet chittered at him. Pitch grabbed the wisp from his hair, causing Scarlet's cheerful humming to morph into a tiny screech. 'I want you to stay back, do you hear. Everyone shall be pissed off with me if anything untoward happens to you. Never mind me, of course.'

Scarlet stood on stubby little legs on his palm. Those wretched, wide-open eyes the creature insisted on giving itself stared at him vacantly. Scarlet crooned, a sound intolerably close to sympathetic.

'Go on,' he tossed his hand, forcing the wisp to fly. 'Get away until I say it is safe.'

Scarlet did partly as ordered. Putting a few feet between them, crossing tiny stubby arms as it fluttered. Pitch interpreted it as meaning it would go no further. But he was not going to waste anymore time arguing. Besides, if this went wrong, it might be useful to have a messenger who'd gather help.

Pitch winced at the thought. What the blazes had happened to him? Fierce warrior of the Hellfield who hadn't given a fuck about his own legion half the time, now reliant on a creature no bigger than one of his balls to race off and cry for help if the need arose. Help that *would* arrive. But this growing reliance on assistance was dangerous.

A flaw to be flaunted by enemies.

Pitch was vulnerable if he did not take care of things himself. And if *he* were vulnerable, so would Silas be in turn.

He stalked closer to the bed. The simurgh rose to its feet, or rather, foot. One claw still curled up, blackened and useless. The Cultivation stretched its wings, the way of someone waking from a decent night's sleep.

'Well? Go on then.' He glared, adding a touch of flame to his gaze. 'You shall have to lead this. I have no idea how to put you back.' Another roll of the stomach came at that, and a sense of the empty place inside him flexing. A terrible combination of feelings, really. 'Do what you must, and know that I'm not pleased with it in the slightest.'

But it made sense. They could hardly ride out with the simurgh sitting upon his shoulder.

The bird stretched its swan-like neck, and arched its expanded wings. Truly, the creature was beautiful, even with its blemishes and colour-drained scars. But it was also fucking big. And he had not forgotten how agonising it was, to have it torn from him. Before his fears took too great a hold, Pitch stretched his hand towards the Cultivation.

'Do it. Get on with it. Return to me.' Was it that simple?

The answer seemed to be no. Unblinking topaz pinned him, the creature resettling its wings. Making no move towards him.

'Fuck's sake, just do it, will you?' Before he lost his nerve. He reached for the creature.

The simurgh made a disconcerting noise, like the distant bellow of a bull. There was such power there, despite the sound's faintness. The simurgh's tail lifted and fanned out, the myriad of pastel colours mimicking the spread of a peacock's tail. The Cultivation shifted back, hopping on its one undamaged leg.

The tips of its fanned tail tilted forward, and down.

Like spear tips aimed toward an enemy.

Realisation brought a twisted smile to Pitch's lips. 'You don't want this either, do you?'

But amusing as it was, the simurgh's reticence was also exasperating. He was not going to beg for the wretched, fucking thing to come to him, but nor could he leave this room without their rejoining. He knew it as certainly as he knew that if he delayed too long either Sybilla would return, or Silas would come looking for him. And he was in no mood for anyone, especially Silas, to see him writhing about, with feathers sticking out his damned gob. If that was how this bloody process played out.

'Get on with it. You may have all the freedom you want, once we get you to the Sanctuary.' For the first time, he allowed himself to toy more thoroughly with the idea that perhaps...just perhaps...his part in this would end once the simurgh was delivered to the Sanctuary. That his freedom was not the illusion he'd always imagined.

And it was that thought that had him lunging.

'Come to me. Now. I command you.'

He grabbed at whatever first came to hand. As it turned out, it was the simurgh's slender neck. The growl that came from the creature would make any troll envious.

'Shut up,' Pitch hissed.

A blast of something unseen, a torrent of power, ran beneath the pretty skin and nearly launched Pitch's Christmas dinner into the room. He hissed again, this time with sheer discomfort.

The creature thrashed, and Pitch was dragged across the bed, holding on for dear life. The simurgh pulled them to the far edge, and they tumbled off, taking quilts and pillows with them. The girth of the creature's neck was no more than that of an actual swan, but Pitch had the sense of holding on to something much, much larger. Overwhelmingly enormous.

Pitch landed on his hip upon the hardwood floor, and promptly bit his tongue.

'Fuck,' he said through a mouthful of warm blood. 'Fuck you.'

The urge to let go was intense, but he knew only a part of that urge was his.

The simurgh was mammoth, far more than its form belied, that much was true. But Pitch did not wish to give up now.

'I don't like it,' he grunted as they rolled, and something fell from the bedside table, 'any more than you...but we are too close...'

He'd been ruled by this confounded arsehole of a creature and its powerful magick, for too long.

He was tired of being overruled.

'Still yourself, you fucking imbecile.' The simurgh's attempts to escape him had them rolling again, and he ground his shoulder into the knotted fringe of the rug. 'We are on the same side. Stop, damn you.'

The next bodily shift saw Pitch's legs slip beneath the bed. The simurgh's one good claw found purchase on the wooden bed frame. Stunning pink diamond talons dug in.

There was a violent wrench upwards, and Pitch's groin was slammed into the bedframe. The shock of pain through his balls was truly eye-watering, but there was little time for crying over such things. The sudden stop had thrown the simurgh off-kilter, and in that pause as the creature gathered itself, Pitch tried to wriggle beneath the bed once more, as a way to anchor himself down.

The simurgh recovered too quickly, and flew upwards once more. Glass shattered as the tips of its wings hit the window, and Pitch's knee met the solid mass of the mahogany bedframe. His kneecap dislocated, before his shins were dragged at a painful angle against the immovable solidness of the four-poster. The simurgh pecked at his arm, not breaking skin, but giving very clear encouragement to let go. The pastels of its feathers shone brighter, causing him to blink against their brilliance.

'Stay still, curse you.'

The downdraft from sweeping wings ruffled his hair, and Pitch was drawing his flame to hand, ready for more drastic manners of control, when Scarlet flew in, nearly blinding him entirely with its added glare.

'Get back!' he shouted.

But the simurgh was not the only creature ignoring him. The wisp darted off, right up close to where topaz eyes were luminous, and a golden beak was parted, ready to strike. Pitch squeezed his eyes shut against the onslaught of pretty hues: sunrises, sunsets, fields of lavender and groves of fruiting lemon trees.

The wisp began to hum. A tuneless sound that rose in volume; slowly, assuredly, over the frantic clawing and beat of pink wings. The intonation was deep—astonishingly so for such a tiny thing—and it was not a melody, nor a language. At least, not one he knew. This was more than either, greater than their sum; it was the rumble of the earth as it quaked, the groan of an ancient tree as it fell, the crack of a glacier. And all came from a creature that could be swatted from the air like a fly.

The sound touched at his ribs, at his sinews and that empty place inside.

His body hummed, not with the power of the simurgh, but with this strange sonority.

Pitch, still barely able to see, had the strangest compunction to still, and listen.

So did the simurgh.

The creature gave up its manic efforts to flee him, relaxing in his grasp. He softened his hold as the beast settled on the rug beside him, lowering its head, all the fight leaving it. Pitch blinked his eyes open. The light was not so harsh now, as the simurgh calmed. The Cultivation glanced at him, but only briefly, for its attention was all for the wisp.

Pitch released the simurgh, and dragged his legs from beneath the bed, rocking onto his knees. He stared, as the Cultivation was doing, at the tiny creature who perched on the fallen pile of bedclothes, like a victorious mountaineer upon a linen Mount Everest.

Scarlet did not hum, nor sing. They played a harp. Surely the smallest harp in the world. One of tangerine, glowing like a tiny setting sun in the wisp's hold. Scarlet plucked at strings no thicker than spider's web, and in fact, Pitch was quite certain that is exactly what they were.

The wisp swayed back and forth, like a rainbow metronome, strumming at the harp with fingers like bloated little sausages, setting off those deep, resonating, Earthly notes that tickled at Pitch's ribs. Scarlet saw him staring, mesmerised. The cheeky sod blew him a kiss.

He laughed, of all things. And the simurgh settled itself like a dragon at the base of its pile of treasures, its gem-eyes never leaving the wisp atop their makeshift mountain.

Scarlet hit a particularly lovely note, one of a low bass register, the boom of a distant thundercloud, that sent delightful shivers up Pitch's spine. It was a massage upon the senses. The wisp jerked their chin, once towards him, then another down at the gazing simurgh.

The will-o'-the-wisp repeated the move. Their intention clear.

'I am *trying* to put it back, but you might have noticed the beast is not so keen,' he whispered, like an irate librarian. 'All well and good that you've calmed it...but that doesn't help me with –'

The simurgh suddenly moved, shook itself hard, feathers coming loose and filling the air so thickly that Pitch shrank back, squinting, trying to see what the blazes the damned thing intended now.

The fucking thing had best not fly off, not after all this.

Scarlet's strumming altered, the resonance giving way to something lighter. The lift of the storm, the melting of the ice.

The clarity of morning as it dawned.

Pitch's vision cleared.

The simurgh had not flown off. It perched upon the bed, standing upon its one decent leg, the other held curled and close to its violet belly.

But it was not the same creature he'd seen when he entered the room. There would be no holding onto this swan's neck.

The simurgh had shed more than its feathers.

The Cultivation was translucent. Its corporeal form was gone.

The harp playing ceased. Scarlet's small mouth hung open as it stared with its horrid lifeless eyes at the simurgh.

Pitch remained on his knees. He did not shift when the wildness once again lifted its wings. This time it did not seek to strike at him, but rather, embraced him. Wings wrapped about him, soft to the touch as clouds.

Enormous clouds that stretched on with an endlessness that made Pitch breathless.

The sense of the ancient about this bird, gods, it made his heart stumble.

The simurgh...what the simurgh truly was...was fathomless.

Pitch shivered. Not fear, not exactly. He was wary...cautious...a little dry-mouthed at the thought of taking in this monstrosity.

He knelt before the infinite. But did not fear it.

Pitch had lived with this creature for a long time.

He had *contained* this creature within him. Found a way to live without being swallowed by the gaping depths of its existence.

Pitch pushed up off his knees, hearing the crack of joints as he did so. There was no pain, but there would be.

He lay down upon the bed, finding his place beside the wild and terrible beauty of the simurgh.

A topaz eye was fixed on him, more like a gemstone than ever, now that the creature had shed its corporeal layers.

'I'm ready. Hurry now.'

The intangible wings brought their endlessness near.

The simurgh rose into the air, drifting just a few feet above him. Pitch's fingers curled into the remaining sheet, clutching at its useless protection.

He was not afraid of pain. Gods knew he'd felt enough of it to grow accustomed to its company. But he was tired of being its whipping boy.

The simurgh bore down on him. Silent as falling snow. Spreading wings wide, its primordial presence the slow descent of the morning star. Far too much for him.

Pitch bit at his lip.

Fuck, he did not want to do this. But what choice was there? So close to the end? He suddenly abhorred his choice to do this alone. To keep Silas away.

Something touched at his knuckles. Warm. Gentle.

He dared look down.

Pitch nearly embarrassed himself with a cry of relief. Scarlet was there. Wriggling in between his clenched thumb and forefinger. Laying their head against his hand, and crooning whilst they caressed the curve of his knuckle.

The wisp did not stop, even as Pitch's back arched, and his teeth cracked, even as he held in screams that punched at the back of his throat.

The simurgh's return was only marginally less painful than its removal, forced as that had been. The agony was exquisite, but it was not his alone. The Cultivation's movements were not fluid, there was a resistance there. Pitch swallowed, seeing for the first time what his own self-absorption had blinded him too. There was not one prisoner to Seraphiel's machinations here...but two. Some part of this being, this magickal creation, knew itself bound, and did not enjoy it. The primordial flame perhaps? Too ancient and powerful an entity to submit to being kept in a cage.

With diaphanous wings jerking unbecomingly, the simurgh began to disappear into him, sinking into Pitch's skin as if it were a pale sea.

Submitting, albeit with obvious protest, to its cage once more.

Perhaps knowing, as he did, that the only way for them to escape one another was to reunite now.

The creature's ruined claw dragged at his skin, the injury striking like a branding iron where it sought to enter him. Pitch flung up his hand, sending Scarlet scattering. He grabbed at a pillow, covering his face so he could release the scream that no measure of pressed lips could suppress.

The agony echoed through him, made his marrow fight to be free of its bones. His tendons stretched, straining to free from where they anchored his joints.

This was not right.

This was most certainly not right.

He had underestimated the damage done to the simurgh by Azazel.

And it hurt. Sweet taints of all the highest Celestials, it hurt.

Until it did not.

The Cultivation's broken parts finally drew into him, and he sobbed. Scarlet returned, with a warm touch that soothed; a glow that worked at loosening the tightness of his muscles.

The pain wrought on him by the damage done to the Cultivation was no small thing.

'Find Silas. We must go now,' Pitch rasped.

The journey to the Sanctuary needed to be swift. So they'd learn sooner rather than later, if this whole fucking quest was in vain.

CHAPTER 14

In the gloom of the dwindling afternoon, only Herbert and Phillipa had stood waving them off. The boy was none the worse for wear after his run-in with the goddess, though he'd been found fast asleep in his bed, rather than the stables, and was too groggy to join their impromptu Christmas dinner. He was a tad sniffly, perhaps a bit feverish, but really did not need any of the worried looks that Silas sent him.

'Is he dying?' Pitch had asked, a bit harshly.

'No,' Silas had cried. 'Of course not.'

'Then stop fussing over him.'

Herbert had left Silas with an odd parting message. 'Don't let them distract you, Mr Mercer. They do not sing louder, you now hear more keenly.'

'Silas?' Pitch had frowned at the odd comment.

'Nothing to worry about. Do you need a leg up onto Lalassu? It's not so easy with her being bare-back.'

That of course had been the perfect distraction. 'Of course I don't need a bloody leg-up.'

Phillipa's send-off was not entirely heart-felt. The ghost was upset with their decision not to utilise her carriage. Tied as she was to the Lady Howard's coach, it meant she could not travel with them. The usually jovial ghost was glum as she watched their small party depart. Even when

Silas thanked her solemnly for all her assistance, he was met with a scowl and a huff, and a fold of arms over the garish gunshot wound on her belly.

'Just don't do anything foolish, now.'

Silas had promised he would not, but they all knew it was a promise already broken. This final journey was foolery of the highest order.

The Struggle was just as its name suggested; a seemingly endless wind of road that grew in its steepness as it traversed the Lake District. Its ascent began right from the outset, on a curving road amongst the houses, at the heart of Ambleside. It would have been quite easy for all the others to send them off, but there had been no messy, and gods-forbid, teary farewells.

'Do you think they have begun the party yet?' Pitch asked after an hour's ride; still trying to find a comfortable position on Lalassu's bare back. He'd lied, of course, when insisting to Silas that he was fine, earlier. The simurgh's presence made his insides clench and twist. 'I expect they are cups deep in champagne to celebrate their freedom from our troubles.'

When no reply came from Silas, who sat behind him on the mare, Pitch nudged him with an elbow. 'Are you still angry with me?'

'Hmm?'

Pitch sighed. 'You're not paying me any attention. Would you prefer Charlie to ride with you?'

'What? Of course not.' Silas adjusted his seat, his thighs pressing firmer against Pitch's. 'I want you with me. And no, I am not angry at you still, nor was I before. I just would have liked to have been with you, to support you, when you took back the simurgh.'

The ankou had most certainly been angry, not at Pitch perhaps, but at his own perceived sense of having failed somehow, in not being there.

'It was all over and done with quickly. Barely noticed it.' Pitch repeated his lie, even as the simurgh's claws seemed to dig at his innards. 'Besides, you could support me now, if you like?' He wriggled his backside to make his point, but received not a wit in return. 'Silas, whatever is the matter with you?'

'Christ, I'm sorry.' The ankou nuzzled at the back of Pitch's head. 'Forgive me. I'm a little fuzzy headed. Perhaps too much wine at our meal.'

'Perhaps.' Though that seemed wholly unlikely. The meal was hours past now.

Silas delivered a few gentle kisses behind his ear, and Pitch decided to let things lie. He could not blame the ankou if he needed a moment or two of peace.

Pitch toyed with the multiple draping collars on his carrick coat, enjoying the fineness of the beige wool. He'd done far better with a riding coat than Silas, who'd been given a plain black cape to go over his equally dull blue frock coat. His gaze drifted to Charlie who rode up ahead through the misty late-afternoon. The lad wore an identical cloak to Silas's, although about twenty sizes smaller. He was easily managing the brown horse, a solid, reliable mount who did not so much as chomp at the bit. In fact he'd heard Charlie encouraging the nag along a few times when it lagged behind on the strenuous climb.

'Are we there yet, pray tell?' Pitch ventured, knowing it would cause Silas to huff with laughter, and Charlie to roll his eyes.

He was wrong on both points. Silas made a faint noise, nothing whole-hearted, and it was the lad who put on a grand show of fake laughter. 'Ah, now I see what it is that Silas adores in you, Tobias. You are utterly hilarious. I can barely stay in the saddle for all the laughter.' The insincerity was masterfully delivered, Pitch would give the lad that much.

'Twat,' he returned.

'Arsehole.'

They casually threw deprecating names at one another, and though Pitch was certain Silas would intervene, he took far longer than expected, and even then sounded awfully distracted with his soft sigh and call on them to desist.

'I shall declare myself the winner of that round, Mr Astaroth.' Charlie's smile was genuine, the sparkle in his striking blue eye evident. The lad was a little force of nature. Small in stature, but rather large in terms of guts and balls. More so than many others Pitch had met. And a very decent rider to boot.

Another strike of pain found Pitch's belly; the muscles in his torso clenching in one sharp action. Silas was too distracted to notice the tiny flinch, but Pitch's other passenger felt it well enough.

Scarlet peeked from the confines of his pocket, wide eyes lifted to meet his.

'I'm fine,' he mouthed.

The wisp folded its arms and tilted its head. A universal sign of disbelief. Pitch poked out his tongue, and then shifted his arm so Scarlet was blocked from view. Silas mistook the move for a fault on his part, widening his elbows, giving Pitch space.

'Sorry, was I holding too tight?'

'No, Scarlet was shifting about, that's all.' Pitch urged Silas's elbows down. 'Don't worry so.'

'Then perhaps don't give me reason to.' Silas's new forthrightness only made him more appealing, but here it was imbued with a testiness unlike him. 'I won't be happy if you are keeping any discomfort from me.'

'I know that. And I assure you, all is well.' Pitch knew he saw right through his insistence that the regaining of the simurgh was no trouble, but with Silas already in a distracted state Pitch was not about to whine about a belly ache. 'And certainly for the best, is it not? Imagine that colourful bird flying with us, or sitting on the back of a horse. Hardly commonplace. We'd have half the county coming out to peer at us.'

'There's no one for miles.'

'How can you bloody tell? This mist is worsening.' The landscape was a white blur. On the occasion that it shifted, they saw themselves surrounded by rolling hills, endless sweeps, rising ever upwards, the occasional flock of sheep showing as whiter blobs amongst the milky scenery.

'Do you think an elemental assists us?'

'No. I think this just a fine example of dismal English weather.' Pitch wiped at his nose where moisture beaded. 'Now, truly, if we are talking of keeping things from one another, perhaps you'd like to elaborate on your mood?'

'There is nothing to my mood.'

'Fine. There was nothing to the return of the simurgh, either.'

'Pitch.' The single word dropped hard, like the clang of a grandfather clock, resolute and dominate. And all at once it seemed completely ridiculous to carry on the charade. Besides, the ankou would chew his ear off for the rest of this journey if Pitch did not open up now.

'I don't feel well. There you go. I feel quite shitty, in fact. And having the Cultivation return hurt like all the fucking hells...' He paused to take a breath. Scarlet gave him a pat from inside their pocket hiding place. 'I think the damage done to the simurgh is partly to blame. The ruined claw was not the most pleasant of things to absorb.'

The reunion had been harsh enough, but he'd not been prepared for how awful he'd feel after it was done. He felt as though he'd eaten bad oysters, truth be told.

Silas said nothing for a while, merely nestled in closer, and brought his arms in with a firmer embrace.

'Thank you.'

'For what? Feeling like a dog's breakfast? Your fetishes are not what I expected.'

He felt rather than heard Silas's amusement, something in the shift of the man's broad shoulders. 'Of course not, my lovely fool. Thank you for telling me.'

'Well, you were being tiresome. It seemed the best way to shut you up.'

Scarlet jabbed at him—with a bulbous finger, he hoped—and Silas's breath huffed against his ear.

'You are so thoughtful.'

Charlie twisted in the saddle. 'I can barely see the road, I'm worried I shall miss the turn off.'

As if to accentuate the remark, a particularly dense buffet of mist swept across the road. There was hardly anything left to be seen of either Charlie or the brown horse.

Pitch was hardly surprised when Silas sucked in his breath.

'It's alright Silas, he's only a few strides ahead.'

'No...it's not that.' He bit the words between his teeth, and jerked at the reins. Lalassu lifted off her front feet, and veered sharply to one side. Pitch lunged for a fuller handful of her mane, instinct pushing him, despite the fact there was no fear he'd fall, with the horse's mane pinning his legs, and Silas steady behind him. 'I just need a moment, Lalassu, release me.'

Freed of the mare's bracing hold, Silas swung his leg over her rump and dismounted.

'Silas? Are you all right?' Pitch struggled to free himself too, but Lalassu was being damned slow about it. 'Come on, you little shit. Let me down.'

'No. Hold him, Lalassu.' Silas leaned forward, bracing his hands to his knees. 'We'll carry on in just a moment. I'm fine…I'll be fine…I just need to catch my breath. They are terrible to listen to.'

The countryside could not have been any quieter.

'Is this something to do with what Herbert said to you, before we left?' Pitch demanded. 'Who are you hearing, Silas? It's not what the Herlequin did to you again, is it?'

Silas shook his head, his dark curls like heavy curtains concealing his face. 'No. This is not manipulation. And I am not afraid.'

'Then what do you hear?'

The ankou straightened. It still astonished Pitch how grand the man was. Every day he seemed greater, more imposing. 'All of them. All of the dead.'

CHAPTER 15

Silas had not lied about being unafraid, but he *was* overwhelmed. The warning Izanami had sent him, through the child Herbert, had hardly been sufficient.

Do not let them distract him? How the bloody hell could he prevent it?

The whispers had begun the moment they had left Ambleside. Grown to quiet conversation an hour later, and grown again to the louder hubbub of a drunken tavern an hour after that.

Whatever protections Izanami had set around the graveyard of Ambleside was not evident here, and Silas suffered for it.

The cacophony was ridiculous. As if he stood in the busiest train station in London, and every passenger held a blasted mega-phone, their melodies pounding the airwaves, each fighting for dominance.

Despite the maelstrom of sound, if he focused just so, he could name each melody.

All manner of dead were here.

There were the simple lost souls, those trapped by their grief, a murderous end, perhaps, a regret so powerful it kept them from finding peace, from wanting to move on. Their quiet notes were near drowned by the sharper trills of the hungry ghosts; the ravenous souls of the worst of mankind, the murderers, the violators, the ones who hunted down the weaker souls and devoured them. Then, over the top of it all, was the bombastic notes of the Blight-stricken teratisms.

It was not a concert Silas enjoyed; all the less for how it made Pitch's voice so small. Barely discernible as he begged to know what ailed the ankou.

Silas would answer–he was desperate to do so–he just needed a moment to gather himself. To understand this newfound intensity.

The goddess had done too well in resurrecting his strength. She had made him too much in her image.

You shall hear more keenly, Herbert had said.

'One moment, just one moment.' His words were a whisper among shouts.

Silas kept his eyes shut. Needing the stillness behind his lids.

That was not what the goddess had said.

Her words, from Herbert's lips had been: *it is not they who sing louder, but you who hear keenly, once more.*

He inhaled, drawing in the centuries, filling in a fine crack of lost memory.

He listened to the death that surrounded him. That had *always* surrounded him as the Pale Horseman. A calamity of the collision of life and death. 'I forgot how to listen.'

His words were instantly consumed by the chorus of the dead; picked apart by the messiness of their nature.

A touch landed on his shoulder, and the furore dimmed. The manic discord lowered its volume.

'Silas? Is someone hurting you?'

Charlie stood by his side, the lad whose blood anchored him more securely to the land of the living. Blood that provided a quiet place, where a lost soul might remember himself.

Silas exhaled, breathing into the space where he existed in the world. A place that housed neither the dead nor living. And he understood; the subtle slink of returning memory warming his mind.

'No,' he said. 'It is not me they harm. I had just forgotten what it was to hear them. I have forgotten how to listen.'

He placed his hand over Charlie's. The lad frowned with confusion, and Pitch cursed at Lalassu when the mare held him fast on her back.

'Start making sense, Mr Mercer, or I swear I'll burn myself clear of your nag.'

Both of his companions were easily heard now, the din of the dead was pressed to the background by Charlie's touch. While there was sense to be made of his own thoughts, Silas listened.

And remembered.

And understood how much violence had been done to the dead, since last he'd ridden with his scythe.

Stronger now, clear-headed, Silas looked to Pitch. 'I can hear all the damage done. The ruin the Blight has made of the melody that should run peaceably between life and death. The goddess warned me how great it had become, but I hear it myself now.' He could not suppress a shudder. 'The Blight knows our threat, and it does not like us. Izanami seeks to make a haven for those most vulnerable, Sybilla shall take her place among the ankou...' He paused, listening anew.

'Sybilla?' Pitch's fingers were aglow, but he'd not made good on his threat to burn Lalassu's mane, thankfully. 'You told me she had come over unwell again, and that was why she did not ride with us. When the fuck were you going to tell –'

Silas held up his hand. 'Hush. Please.'

There was something there. Distant. Sweeping through the noise, like wind through a wheat-field. But so desperately faint. Charlie shifted, and Silas tightened his grip on the lad's hand.

'Wait.'

Silas closed his eyes, shaping his senses towards that faint whisper. Sifting his way through the clamour, the chaos that had been more of his making than that of the souls. But now his old mind, ancient and tired as it had been, was rejuvenated by Ambleside's dead. Revived in its ability to understand the notes he heard.

Teratisms, certainly, but they could be counted among those who had learned to struggle against the grip of the Blight.

'What do you wish to tell me?' he whispered. 'Speak up, just a little louder.'

Silas squeezed his eyes tighter shut, sinking down into that fathomless place in the darkness where the quiet held court. He drew the whispers to him there. Encouraged them closer.

Ankou of the Pale Horse.

'Yes. Are you there?'

The noise that came was grating, the slash of the needle on a phonograph, the rusty drag of a prison cell door.

Interference. Whoever sought to reach him had those who wished them stopped.

For all the teratisms he had saved, converted, there were many more being birthed anew by the Blight. But Silas had experienced a rebirth of sorts, too; he was not so feeble now.

He let go of Charlie's hand. And sank into the ocean of sound before him.

If the teratisms could not reach him, he'd move closer to where they were.

Silas wove his mind through the tangle of death notes, through the anguish that drifted there, ever-present, through the rotten grief and profound regret that the Blight stirred.

'Are you there?' he asked again.

We are, Lord Death. Here at the graveyard.

Which bloody one? Silas wanted to shout. Make your damned point. But he caught his fury in time, reeled in it, and let gentler thoughts go ahead. 'Where might you be? What do you need me to know?'

The sombre tunes surrounded him; death notes that lashed out at the intrusion of his own melody. There came again the cringe worthy grating, the harsh crunch of cog wheels being broken.

'Speak now. Quickly.'

We stand by the church you bade us guard. Where the witches lay.

Silas's shock nearly cost him the frail connection he held. These were the teratisms who'd aided Sybilla and the Dullahan in keeping open the entrance to the cockaigne; still at their posts, just as he'd asked. 'And what do you know?'

The answer was nearly buried beneath an onslaught of targeted grief, a wave in the ocean that sought to catch Silas in its whirlpool.

But familiarity not only bred contempt, it bred resilience. Silas was no stranger to the machinations of the Blight.

'What do you know?' His note resonated through the depths, an ironic lifeline, one the teratisms clung to now.

An angel came for the bones of his kind, those beyond the church.

'In the cockaigne? Someone has entered?'

Yes.

'Who is it?' Christ, were they not done with nefarious angels?

A great one. White as lightning. We will not go closer. He frightens us. He frightened the fae.

'The fae? Do you mean the Dullahan?'

The angel took the fae from the glass. Freed him. Wanted answers. The fae gave him lies, to save himself. Told him it was the Daemon King's doing that trapped him there.

'What does the angel want?'

To know where the simurgh has gone.

The roar of the crowded ocean of death gathered greater strength. The clamour of anguished voices, of lives lost and spent unwisely, grew louder, goaded on by the Blight. Silas held his eyes closed so tight his cheeks stung with pain. His ears bled. The warmth of it unmistakable. But he did not have enough.

'He knows of the simurgh?' Silas hummed with frantic energy, desperation that sputtered useless questions from his mouth.

He knows much, Lord Death.

'Tell me more. Do you have a name? What was the angel's name?'

Michael.

The Blight drove in, and deafened him.

Silas was hurled from the depths to which he'd sunk. A bodily throw of the mind that sent him tumbling, only to be caught before he'd had chance to draw a breath.

Pitch held him, Charlie stood over him. The lad clutched his hand to his chest, his worry clear.

'Are you hurt?' Silas knew he spoke aloud, but he could barely hear himself. He sounded as though buried beneath snow.

He had to translate Charlie's reply through the reading of the lad's lips. *I'm fine. What of you?*

Not terrible here perhaps, but elsewhere far more dire things stirred. Pitch's breath against Silas's hair told him he was being spoken too. He shifted, rocking onto his knees. The fog hung like sheets around them, and the fire in Pitch's eyes had it glowing.

The daemon touched his fingers to Silas's ears, and they came away bloody.

What the fuck is happening? Silas read the question on perfect, cupid-bow lips.

But he countered with a question of his own; unsure how loudly he spoke, for his hearing was still as though buried beneath great muffling layers. 'Who is the angel Michael?

The flames at the heart of Pitch's eyes flared. Heat flowed from him, making the fog shift and sway.

'He is one of the Seraph.'

CHAPTER 16

Lucifer should have returned to White Mountain, as he'd told Vassago he intended. He'd not lied to the prince. Arcadia *was* Lucifer's destination.

But, by the Celestials, he was spent, and in no mood for the political strife of White Mountain's halls. The encounter with Azazel's divine magick had stolen something from him, and the strength it had taken to hold back Wrath so that Silas and Vassago could escape the cockaigne, had pushed him over an edge of exhaustion he'd not encountered before.

So he sat in the stench of humanity, in a tea-house in Slaidburn, a small village north of Newchurch-in-Pendle, little more than an hours ride from the cockaigne, and all its tumult.

The woman who owned the tea rooms had approached him after he'd been staring into a cup of black tea for the better part of two hours. His scones untouched, the clotted cream forming a crust. He slipped the trumpeter endlessly between his fingers, the metal cold, its power extinguished. Now, it truly was no more than it appeared: a slender whistle of silver. The cut on his palm, made from the blade of his own vestige as he'd fought to secure the cage, was really the only evidence of the entire debacle. And it made itself known, the skin bright pink and throbbing around the gash.

'Do you enjoy a hunt, then?' the proprietor had asked on the first day, when she'd mistakenly believed herself worthy of being spoken to.

'Do you have rooms?' He'd slipped the trumpeter back into his pocket.

She'd smoothed her skirts, unruffled by his brusqueness.

'Certainly do. There's one sitting empty. Would you like it?'

'Do you have a library?'

She'd blinked, but barely paused. 'Not as such, but I can get a hold of some reading material if you'd like. What takes your fancy?'

'Fairy tales.' Now she blinked again, with an added small smile.

'Is there a problem?' he'd glowered.

'No offence intended, my apologies. I just hadn't thought you…never mind.' Smart woman. 'Fairy tales it is. I'll see what I can do.'

She'd not spoken more than a handful of words to him since. And had brought him several volumes of Grimms' Fairy Tales–which he already had in his private collection at his residence in Arcadia–along with a pile of penny dreadfuls.

For two days he'd lingered. Reading. Sipping black tea. Picking at scones. But never fully falling into the lull of the tales that normally soothed him.

His hand ached.

The gash from his own vestige had not yet healed. Its line across his palm remained: a dirty grey cut with thin veins of black spreading from it. An oddity which concerned him, but one likely to be rectified on his return to Arcadia.

He simply had to decide when that return would be.

Lucifer took another sip of tea, and looked out through the iron-wrought window. The proprietor had shifted the small table and chairs that had occupied this space elsewhere, and moved the armchair he favoured to rest there instead.

He had simply thought to catch his breath, amongst quieter folk. Sit with the dullness of the purebreds, before he presented himself to those of Gimli Hall. Before he took a knee before Enoch's Ophanim throne; the throne beneath which the Creation Flame burned, guarded by the Eternal Wheels which spun in perpetuity, their nekhri surfaces covered in a thousand watchful eyes.

But he'd not been ready for those eyes, or those of the court, who would devour his every word, digest it, and then spew it back at him with a thousand questions. The Higher Angels would not take news of Gabriel's betrayal well. Nor of Iblis's existence, and the scourge of maleficium festering beneath their very noses. He would be challenged; he would face torrid accusations. The angels and daemons held an uneasy alliance. The Archangels would rage. Would always assume a king of Daemonkind sought to extend his power. Would always spoil for a fight.

Who did not, in Arcadia?

He'd be challenged.

Why had Lucifer not called on any Angelic assistance? Had the Lord Enoch truly gifted him the trumpeter, or had Lucifer stolen the Lord's Wrath? What proof did he have that Gabriel was a turncoat?

Lucifer had no idea what support he could rely on from Enoch. Arcadia's master never shared his designs. His workings were unknowable.

And his nature was devastatingly mercurial.

Who was not to say that this would be the moment Arcadia's master would rid himself of a daemon king who knew a dangerous secret?

It was not beyond the realm of possibility that Enoch had not given Lucifer free will out of a genuine desire to allow Seraphiel's plan to fruition, should the fates allow, but to bring about the demise of the one daemon in Arcadia who knew the Lord of Arcadia had killed his favoured angel.

Lucifer drained his tea cup. He'd barely set it down than the woman replaced his tea pot with another. She was remarkable in that way: knowing when a refill was needed, saving him the need to utter a word.

It was Lucifer who used words today. His throat dry with disuse. 'I wonder if I might have a boiled egg?'

The woman's face brightened. Strange creatures they were. 'I'll see to it, right away, sir. Toast, too?'

'No.' Lucifer returned to his penny dreadful, where a dubious barber was breaking necks, so as to make pies.

'Right then.'

She turned away, but did not move. He shuffled his thin papers, coughing in the hope she'd move out of his space.

'Can I help you?' Her voice wavered.

Lucifer raised his gaze from one nasty piece of work, to another.

The man who had entered the comfortable rooms cast a silence over all its guests. Tea cups hung halfway to mouths, crumbs remained spilled in laps with hands raised in the process of dusting off but going no further. Only the fire dared to keep crackling.

'Michael.' Lucifer folded his penny dreadful, placed it carefully upon the table. He wished there had been one more swill of tea to drink so he could delay his rise further. 'Would you care for tea and scones? An egg perhaps?'

The Seraphim appeared as a mortal man, but made himself no small creature. Imposing and dominant, as the angels were in true form, Micheal was a great bruising chap who'd be more likely to bodyguard a crime gang's leader: hair cropped so short he appeared almost bald, a protruding brow creating a shadow over his dark eyes. Though none of the purebreds could see the angel for who he was, he doubted they'd be more any more fearful if they could. So much threat rippled from the man.

But they were not the target of Michael's ire.

Lucifer poked the proprietor in the shoulder. 'Go on then, see to those eggs.'

She jumped, muttered something, and left. Or rather, fled. Other customers chose then to leave behind their hot brews and sweet cakes. The strangest thought came to Lucifer as he watched Michael clear the room without uttering a word: how Vassago would have been appalled to see all the cakes so abandoned.

Gods, he must be weary to have such ideas. His hand pulsed with pain.

'Is there something you'd like to discuss with me, Michael?' He gestured to a now-vacant chair at a neighbouring table. 'Would you like a seat?'

'What are you hiding, daemon?'

'Good day to you too, angel.'

The growl that came would have made the Brothers Grimm proud.

'Gabriel used his halo to reinforce a cage in that cockaigne,' Michael's words held their own sparks. 'What did it hold?'

Well, at least he'd not have to prove Gabriel was a duplicitous arsehole. Lucifer had assumed a clean-up crew would arrive at some point, to extract the angel bones from the cockaigne, but he'd thought it would be longer before the Wrath had subdued enough to do so. And that it would be another archangel acting as housekeeper. Michael was the very last angel he'd wished to have here.

'I saw no prisoner. It was empty.'

'Liar. Think carefully before you speak again.'

'Do you not have better things to do than interrupt my breakfast?

Michael moved through the room with the grace of a wrecking ball. Without touching them he swept aside chairs, a table, a pot plant that had the misfortune of dipping its fronds in his way. The angel was barely restrained beneath his human skin.

Lucifer seated himself, and crossed his legs. If he'd not done so he would have likely fallen into his seat anyway. The pain in the wound was astounding.

Pulsing with each step the angel took. Making his vestige, where it was embedded in his finger, hum with discontent.

Michael arrived at Lucifer's side in a heart-beat. His shadow cast itself throughout the entire room, darkening the light coming through the panes. The purebreds always wrote of the angels as creatures of light. The Seraph were brightest of all, but that did not mean there was no blackness to them.

'I have scried their bones, Lucifer.' He drew three shards of white from his pocket, brandishing them like some macabre fan. A fingerbone was recognisable, but the other two Lucifer could not discern. 'Azazel lives, his bones hold his secrets, but Gabriel and Iblis...' The blankness of Michael's face made his words ever more chilling. 'I know what these angels saw as they took their last breath. The Death Wish is not the only power to be found in the pause between life and death, and I amongst my brothers am the most talented with the bones. Vassago does not lie rotting in the abaddon.' He closed his hands around the angel bones. There was a crack, a snap, as he tightened his grip. 'He does not pay for his sins as he should, does he, daemon?'

Lucifer tried to mimic the angel's blankness, but by the gods he feared he did so none too well. 'If you are so all-seeing, then I need not answer that.'

The seraph moved with sickening speed, snatching up Lucifer's hand. He cried out in surprised protest, and summoned his flames. The crawl beneath his skin was unpleasant. The burn unusual in how it caused him to shiver.

'Raise your flame to me, I dare you.' Michael's spittle hit Lucifer's cheeks like chips of ice. 'Give me another reason to strike you down, here and now, without need for White Mountain's sentence.'

Lucifer sunk the fire deeper beneath his skin. Micheal drew in closer, bringing shadows with him, causing the wood beams to groan as the walls shifted around him.

'Where is the simurgh, daemon?' He traced his finger around the gash on Lucifer's palm.

'I left it to Wrath to deal with.' Michael's presence was a terrible pressure on his chest. He struggled to keep his thoughts in a row. If the angel had only witnessed Gabriel's last moments, he could not prove Lucifer's words true or otherwise.

'Where is the simurgh?'

'I don't know.' The truth had a way of flowing more easily.

Michael turned the bones to powder in his tight-hold, letting them sift between his fingers and fall down onto the penny dreadful laid out on Lucifer's lap. 'Iblis and Gabriel deserved what you did to them, they deserved our lord's Wrath. They were traitors, both. But what are you, Lucifer?' His finger kept working in slow ovals around the wound. 'I saw what they took from your spawn, a prince who should have been put to death the moment he raised his vestige against a Seraph. I saw you bring down an Archangel to protect something that does not belong to you, and might well destroy everything my brothers and I have set in place to contain the halo. Don't be more of a fool, daemon. I know the Cultivation does not remain in that cockaigne.' He brought his hand, white with angel dust, to Lucifer's throat, and wrapped his fingers around it. The pressure he brought to bear forced Lucifer to his feet. Lucifer's innards drew tight with knots. His flame twisted and riled against the fear that swept through them. 'The madness of Seraphiel has stained you, but it is our mistake not to have paid greater heed to how deeply you were enraptured by him. The lengths you'd go to, to keep his dangerous, fanciful delusion alive. And now, it has killed you.'

'Perhaps glasses are in order, I'm alive.' Lucifer rasped against the angel's chokehold. 'And you'd do well to reconsider destroying a King of Daemonkind, one who carries the lord's trumpeter, proof I had his Blessing in this.'

Michael smiled, teeth of purest white gleaming. Slick as blades. 'Our lord's Blessings come in many shades, so few of them pure. Will he come for you when your suffering becomes too much? And it shall, for you have stood far too close to the Primordial Flame, daemon.' He lifted Lucifer just high enough to ensure his tiptoes only reached the floor with much straining. 'Where is the simurgh? I'll ask one last time, before I give you no choice.'

'I told you. I do not know.'

'No. You don't, do you? I see that now. And more is the pity for you.'

Michael dug his fingers into the wound on Lucifer's palm. The bellow it drew forth must have reached all the way to Arcadia. It certainly cleared the tea-room of lingering guests, who added their own cries to the hue.

Lucifer's roar shook the windowpanes. He sought to ignite his vestige but the angelbone lay stagnant. He shot raw daemonic flame from his other hand, wild and lashing, catching Michael square in the chest.

The blast sent them both flying through the tea rooms front wall.

Michael did not release his clawed hold on Lucifer's hand, and it was impossible to work himself free, no matter how vigorously he tried.

They shot out across the road, and into the open field opposite. 'Your blood reeks,' Michael snarled in his ear, 'of forbidden things, daemon.' They carved a deep gully into the earth with the slide of their bodies, churning the grass to nothing as they tumbled and fought. White fire, orange fire, burning the field to a carpet of cinder. 'Of maleficium and divine magick but it is the stolen fire that shall kill you. It crawls through your blood, and soon you shall know why the Primordial Flame is for the gods' alone.' Michael's hiss gave off steam, his human skin splitting open with the impossible task of holding in all he was. Angelfire poured from the tears. 'No corporeal creature survives long once touched.'

Lucifer fought, letting his fire surge, great infernal wings fending off the light that sought to douse them. He fought, through fatigue and horror, through something akin to fear, striving to resist the angel's ministrations. But this was a Seraph. One not worn down by all Lucifer had weathered. And Michael had realised it before Lucifer himself. The chaos in that conservatory–in the heart of the Erlking's hidden realm–a storm of maleficium, divine magick and ancient flame, could not be weathered without consequence.

A brilliant burst of Angelfire stole Lucifer's vision. It was a fleeting moment, and it was all Michael needed.

The Seraph pinned him down, shoving himself between Lucifer's legs. Crushing his fire into the earth.

He tore at his trouser leg.

'The thigh, was it not?' Michael hung like a sun above him. 'That is where they took the piece from you that made him, if I recall.'

Lucifer opened his mouth to protest, and Michael shattered his jaw with a casual strike from an Angelic wing. The break was nasty, and would be slow to heal. But with that strike Michael had rid Lucifer of any lingering doubts; he'd do anything in his power to see Vassago afforded the chance to test Seraphiel's Cultivation now. Lucifer did not take kindly to this sanctimonious prick's bullish behaviour.

Michael dug his fingers into Lucifer's human flesh, sinking them into the daemonstone beneath, and the scar embedded there; the place where Lord Enoch's blade had cut away Lucifer's flesh and cast the piece into the Creation Flames, so a new Dominion Prince could be made.

Michael leaned on him, crushing bone and lungs and all those feeble vessels of humanity.

'You could have just taken me to him, Lucifer. Avoided all this unpleasantness,' he said, his brilliance glancing against the low lie of the clouds. 'I see it very clearly now.' He slumped back onto his heels, holding Lucifer's scarred daemonstone like some rocky heart in his hand. 'That day upon the cliff was a result of my brother, the fool, becoming the architect of his own demise. The Cultivation is in the Dominion Prince. And Seraphiel lost control of his creation.' He shook his head, and it was like a shower of stars. He studied the piece of Lucifer he held. 'Now I will see that Cultivation destroyed. This entire, farcical episode shall be done with. And this piece of the sire shall lead me to the wretched spawn. I will see your crown stripped from you for your part in all this, Lucifer. You will pay for your blind devotion.'

He pressed down on the place where he had dug part of Lucifer away, pushing himself to his feet.

And when he swept his wings, he let them crash their way across Lucifer's body, striking him from importance. From consciousness.

In one final act of degradation, he stooped and grabbed Lucifer's finger, where the vestige burned like a hot ember in his nail. Despite all his attempts during the battle, Lucifer's vestige had not ignited as it should; had not amplify his daemonflame to give him greater defence against an all-powerful angel. Michael snapped the finger so decisively the entire digit broke free with a clean tear of flesh.

The Seraph rose, the brightest star in a sky not yet touched by any other. And blackness stole Lucifer from his senses.

He had no inkling of how long he lay there. Half pressed into the earth, shattered and picked at like carrion. Long enough to know some of his bones had healed, but far from enough. The faint tinkling of bells found its way into his dazed mind.

'Gods,' he breathed, through swollen lips and throat, but grateful he could speak at all, his jaw bone having knitted its break.

His eyes fluttered open, and even his lashes seemed to ache.

A new darkness presented itself to him. A darkness that moved. Nudged at him. Snorted in his aching face. Touched at his torn-open hand with a hoof studded with nails.

Lucifer sat up, far too quickly, finding every rib not yet knit together, and collarbones that poked at flesh where they really shouldn't.

The Dullahan's black stallion screamed, every bit the war horse.

Chollima went to his knees, lowering his great bulk to the ground, tossing his head, sending the reigns to within Lucifer's reach. The message was crystal clear. Get on.

'I mount, and then what?' Lucifer wheezed, dreading the punishment that would come with trying to get to his knees, let alone his feet.

'He's a horse. Fae horse, sure, but not going to talk back to you.' The rather shrill voice belonged to the tiny creature sitting on the pommel of Chollima's saddle. A pixie, if Lucifer was guessing correctly. One that looked to be several twigs twisted around one another. 'Are we going to find him or not? You are looking for Silas Mercer, aren't you?'

Was he? If he wished to find Vassago, then the answer was yes. He doubted Enoch himself could separate the two. But maybe Lucifer was best to just stay here, like an old stump rotting in the soil; let his wounds heal over and let the rest play out, without his hand in it. Allow Michael to go ahead and, as the angel had described it, let this entire, farcical episode be done with.

The stallion knocked at him again, down low and far too close to where there was a damned great hole in Lucifer's thigh. The tinkling of tiny bells was evident again.

'Stop it,' he snapped.

'He wants you to get up.' There was more than one piskie in the horse's mane. This second one was woven from stouter sticks, with three dew drop eyes and white flower petals in some semblance of hair.

'I'm well aware,' Lucifer snarled.

'Then why aren't you moving?'

'I would say that is self-evident.'

'Bit beaten up, aren't you?' This came from a hobgoblin of all things, peeking from behind a refuge of ploughed earth. 'Scruffy, dirty too. But we probably don't have time for bathing. The angel flew off pretty fast.'

Lucifer cursed at the waning afternoon that settled around him. 'How long ago?'

Several gnomes pushed their heads from the soil, which formed peaked caps on their heads. "Not more than ten minutes,' one of them said. 'Are we going?'

'Going where?' Lucifer's voice lifted with tired exasperation. 'How can the likes of you find them?'

A plethora of indignant gasps erupted from the ever-widening audience, the bells tinkling madly. 'Just as well we aren't doing this for your sake. The likes of us are all too small to be noticed by the likes of you. *That's* how we can find them. Because no one gives a damn if we see things or not.'

'Also, Chollima used to be ridden by him who is the Erlking, but the horse is free now. Still carries the duty-bind to the ankou, though. So that helps.'

Lucifer had not one ounce of energy to correct them on the fact Chollima's rider, the headless horseman, was no king. He sat with both hands cradled in his lap, one with its amputation, the other with its crippling cut. Both now cauterised, both still aching. This was likely the most rotten he'd felt in all his long years.

'And,' another of the gnomes chimed in, 'the kodama will send word through the trees to guide us. Them boys saved the Forest of Dean after all, so the trees like them a lot, which means we'll know the shortest way. Least we can do for those fellows.'

The hobgoblin bravely stepped from behind his pile of dirt. 'Them angels killed my second cousin, six times removed, down Mordiford way, too. Tried to blame it on that daemon the ankou likes, dirty rotten scoundrels.'

A crowd, a human crowd, was gathering on the far side of the field, the faint murmur of voices reaching him. The very last thing Lucifer wished to do was find himself trapped amongst frantic village folk. They had a history of using pitchforks to stab at anything they did not understand, and he was done with being the object of assault.

The tinkling of tiny bells drew his attention back to his smaller audience. Chollima's reins were held aloft by a small group of ethereal little creatures, no bigger than the finger that Lucifer had lost, and with silver hair that flowed like quicksilver down their backs, the strands tinkling like bells. Peri. He should have guessed from the bells, but the nymph-fae hybrids were such rare folk he'd never glimpsed one.

A string of peri held Chollima's reins aloft, so that they dangled as though held by an invisible rider.

Lucifer groaned, at himself, more than at the presumptive creatures.

The blame for this entire, farcical episode, must, in great part, be laid at Lucifer's own feet. His actions had revived an angel's harebrained scheme.

Lucifer should have laid everything to rest, Seraphiel included.

Should have; but could not. Even now, barely conscious, he intended to chase after a Seraph. Mad, did not adequately define him.

Lucifer crawled on hands and knees to where the Dullahan's black stallion sat waiting. He took Chollima's reins from the peri, who made music as they fluttered away.

With an undignified amount of assistance from this strange gaggle of creatures, he dragged himself onto the back of the black stallion. And did his level best not to pass out as the horse galloped him away.

CHAPTER 17

Lalassu held Pitch and Silas securely, their legs and lower backs wrapped in her storm-cloud strands as she travelled along the road at a gallop. Silas's eyes watered. The air, which had been cold enough to begin with, now turned icy with the pace. The blood that had run from his ears was dry and stiff along the sides of his neck, on the left more than the right, as Charlie had insisted on trying to clean him up a little before Silas demanded that both he and Pitch stop fussing.

He had some inkling how frustrating all the coddling he was accused of, could be.

Up ahead, between the ears of the brown gelding, Scarlet was a minute beacon of rainbow light, having decided that being pressed in Pitch's pocket beneath the layers of horsehair was not to their liking.

Silas was almost thankful for the presence of the brown horse that Charlie rode. The gelding held no magickal properties, so Lalassu could not launch into her insanely quick pace. Which meant their noses and lips were not in danger of freezing off in the wind blast it produced, and their nethers were not punished further upon her bare back. But it did concern him that the mare could not seem to navigate her way without the lad ahead. Lalassu did not try to overtake Charlie and his mount, and she'd shown them nothing in her mane to suggest that she knew the way.

'Was Sanu with you?' Silas said, too loudly, as he struggled with the whispering voices that remained. He was improving though, according to Pitch, and not yelling loud enough for all of London to hear now. Silas's worries could be thanked for that, along with his improving ability to place the hum of the dead at the far edges of his mind.

'Yes, she is with Edward, I promise,' Charlie returned. 'What worries you?'

He huffed with dry, unamused laughter. 'What does not? It's just that I assumed Lalassu would know the way, too.'

'Likely Sanu knows I'm with you, and is refusing to make this easy.' Pitch offered, with no more amusement than Silas, but laughing all the same.

Neither of them voiced what Silas was certain they both pondered. Was the angel already close enough that Sanu did not dare betray her exact position to her mate?

Silas's mind was a whirl with what he'd learned from the souls. Michael, the Serpahim, knew of the simurgh. Did the angel hunt them even now, or was he focused upon finding Lucifer?

'Did Lucifer say he was returning to Arcadia, when last you spoke?' Silas pressed his mouth close to Pitch's ear. 'Will Michael return to White Mountain?'

'Lucifer said he would be returning,' Pitch's concerns manifested a slight tightness in his body, a change that Silas found himself intimately attuned to now. 'But who fucking knows what that bastard shall decide to do. I don't have Tyvain's godsforsaken cards.' His back pressed against Silas's chest as he took a deep breath. 'To be fair though, if your souls speak truly, and Michael is having to take headless fae from windows to glean information, it shows that Lucifer did not run back to Enoch and spill everything about what is happening here.' Another breath. 'The souls said Michael knew of the simurgh, that he wanted to know where it had been taken...but did they say he knew of me?'

Silas brought his arms in tighter about Pitch. 'No, they didn't.' Relief came with that; what felt like a small victory. 'And Byleist would never betray you to the angel.'

Pitch made a small hitched sound. 'You cannot say never. I know you think the sun shines from the Dullahan's arsehole –'

'That is absolutely not –'

'He was brave, and noble, I'm not denying that. He went to great lengths for you, but to be interrogated by a Seraph…well, I doubt even I would not succumb and let something important slip.'

Silas swallowed, his mouth suddenly dry with thought of such torture. 'I should have asked more of the souls…it sounded to me that Michael had already moved on from Byleist…Christ, I did not ask them if he survived.'

Pitch managed to find a gap in Lalassu's mane, and pinched Silas's thigh, bringing him back to where panic sat shallower. 'Stop tormenting yourself. If you'd stayed any longer in the state you were in, I think your brains would have seeped out of your head. And I would not enjoy an empty-headed ankou in my bed.'

Silas nestled his chin upon Pitch's shoulder, Lalassu's gait so smooth there was no danger of chipped teeth. 'I'm sorry that I frightened you. The voices overwhelmed me so quickly, I had no time to even realise what was happening. I think Izanami protected me from their clamour in the village.'

'Pity she didn't see fit to stuff deathly cotton in your ears out here. She is a mercurial wench, like the rest of the gods…and Lucifer. Let us hope he is deep enough into the halls of White Mountain that Michael cannot draw information from him in the ways he prefers. Which is to say, painfully.'

Silas lifted his head, watching the road ahead, and Charlie upon his horse. The gelding was doing well with the punishing ascent and quick pace. 'It is not a pleasant state, in the world of the dead, my love. They are being greatly burdened by the Blight, ever more so than before.'

Pitch covered Silas's arm, where it remained at his waist. 'And your burden grows with it, too, no doubt. I shall be glad to reach this infernal Sanctuary, if only to see that heaviness lifted from you.'

Silas breathed in the dank scent of Pitch's hair, the hint of the grave still clinging there. Soothing to Silas's peculiar tastes. He chose to relish what it was to be able to hold and comfort the daemon at all. Not so long ago, he had feared they would never sit so closely again.

'No much further,' Charlie shouted. 'There's the Kirkstone Pass Inn, look!'

And for the first time in quite a while, they could actually see what lay ahead. The fog thinned where a solitary building sat atop a long-awaited crest. The pub's name was clearly written upon the signboard hanging outside, but to Silas's untrained eye it was no better than chicken scratches. Lights gleamed inside, sending square patches of illumination onto the road. No one sat at the scattering of tables outside, the evening being far too cool.

Beyond the Kirkstone, down into the valley behind, the fog spread itself thin, revealing more of the countryside than they had seen on the ride so far.

Stark and near-bare as those hills were, the sight was no less breathtaking. Though still absorbed by his troubles, Silas's heart stuttered to see the majesty of the landscape.

Charlie's horse slowed, into a canter, then a trot. And Scarlet's light suddenly extinguished.

'Everything all right?' Silas called.

'We can't stop for an ale, you know,' Pitch added. 'Tempting though it is.'

'The gateway is not far from here, I don't want to miss it,' Charlie called back. 'And there is also a carriage approaching, if you must know.'

Silas had been too absorbed by the sights to notice the dark looming presence of the simple berliner, with its pair of dapple greys. Lalassu went from gallop to walk, barely interrupting her steps with a transition to trot, which made for bloody uncomfortable riding.

He did not begrudge Pitch the foul language as they jerked about. The mare set herself near to one of the unused tables of the alehouse, where the road swelled out like a toad's belly either side, to allow for those stopping at the Kirkstone. The carriage's passengers were not among them, though. The carriage driver slowed his dapple greys' trot to accommodate the steeper decline, and continued on, barely glancing at the huge horse with her dual passengers, on the roadside.

'Here we are,' Charlie's voice rang out, but the lad himself was harder to find. The fog had swept in again, nudged by the gentle but icy breeze. 'Come on, this way.'

Lalassu moved on, and Silas could only assume the mare saw far more than he did, for she was back at a trot in no time. Taking them across the road, travelling alongside the low-set rock wall that hugged the Struggle into the gloom ahead. Night was moving in fast now.

A ball of light appeared up ahead; Scarlet illuminated once more. Silas sucked in his breath. If Scarlet still sat between the brown horse's ears then the wisp was far too low. For one horrid moment he imagined Charlie and his mount had somehow fallen down a hillside.

'Charlie?' he called.

Lalassu veered sharply left, and jumped, straight over a dilapidated cross-beam gate. Neither of them were in danger of falling off, but the sudden move made Silas's neck crick, and Pitch squeal with surprise. Both of them slid an inch down the mare's bare back as Lalassu launched herself skyward. She sailed over the low fence, jumping much higher than really needed.

Charlie was someway ahead, down where the landscape flattened out, and he could afford a canter through the barrenness of the sprawling fells. The fog did not seem to like the lower lay of this land, and reduced itself to a lighter mist, though the air remained damp enough to have Silas wiping at his face, and Pitch muttering about being uncomfortably wet, and not in a happy way.

They gained on the brown horse easily, where the lad rode with certainty, lying low, arms lifted high up his horse's neck, hands coaxing, body utterly still despite the pace.

The fells rolled on endlessly, decorated only by rocks and boulders, thin grass and clinging moss, but with solid enough ground to not risk the horses' fetlocks. The air forced itself into Silas's lungs, giving him no option but to breathe deep. Scarlet was a guiding light ahead, hovering above Charlie now, apparently enjoying the pace as much as the horses appeared to.

After a time, a small lake spread out to their left, its surface changed to black by the encroaching evening. Silas did not enjoy where his mind went, upon seeing the water. He very much doubted Blood Lake would look so simple and surmountable. But he only had to tune in to the ceaseless whispering at the back of his mind, the voices of all those unhappy dead, to find his resolve once more.

'Gods, I wish we could keep this up,' Pitch spoke, breathless, but happily so. 'Just carry on riding until we toppled off the edge of the world and no one could find us.'

He tilted his head, as though seeking to read Silas's expression when an answer did not come straight away. 'What do you think? Shall we sneak away when Charlie's not watching?' His laughter was fractious, his mirth utterly false. Silas kissed the hard line of his cheek, wishing their position practical enough to find his lips.

'I am game if you are.'

Lalassu nickered, giving them scant warning of another impending jump. Smaller this time, a pile of gravelly rocks, and once more they were soaring, before a return to a canter across the lonely landscape. They managed another fifteen minutes or so of fast riding, before Charlie's horse stumbled.

Lalassu's mane whipped out, finding the brown horse before the gelding's nose could touch the ground, pulling him up and out of a dangerous fall. So much so that the horse thrashed about with hooves lifted off the ground. Charlie cried out in alarm, and Lalassu adjusted their measure.

At a halt, safely grounded, the gelding's sides heaved, and white foam flecked it's mouth and chest. Scarlet patted at the horse's muzzle, squeaking in their indecipherable language, but clearly consoling the animal.

Silas wriggled against Lalassu's hold.

'Hardly the place for that, my dear,' Pitch declared.

Silas flicked a finger at his ear. 'I'm concerned for Charlie and his mount.'

'Of course you are,' Pitch sighed.

But Lalassu did not release them.

'I've pushed the poor thing too far, I'm not proud to say,' Charlie jumped out of the saddle, running a hand down the sweat-soaked shoulder of his horse. 'But we are so close. Look, you can see the outline of the hill we are headed for.'

He pointed, straight ahead, where there was indeed the shadow of a rise. Silas startled to hear Charlie cry out.

'Bloody hell!'

Lalassu had fixed her attention on Charlie, and wrapped him her tail; lifting him off his feet.

'Wait, wait. Let me unsaddle him,' Charlie cried, fumbling at the girth in an effort to unsaddle the exhausted horse. Lalassu obliged, allowing the lad to remove the bridle too, leaving all in a heap on the ground, and the gelding, sweat-stained, but free.

With a squeal of trepidation, Charlie was drawn back towards the mare.

'No, not with us. There's no bloody room,' Pitch declared.

And he was not truly wrong. Nevertheless, Lalassu lowered Charlie onto her rump, where he was very near to the dock of the mare's tail. If not for the pale horse swaddling him, Charlie would have been in real danger of sliding straight off, but as it was, the lady's horse settled them all in a precarious cocoon; one illuminated by Scarlet as they came to sit on Pitch's shoulders, right beneath Silas's chin.

'A little duller, Scarlet, if you don't mind,' Silas said, squinting until the wisp did as he asked.

Lalassu set off at a brisk walk, neighing and receiving a return from the brown horse which began to graze upon tufts of grass between the rocky ground.

'This is truly not the threesome I had in mind for us, Silas.'

'Please don't,' Charlie sighed. 'I'm being squeezed so tight, it really won't take much for me to throw up.'

'Please don't.' Silas repeated the lad's words back to him. 'How far do you suppose?'

But any answer was lost when Lalassu decided, in her wisdom, to instigate a trot. There were cries and curses from all three passengers, most vocal from Charlie who truly was in a terrible position upon the mare for such things. How Lalassu could stand all the banging about on her back, uneven tempos at that, Christ only knew.

The ludicrous journey went on for a near intolerable ten minutes. The hillside they had seen as a shadow drew ever clearer. A fell of considerable steepness, slate spilling down the slope like grey tears, whilst crags of gathered rock sat higher up. After another few minutes, when Pitch was threatening to burn himself free if the trotting did not stop, Lalassu finally drew to a halt.

There were groans of relief from everyone. Silas peered up at the hillside.

'Now to top this delightful day off, you are going to tell us we need to climb that wretched mountain, aren't you, Charlie?' Pitch fumed.

'It's more of a hill, but yes, I am, I'm afraid. There's the Priest's Hole, that darkness there at the top.'

It was barely visible, but if Silas squinted just so, he could imagine he saw evidence of the cave high up. Very high up.

Lalassu released them. Charlie simply slid off over her tail, Silas went next, offering Pitch an unnecessary hand, but the daemon did not berate him for it. He jumped off Lalassu, and his free hand went at once to his groin.

'Thank the gods I still have an arsehole for you to play with, Silas, for my balls are flattened beyond measure.'

Despite his own discomfort Silas chuckled.

'Ready?' Charlie had already made his way to where the scattering of shale was thickest. 'Be careful, the rock slides easily.'

'Did you hear that, Silas? No lumbering. You must be nimble, because if you slide back down into the valley, I'll not be coming after you.'

They both grinned at the obvious lie.

'Fair enough. Will you be alright with the height, though, or shall you faint, as you are prone to do?'

'How dare you, sir.' Pitch put on a show of righteous indignation and followed after Charlie, who had already begun to climb. At first, the prince refused to use his hands to balance himself on the steepness, and it made for amusing viewing. Watching Pitch's arse was pleasant distraction from the incline, which was rather more formidable than Silas had anticipated. Lalassu picked her way carefully behind him, which was comforting, as he doubted the mare would allow any of them a dangerous slide. The Pale Horse had the advantage of her tail for extra balance, the strands spread behind her like the roots of a ghostly tree.

The traipse up the hillside loosened shale, and several times Silas had to adjust his course as either Charlie or Pitch dislodged stones and sent a cascade down the slope.

They scrambled. There was no more dignified a word for it. All three of them on hands and knees as the soil gave way to craggy rock which was as likely to offer a foothold, as to twist and break an ankle with its crevices.

But the darkness of the cave drew nearer each time Silas paused to glance upwards. They were making decent headway, with Scarlet the only one among them who was travelling easily, sitting upon Pitch's shoulder, despite his chiding of the wisp for it.

'Nearly there,' Charlie panted. 'Only a few more feet to go.'

Silas went to answer. A rush of trepidation swept him, as surely as the breeze itself, cold in his blood, churning fear. Lalassu snorted, and stone clattered behind him as the mare stomped. He turned.

'Look out!' Pitch shouted.

Silas was enveloped by a storm-cloud of Lalassu's mane, a surge of horsehair that rose up high above him, and curled forward like a giant crashing wave. Silas lunged forward, throwing himself towards Pitch who in turn had also lunged for Charlie, grabbing at the lad's ankle. Dragging him down the rock.

'Pitch, what the hell are you doing?' Charlie cried.

The blast struck a heartbeat later. An enormous shift of air that flattened Lalassu's mane against them, like a thick, wet blanket, pummelling them into the hard rock. The mare went onto her knees, a strangled, terrible wheezing sound coming from her but she held their cover valiantly.

Incandescence engulfed their position, a brilliance that dared any eye to remain open.

'What is happening?' Silas bellowed, blinded, but reaching for where he'd last known Charlie to be, protected beneath Pitch's body as the daemon covered him.

'This is gods-damned angelfire.' The brilliance of white was now shot through with flame. 'Michael has found us.'

CHAPTER 18

Michael must be drunk. Or he'd become a fucking terrible shot, since last Pitch had been anywhere near him in a battle. Charlie sought to lift his head from the ground, where Pitch had the lad pressed beneath him.

'Stay down, idiot.'

'Who is out there?' Charlie's voice quavered with distress.

'A bastard. Where is Scarlet?'

'I don't know.' The lad slipped in shale, causing a new rivulet to run.

The ground shook with another blast, another shockingly bright explosion that caused Pitch to blink through tears.

Another miss.

What the fuck was going on? They were sitting ducks, here upon open hillside, and yet three strikes now had blown wide. Each time, the shot of angelfire sent off a shower of stone, hot as embers, which must have been terrible for the mare to endure, but Lalassu held their canopy fast.

'Let me out, you daft nag.' Pitch did not dare extend his flame too far, for fear of giving the horse any more to contend with, but Lalassu was giving him no way out. 'I can deal with him.'

Which was actually part lie, he had no real clue what he could do against a Seraph; but he was useless here, beneath the horsehair. And his fury was difficult to manage. The cunt of a sire of his had betrayed them again. How else could this prick have found them?

'It's a Seraph, Pitch.' Silas was on his knees, hunched over, his hands hovering over Charlie's head; a rather useless shield against nothing, as so far nothing had pierced Lalassu's protection. Pitch was squeezed uncomfortably between them, his body laid flat against the lad. They were a ridiculous, stacked pyramid. 'Are they not the highest of angels?'

'Yes, but that has not stopped me before. And a direct strike will be more than your horse can bear. I need to get out, Silas.'

Another blast rocked their world. Pristine white light seeped through the tiny cracks in the Pale Horse's mane. Lalassu screamed, and for a terrifying moment Pitch thought the mare had been struck, but it seemed she was just as pissed off as he was. She rose to her feet, keeping them beneath her veil. Silas eased back enough that Pitch could slip free, scrambling to one side as Charlie coughed and spluttered, his face darkened with being pushed into the ground by the pressure of a daemon and ankou atop him.

'Climb.' Silas's commanding tone brokered no argument, even if Pitch was inclined to protest. 'Move now.'

Strands of horsehair touched at their backs, like guiding hands to urge them upwards, and Lalassu wound a particularly thick strand about Charlie's waist, preventing the lad from an outright fall.

'She could have done this from the bloody start,' Pitch said, though none bothered to reply.

Together they laboured on hands and knees, clawing ever higher whilst their poorly-aiming assailant took their time with their next shot.

'Something's not right, Silas.' Pitch and the ankou moved, side by side, just behind Charlie who puffed as he hurried to make his way up the unforgiving slope. 'Michael does not miss.'

Once again a blast came. Once again, it struck near enough to make a blinding flash, and send the shale rattling and cascading, and generally making their day preposterous, as they sought to climb through the instability.

But there was a difference this time.

Amber and vermilion hues joined that of the stark white.

The flaming shades matched those dancing beneath Pitch's skin.

'Fuck,' he whispered.

There was a reason for Michael's ineptitude, and it was not inebriation.

Pitch's distraction caused him to stumble. His knee met a lip of rock with eye-watering force. Material ripped, and skin tore, but before he had chance to finish a curse Silas grabbed him by the waist, keeping him steady, despite the ankou's own awkwardness of angle.

'What is it?'

'There's a daemon out there. They have to be the reason that arsehole can't seem to strike a target.'

'Lucifer?'

Likely, but the intensity of the flame was not as it should be if the King of Daemonkind were responsible. 'I'm not certain.'

The shifting, rocky ground gave way to a flatter surface, covered with thin grass, and softer soil.

'This is it. The cave is here, I remember all this grass.' Charlie found a turn of speed, straining against Lalassu's more cautionary pull. 'Let me go now, we're here. It's just here.'

A blast of angelfire sent everyone diving for cover.

'Let me see, damn it.' Pitch grasped at Lalassu's mane, and the mare obliged him, parting her strands just so. Pleasing as the view was, it did not give him hint of either angel nor daemon. Only will-o-wisp. Scarlet danced about, stubby hands bloated to make them more visible. As though anyone would need guidance towards the roughly built wall that bordered the entrance to a low-roofed cave.

'See, do you see it?' Charlie's laughter bordered on manic.

Pitch gave no answer, for only a blind man would not notice the Priest's Hole. Lalassu peeled back her mane, letting it fan upright behind them, giving them room to finally get to their feet. Charlie found a turn of foot that was impressive, clearing the short distance to the cave first. Scarlet squeaked and chittered like a lunatic, waving them in.

Silas turned to reach for Pitch, who slapped his hand away.

'Go. Go. I'm right behind you.'

The wall was barely deserving of the name, made from the shale which littered the area, and clearly man-made. Likely a wind-break for any fool who decided to hike this way and found themselves overnighting in the inhospitable landscape. Perhaps the long-dead priest who gave the place his name was the first fool among them.

Charlie slipped through the gap in the wall towards the right hand side of the mouth of the cave.

'Edward!' he cried. 'Edward?'

Pitch did not enjoy the note of consternation he heard. Nor how Scarlet's colours bounced against the back wall of the shallow cave. This was little more than a shelter carved out by the incessant scrape of the wind. There was no continuation, no tunnel to lead them to wherever this confounded Sanctuary awaited.

'Charlie, where is Edward?' Silas had to bend to enter the confines. 'This is a dead end.'

'No, I promise you. It's not.'

The ground rumbled, and shivers of dust fell from the roof.

'Pitch, get inside,' Silas said, whilst Scarlet went into a maddened dance which clearly said much the same thing.

'No, I need to see...oh!'

Lalassu shoved him into the cave, sending him into an undignified stumble from which Silas saved him. The ankou edged them both out of the way, so that the mare too could enter. She barely fit, her head lowering, her heavy breath shifting the dusty floor.

Pitch shook off Silas's hold and crouched behind the layering of shale. He narrowed his eyes against the dying glare of the last blast. The view, as it dipped into nightfall, was admittedly, stunning; the roll and dip of endless hillsides, barren but no less beautiful for their dominance of the landscape.

A landscape that was streaked with scorched earth: like the markings on a tiger's back the burns of an angel and daemon's battle were cut into the ground.

Pitch stood, leaning his hands upon the wall, craning his neck to peer down the slope.

'Pitch, be careful.'

'Do you see that?' He ignored the ankou's warning. 'Down there, a horse.'

And a rider.

Flaming. Dazzling. Though rather unsteady in the saddle.

Their fire-hues glanced off the coat of the black horse beneath them.

Silas drew in a breath, and though he did not lean out as far as Pitch, he too strained to catch a better glimpse.

'Is that Chollima he rides?'

'Who the blazes is Chollima?'

'The Dullahan's horse.'

'If he does so, he does not do it well.' Pitch squinted, taking in how precarious the daemon appeared on the horse's back. His flames were vibrant, splaying from his back in the imitation of wings so many among the elite of daemonkind preferred, but those wings swayed alarmingly, their tips almost touching the ground at times. 'There is something wrong.'

'Has the angel struck him, perhaps?'

'Most likely.'

Behind them Charlie still called on the lieutenant.

'Let us in, Edward. What is wrong?'

Pitch peered at the sky. 'Where is the angel? Do you see him, Silas?' There was a deep silvery-grey as day and night exchanged ownership of the light. The first of the stars were hinted at. An angel would have been the brightest among them, magnificent where the night lights were mediocre.

The sky held no magnificence, so far as he could see. Save perhaps for the half-moon that waited for its time to take charge of the night.

'Nothing of note.' Silas replied. 'Do you think Lucifer might have chased him off?'

'Chased off a Seraph?' Pitch nearly choked on bitter laughter. 'There is optimism, and there is stupidity, my dear. Especially considering Lucifer barely seems able to keep his saddle.'

Scarlet tugged at one of the layers on Pitch's carrick coat, hauling at him so he might go deeper into the cave. 'Stop it. Do you not see the stone? Am I to walk through it?'

The wisp made a despondent sound, which to Pitch's ear was recognition of the fact that they were now holed up in little more than an indent in the rock. No more a cave than a decent wardrobe. If they had been sitting ducks before, now they were fish in a barrel.

Silas touched Pitch's arm. 'Stay low, I'll see if I can assist Charlie.'

'By what? Punching a hole in the rock? We are clearly in the wrong Priest's Hole.'

'We are not,' Charlie snapped. 'He's here. Sanu, too.'

'Then they wish to see us roasted alive by angelfire. I told you, Sanu despises me.'

He threw flippancy and vile humour up like a shield, sheltering behind his tactlessness, while sickened by the notion that after all this, after coming so far, there was a very real chance he'd see Silas and Charlie, Scarlet and Lalassu die at the hands of a raging angel.

The notion both sickened, and fuelled him. Lucifer may seem like a drunkard in the saddle, but Pitch was anything but. And even Michael's performance left much to be desired.

In contrast, Pitch was revived. Strong as he'd ever felt. And he had a far better understanding of the power he carried. A power that lay quiet, still, watchful and ready.

He'd not see his friends and lover incinerated, because he'd simply sat here.

If Lucifer was fighting, so too would he.

With Silas's back turned, his attention upon Charlie, Pitch straddled the wall. And stepped out of its shelter.

He knew it a mistake, the moment the cool air ruffled his hair, and a shadow flittered above.

'Vassago, no!'

Lucifer's cry filled the valley, bounced from the hillsides and roared into the cave behind him.

The world lit brilliant white.

Lalassu's scream joined that of Lucifer's. The entire world sounded like the wail of a banshee.

Pitch turned, his flames pouring from his hands. Catching a meagre glimpse of the descending angel, a falling star with hint of Michael's human silhouette at its core. The Seraph unleashed a torrent of angelfire, cutting open the earth like a hot knife through butter. A great force ploughed into Pitch's side, pushing him from the path of Michael's downpour.

The waft of charred flesh was sickening, the agony of the mare forever scorched onto his psyche.

Silas screamed his name, the ankou's desperation terrifying.

Pitch hit the ground at a horrendous velocity, and tumbled. His head glanced against sharp rock, his clothes shredding, his coat slapping at his face as his fall gained momentum.

The terrain jabbed at his lungs, stealing his breath, his own flames licked at his skin as he struggled to gain some semblance of control.

'You fucking moron,' he roared, at himself.

His terror, his fury, braced him, he threw out his hands and grabbed. At anything. Something. Whatever would end this sickening arse-over-tit descent.

But in return something reached for *him*.

Tiny gasps, grunts and straining, joined the clattering of stone and pouring of soil. And the maddened descent slowed. There were pinches at his arms, at his legs, as though he'd just landed in an ants' nest.

'That's it, you've got him.'

'Careful there, Boyd.'

'Stop bossin' me about, Leslie.'

'Get the fuck off me,' Pitch shouted, finally finding purchase, lodging his feet into some rock that did not simply just roll with him this time. 'Let me go.'

Not ants, but gnomes. A veritable battalion of the blasted things, poking from the ground through crevices, and for the luckier ones, bare patches of earth. Each held a handful of Pitch's clothes.

'What are you doing?' he demanded.

'Saving your bloody arse, you ungrateful sod.'

The strangeness was far from over.

'Vassago, look out!' Lucifer and Chollima were at a flatout gallop towards where Pitch had come to rest, down very near the bottom of the slope he and the others had just worked so hard to surmount.

The daemon king had shimmering wings of flame behind him, stunning, but not nearly as vibrant as they should be. Lucifer was injured. Oddly, there was more vibrancy around his body. Silver light.

'Get up, he's coming back.'

Lucifer gestured skyward. And rose from Chollima's back.

Lifting higher. Coming out of the saddle entirely.

Lucifer flew.

But daemons could not fly.

His body glowed silver, and as Pitch followed his skyward drift, the tinkling of silver bells rang out.

'Gods,' he whispered.

Lucifer was covered head to toe in a glimmering layer of peri, the tiny creatures of the woodlands, normally frightened of their own shadows. Here, giving a daemon true wings.

Pitch's gaze shifted higher, and all else was forgotten.

The angel came at them like a comet, a glowing ball of destruction that Lucifer rose to meet.

Pitch staggered to his feet, his flames igniting. Blazing with a crisp intensity that his sire's did not.

Michael took aim at the King of Daemonkind.

His blast was mighty, every bit intent on ridding the world of the daemon who threatened him.

But Lucifer was not alone this day.

And nor was Pitch. The simurgh brushed a lazy stroke against his insides, and Pitch's grin was a vicious, greedy lift of his lips.

Sire and spawn counterattacked as one. Pitch's brighter flame, the very heart of a volcano, engulfed the lesser blast of the king; a unification of power, a joining of Dominion Prince and kingly Majesty.

CHAPTER 19

The radiance of daemonflame met the striking brilliance of angelfire. The collision was catastrophic, and the ensuing shock wave
massive enough to shake the moon on its axis and make the mountains
tremble.

Lucifer's scream was not entirely forged from pain. There was victory
there, too, triumph and battlelust. The colliding power sent him hurtling
back to the earth, whilst Michael shot up into the invisible depths of the
night, ever more the comet.

Pitch had less distance to travel.

He slammed against the ground, forming his own crater; the dirt
splaying up in a high, scattering wave.

Lucifer's body hit the ground somewhere nearby, the thud holding a
finality that quickened Pitch's heartbeat, but he could not move a limb;
his body rife with the counterflow of the attack, his own flame an inferno
within. The simurgh goaded it on, hungry for more.

Pitch rolled himself over, dug his hands into the heated dirt, and began
to climb out of the hole he'd created. His clothes were in absolute tatters;
it was a miracle he was not emerging naked. Pitch struggled, just shy of
the lip of the crate, the simurgh violence throwing him off-kilter.

'Enough.' He ground his teeth against the violent stirrings. 'It is done.
Let me be.'

The brush of something against his hair startled him and the jerk of his head made his neck ache.

Chollima stood over him, reins dangling within reach. He grabbed at them and allowed the stallion to haul him fully out of this unsuitable grave. Lucifer lay down at the base of the slope Pitch's impact had made. The king was alive, though in no fine form, his skin smoking, most of his clothes burned away; some fabric remaining around his waist giving him the appearance of wearing blackened shorts.

Pitch sought to find his bearings. To find the cave, and Silas. The ankou was halfway down the slope, sliding in his haste.

'Pitch? Thank god. Are you injured?'

'No. Stay up there.' Pitch peered past him. The scythe had reshaped to a large panel, like something from the side of an ocean liner; certainly big enough to cover most of the entrance to the caved. 'Lalassu...did she...where is she?'

But he found the Pale Horse before Silas answered. Pitch's blood cooled. His flame stuttered, as a surge of something hard and vile and painful overcame him. The simurgh slunk into the depths, as though it too could not bear to witness her state.

Lalassu was down, on her side; a grievous burn consuming her flank and a great portion of her belly. A dark and dangerous scourge across her storm-green coat.

'Is she...' He couldn't finish.

'She's alive, but her injuries are severe.' Silas was reaching for him, but Pitch shrank away.

'That is my fault.' He took one step back into the hollow in the earth. 'I shouldn't have gone out...I should have stayed.'

'Give me your hand, Pitch.' Silas cursed as loosened rock made his footing precarious.

Chollima pulled at the reins that Pitch still held, snorting softly. 'I didn't listen...Gods, what have I done?'

'Michael is the reason she lies there, not you, Pitch. Give me your hand. Let us go.'

But he couldn't. Silas was lying. With the best of intentions, but lying nonetheless. Michael was not the reason the mare was down. The fault lay with Pitch. With his fool-hardy, ill-planned actions.

'Go you fool.' Lucifer's rasp dragged Pitch from his horror.

The king swayed on his knees, scorched to a mere shadow of himself; his stance giving Pitch full view of an appalling wound upon his thigh. He was a grievous sight to behold; with so many bruises upon his skin that barely any pale flesh remained, and his eyes sunken, no hint of a spark there at all.

And he was missing a crucial finger.

'Your vestige,' Pitch gasped. 'Michael destroyed it?'

'He took it,' Lucifer spat. 'As he took the scar where my flesh was taken for your creation. That is how he found you.' He lost himself to a violent coughing fit, one that projected dark fluid onto the ground around him. Fluid that blinked out some of the specks of light surrounding him. It was as though diamonds lay there in the dirt and rock, highlighted by the strengthening glow of the moon. Pitch blinked. Not diamonds at all, but rather the fragile, minuscule bodies of the peri. Those who had helped a daemon to soar. 'Leave...before he recovers enough to return.'

Silas's shadow was large and encompassing; comforting with its sheltering darkness as the ankou reached him. 'Pitch, please. We must go.'

A whinny set Pitch's heart racing, his hopes soaring higher than the bastard angel who'd brought them so low.

'Lalassu?' Pitch gasped.

But it was not the Pale Horse who heralded them.

Sanu had emerged from the cave. Silas's scythes having parted enough for her to emerge where the man-made wall was lowest. The wall that Pitch had so foolishly climbed. She stood over Lalassu, lowering her head to touch at her downed companion.

Lalassu tilted her nose to find the other mare, and Pitch's breath hitched to see it was as Silas had promised. She lived.

Chollima answered the Red Horse's call, and pushed at Pitch's arm, urging him forward. Silas waited with arms half-lifted, treating Pitch in that way he sometimes did, as though he were a skittish horse himself, ready to bolt.

But they had long ago run out of places to run. And Lucifer was right, Pitch was a bloody fool if he lingered.

He'd brought about the downfall of the djinn horse, and now he stood here in the open, lit by moonlight, in a landscape where a seraph licked his wounds, and those who travelled with him were vulnerable.

Where a daemon king lay stripped and wounded and hardly recognisable.

Lucifer would not survive, if Michael did.

'We can't leave him here,' he said.

Silas nodded. 'Shall I carry him?'

'Don't you dare,' Lucifer hissed. 'You will leave me. Do not disgrace me with your pity.'

But Silas understood. He always did. The ankou turned his attention from Pitch, albeit with a reluctance he made no effort to hide, and crouched beside Lucifer.

'Can you stand at all? Or shall we have Sanu –'

'Are you deaf? Get on with you. Don't touch me. I warn you,' the daemon hissed, and grimaced, and spat more of the dark spittle. But the fact that he did not get to his feet, nor even try, told Pitch enough. Lucifer's wounds were nefarious.

With his own back still aching from his meeting with the ground, Pitch took one arm, whilst Silas took Lucifer's other, and together they began the laborious climb carrying the king between them. Chollima followed behind, picking his way carefully, supporting Lucifer when the shale slipped beneath Silas's feet, or Pitch stumbled against a rock he'd not had the foresight to notice.

As they struggled along, Lucifer berated them, and insisted they release him at once.

Pitch gave his sire a withering look. 'I'm blamed for one seraph's death, perhaps now another. I'll be fucked if I'll add a daemon king to my tally. Now shut your fucking mouth.'

After a few more feeble attempts at protest, Lucifer fell quiet, his chin bobbing at his chest, his body weight suddenly more cumbersome.

'Is he still conscious?' Silas asked at one point.

'No, thank the gods.'

'He's a grumpy one to be sure.' A hobgoblin with swollen cheeks and a red-tipped nose was seated upon Chollima's saddle, appearing from apparently nowhere. 'But to be fair, that other angel gave him a right seeing too, and I don' t mean in the pleasurable way.'

'Gods, how did the daemon build such a following of miscreants?" Pitch's thighs strained with the load and steepness. Each step drew them ever nearer to where Lalassu lay, with Sanu standing guard. The red horse watched him, he felt keenly the sharpness of her gaze.

'We found him, not the other way around. Though truth be told, the altercation was hard to miss. And when we heard it involved Silas Mercer, well, we couldn't just stand by. Such a good fellow you are, putting up with troublesome company and all.'

'Stop with that.' Silas scowled at the ground; most of Lucifer's weight rested on him. 'Pitch is as decent and brave as I. More so. And you'd do well to hold your tongue if you are going to say anything else to the contrary. He has endured more than you or I could ever hope to survive.'

Pitch flinched, thankful for the bulk of Lucifer between them, so he could avoid the look he knew Silas directed at him. The one that said he believed every word he'd just spoken.

'That's what Billy's cousin Gilmore is always saying. He works down in that Holly Village he does, and says he's never seen a fellow in more pain and yet still standing. Says you're a right prick, Mr Astaroth, but one who has a heart he tries to hide. They've seen it, mind you, down in the Forest of Dean, and in Sherwood. Your heart that is. But we aren't sure why you need to be so darn wild and frightening and bloodthirsty.'

'Another word,' Silas growled. 'And you'll find there are two such creatures in your midst. Help us, or leave us.'

The hobgoblin said not another word. Who would dare after such a command? Pitch allowed himself to thrill, just a little, at being the object of the ankou's formidable defence.

Sanu sent aid, in the last few feet, by way of the threads of her mane. She wove them about Lucifer's middle, and took most of his weight, doing a decent job of keeping him somewhat upright. Pitch stepped away as the horse and ankou took over Lucifer's care.

Then, there was no more time to avoid Lalassu, and her frightful, sickening injury. The halo's burn was not so different to that which marked Sybilla's skin. The curious green-grey of Lalassu's coat replaced with vile black tightness that still smoked. Her eyes, usually the colour of a daisy's middle, were dull. The glow that reflected from them came from Scarlet, who sat in the hollow beneath Lalassu's ear: where the curve of her cheek met her neck. The wisp crooned to the horse, humming in their nonsense way, for which Pitch would be eternally grateful, because he felt it...the comfort in the sound.

He sank to his knees beside the Pale Horse. His stomach a painful knot, his throat, his body, aching with what it was to see his mistake laid out so plainly.

'What do we do?' His hands hovered over her muzzle, but he feared touching her. He'd done damage enough already. 'How do I take away your pain?'

Lalassu lifted her nose, stretching towards him. Pitch drew in a shaking breath, and gods, his eyes pained him. He shuffled nearer, and the Pale Horse rested her head in his lap, a heavy sigh leaving her. Scarlet sang softly, the nearest to a discernible tune he'd yet heard from the wisp. Lalassu's eyelids dragged, the horse fighting the urge to sleep.

A shadow cast across them, but Pitch dared not look up.

He knew Silas stood there, and it was difficult enough to look Lalassu in the eye.

If he glimpsed blame, or pain, or grief in Silas's gaze, Pitch would not find his feet again. He bowed forward, touching his forehead to the mare's cheek. She was warm. Her scent that of horseflesh, and summer days and wide open fields.

'I'm so sorry,' he whispered.

Scarlet hummed their comfort. Silas knelt down beside him, one broad hand laying gently on Pitch's back, the other caressing Lalassu's nose. The ankou's breathing was shallow, unsteady. His tears made dark marks against the mare's pale coat.

'I'm so sorry,' Pitch said, again.

'She knows.' Silas rubbed his back, and kissed his hair. 'And I know, darling.'

Go on now.

Pitch didn't flinch at the voice, though he could not say who it belonged to. The lady perhaps. Lalassu's own. One or the other. Both. He nodded, rubbing his forehead against the coarseness of the mare's pale coat, the pressure behind his eyes unbearable.

It did not matter where the voice came from, only what it encouraged.

Pitch sat up, and with a gentleness he'd not known himself capable of, settled Lalassu's head against the ground. The mare sighed again, and her mane lifted to caress his cheek. The pain behind his eyes intensified. A single, caustic tear pressed itself free, tracing a harsh mark down his face.

Red strands caught at it. Wiped it clear. Sanu stood over him, absorbing the hurt that ran from him in that watery way Pitch had always so derided in humankind.

Silas held him tightly, and drew him to his feet.

'We must go.'

Pitch nodded, numb, and yet more sensitive than he'd ever known. He could not catch his breath, a pressure at his lungs that felt insurmountable.

The Red Horse traced her mane down his chest, over the strips of shirt that remained, and Pitch found his breath came much easier. He gulped at it, coughed as it filled lungs he'd forgotten to use. He gave her a grateful nod, and wished he could work his throat enough to say more.

'Easy now, love.' Silas guided him towards the mouth of the cave, his cheeks shining with spilled tears. 'Izanami herself shall guide her home, when the time comes. She gives me her word on that.'

Pitch staggered, only now understanding the weight of what Silas carried with him every day. Indeed, what any who were human, and prone to grief, must carry. He'd thought himself familiar with loss, he'd imagined he'd grieved when Seraphiel fell. He'd not known true sorrow.

'We can't leave her like this.'

'Nor can we stay. She is not alone, and wishes us onwards.'

Scarlet came to sit on Pitch's shoulder, warming his neck as they nestled in close.

Pitch looked back only once; when Sanu called to him, her bray sending gooseflesh rising.

He lifted his hand, and fare-welled a horse he had never deserved, but who had carried him so well, nonetheless.

Chollima stood with her, guardians either side of the fallen Pale Horse. Fae magick made the black stallion's coat gleam with sparks of blue. The earth was busy with movement, the gnomes and hobgoblins gathering around the mighty djinn steeds. Already the natural world was claiming one of their own. The moss grew upon Lalassu's legs, and over her hindquarters. Already covering over the terrible damage done.

'They bury her while she still lives,' Pitch said, his pulses pounding. 'We cannot leave her.' He tried to go back, working against Silas's hold.

'It is her command I follow.' He was the firmest he'd ever been, in voice and deed. 'Do not go back. Do not waste this gift she gives us. She will return to the earth, and find new life there. It is the way of things, for all creatures of nature. And the djinn are nature at its purest. Keep on, my love.'

Sanu wove her mane in with Lalassu's, their tails intertwining too. Together, as always, they weaved their magick. Building a forest of horsehair; a formidable barrier that crept over the shale and dirt and rock, like jungle vines and errant ivy, growing, concealing, taking on the shades of the moss and lichen. Just as those truly of nature took over the Pale Horse. Claiming her once more. Their plant life feeding off the djinn life she gave them.

The miraculous forest pushed from the earth and rose to consume what the wind and weather had stripped bare; moving up over the shale and climbing to reach the cave. The entrance vanished behind a wall of greenery; as deep and impenetrable as all the forests of the British Isles combined.

Pitch stood in the shadows, clasping Silas's hand, feeling him tremble, hearing his tears begin. The light grew dimmer, the air warmer as the entrance sealed over.

The lady's fine horses, those formidable agents of the djinn, protected them to the last.

CHAPTER 20

Silas held on to Pitch in the darkness, and wept. The tears seared from him: acidic and hurtful and exhausting. What a great and priceless gift Lalassu gave them; using the last of her reserves to serve their cause. Giving the last of her magick so that an avenging angel would find his way barred.

Silas mourned the Pale Horse, despising how little time he could give to her, for this was far from said and done, and he'd not waste the chance she and Sanu now gave them. But Christ, he wished his humanity not so dominant; so ready to give him pain. How much easier it would be, to lose himself in the monstrosity of his Nephilim nature; or be so thoroughly Death's messenger that the mare's loss did not cut into his very soul.

Pitch shook in Silas's arms. His clothing was mere shreds, but it was not the cold that caused him to shiver.

Silas held tighter, as his own tears refused to dry, and sought to console the prince in what small way he could. Pitch's guilt would fester, and Silas could not allow that extra burden upon shoulders already so laden.

Illumination arrived. A flickering of a torch, a quiet footstep.

'I'm so sorry,' Charlie whispered. 'Is there no hope?'

Pitch tensed, pressing his face firmer into Silas's chest. Scarlet resettled themselves in the prince's hair, offering up all her pretty colours to placate him.

Silas shook his head. 'Not this day. But she will not suffer. Sanu, and Chollima and the natural folk, will see to that.'

The whispers of Lalassu's death note still rung in his ears. Their melody would never leave him.

'Oh, Silas,' Charlie's voice broke. 'She was so wonderful.'

'There will none other like her,' Silas said, rocking gently on his heels, while Pitch hid against him. 'Where to now, Charlie?' Silas glanced over his shoulder, back to where a shield of darkness now blocked sight of endless hills, and awful tragedy. 'Lucifer?'

'I've taken him to where Edward waits. He's badly injured after what he did for us.'

'Then let us make haste, so no efforts are wasted.' Silas nodded. 'Take us to them, Charlie, and quickly now.'

They had lost the mare, Lucifer was wounded; but had it all been enough to lose the Seraph?

'I will show you the way. It is open now.' The lad looked pained, ducking his head. 'Silas, if I'd been faster about getting us here. If I'd made Edward hear me sooner...'

Now Silas saw he was dealing with not one, but two souls laden with guilt.

'All right. Both of you, listen to me.' He gently pried Pitch away so he could look him in the eye. 'What has happened, is not the fault of either of you. Do you understand?'

Pitch would not look at him. Charlie shifted uncomfortably, and the torch light flickered; sending darkness and light shuddering against the depths of the cave. Silas peered up the way the lad had come; not a shallow cave anymore at all, but a long stretch of tunnel whose end was so far off it was not lit by Charlie's torch.

Pitch tried to free himself. 'Then who do you blame, Silas?' His words reeked with bitterness. 'Lalassu herself, perhaps?'

'Of course not. But what is done is done. And have you forgotten who gave you reason to step from the cave to begin with, who struck her down? That angel is the villain here.'

Pitch shook his head. 'But that does not mean I wasn't a fool.' He pulled out of Silas's grasp, and wrapped his arms about himself. 'Can we just be done with this. The sooner I am at this fucking Sanctuary, the sooner you can all move on, and know some peace.'

A flush of anger warmed Silas; such despondency did not suit Pitch at all, and it would get him damned-well killed. He needed the fight, the fury and arrogance that seemed drained from him now.

'All right, that's enough.'

'Leave me be, Silas. I'm in no mood for cheering.'

'And I am?' he stormed, grabbing at Pitch's arm so roughly the daemon had no choice but to show some life and fend him off. 'Stop talking like that.'

'Like what?'

'Like we are so much better off without you, I'm sick of it.'

Pitch ripped his arm from Silas's hold, a hint of light emerging in his eyes. 'I got your fucking horse killed, Silas,' he shouted.

Scarlet, wise creature it was, fled from Pitch's hair, and dashed to Charlie's shoulder instead.

'She made her choice, as you made yours,' Silas shouted back. 'We all make errors in judgement, Pitch.'

Too bad if Michael searched for them outside, his hunt would be over now; he just had to listen for the shouting.

'Not so constantly as I, nor so dangerously.'

'Bullshit.' Silas was high on anger now; but it was not aimed towards Pitch. 'What of me? That imbecilic oaf you so often deride, and with just cause. If I'd not bumbled about, if I'd set myself with more resolve sooner, sought out answers, instead of playing dumb. If I'd learned my truth, instead of remaining the simpleton, the coward, I appeared, then how many more souls might I have saved? So many have suffered because I was afraid. Of a fucking bathtub, no less.'

'Silas you –'

'Not now, Pitch. By god, you shall let me have this rant. You should have let me blasted-well drown in that moat, at Goodrich Castle.' Silas winced, stomach turning at how fearful he'd been, clinging to Pitch's back. 'It might have knocked some sense into me, way back then. I'd have been strong enough to protect you from Gidleagh Park. Christ, Pitch I shall never forgive myself for that place, for being so easily manipulated, for letting you down. And Sherwood Forest…' Silas struggled to catch his breath, caught off-guard by the ferocity of his pent up confessions. He'd underestimated how badly the guilt ate at him. 'No...there is no forgiveness for an error of judgement that saw me play with fucking asrai, rather than be there when you needed me. I profess to love you, and yet you endured hell because of me.'

'Stop,' Pitch bellowed.

The echo filled the chamber, reverberating down into the unknown path beyond where Charlie stood. He could not decipher the look on the lad's face. Perhaps he was wondering what sort of a man he was tied to, whether he was as good as those stupid gnomes declared.

Silas turned away, his breath coming in shudders. He thought he might be sick. In the silence that fell, he heard the trickling flow of water in the distance.

'So here we are,' Pitch said, quieter now. He cleared his throat. 'The sorriest pair of saviours a world could hope to have.'

Silas huffed, and rubbed at his face. 'The sorriest indeed.' He did not regret his outburst, much had needed to be said, but he did resent how drained it made him.

'You seem so determined to win this battle of regret,' Pitch said, some strength returning to his voice. 'If I concede, might I ask one thing of you?'

Despair made way for cautious amusement. 'What would that be?'

'I ask that you remember what I say now, when next you are overcome. I did not endure hell because of you. I *survived* it, because of you. Because I knew what you evidently fail to recognise in yourself. That you are no coward, Silas.' His slight, wry smile was a welcome sight. 'Though perhaps deserving of the title of oaf, at least so far as your declarations of affection for me are concerned.'

Silas inclined his head, some of the pain abating. 'Perhaps you are right. We shall see.'

Their eyes locked, fixed upon one another in such a way that nothing else seemed to exist in the world. Not even an all-powerful angel, bent on striking down their errant quest.

Charlie shuffled his feet, and coughed. 'Gentlemen, I'm sorry, but we must go on. Will you follow me?'

'Of course,' Silas said.

'As though there is a choice.' Pitch returned, but there was only the merest hint of bitterness in the reply. 'Lead on.'

Scarlet leaped off the lad's shoulder, dancing circles in the air around Charlie's head; before racing off into the stretching darkness behind him. Their rainbow hues grew smaller and smaller, fainter and fainter.

Without a word, Pitch looped his arm through Silas's, and they made their way together.

The tunnel was not great in length, the trip short and easy. The passageway opened up into a much larger chamber, one whose roof was entirely made of clear quartz. The light from Charlie's single torch seemed to fill each of the jutting prisms, casting a golden sheen over everything.

Pitch inhaled. Silas looked to him, only to be scowled at before he could enquire if everything was fine.

'Let's go.' Pitch walked on ahead of him.

Silas had been right to think he'd heard water earlier. The chamber held a great body of it; bigger than a pond but shy of a lake, and clear enough to see that the quartz that covered the roof lay there beneath the surface too, glowing golden as the rest.

Edward waited for them. He sat by the edge of the deep water, upon a rock that looked very much like hardened lava; with its bulges and layers. Lucifer lay slumped at the base of that same rock, and Edward's hand upon his shoulder was likely all that prevented the unconscious king from ending up flat on the ground.

'Silas, Tobias. Thank the gods, you've made it.' He gaze flitted to Silas. 'And I'm so sorry.'

Silas nodded, thanking him for the condolences, but he could not linger in that place of grief, now. 'You know then that the Seraph Michael pursues us.'

'I do.'

There was no time to be wasted in asking how. 'Can he enter this place?'

'No,' Edward said with conviction. 'Not as things are. But that may change.'

His gaze moved between Silas and Pitch, pausing there on the daemon; as though he could not quite believe his eyes.

'Are you well, Edward?' Silas pressed.

He laughed, a good sign in itself, but it was none too hearty. 'As well as can be expected. I'll be grateful for the end of this journey. And it is close.'

He reached into the pocket of his heavy wool coat; the fit was much too large and swamped his frame, a high collar reaching above his jawline, as though to swallow him. Despite the thickness, Edward shivered. He withdrew an item Silas thought he'd seen the last of.

Pitch groaned. 'That bloody watch.'

It was indeed the pendant watch. The one that had been in so many important hands: passed from Edward to Pitch, a lover's gift, from Seraphiel to Lucifer, a dying angel's secret, and finally from Lucifer to Pitch, a talisman that had ignited a spark Silas still struggled to understand. The watch had somehow made Edward a prophet of the Serahp; and seemed to have brought to life the angel who had been thought long-dead. But were they dealing with remnant power from Seraphiel, or true resurrection?

'I need to pay the fare,' Edward grunted as Charlie helped him to his feet. 'Then we can move on.'

'The fare? To whom?' Pitch said.

'The ferryman.' Edward stepped into the water, not bothering to remove his shoes, nor roll up his trousers. Charlie went with him, muttering about the cold being the last thing Edward needed, but the lieutenant paid him little heed. He held out the watch, as though he meant to drop it into the water. 'I hail ye, ferryman. And bid you, tell me, what price shall I pay?'

Pitch and Silas glanced at one another. 'Has his mind finally come undone?' Pitch whispered.

The boat appeared before Silas could offer a reply.

Not there, in one blink, and there upon the water, in the next.

A simple craft, not much more considerable than a row boat, and just as open to the elements. The wood was plain, a brown that appeared ever duller in contrast to the golden elements of the chamber, and greatly at odds with the singular passenger it carried.

They stood at the bow, holding a long, curved staff which held a glowing lantern above their head. The passenger was clad in armour; the pounded metal sheets of a by-gone day. The silver grey did not reflect the glow of the lantern, even though that light was bright enough to make Silas squint.

'Gods,' Pitch breathed.

And Silas saw his mistake. It was not simply the lantern that glowed.

Edward was radiant. In the way that Pitch was when the flame hinted beneath his skin. But where the daemon's light held all the hues of fire, Edward gleamed gold: of wheat fields under a summer sun, and the grandest crown of monarchy polished to perfection.

Charlie raised his hand to shield his eyes, and Scarlet, seated as they preferred upon Pitch's shoulder, made a quite sound of awe, their own colours subdued.

'Do you have the fare?' The ferryman's voice caught Silas off-guard. Not a man at all, but a woman of melodic voice was hidden behind the grill of the face-plate.

'I have the fare.' Edward still held the watch raised, its pewter darkening against the glow of his skin.

'A single coin shall pay your way. Do you have that coin?'

'I have the fare.' Edward repeated, and there was a sense of rhythm to the exchange, like the unlocking of a vault by way of voice, rather than key.

Edward turned the watch over, and placing it on his flattened palm. He touched at it and a soft click preceded the unlocking of a clasp; and the lifting of the rounded back on a hinge. Edward drew forth a gleaming gold coin, one nearly as wide in circumference as the watch itself. He held it aloft.

The coin shone like a piece of the sun. And the water frothed where Edward and Charlie stood. Silas edged closer, fearing the water's violence.

Pitch held him back. 'Let them see it through.'

Silas waited, and watched.

The boat drew closer, ever silent. The armour-clad ferryman still held their staff, still rested their foot upon the bow; the armoured footwear held an exaggerated point at the toes.

Edward stepped forward, pressing Charlie back with his free hand when the lad sought to follow. Silas dashed forward, despite Pitch's hiss of annoyance, and pulled Charlie back to the shore.

The lieutenant took only a few steps, and halted when the water reached his knees. The frothing and bubbling remained at a simmer, no worse, whilst Edward held out the coin.

The ferryman did not slow the boat, if they had the means to. No oars, nor sail assisted this captain. Charlie tried to wriggle from Silas's grasp, fearing the lieutenant at risk of being run down.

'Wait, one more moment,' Silas whispered.

Edward raised his free hand, his fingernails incandescent. The boat slowed, its prow drifting until it was perfectly aligned with the lieutenant's waiting hand. The bow nestled into his cupped hand, and the boat stopped, as though it had never moved at all.

The frothing of the waters extended to surround the boat, small waves chopping against the sides.

'I have the fare,' Edward said, once more, with hints of an echo upon his voice. He lifted the coin.

The ferryman bowed forward. Their armour made no sound, no rasp of metal, nor creak of joints.

'The fare is duly paid.' They took the coin. Their lantern flared, a blinding flash of gold that quickly dimmed. 'I shall take you where you seek to go, your grace.'

The water returned to smooth and crystalline. All the radiance that had engulfed Edward vanished. He staggered, pressing both hands against the hull. There was no holding Charlie back this time, and he slipped from Silas's hold. With speed as freakish as his strength, he caught the lieutenant before his arse had touched the water.

'I'm all right, Charlie.'

'Bullshit.'

Edward laughed weakly. 'Everyone must get in the boat now.'

'Fine, but you first. I want you out of this cold water.' Charlie shifted his grip, seeking a hold beneath Edward's arms so he might lift him. Silas had barely taken a step to assist when the ferrymann took control. They let go their staff, though it remained starkly upright, and grabbed

Edward's wrists, metal-clad fingers finding a hold, before lifting the lieutenant from the water.

'Hey! What are you doing?' Charlie cried. 'Be gentle with him, he's not well.'

The ferryman gave no indication they had heard, and lowered Edward onto the bench seat at the front of the boat, where he slumped forward with a groan. The boat did not rock as Charlie vaulted aboard, settling beside him.

'Right, us next I suppose.' Silas could not entirely chase away trepidation at boarding a boat. One that was not so very different from those he recalled on the loch.

He glanced back. Pitch stood with his head lowered, his hand upon his belly.

'Pitch?'

'The simurgh is restless, that's all,' Pitch said, without raising his head. 'The ferryman addressed him as *your grace*. Did you hear?'

'I did.' Silas nodded. 'What do you make of it?'

'Nothing. Everything. I'm not sure I wish to know the answer.' Pitch lifted his head, hints of ember glowed. 'How will you fare, being on the water?'

'Fine, fine.'

Pitch's crooked smile was uncommonly gentle. 'About as fine as I am with returning to the Sanctuary, I suspect.'

'A reasonable deduction.' Silas's returned smile was not as steady as he would like.

Scarlet peeked from behind tangled waves of hair, waving at Silas as the prince stepped closer. 'If you like I could use a little enchantment to distract you.' Pitch's wink made Silas's pulse skip. Christ, it was tempting, but he shook his head.

'I need no enchantment to be distracted by you. In fact, here, take this. Clothe yourself.' He slipped off his black cape. Dirtied and ripped as it was, it was in far better condition than Pitch's own clothing, which allowed much of his chest to show. 'I'd not forgive myself if anything untoward happened because I was absorbed by lust.'

'Lust?' Pitch's eyes widened, as he slipped the cloak over his narrow shoulders. It swamped him. 'My dear fellow I had thought to enchant you with poetry, that is all. You speak as though I would suck you off in front of the other passengers.'

'You would.'

Pitch smiled sweetly. 'What a pleasure it is to be known.'

'Will you lot hurry up,' Charlie cried. 'Or shall I come and carry that poor man myself?'

That *poor man* was one of the mightiest daemons in Arcadia. Though this was not his finest day. He was as Silas had first seen him. Leaned up against the rocks, eyes shut, his long legs gathered up, knees touching his chest. There was something inordinately child-like about his position.

'I'll see to him,' he said. And he'd enjoy a few more moments land-bound. 'Pitch, get on board.'

Silas gathered up the fallen king, surprised by how heavy the lithe man was. He had to brace himself before pushing to his knees, and could not stop the grunt that came with lifting such weight.

'Can you manage?' Pitch was already in the boat. As far from the ferryman as he could make himself, standing between the last bench and the stern. But the boat was small. If they had both leaned in, across the four rows of seats, Pitch and Charlie could have touched hands.

'Of course I can manage it. But help me with loading him into the boat.'

Silas waded into the water, inhaling at the crispness of the water when it engulfed his boots and hit his shins. There barely seemed enough depth to the water here for the boat to float at all. Perhaps it was hitting the bottom, and not a preternatural stillness that meant the boat did not so much as tilt when Silas lifted Lucifer over the side, and Pitch changed his position so he might assist. The king did not move, nor utter a sound, despite the man-handling.

They placed the daemon in the near centre of the craft, where the gap between the benches was slightly wider. Silas hauled himself aboard as soon as Pitch had a decent hold. The prince placed Lucifer on his side, and perhaps was not as careful as he could have been, for there was a thump of the king's head against the wood.

'Careful, daemon.' The ferryman's command resonated from behind their visor. They looked to Edward, as though expecting the lieutenant to add to the reprimand. But he and Charlie sat close, locked in whispered conversation. 'Be seated. Now.'

Pitch was already seated, and he grabbed Silas's hand, encouraging him down. They sat close, and Silas was grateful that the prince made no comment about how tightly his hand was held by a nervy ankou.

The ferryman reset their foot upon the bow–a position either favoured, or necessary, it wasn't clear–and wrapped their gauntlet around the staff. The boat swung about, a gentle move that nevertheless had Silas grabbing at the lip of the bench, holding fast. Scarlet hopped from Pitch's shoulder to his own, climbing the curve of his neck to pat at his earlobe.

'Dreadfully annoying, aren't they, Silas?' Pitch rolled his eyes.

Scarlet chittered at him, and their indignation needed no interpretation.

'I'm happy to have Scarlet with me.' There was something soothing in how determined the little creature was, how unperturbed by all they faced. He'd borrow what he could of Scarlet's resolve. For all the changes Silas had undergone, this mass of water still managed to fill his belly with unwelcome butterflies.

CHAPTER 21

The boat glided over water that grew greater in depth. The Ferryman used no visible means of propulsion–no oars or pole–and stood utterly silent with their lantern, which did not sway on its hook as they moved.

The light it cast did not reach the quartz in the water as before. The depths grew in their fathoms. Pitch watched Silas's observance of it with an ache that helped draw his thoughts from the pains of Lalassu.

'Silas, stop looking over the edge.'

The ankou was trying awfully hard to be stalwart, but the brave man had a limit to his courage. Pitch could not blame him for that; endlessly dying through drowning must wear down a fellow.

'I thought I saw a fish, that's all.'

Scarlet's answering snort said exactly what Pitch had been thinking. 'Bloody rot. Now look at me, and forget all else. I know you adore staring at me. Come on now.' He pressed at Silas's cheek, urging the ankou to turn away from the water. 'Look at these lips, how plump they are, how ripe for biting at. You do so love to bite them, don't you?'

Silas took a breath too long to answer. 'I do. I do. But you'd tell me if I do too much?'

'Don't ruin the mood, lover. Now, what else of mine do you like in your mouth?'

Pitch took his hand; their thighs pressed, their ankles touching, Pitch practically buried into his side. But Silas, damn him, still seemed distracted; blinking too fast, as though he fought an impulse to gaze once more at his nemesis.

'Shall I give you a clue?' Pitch asked.

He took Silas's free hand, where it gripped the edge of the seat for dear life, and made a great show of dragging it slowly up his own thigh, taking it all the way up to where a slip to the right would land it upon the soft bulge between Pitch's. He considered asking again if he should use his enchantment to smooth out Silas's distress.

'I'm fine,' Silas said, quietly, resisting Pitch's efforts. 'And though your cock is quite possibly my favourite thing in all the world, I truly am fine. I don't need a distraction.'

Which was such a terrible lie even Scarlet's motionless eyes seemed to roll.

'Who said anything about you?' Pitch would not give up without a fight. 'Perhaps I am feeling unsettled and wish you to tend to my needs.'

'Here, and now?' Silas spluttered, and his ridiculous blinking ceased. 'Are you mad?'

'Perhaps. Highly likely. Now, come on. I am feeling very rejected right now.'

He tugged hard and managed to land Silas's hand right where he wanted it. Finally the distraction was enough. Silas jerked with laughter; a low rumble, not unlike distant thunder. 'You are utterly ridiculous.'

Distracting, actually. Pitch gave himself a private pat on the back for a job well done. Silas was still chuckling, and now laying kisses upon Pitch's hand. Breathing; the ankou had remembered how to breath.

'Is everything all right back there?' Charlie twisted in his seat. 'What has come over you?'

'Nothing has come!' Pitch raised Silas's hand, like evidence in a courtroom. 'That is precisely the issue, dear boy. This hand is going to waste, despite my pleas.'

Even Edward managed a soft smile. The ferryman of course ignored it all.

'Stop it,' Silas pleaded. 'Charlie pay him no attention. I beg you.'

'No need to beg.' Charlie shook his head, and turned back to where the way ahead lay.

Pitch would obviously say nothing to Silas, not now he was calmer, but he'd noticed that for all this time moving forward the boat had not drawn any closer to the far side of the chamber. He glanced back the way they had come. Ground had definitely been covered, for there was no sign of the shore or the rock where Edward had been sitting. There was only water. With its dome of quartz above. Spreading out in all directions.

'Ferryman,' he called. 'How long shall this journey take?'

'As long it needs to.'

'Arsehole,' he muttered. 'Those of an overly philosophical nature should be burned at the stake.'

'Perhaps a bit harsh,' Silas smiled. 'But I am not in full disagreement.'

They fell to silence. Pitch ran his thumb over Silas's fingers, thinking of Lucifer's injury. He didn't realise he was being too rough, too vigorous, until Silas stayed his hand.

'Are you trying to take off some skin?'

'What? Oh, no. I was just thinking about Lucifer.'

'Rather enthusiastically.' Silas wriggled his fingers. 'Where was your head?'

And because he was getting much better at telling Silas what was on his mind—for the most part—he said, 'Michael took his vestige. It was hidden beneath his fingernail, and that cretin angel decided to simply remove the entire digit. I have no idea how Lucifer managed to put on such a show back there, but I'm not surprised he's been unconscious this long.'

'Christ.' Silas surveyed the king where he slept. 'That must be terribly painful.'

'It is, though it will dull. And losing his vestige won't kill him, but he shall feel like dog shit for quite some time.' Pitch tried to withdraw his hand, but Silas halted the retreat.

'You don't still feel that way though, do you? You don't have your vestige.'

'Thank you for stating the bloody obvious.'

'That came out all wrong –'

'You don't say.' This was not quite as fun as making lewd comments to keep Silas's mind off the boat situation, but Pitch would roll it. The waters beneath them were notably deeper, the edges of the chamber stretching farther away as they journeyed, seemingly, to nowhere.

'Forgive me.' Silas tried to back himself out of his corner. It was delightful to watch. 'But you are not forthcoming when it comes to what ails you. Has it pained you all this time?'

Pitch shrugged. 'I can't really tell, on account of my plethora of pains. To begin with, I am in the worst type of pudding club.' He slapped at his stomach, making much theatre of it; rewarded with the sight of Silas fighting a grin.

'A pudding club?'

'That's what those of us in this delicate condition call it. I'm expecting a bouncing baby bird, any day now.' He twisted his arm to jab at his back. 'And let us not forget that I also had an angel turn me into a daemonic target, and his aim was horrid. That strike rather hurt, too.'

Silas might have only seen the true wound once, but that was evidently too much for him. His unhappiness made his shoulders slouch. 'I cannot imagine what pains you have tolerated.' He lifted his arms, intending another of his plentiful hugs, probably.

Pitch waved him off, frightening Scarlet who evidently thought themselves about to be smote, and zipped off the ankou's shoulder to dart over to the slumbering Lucifer.

'Honestly, Sickle. You must not...Ah!' The blistering pain struck hard and fast. Pitch buckled forward, his hands landing on Silas's thigh, gripping hard. 'Blast it.'

'Does the simurgh hurt you? Pitch, answer me.'

The answer was yes, a resounding yes. But he'd not say so.

'No...I mean, it pinches, quite vigorously. But nothing I cannot handle.'

He hoped. The wildness was living up to his memory of it. Those days in the past–before they had found something of a truce–when it used to batter at the cage he'd forged in his gut, demanding escape.

Pitch exhaled, every bit the expectant mother breathing through her pains. 'There, see it has passed.' He plastered on a grin. 'Perhaps it was too many Brussels sprouts at the last supper.'

Silas gave him an unimpressed look. 'You refused to eat any.'

'So I did. Foul things.' He shrugged. 'Perhaps this blasted thing simply knows where we are bound. Perhaps we are closer than it appears. Silas don't look at me like that. Do you truly think he'd have us brought all this way, only to give me an aneurysm at the very last stage?'

That did not go down well. Horror marked Silas's face. 'Christ, Pitch. I have no bloody idea what this blasted angel intends, but do we put such a thing past him?'

He glanced at the water, as though considering throwing them both overboard and making a swim for it.

'Gods, man. It is fine. I'm fine. Perhaps the simurgh gets sea-sick, I don't fucking know. But it's done with now, alright?'

It was so far from done with that Pitch could barely feel his pulse; the beat was so rapid it blurred into one long hum.

They were getting closer. He knew it. The blasted Cultivation certainly knew it.

And he was not ready. He would never be ready for this return. To a place he could barely recall; and wished he could forget.

He glanced ahead at Edward. Thinking of how the ferryman addressed him with such title. The simurgh had shifted then too, when the coin was exchanged. A curious roll of movement unlike any he'd felt before. Not a struggle, not a vie for freedom, as he'd felt just now. He wasn't sure what to make of that last pain.

But as he stared at the lieutenant, Pitch realised he had missed something equally, if not more, intriguing; the chamber had become a cave once more. One with an open mouth.

Charlie spied it at the exact same time. 'Look, the way ahead is open. I can see outside.' He stood up, a hand on Edward's shoulder for balance, despite the stability of the boat. 'Are those mountains?'

They bloody well were. Beyond the yawning mouth of their chamber, the sky held hints of dawn's palette; silver dominated, but with tinges of blue and subtle pink evident. Pitch might have wondered how a whole night had passed, were he not captivated by the rest of the scenery; mountains, indeed. They were snow-capped and sharp-tipped, commandingly high; ringing a vast body of water where islands lay further out. There was no hint of any settlement on the isles, certainly nothing that might be a Sanctuary; their foliage stripped of green by the encroaching winter and left stark and uninviting.

Silas sought to get to his feet. Pitch slapped at his leg. 'Stay down. Don't you dare rock this boat.'

'Do you recognise anything, Pitch? Do you see it? The Sanctuary?'

'No, I recognise nothing.' Pitch stifled his bitterness. 'I was not exactly allowed out for safari. And no, I don't see the Sanctuary.'

He was not sure if he was relieved, or furious.

'Charlie, please. Be careful.' Edward urged the lad to sit down, but Charlie was feverish.

'No, wait. That land....those peaks. I think I know...' He cut himself off, with a frustrated cluck of his tongue. 'No. It can't be.'

'Can't be what, Charlie?' Silas demanded.

'Sit down.' The ferryman spoke for the first time in gods knew how long. 'Now.'

Charlie sat quickly. Edward turned. Not to the lad, but further on around; to Lucifer who slept on through all. The lieutenant gazed down at the king, and said, so softly it was almost missed. 'Almost there, Luci.'

When Edward lifted his head Pitch had a moment's sight of his face; the white gleam of angelfire hinted there in his irises. Pitch flinched.

And in that second it took to do so, the chamber vanished.

Their boat sat out upon the centre of the great lake; where December reminded them all it had arrived, the breeze stirring goosebumps and ruffling the surface of the water.

Silas let loose a sudden cry, his gaze fixed toward's the boat's starboard side, his hands braced against the rim, knuckles white.

'Silas, gods, steady yourself man.' Pitch grabbed his arm. The ankou's muscles were tensed.

'Pitch. Oh ,Christ...Pitch, do you see it? That grand house.'

Until then, he'd still been absorbing their sudden shift from chamber to open air, but he'd have to have been blind not to see what Silas pointed out now. There on the shore, perhaps a mile across the way, was a formidable mansion. Its massive pedimented porch was supported by dramatic, paired Tuscan columns; two storeys of classical architecture, with north and south wings, that spread itself unashamedly across the manicured lawns and careful gardens. A boat-shed was further down the shoreline, with a long jetty that stretched like a wooden finger; pointing at them.

He glanced at Silas. The ankou was terribly pale. 'Do you know this place?'

Silas's mouth worked, as though he meant to answer, but no sound came. There was an odd distance in his eyes that made Pitch feel suddenly and terribly alone.

'Silas, please –'

'Charlie, be careful.' Edward's cry turned Pitch's head.

The lad seemed overcome by the very same melancholy that had struck Silas. He stepped over the seat, and would have gone further had Edward not been holding his sleeve. His mouth was agape, his eyes rounded like a deer caught in torchlight. Both of them focused on the damned house. The ferryman had not moved from where they stood, sentinel at the prow. Their armour held embellishments of gold that Pitch had not noticed before.

'No. No, this cannot be.' Charlie let out the strangest sound, something layered with both anguish, and joy.

'What the blazes is wrong with you two?' Pitch demanded.

The ankou swallowed, and it looked a painful thing. 'Pitch...that's...' Silas's lashes fluttered and Pitch truly thought the man about to pass out.

'Go on.' He worked at being gentler now. 'What do you see there? Are there souls?'

Silas shook his head, still intent on the shore, as the boat drifted ever silently away, headed out deeper onto the lake.

Charlie spoke first. 'That is Rossdhu House. That is where I was born. My home.'

Finally Silas moved. His eyes dark as they set on the lad. 'We are in Scotland.'

Charlie nodded. 'This is Loch Lomond.'

Silas turned his attention back to the water, which lay like a sheet of pewter around them. He leaned over the edge, his fingers hovering just above the surface. He trembled. Pitch sat close enough to know Silas's entire body shook.

The cold seeped into Pitch's bones. He recalled their pillow talk, all the ankou had said of his demise. A loch. A jetty. A drowning.

And he could barely catch his breath for knowing. 'Silas...is this the place?'

The ankou seemed smaller, more in need of Pitch's presence. He touched his hand to Silas's shoulder.

'This is the place. My loch.' The ankou's voice was the quiet approach of a storm. 'My grave.'

CHAPTER 22

Silas knew Scarlet was with him, working away with tiny pats against his neck, somewhere beneath the layers of his hair. Trying to soothe. He knew Pitch sat pressed against his side, sending what warmth he could, to a man of the grave. Charlie was there too, reeling with his unexpected, perhaps unwelcome, return home.

But Silas felt a world away from them all.

He stared down into the water, and felt the centuries roll in its hidden currents. His memories of this place had been fear-riddled, engraved with unspeakable terrors, ones that seemed impossible to surmount, to ever shed.

Silas dipped his fingers into the water. Let them trail through the murder and anguish and misguided vileness that clung to each and every drop.

The scythe shifted against his finger, as though seeking to rise higher and avoid the wet memory of his constant demise here.

But Silas felt no need to recoil; only a driving need to let go this fear. It's claws did not sink so deep anymore. He was the Pale Horseman. He was more than a drowning man.

His fingers curled with thought of Lalassu. Of the angel who had destroyed her. And discovered how much harder it was to be fearful, when one was enraged.

Michael had sought to destroy Pitch, too. The daemon who now whispered quiet words of comfort, gentle reminders that he was at Silas's side, and would not leave. This was the creature who had truly changed the colours of Silas's world.

He leaned into his lover, his prince, but said nothing.

Silas slipped his hand deeper, to the wrist now. The tonnage of the past brushed at his fingertips, and made him shudder. His grave lay beneath him. Dark and cold and, it had seemed, endless. That was what had frightened him most. The eternity of solitude. The inevitability of being catapulted between life and death, over and over, until he was lost to both worlds. There had been nothing–no one–to anchor him before.

'Silas, please. Sit back, will you?' The daemon's concern was precious. And unnecessary.

'It's all right.' The voice that left Silas bore traces of all the men he had been; dead, and alive. And he had needed each and every one of them to form the creature who now trailed his hand through these deathly waters, daring the depths to reach for him one more time.

He was ready. To repel them. To make them wait.

The lives he'd lost trickled through his fingers, slipped around his palm like seaweed. They sat on the bottom like submerged tree trunks grown thick and unrecognisable with detritus. Bones were there too. Many more than Silas's own. This was an old loch, and death an ancient part of it.

To Silas, it did not seem at all strange now to find himself here: returned to where it had began, as the end approached.

The ferryman guided them deeper out over the loch, heading towards a tiny island which sat nearer to the middle of the loch than the rest of the greater islands beyond it.

A speck of land, defying the unfathomably deep waters

Waters Silas knew intimately.

With his hand still submerged, his fingertips numb with the cold, he raised his head.

Found a shoreline carved into his awakening memory.

There, the jetty that had seen him fall.

There, the lawns where the woman in lavender and the young man had run to him.

The echoes of the estate and its gardens had clung to his dissolved memories; and refused to be lost with all the others.

He'd walked those halls therein; tending to the potted plants that held their fronds towards light that filtered through expansive windows. He'd eaten at the table where working folk gathered, and tended many a fireplace in those wood-panelled rooms.

The details weren't sharp, time had dulled them, polished them down to worn stones with no facets, no pin-points he could prick his finger upon.

But he knew.

Silas knew this the place, the way he knew certain things in his life. A short list: he had died in this loch, he was Izanami's servant, he was a man of the outdoors, he had an affinity for all the beauties of the garden, a taste for brandy, an appetite for women *and* men. He had the rhythm of a rabid badger when it came to dancing, but above all else, he knew he'd not held a desire for any other, like that he harboured for the daemon by his side.

The one waiting with uncommon patience for him to speak. Pitch rested his head upon Silas's side, burrowing into him.

'This is the lake in my nightmares, in my dreams,' Silas said, while the water swept through his fingers. 'This is where my brother drowned me, while the Flood waters fell.'

Pitch's heat strengthened, and Silas's fingertips defied the freezing water. 'My dear man, I don't...I don't know what to say...' That he was seeking to say the right thing at all bore witness to how a wild prince had softened.

'How is this possible?' Charlie very rarely sounded as small as his stature. The lad suddenly laughed, high and hard. 'What a stupid question, really. After all I've seen. And it doesn't even bear asking how we travelled so far so fast. But do you know this place as well, Silas?'

He was still on his feet, still gazing back towards the shore which grew ever more distant.

'Do sit down, dearest,' Edward insisted. 'Give yourself a moment to breathe.'

'You too, Silas. Breathe.' Pitch's whisper was like a caress. 'You are rather more blue around the lips than I would like. Take a breath, perhaps another after that.'

'Silas?' Charlie's voice seemed to drift down a tunnel. 'Have you visited my family estate?'

Oh Christ, how he had visited. 'I have. It was my...' Home? That was not quite right. 'I worked there, for a time.'

'What a remarkable coincidence. But surely before I was born, for I feel certain I would remember one such as you coming to call.' Charlie's words echoed with confusion. 'I feel like...well, this sounds foolish, but it is as though I have never *not* known you, Silas. I'm not making any sense, am I? Bloody hell, what a time this is.' He imitated Pitch, in slumping against Edward's side, and found equal welcome there. The lieutenant, drained as he was, wrapped his arm about the lad. And Silas felt a surge of gratefulness, of contentment, that such closeness had been found. 'Do you think you might visit, Edward? Once life is not so peculiar?'

Charlie's wistfulness suited the strange hues of the day.

'I would like that, very much,' Edward said, thickly. 'Once life is not so peculiar.'

'You should be there with them, Silas.' Pitch's voice warmed him, every bit as his touch. 'There must be so much you hope to learn. Once I am delivered, I shall have the ferryman return you, I promise.'

The words snapped Silas's trance like a squall against a sapling. He looked at Pitch, for what felt like the first time in an age.

'When the time comes you shall be with me. We will both return.'

Pitch's nod was a gentle brush against Silas's arm.

The boat struck uncertain waters and the calm, mirrored surface was devoured by a sudden roughness. Charlie let out a cry of surprise, and Scarlet a chitter of indignation, as a fine spray of water doused all in the boat. They rocked with vigour from side to side and Silas's throat ran dry.

'Hold fast. We approach.' The Ferryman's lantern did not sway, despite the motion of the boat as it moved through the waves.

The smaller island was very near, and the boat clearly headed towards it. A structure was visible upon the land; broken shapes at through clinging vines and winter-stripped branches. A ruin, most likely. Its shape teased at Silas's memories: bringing forth notions of exploration on summer days, and kisses stolen against moss-ravaged stone.

'That is our way.' It was Edward who spoke, but with the oddest tenor, like the boat still drifted in that chamber and echoes swelled his words.

'Inchgalbraith Castle?' Charlie asked.

The boat roiled with the waves. Silas breathed against the ill-feeling that came. His ancient fear still teased at him; it was tattooed deep. But he'd never allow it's head free here.

'That's not a bloody castle, it's ruins,' Pitch sneered, but he was not wrong. 'Nor is that speck of land worthy of being called an island. I could not toss my head without my hair getting wet.'

'I won't disagree with you, Tobias,' Charlie said. 'The castle has been in ruins for centuries...and it makes for a very uncomfortable hiding place, I can vouch for that. I ended up with leeches one summer.'

'That is our way.' This time it came from the Ferryman. Their armour glistened, and Silas took note of how much brighter the hints of gold embellishment were now, even though the light was no different than before; still gripped by the cusp of a dawn that did not seem able to spill.

'That is the best the Seraph could do?' Pitch mocked. 'That speck of a place is what we have fought tooth and nail to reach? We are being made fools of. This is no more a Sanctuary, than I am Queen of England.'

Edward turned. The sheen of the Ferryman's armour cast a halo of golden light around him. He studied Pitch—there was no other word for it—studied him as though seeking to glimpse the heart beneath his ribs. 'Then a queen you are today, Prince of Daemonkind. Hold fast, now.'

The boat lurched forward at a shocking pace. Silas toppled back. Surprise allowed the stranglehold of his fears to tighten; a torrent of panicked thoughts to rush forth.

He would fall overboard. He would drown.

He would not be there for Pitch when he'd promised.

And Charlie would try—as all his ancestors had tried—to rescue Silas; but he would fail now, as they had failed then.

They would all watch on, as the waters claimed Silas for the thousandth time.

His shout of horror and age-old fear became a roar of refusal. His topple backwards a violent opposing shift forward. He dragged Pitch with him.

'I'm not going in this fucking water again.' Silas shouted, screamed it really, and bloody hell it felt sublime. 'Not again. It is done.' More words untangled from the depths he held within. 'Damn you, Otis. You fool. I forgive you. I forgive you.'

Silas slumped forward, chest heaving, the weight of a prince against him.

No one spoke. He'd said enough. The boat still roiled and dipped in the churning water. Water dripped from Silas's lashes, ran from his hair down his neck. But the archaic knots of his past had come undone, the ashes of his fear scattering with the increasing wind.

'Who is Otis, Silas?'

He raised his head, finding emerald eyes watching. 'He was my brother.'

A shadow shifted in the daemon's eyes, a tiny flare of his flame. 'The man who cast you into the water.'

'Yes.'

'And you forgive him.'

'I do. What alternative is there?'

Pitch considered it, water drops like diamonds on his cheeks. The Ferryman steered them through the troubled waters, the sun-glow of their lantern lighting the way.

'You could hate. It is what so many others do.'

'I do not wish to be like others.'

The sway of the boat pushed them together. 'There has never been another like you, my Sickle. Izanami was no fool.'

'Nor Seraphiel.'

Pitch took it as the compliment it was intended, and offered a grim smile.

The smack of a wave against the hull sent up a fresh, more vigorous spray of water and all the softness left the daemon. 'Gods! You, at the bow there, steady this fucking craft, or I swear by the taint's of all the fucking angels I'll come down there and roast you in that ridiculous armour.'

The silence, and utter indifference of the Ferryman only infuriated Pitch further, and Silas wrangled with a prince who spat all kinds of dark intentions for the guide's staff.

The splash and slap of waves worsened. Charlie yelped, and both he and Edward braced their hands against whatever solid piece of wood was nearest. Scarlet had entirely disappeared, inside a pocket no doubt. Silas was beginning to wonder if there was not more of the loch inside the boat than without when the frothing waters suddenly found peace.

The change from rough to smooth was instant. A startled mewl came from the prince. 'About bloody time.'

Silas blinked, swiping at the wetness in his beard.

The loch was returned to smooth as glass, but did not retain its pewter of earlier. The water here was white as milk.

Inchgalbraith was nowhere to be seen. The tiny island ruins were gone. And in their place a land mass far greater than all the other islands in the loch combined.

At the heart of the spread of land was an enormous structure. Castle was not fine enough a word. This was a palace. Superb, enormous. Richly decorated with a multitude of gold-tipped spires and whitewashed walls with a subtle lustre.

'Oh my,' Charlie gasped in the sudden quiet. 'That is beautiful.'

There was no denying it.

Pitch sighed. 'Now, this is far more suited to that vainglorious prick Seraphiel.'

'It's like something out of a fairytale,' Charlie whispered. 'I used to think I could see gold glinting off the islands at sunset. I watched as often as I could, and imagined there was a pot of gold here I could find and steal, so I could run away.' He laughed, a little dreamily. 'But I never imagined anything like this.'

Silas wondered if anyone had ever imagined something like this.

The palace was overlooked by a towering mountain range, snow capping the peaks; just as they'd seen when they set out over Loch Lomond.

But this was not the loch now.

Silas's grave lay beyond the veil that hid this place, and he welcomed the distance forged.

The slide of the boat slowed as the new shore approached. A white sand beach lay like a thin ribbon between the milky water and a tangle of spindly trees, their trunks ghost white, their leaves gold and big as maples. Beyond them, the palace was a great hulking presence. Edward rose to his feet, with Charlie at his side. Silas stared at the dry state of the man: not a single wet hair upon the lieutenant's head, whilst the rest of them were soaked through.

Edward turned to face them. His eyes held pinpricks of gold light, the spark of the angel within, well alight.

'You took your time, Dominion.' It was not Edward who spoke. A man could not carry such a tone as this.

Pitch surely knew, but that did not stop him from being riled. 'That is my greeting? You complete cu–'

'Enter the Sanctuary. Delay no more. Time does not favour us, Prince Vassago.'

Edward's eyes rolled back in his head, and he collapsed into Charlie's ready arms.

CHAPTER 23

Pitch fought Charlie for the right to lift Edward from the shallow cradle of the boat.

'I could manage him. Careful of his arm, slow down!' The lad buzzed about him like an irritating fly, moving hanging limbs, adjusting the lieutenant's shirt when his position bunched it at his chin. 'Let me fix it, he won't be able to breath.'

Pitch knew his eyes aglow, and gave no shits at all. Charlie did not frighten easily. 'Get out of the way.' He stepped one foot on the edge, calculating the depth. Not substantial; he knew that from Silas already being in the water. But the ankou was so blasted big, Pitch might end up submerged if he assumed things, and there was the milkiness of the water to contend with. The bottom was entirely hidden.

'It is shallow.' Silas stood just shy of knee deep. The ankou had not hesitated to leap overboard. Brave bastard he was now.

'Watch his head.' Charlie was not to be satisfied. 'Don't let it loll about like that, damn you.'

'You've met your match in coddling, Silas.' Pitch elbowed the lad out of the way, lifting Edward at an angle, so could see where his feet would tread. 'Tend to Lucifer, Charlie. And leave me be.'

'Don't jump from the boat, Tobias. No! Don't you dare.'

Pitch jumped. Hardly an Olympic effort, and more of a long, reaching step. One steadied by Silas's hands at the small of his back.

'I'm fine,' Pitch said, more sharply than Silas deserved. 'Help Charlie.'

The ankou did, as so often, what Pitch asked, and turned back to the king and the lad.

The water was warm as shallows in summer, and moved more languidly than true water should. Underfoot, the ground was pliant as damp sand, but crunched, oddly, like eggshells.

'Gods, you are such a fool, man,' Pitch whispered to the silent lieutenant. 'You would not be here if you were not so determined to make a friend of me. You would be no one's puppet, and I'd not feel sick with guilt every time I laid eyes on you. Whatever form he takes, Seraphiel is not worthy of you.' He dragged in a breath. 'I'm sorry, I'm so sorry this happened to you. I'm sorry this happened to you all.'

Edward opened his eyes, mere cracks, through which only reassuring grey was evident. No angelfire. No intrusion. 'This is not your fault.' His lips were cracked, a tiny bubble of blood upon the bottom. 'You do not need anyone's forgiveness, least of all mine. I love you, Tobias. You are and will always be, my friend. And I have no regrets. None.'

'You are mad.'

'I think I can be forgiven for that.'

Pitch gave him a placating nod. 'I'll allow it, considering.'

Edward's smile had always been a sweet thing to see, and this was no different now, even as Pitch worried it might be among the man's last. 'How charitable of you.'

Laughter, it turned out, was beyond a beleaguered prophet. Edward convulsed, fresh blood striking beneath Pitch's chin.

'Shit, Edward? Gods, Edward, can you hear me?'

'What's wrong?' Charlie called. 'Pitch, is he alright?'

Edward's convulsions strengthened, and he jerked in Pitch's hold. His eyes returned to rolling in his head, a horrid gurgling coming from him. Twice Pitch was struck in the face, and once he nearly lost his footing altogether when a spasm coincided with him stepping into a hidden divot in the soft, gritty sand.

The churning of water behind announced the rush forward of the ankou.

'Silas, is he...gods, tell me he is not...'

A shake of the head sent dark curls shifting. 'He is not dying, Pitch. I'm not sure what this is, but it is not death.' He turned. 'Ferryman, where is the path.' Silas made a sound of annoyance. 'That bastard. He's left us. Do you know the way, Pitch?'

There was nothing but genuine enquiry in his tone, but nevertheless Pitch snapped at him. 'No. I don't know the fucking way. I wasn't exactly let out to take strolls.'

A heavy hand laid on his shoulder. 'I'm sorry. Forgive me.' Of course Pitch did. None of that, nor this, was Silas's fault. 'We will find our way.'

Edward had stilled, his hands curled beneath his chin, his face a terrible shade of grey. But he breathed. Pitch could hear him rasping.

They emerged from the water.

'It is strange, is it not,' Pitch said. 'How close you and I might have been here at times.'

'No so close as we are now.' Silas slipped an arm around him, escorting him up onto the narrow sliver of beach. 'Do you suppose it coincidence, or divine purpose, that led the goddess to choose me from a loch so near to a Seraph's Sanctuary?'

Pitch stared at the tangle of slender young trees up ahead, pondering the question. 'I'm not sure how long the Sanctuary has existed, but I don't think it coincidence, no. It is more likely that this place holds some power.'

'What sort of power?' Silas cast a glance over his shoulder. 'Are you sure I can't help you Charlie?'

'Do I look like I need help, Silas?'

'No, you don't.' He smiled, and his gentleness always managed to melt something in Pitch. No matter the circumstances. He became the focus of the ankou's attentions once more. 'Forgive me. Go on, what power do you think is here?'

Pitch shrugged, more to ease the tension in his shoulders than anything else. 'At a guess, perhaps one of the seals is nearby. Three were set, and Seraphiel was responsible for one. I don't see why else he'd be so intent on bringing me here otherwise. Do you sense anything of the Blight?' But he knew the answer already. Silas was untroubled by souls. Pitch felt that he knew the man well enough–knew each tick of his jaw, every flicker of his eye–to know if Silas were in any distress.

'No.' Silas did not let him down. 'In fact, there is more peace here than I experienced before we found the Priest's Hole.' He touched at his ear. 'Though my ears are still ringing. Their din was terrible.' Silas sighed, and rubbed at Pitch's back. 'I wish I had been able to find my way out of the loch, so I could have saved you from this place.'

Pitch laughed, and Edward made a small sound of discomfort at the sudden jolt. 'Truly, you are the most sopping romantic I've known, and I've known my share.'

'Oh, my dear fellow, I have barely begun. Once we have settled this matter, prepare to be swooning, noon and night, as I court you with an extravagance and charm of which the poets shall write, for ages to come.'

'Do you have a fever?'

'Only one that burns for you.' Silas's wink was ridiculous.

'Charlie, hurry up at once. Silas is trying to kill me.'

The lad was close behind, not even puffing with the effort of carrying the king of Daemonkind; carrying Lucifer in such a way that his knees were very close to his chest, no doubt in a bid to keep his feet from dragging in the water thanks to the lad's small stature. Pitch hoped for Charlie's sake that the king wouldn't wake soon. He'd not be pleased at being carried about like a bundle of rags. A bundle of rags being made a home for a will-o'-the-wisp, no less; Scarlet was there, half hidden by collar and hair, their glow subtle, a singular colour, a soft yellow, as though they sought to match themselves to the glint of leaves and air.

'It sounds like a blasted lovely way to go,' Charlie said. 'If you ask me.'

'Well, no one bloody asked you,' Pitch huffed.

Silas's low laughter held the gravitas of mountains. And Pitch grinned back at him. They were both acting a little mad; holding a nervous energy that needed placement.

Stupid sweet talk might be the only thing holding them both together.

They halted, just short of where the coarse sand gave way to the delicate velvet of verdant moss, and the gathering of trees; with their grand golden leaves and bone-white trunks. The thickness of their crowding was substantial, and at a glance Pitch could see no evident way through.

'Are we supposed to chop our own path?' he muttered.

Silas moved closer to the woodlands, where many of the trunks wrapped one another like serpents, whilst others stood straight as pillars. He strode up and down the beach, frowning, and muttering about how there seemed no visible way. The leaves shifted with a wind that did not reach them, Pitch felt no brush of it against his skin.

'Perhaps it needs a taste of your blade,' he called, casting an anxious glance down at Edward. He preferred the man thrashing about, to this new...deadness. 'Cut the fucking trees down, and let this be done with.'

The axe was not required. Scarlet whisked from their place at Lucifer's collar, and flew straight past Silas who was pushing at a tree trunk, as though considering simply shouldering his way through. Pitch had no doubt it was possible.

Scarlet chirruped, their colours pulsing with the rainbow's spectrum, though the yellow hues shone brightest of all, as though intensified by the damned amount of gold in the surrounds. Scarlet vanished between two trees that curved in towards one another like dancers bowing.

'That's too small a gap,' Charlie said. 'For me, let alone Silas.'

The ankou traipsed the line between sand and moss, moving to where the wisp had entered.

'Scarlet?' Silas leaned in towards the bowing trees. And took a step.

He promptly disappeared. Charlie gasped. Pitch scowled, gripping Edward tighter, letting more flame tease at his fingertips.

'Silas?'

'Illusion, another blasted illusion,' The ankou shouted, and stepped back into view. Scarlet perched on the top of his head, waving bloated fingers, as though they'd been missing for months. 'Rather clever though. Come on, this way.'

'Go on, Charlie.' Pitch nodded the lad ahead.

Silas vanished again, and then Charlie and his daemonic passenger did the same. Pitch stepped up to the bowed trees. They were not, as it had first appeared, side by side at all. But rather one was set at a short distance behind the other; and the gap between them allowed glimpse of a pathway. Silas and Charlie stood waiting, another tangle of trees just behind them, but, Pitch suspected, another gap was to be found there.

A trick of the eye; a well-loved trademark of the fae.

Pitch had not stopped to think of the builder of this Sanctuary. Which of the Children of Melusine held such an enormous secret? Their coffers must be overloaded; if the angel had not killed them the moment the last stone was laid. He vaguely recalled Bess speaking of a missing sibling, on a night when he'd paid more attention to his whisky and winning hand than to idle chatter. Pitch had little interest in the Children, save for when they built places like the Fulbourn, or the Crystal Palace. Then he would quite happily murder them himself.

Pitch adjusted his hold on Edward, shook off some of the gritty sand clinging to his own boots like burrs to trousers, and moved deeper into the woodlands.

Scarlet led the way, quick to discern where the gaps lay. Something of a marvel, really, for Pitch's own eye was fooled every time, disbelieving there could possibly be a way through a tangle of trunks.

He kept his eye on Silas, mostly to discern if the scythe told the ankou anything of concern, and partly because there was comfort to be found in watching someone who took up so much space in the world. Silas's bulk filled the pathways. He had to turn side on to manage some of the smaller sections, whilst Pitch had no such issue; Charlie even less so, despite having Lucifer to carry.

Pitch knew the Nephilim upon the Hellfield, he knew how their size had terrified so many of the daemons in his legions. He could only hope that whatever Angelic power awaited in the palace up ahead, held even just a touch of that fearfulness; at the very least, a caution. One that would keep Silas safe.

'We are here,' Silas declared.

Scarlet emitted a sound that was undeniably one of awe.

Charlie breathed in. 'I thought it astonishing before...but...oh, my word.'

The last to arrive, Pitch nearly ran into the back of the lad who had stopped to stare.

Certainly, it was a sight.

Now they were much closer it was evident that the walls of the palace were not simply white. They were the same milky hue as the water, but with an opalescence that hinted at pastel hues as the light reflected the golden leaves of the woods, and gilded spires. The gold on the spires was polished to a shine, making pointed suns up high, reaching towards a sky that was low and close and white as a bride's veil.

The air was crisp, clean, generous on the lungs, as it would be if they actually stood in the Scottish Highlands.

How was it possible this place could be forgotten? Pitch winced, searching for something–anything–that might strike him as familiar.

The lay of the garden certainly wasn't. It could have been plucked from Versailles itself. In fact, he'd wager the architect had either stolen ideas, or built both places. The hedges were topiary of the highest and strictest order, the pebble pathways cut in circular patterns, the marble fountain at the centre–a burly man in a chariot with two wild-eyed stallions leading him forth–was worthy of any monarch's palace. White rose trees pinpointed each corner of the rectangular yard, their blooms far too large, and nonseasonal, to be natural design. Scarlet landed upon one, and disappeared into the petals, the flower was so large. Everything was immaculate, not a white pebble out of place on the pathways, not an errant leaf fallen. It felt almost a travesty to walk upon the path.

There was something to the white and gold theme that was unsurprising, but nothing else of the place gave him a sense of familiarity.

They gathered in front of the statue, facing the front entrance. A green-gold doorway, the electrum metal a product of silver and gold mixed together, marked the entrance into the palace. It was, of course, imposing; the height of one and a half Silas's, with a massive ornamental door-knocker at its centre. The design was of a pheasant, with the lengthy tail exaggerated here, so that it almost swept the ground. Gold, of course, the entire thing, though it was not so polished as everything else around it.

'That's a pheasant,' Silas said, as though none of them could know that. 'Quite remarkable workmanship, don't you think?'

Charlie and Pitch hummed in vague agreement. And they all just stood there. Pitch and Charlie with arms laden, Silas with arms folded, and Scarlet squealing with delight as they jumped from bloom to bloom. Someone really ought to move. Pitch considered it, and decided it was really quite pleasant just where they were. He hefted Edward, shifting the man's weight, which was far too paltry.

'Knock on the damned door,' Lucifer coughed.

Charlie screamed, nearly dropping the daemon who had been utterly motionless until that moment. Silas only just managed to step forward in time, preventing an unfortunate fall upon the pebbled ground.

The king groaned at the sudden movement, coughing again, and expelling a rather foul substance, red mostly but with hint of black combined. Silas cast him a look, oozing with his confounding concerns.

'We must get him inside.'

Pitch was very aware of that. But this threshold felt enormous. He nodded, but could not bring himself to take a step. Charlie was watching him, as was Silas, and both waited.

'Too late for pause now,' Lucifer spluttered, his lips stained with the vile fluid that he'd coughed up. He truly was more pleasant company when he was more dead. But most disagreeable was the fact that he was quite right.

He glanced at Silas. There was no judgement to be seen there, no impatience, or worse, disappointment that he found Pitch lacking. A little of his terror subsided, giving his thoughts time to resettle. Of course he knew why he was here. This world, Silas's world, Charlie's and Edward's too, might be free of the scourge of the Blight, if Pitch just stepped across that threshold.

Still, it was not until Edward whimpered, his face scrunched with silent pain, that Pitch finally nodded.

'Let's go.'

The ankou's gaze lingered another heartbeat. Pitch sent a silent prayer to worthless gods that Silas would not ask him if he was alright. The answer was no. Very much no. The catastrophic incident with Lalassu had caused something to slip inside Pitch. Like the earth splitting after a tremble from its core. Doubt had slunk in when the Pale Horse fell. Festering in the cracks that formed inside him.

He'd been a fool to think he could slip free of the yoke of the Berserker Prince. Pitch acted on violent impulses still. He remained a selfish prick whose chaotic nature brought terrible harm, and yet here he was.

Letting Silas give him a grim but understanding smile.

Letting the ankou walk ahead. Allowing him to approach the threshold that Pitch himself could only yet stare at.

And his lips, damn them, would not part to tell the ankou to stop. To stay away. To leave while he still could.

Silas strode ahead, steadfast, whilst Pitch roiled. The ankou took the handful of wide splayed steps two at a time. He took hold of the pheasant's tail, up near the base of its body, and glanced over his shoulder.

'Ready?' Silas said, brown eyes soft and full of kindness.

Pitch should never have allowed him here. Certainly never should have gone along with the ankou's notion that this task was best done together.

Before Pitch's cracks could widen further, he shrugged on his familiar, acerbic guise. 'Get on with it, you oaf. It's a door, not the Seal itself. I don't understand why we must knock at all. Fucking dreadful hospitality.'

Not a one of them reacted to his little temper tantrum, none recoiled, nor told him to fuck off.

He talents were embarrassingly rusty.

Silas lifted the knocker and let it fall. The clang that rang out was not the heavy clack of metal on metal that Pitch expected. Instead, the pretty notes of a windchime filled the air: tinkling delicately, where all else of this place seemed so solid and robust.

Barely had the melodious ringing begun than the green-gold door opened, swinging inwards. Silas backtracked down the steps.

A woman stood silhouetted by the glow from within, her figure like something brought to life from a Reuben painting: a generous swell at the hips and breasts, with the slightest of narrowing at the waist, accentuated by the ruffling of a modest peplum. She did not acquiesce to the dress expected of her sex, and instead wore what appeared to be stockings with melon hose. If Pitch's assumption was correct–and in clothing he was rarely wrong–her costume was at least a century out of date. The finer details were ambiguous, as the light cast her front into shadow, but her aura, subdued as it was beneath the greater brightness, told Pitch a grand story indeed.

A Child of Melusine.

She was a sister to Old Bess. And, less pleasingly, to Palatyne.

Though who she was, he could not say. The Children of Melusine were multiple in number. And their allegiances varied wildly: Bess pledged himself to the Order, Palatyne had been bought by the Morrigan, or the Erlking, perhaps. And Seraphiel had lured this creature into his employ.

Silas glanced at him, and mouthed a single word. *Child?* The fact he made a question of it gave Pitch reason to think her naming melody was as contorted as her aura. Pitch nodded.

The Child's colours were right, for the most part, but there was an unusual amount of sunflower yellow in the design, that was foreign to the half-fae's usual presentation. As though the Sanctuary's heavy gold accenting had tattooed itself upon her.

The woman bowed deeply. 'Your Grace, the warmest of welcomes to you. Long have I awaited the return of your presence.'

'Me?' Pitch frowned.

She righted, a soft tinkling joining her movement, the click of jewellery somewhere on her person.

'No. Though your return, your highness, is just as longed for. It is the point of everything, after all. You do not remember me, I suppose?'

'You suppose right.' Pitch glared, in part because she was infuriating, and partly because his lack of memory formed a hard ball of tension in the pit of his stomach, near where the simurgh huddled, as unhappy about things as he was.

Silas glanced between them both. 'You were here, when Pitch was held by the angel?'

'I have been here since I built this Sanctuary. I have served His Grace for several centuries,' she said, an airiness clinging to her words.

'Then you knew him a prisoner?' Silas's voice held an angry tenor, all the more ominous for his deep tone, but the Child was unmoved.

'Prisoner? That is too harsh a word.' She shrugged lightly. 'He was confined but not neglected, I assure you. However ferocious his incubus appetites were, His Grace was most generous with seeing that his vessel was sated. He needed you in fine form, after all.'

An actual growl came from Silas, and his step forward held all sorts of menace. As rousing as it was to see the ankou ready to throttle the half-fae for his sake, Pitch edged Edward's feet, so that Silas would have to push him aside to go any further. The ankou would do no such thing. His glance was filled with displeasure though.

'My Lord Death,' the Child continued, unflinching, despite the obvious dislike of a very large man. 'Might I offer my condolences on the loss of your mare? The Lady of the Lake mourns with you. Do come in.'

Silas deflated at once, and Pitch's fingers dug a little tighter against Edward's body.

'Satine is here?' Silas asked, carefully.

'Not entirely. Not as you would think.'

Intolerably nebulous as always, the fae. But Pitch had no chance to snap at her, much as he desired too, for Lucifer had found energy enough to protest at Charlie's handling.

'Set me down, blast you.'

He gave the lad small choice in the matter. Charlie grimaced as he tried to avoid being struck in the face by the preposterously unsteady king, who had to lean on him heavily once he was set on his feet.

'Is he here?' Lucifer demanded, looking dreadful with his stains of blackened blood.

'In a manner of speaking, your majesty.' The Child inclined their head and stepped aside, moving out of the glare that hid her, revealing attire that was unmistakably from a bygone century: a lacy ruff circled her neck, and sheer white fabric covered her shoulders and chest, meeting heavy burnt orange material with pearl bead-work and slashed sleeves which hinted at satin beneath. Her hair was braided and looped beneath her ears, with a pearl hairpin atop her head that shone with topaz stones. And yes, it was most definitely white stockings and orange and gold hose dressing her lower half. 'Though not as he would desire.'

'Don't befuddle us with your cryptic fae-speech, blast you.' Lucifer managed most of it without coughing. He paused to spit, more distasteful black dollops. The bruising at his jaw was a grotesque mottling of rusty brown and mould green. 'What is your name, Child of Melusine? Who vexes me so?'

'I am Jacquetta.'

Silas breathed in, and Pitch glanced at him. 'Do you know her?'

'I know *of* her. You are the lost Child,' he said, with the wrinkled forehead of someone in serious thought. 'Your sister Palatyne thought you dead, buried in a cornerstone by the angel, to reinforce this Sanctuary.' He glanced at Pitch. 'I was informed at the church after we escaped, but had given it little mind. Palatyne had told Old Bess it was the reason for her siding with the Erlking.' He looked back to the woman, his gaze hard as marble, his commanding tone never more impressive. 'That alliance nearly cost Pitch his life.'

The Child, Jacquetta, showed the first sign of anything but smooth indifference. Her hand lifting to the ruff at her neck. 'I am neither buried, nor dead. And it insults me, that she imagined me so fool-hardy. I serve a righteous angel, but I imagine Palatyne served only her own avarice. The UnSeelie Court glitters brightly. She would be easily swayed, and it has nothing to do with concerns for me. Forgive her, your grace. My sister's head is easily turned by material things.' She spoke all of this to Edward, who had gone back to his terrible stillness in Pitch's arms.

'That half-fae matters not. The prince lives.' Lucifer grunted, his vestige-less hand curled into a fist, and pressed to his chest. Scarlet, bravely or stupidly, flew in close to fuss about him like the tiniest of nurse-maids. 'I ask you again. Now speak plainly. Is Seraphiel here?'

All the mightiness of the king could not hide the frailty behind his words. The uncommon desperation that embroidered the question.

'The purebred holds the answer to that,' Jacquetta remained enigmatic. 'And the prince holds the purebred. Will you step forward, Prince of Daemonkind?'

There was only one answer, of course; they could not stand on the doorstep forever. And truly, what choice did he have? But the weight of this answer felt tremendous.

'By the Celestials, Vassago. Why do you wait? Move.' Lucifer shoved Charlie aside, and the lad nearly took a tumble down the steps. Scarlet was their rescuer, whipping in behind the lad to catch him.

Silas stood tall and imposing, unafraid of Lucifer. 'Do not touch Charlie again. And Pitch will move when he is ready. Give him a moment.'

'You don't have a moment, your highness,' Jacquetta replied. 'Or rather, the prophet does not.'

'His name is Edward.' Charlie spoke up, Scarlet nodding emphatically as they took a seat on the lad's head.

'His name shall be on a tombstone before long,' Jacquetta declared.

'That is a lie!' Silas's words boomed like Big Ben's toll. 'He is not dying.'

'You do not know what he is, Lord Death. There have been no prophets of a Seraph before him.' Jacquetta's brown eyes sparkled as she stared down at Edward. 'His Grace is truly a wonder.'

The lieutenant moved, and his eyes fluttered open. The calming grey of the man himself.

'Edward?' Pitch said.

'It is you who is a wonder, Tobias.' A harsh, painful whisper. 'And he knows it. He has always known it. It is why you were chosen.'

A wonder? Edward was truly delirious then. Pitch's thoughts filled with Lalassu, with the horse's scream as the angel struck. An angel who might yet find his way here, and destroy everyone in this Sanctuary. Everyone who was here because of Pitch.

'Take me to him.' Lucifer made a shoddy job of the last step, tripping on its lip, grabbing at the doorframe. 'Now, Jacquetta. Which way to your master?'

'I will show you a way, but it will not be the right way, without the prophet. Or the prince.'

'Pitch, do not let them rattle you.' Silas was right there. He regarded Pitch in the only way he seemed to know how; as though he were delicate and precious as a masterpiece. 'I will be at your side, come what may. I promise you.'

Pitch stiffened. That was the whole damned, fucking problem. Silas was a man of his word. Edward exhaled. A frightening sound of release. He went limp again, boneless in Pitch's arms, returned to his bare existence once more.

If the Child said nothing else of worth, it was that Edward's time was short.

And Pitch would not see another of those who had followed him, fall because he'd made a wrong move.

'You shall be free of this, Edward.' Pitch hissed beneath his breath. 'Let it be done.'

He walked up the stairs, crossing the threshold with Silas and Charlie and Scarlet at his back.

CHAPTER 24

Jacquetta magicked an invalid chair out of thin air. Or rather, from one of the rooms that lined the corridor. A wooden chair–with large iron wheels, a sturdy cane back and made from polished wood without a hint of gold or embellishment–rolled of its own accord at her whispered word, and came to a stop before Pitch.

The Child insisted that Edward be placed there. She insisted too, on wheeling him along, but one glare from Pitch, a protest from Charlie, and the scowl of Scarlet seemed to put paid to that notion.

Pitch took hold of the handles and pushed the barely conscious Edward along. They travelled down a long, wide corridor, one with all the embellishments and grand dimensions of a palace. The glamour and richness of this place could not be understated, its beauty very evident, but Silas found it impossible to be awed by a location that had been such a prison for Pitch.

A prison that, if the prince recognised it, he gave no sign. But that the Sanctuary had an effect on him, was indisputable. Since they had walked into that courtyard with its flourishing garden and ostentatious water fountain, a change had come over Pitch, one that bothered Silas greatly. His sharp tongue had dulled, his propensity to lean into Silas had not been evident. Subtle things. But Silas knew far more of Pitch than the curves of his body, and the devastating beauty of his face. He knew when his lover's thoughts darkened.

Silas blinked. The Sanctuary was the antithesis of darkness. His eyes pained with adjusting to the rather dazzling glow of the building's interior. Silas took a more studied look at his surrounds, needing to distract himself from his concerns.

Of where this walk would lead them.

There were mirrors set into the walls, floor to ceiling, one upon every second panel, adding to the vastness of the space, and accentuating the illumination coming from elaborate sconces on the mirror-less wall panels. The sconces were gold, of course; that hue dominated the decor. Each had four arms, in the form of swans, with long sinewy necks and exaggerated beaks. Four fat white candles sat upon each arm; candles that gave off a far brighter, and indeed, far more golden light than any Silas had seen before.

His gaze did not stray long from Pitch, though. Silas took in the sway of the black cape he wore as the daemon pushed Edward along. Beneath that layer of borrowed clothing was an undeniably beautiful body, but one that had been strained by the trials put upon it. They needed a dozen more meals like the last one shared, to fill Pitch out and put some extra meat upon sharp bones. Silas bit at his lip. To think of such a time, both the past meal done, and those he had yet hoped to share, was to torture himself.

He started at a sudden thump.

Lucifer had stumbled again, his hip contacting the wall. He was ahead of Pitch, and behind the Child, who kept on, and did not look back. Scarlet was the only one who dared react. And their reward was to be taken aim at by the cantankerous, wounded, daemon.

'Piss off.'

The wisp's sigh preceded a retreat. Back to the safety of Charlie's shoulder.

The king of daemons walked, or rather stumbled, along the bare floorboards at the edge of the cream and honey-gold runner that dominated the walkway, propping himself against the walls. He dragged one hand along the pristine panels and left more than a few smudges upon the stark white plasterwork with its gold edging.

When Jacquetta had suggested a wheelchair for him as well, Silas feared the Child about to be turned to stone by the look Lucifer gave her. But there was no doubt he would have benefited.

Lucifer looked wretched. His face was bruised, his moustache scorched clean off at the right side, his cheeks were notably hollow, and the careful styling of his hair long since ruined. More horrid bruising peeked from the parting of his shirt; awful marks of russet and grey at his collarbones. Some other evident marks might have been healing burns, and there was a tear in the king's trousers that revealed an appalling wound beneath, a gouging of flesh causing a shocking hole in his thigh. Worst of all was the damage the king tried hardest to conceal. He kept his hand close to his chest, his fingers curled, but he was already like a drunkard on his feet, and once or twice he'd used both hands to brace himself. Silas had seen the space between thumb and middle finger; the festering cut upon his palm too, red and weeping. A nasty infection, he surmised, whilst wondering how his majesty could be vulnerable to such simple things. But most of all he wondered, and worried, about what the downing of the other Seraph meant for them. Was Michael strong enough to enter the Sanctuary? Or, perhaps worse, did he return to Arcadia to spread word of a prince who had escaped the abaddon? How many legions would be sent to reclaim Pitch?

'Silas? Is everything all right?' Charlie said softly.

Pitch had turned, frowning. 'Do you hear something?'

Silas had not yet opened his mouth to answer them when Jacquetta called out, 'Do try to leave my candles burning, if you will. It shall make it far easier to find our way.'

Silas was utterly lost until he realised how dim it was where they had all come to a sudden halt.

'The candles all went out.' Charlie pointed to the nearest sconce, but no sooner had he done so than unlit wicks burst back to life. Dazzling and causing the lad to shade his eyes.

'Did I do that?' Silas said, glancing behind, where all else seemed fine. Save for the fact that the corridor seemed to stretch in perpetuity; he could see no evidence of the substantial green-gold entrance. The place stirred reminders of The Atlas and its endless staircase, and, less pleasant a thought, the Fulbourn with its labyrinthine passageways.

'You did, twice now,' Pitch answered. 'Silas, tell me, are you hearing something that we should be worried about?'

'No...no, I was just wondering...' Silas stopped himself. Idiot. He would not add to the prince's load even more by talking of vengeful angels. He'd save his thoughts until he spoke with Lucifer, alone. 'Just wondering how much further.'

'If you kept walking, it would be less far for you than it is now.' Jacquetta had not slowed at all and had moved a considerable distance away from them. She stood at a pair of double doors, white with gleaming gold handles. 'Come on. There are three more doors to pass through, three more corridors after this. I am not known for the simplicity of my designs. Don't dally.'

Jacquetta raised her hand, fluttered her fingers, and the doors swung open. A sitting room lay beyond, an ostentatious design with bulging lounge chairs and settees in satins of the deepest gold hue.

Lucifer made a quiet sound of unhappiness, his shoulders hunched, most of his body pressed against the wall.

All at once, Silas could stand it no more.

'Scorch me if you like, your majesty, but I am going to help you.' He spoke sternly, and the nearest candles fluttered dangerously, bending to near horizontal upon their wicks. His shadow cast over Lucifer, darkening the rings of fatigue beneath his eyes. Silas eyed the disturbed candles, and a deep satisfaction swept over him. His body hummed with energy; with power his goddess had made sure was filled to brimming. With Lalassu's loss, and Pitch's distant state, Silas had sunk too deeply into grim thought, losing sight of what was most important.

He was not powerless. Far from it.

Silas took Lucifer's arm. The heat was immediate, searing and intense, and vastly disconcerting. Silas's breath quickened. The candles fluttered once more. But he held fast, and the burning sensation lessened. 'We shall take all day if you insist on this senseless independence. Give me your weight. It is no challenge, I assure you.'

They locked in a brief, silent battle, one where Lucifer held himself rigid, as unyielding as he could make himself. Scarlet came between them, darting straight up to Lucifer, and landing a swift, tiny punch to the end of his nose, following it up with a chittering tirade.

'Good gods.' Lucifer sagged, covering his ears. 'If it will shut you up, I'll let the blasted ankou throw me over his shoulder. Foolhardy, creature.'

The moment he slumped against Silas, Scarlet's high-pitched admonishment ceased. Peace reigned, and Silas's ears rang. But the clever little wisp looked suitably pleased with themself as they returned to Charlie. And well they should. They had given the king an excuse he desperately needed. An ability to accept aid, without saying a word.

And Christ, how he needed the aid.

The king was solid, no doubt–built like a war hammer, where Pitch was the leanness of a small sword–but there was an added heaviness to the daemon that alarmed Silas. Lucifer's naming melody had always been faint, as though it did not deem Silas worthy of listening to it, and had always been laced with notes of grief; but there was a new chord present now. One forlorn and frightening. Silas shifted his fingers, and heat pulsed from Lucifer's body; striking out at Silas's touch, as though seeking to remove him.

Silas drew his breath. Lucifer looked at him. The daemon was tall, and it was not much of a raise of his head needed to meet Silas's eye.

'What bothers you, ankou? This help was your fool idea.'

Silas frowned, trying to fathom the melody that played. Deathnotes, perhaps? But if so, they were like none he'd known. And this was a King of Daemonkind, with Silas an ankou of the purebreds. Did Izanami's reach include such creatures as Lucifer? Or did another god of death hold sway in Arcadia?

'You are greatly harmed.' That much Silas was certain of.

'Say no more, ankou.' The faint hint of flame burned in Lucifer's eyes. 'I am not your concern. Focus on the prince. See him through.'

Silas nodded, shifting his fingers again as the king burned with this strange fever.

Their party carried on, Lucifer muttering every once in a while under his breath, his weight growing heavier and heavier.

When they entered the next room, Jacquetta was already at its far side, standing in front of another set of doors.

Gold was a highlight in this room too, of course. It was there in the thick roped cords that held back velvet green curtains, and there too, in the gilded edges of the furniture. Lucifer exhaled heavily, and leaned them towards the blazing hearth, where a massive painting took up all the wall space above the mantle. The scene depicted an angel, shrouded in flowing white, with tightly curled gold hair and golden wings stretching, upon a black horse whose mane held hints of midnight blue. The angel carried a sword, ready to strike down at a fearsome dragon that menaced him from the ground.

'St George and the dragon,' Lucifer said, hoarse as though he'd smoked a pipe all day. 'He gifted me one very similar, though there is armour worn in mine.'

'Ah yes, the final version,' Jacquetta said. 'He took a long, long while until he was satisfied enough to send it to you. I tried to warn His Grace that purebreds needed more sleep than the painter was afforded, but he'd not listen. The chap would no sooner finish one piece than His Grace decided on a different appearance. The poor sod was painting day and night, until exhaustion claimed him.'

Silas winced. 'The artist died from overwork?'

'I did suggest we allow him to leave when the man started to babble and couldn't keep water down, but I'm afraid my advice fell on deaf, divine ears. His Grace easily forgot those who surrounded him did not hold a strength of his magnitude.'

Pitch's laughter was bitterness personified. 'Oh, you don't say.'

He stared up at the painting, and the emptiness in his expression frightened Silas.

'Do you recognise the painting?' Silas watched him, searching for any sign that memories pained him. But he was closed off in a way that Silas had not known since their very first meeting.

'No, only the arrogance. The light curls do him no favours.'

Lucifer grunted, as transfixed as Pitch appeared to be. 'I disagree.'

Jacquetta hummed where she stood. 'My lord could manage any shade, really.'

'I preferred his hair pale,' Lucifer said, pressing his free hand to the mantle.

'Yes. He knew that,' Jacquetta said.

'So, this is truly Seraphiel?' Silas stared anew at the artwork. Finally, a face to put to all the misery. A face for him to despise. A pity it was not uglier.

'Of course not.' Lucifer's indignation caused him pain, and there was a pause before he continued. 'You are not fit to behold his true form. It would blind you, send you mad, for you are, at your core, a purebred. The Seraph are but one step away from the Celestials themselves.'

'And don't they like to remind us of it?' Pitch muttered.

Silas itched to reach for him, but Pitch had put himself out of reach.

He turned back to the painting, taking in the powerful shoulders, the ripple of muscles along the arm, veins raised where the angel clenched the sword. His face was diamond shaped, his features bold. He was imposing, and fierce, not far removed from how Silas had imagined Seraphiel.

'This is merely one reiteration he chose among many,' Jacquetta said. 'I believe the scene is from one of your favoured mythologies of humankind. Is that right, my lord?'

The king elbowed Silas's side in his restlessness. 'No time for all this nonsense.' He coughed, seeming in danger of another fit.

There absolutely wasn't time, but Silas noted a welcome gleam in Pitch's eye, a sly twist of his lips as he spoke. 'By Enoch's filthy balls, this monstrosity was commissioned for you. A lover's token.' He stared at Lucifer, the delight doing much to thwart the glumness. 'He worked an artist into his grave to bring to life one of your fucking fairy tales.'

The king's anger fed his fever, and the heat stung Silas's hand where it pressed to Lucifer's back. At a great muffled distance, the daemon's contorted melody played out, causing a shiver to run down Silas's spine.

'St George and the dragon is not a fairy tale, you cretin,' he returned, ignoring the snider remarks. 'It is an old legend, from the faith of Christianity –'

Pitch snorted with derisive laughter. 'I could not give a basilisk's cock what old damned book you read of it in.'

'It was not in a book,' Lucifer snapped. 'There was artwork in one of the Bodleian libraries at the University of Oxford. I commented on its beauty when we visited. I did not know he'd worked upon so many versions.' Now a shiver replaced the tremble of rage. 'Superb place, the University. You heathens have no doubt never heard of one.'

There was a strange silence. Perhaps they were all doing as Silas was; trying to absorb the picture of the King of Daemonkind strolling about a library.

'Actually,' Charlie said, cautiously. 'My uncle read history at Oxford, and we visited once. The libraries were marvellous.'

Lucifer's scowl was not entirely mean-spirited. There was some satisfaction there, pleasure in being deemed right. He gave Charlie a sharp nod.

But now Pitch utterly lost his mind. His laughter was strained and high, but anything that was bringing him to life was fine by Silas. 'You took a Seraph to a library? Wait, you demeaned *yourself* so low as to step foot in a purebred library, amongst the stench of old paper and sniffling academics?'

Only Silas heard the stifled groan from Lucifer before he shot back a reply. 'They are the only places of merit in this world. Will you wipe that ridiculous smirk off your face, Vassago, and get on?'

'I'm quite done with being ordered about.' The prince spoiled for a fight, which was encouraging, but not useful here.

If Silas stepped away, Lucifer would fall. The king was desperately weak. Any fool could see it, and Silas *felt* it, beneath his skin, and ringing in his ears.

He caught Pitch's eye, sending a glance down at the king before looking back. Hoping fervently Pitch would not take what was about to be said to be a command or order, ever mindful of pushing the prince anywhere he did not wish to go. 'We are all in need of a place to sit down, to rest. I think it best we move on quickly now.'

The prince's verdant eyes narrowed, never leaving Silas's face. 'Very well, but only because it is you asking. And you shall have to make it up to me later, for losing me my chance at mockery.'

'A chore, but one I shall endure,' Silas returned, relief sweeping through him at hearing the prince so very like himself. Scarlet giggled, the tittering like a mouse's squeak.

'You are quite changed from the creature I recall, your highness.' Jacquetta fussed at the embellished lines of her burnt-orange hose, a defiant hue amongst the golds and white. 'A true lover at your side, and friends, to boot. It is a fine thing to see, but let us hope the Beserker

Prince is not the creature needed for this task.' Seeing the angry twist of Pitch's mouth, she held up her hand. 'Do not misunderstand me, your highness. Your changes are admirable, and your happiness deserved. Yours was a greatly pained spirit. Many feared you, but I did not. You always seemed so very lost to me, and lonely. Now I see that you are neither of these things anymore.' Silas felt her eyes upon him. 'Please, if you don't mind, follow me this way.'

She turned on her heels, slippers of the same hue as her clothing, and left them in her wake.

Pitch was first to follow, pushing Edward along as the man slouched in the chair, eyes closed, chin bobbing against his chest. Silas mostly carried the ailing daemon king, and kept close behind the prince, Charlie and Scarlet, in turn, were right on his heels. They moved into the next room; past huge decorative pots with healthy palms spreading their fronds, past magnificent sideboards, and a remarkable dining table of gleaming marble, set for at least twenty places with crystal glasses and golden cutlery, past a chess board as large as the card table it sat upon. Excess and extravagance were everywhere; candles with long tapered flames lighting each room as brightly as though it were upon the stage.

As they entered the next room, the last, Jacquetta declared, Silas gazed absently at the elaborate tapestries that hung from the walls. Still mulling over what the Child had said about the Berserker Prince. Wishing he understood it fully.

Let us hope he is not the creature needed for this task.

Her meaning tormented Silas, but burned a tiny spark of hope. If she did not know if the wildness of the Hellfield prince was needed, then perhaps this truly was the very last step. Perhaps, and the thought had his pulse thumping hard, they could simply hand over the simurgh after all.

And walk away.

Edward let out a cry, banishing Silas's sombre musings. The lieutenant's body stiffened, wracked by another harsh spasm. His fingers bent to claws as muscles contracted. Charlie dashed past Silas, bumping into him in his rush.

'Edward, it's all right. Edward.'

'Please, hurry.' Spittle flew as the lieutenant sought to speak. Pitch had gone to move around the chair, but Jacquetta's shout sent him straight back to the handles.

'This way, quickly. Move.'

There was no hesitation, no snide remarks, from the prince, nothing but a heeding of the instruction. The Child tore down one of the tapestries, a peaceful scene of flowered meadows and spring lambs.

A stark iron door lay beneath. A coarse, unrefined contrast to the elegance of the rest of the palace, so far. Etched into its surface, in ink black, were the emblematic curls and flourishes of runework. There was no evident door handle.

'He is coming,' Edward spoke, though clearly under duress, his cheeks ruddy, sweat dampening his brow. 'I cannot hold him.'

'Here, come to the door.' Jacquetta stepped up to the chair, and against Charlie's shouts of alarm, she lifted Edward clear.

'What are you doing?' Charlie sought to intervene, but Pitch stepped forward, wrapping his arms about the lad, and dragging him away.

'Let them be, so this might be done.'

Silas tried to catch Pitch's eye, to get a glimpse of any pain that might lurk there. Did the simurgh roil violently within him?

But Pitch kept himself turned, away from Silas's careful eye.

Jacquetta handled Edward roughly, but there seemed no other way as the cruel twists of his body made his movements so erratic. The pair looked to be in a sort of half-hearted tussle, and with Charlie's cries growing ever more fearful, Silas considered stepping in. But Jacquetta was soothing, not demanding.

'Doing well, just a little further.' She moved him another step.

'I see the crest. Please, help me...with my hands, lift them...' Edward pleaded, or rather, instructed. He was not asking for help from any other but the Child. She obliged, clearly knowing what must be done.

'Of course, Your Grace.'

'Stop...calling me that,' he grunted. 'I am Edward, still. He does not...rule me.'

A valiant protest, from a noble man, but his struggle was horribly apparent.

Silas's distraction saw his arm loosen around the king's back, and Lucifer made a stifled grunt of pain.

'Sorry.' He quickly adjusted his hold, taking a handful of Lucifer's trousers to hoist him upright more firmly.

Pitch, with Charlie a wriggling eel in his grasp, frowned at Silas, and the frown deepened when he looked to Lucifer. But Silas shook his head. Now was not the time.

Jacquetta lifted Edward's hand. His fingers were splayed wide, but bent at the first knuckle, which were white with strain.

'There, that's it.' Edward's head jerked to one side, unsettling in how like the ravens he moved. 'Now, Child.'

Jacquetta heaved him forward, his legs bowed, his torso stiff as a board.

Edward's hand landed upon the iron.

The black markings of the runes lit piercing white.

A laborious groan came from hidden parts. The door did not swing open, rather it rolled into the frame, disappearing. Jacquetta and Edward moved across this new threshold, stepping into light as bright as that which had greeted them at the main door.

Like looking into a fledgling sun.

Pitch grunted, cursed, and lost his grip on Charlie, the lad slipping from him. Both dashed forward, one seeking to escape, the other to capture. Edward made it through the doorway, disappearing inside, but Pitch only made it as far as the threshold.

He stopped in its frame, hunching over, a quiet whimper of pain leaving him. His hands wrapped about his belly.

'Pitch, does the simurgh pain you?'

Silas cursed the burden of the sickly king, and was none too gentle about gathering him up, lifting him off his feet so they might move faster. Lucifer's low moan was not pleasing, but Silas did not like how still Pitch was in the doorway.

'What is it? Is something wrong?' Silas winced, Lucifer's heat almost too much to bear. 'Talk to me, damn it.'

Pitch turned. The light made his appearance seem gaunt and haunted. His eyes shimmered, cold chips of emerald.

'I remember, Silas. I remember this room. This is where Seraphiel kept me on my back. And it seems he's found a new plaything.'

CHAPTER 25

Pitch stepped into the room before Silas could touch him. The pained look on Silas's face, a whirl of anguish and sympathy, and unexpected hurt, had given Pitch the impetus to move, when just moments before he'd thought another step, another breath, impossible.

He stepped to one side, pressed his back against the wall.

He could not look yet at the bed, at the figure lying there. No matter how the simurgh battered his innards. Pitch felt himself at the edge of an abyss. And he was not yet ready to fall.

Fuck Seraphiel, and this game he played. If all that Pitch had left in his arsenal was avoidance, then so be it.

The room held a medieval sensibility to it. Jacquetta's clothing was not so jarring now in this space. But the lack of windows certainly was.

Their absence hadn't bothered him in the past. He remembered.

He'd been too preoccupied...or too manipulated...to wonder why the only light he ever saw was that from the candles that circled the huge lighting fixture hanging at the very centre of the room, a piece of metal large and round as a wagon wheel, and held by five link chains. It held twenty candles at its periphery; each as thick as his arm.

Twenty candles, exactly.

He knew. He'd counted them many times: in what he'd always remembered as a drunken stupor, or strong haze of enchantment, or post-coital bliss.

Pitch *remembered* this room: the fawn tiles on the floor that were always warm, the wallpaper with its busy yellow and blue design that reminded him of fleur-de-lys but with sharper tips upon the plumes, the rosewood beams with their thin trims of gold, and the coarse stone mantle with its hearth deep enough for a dozen logs. So dull compared to the florid, Baroque fashioning of the rest of the palace.

No part of which he recalled.

Had he ever been allowed from this room?

Whilst the others bustled around him, Pitch's memories fell over themselves, tangled up their pieces and pushed at him like a frightened herd of cattle. He could not make out their shape and substance.

He could not tell if a single one of them was real.

Pitch sought to keep his breath even, his mind from fraying at the edges. He dug his fingertips into his stomach, pressed down till he felt the warmth of blood. The simurgh quietened, sank deeper, gave him the space he craved.

Only then did he let his gaze settle on the bed: a rosewood four-poster, with black velvet canopy and hangings, perched upon a platform of red-painted wood.

A man lay upon a royal blue quilt, his head against black satin pillows which accentuated the spun-gold of his long, straight hair. Pale skin, a Roman nose and square jaw, with a jutting chin that held a deep cleft. Handsome, defined features; the sort of face that would have caught Pitch's eye, back when he was hungry for senseless desire.

But he had never seen this man before.

He swallowed against the immovable lump in his throat. Pitch had barely made it into the room, whilst everyone else, including Silas, moved deeper.

Pitch and the golden-haired stranger were the only points of stillness in the room. They, and the simurgh; the wildness had moved so far into its cage it could barely be felt.

The ankou approached, having settled Lucifer in an armchair he'd dragged closer to the bed. The king leaned out of the chair, his arse at the very edge. If he moved an inch more, he was likely to fall off. Scarlet took it upon themselves to grab at his shirt collar, hauling back, like the King of Daemonkind was a belligerent, bruised and battered, dog on a leash.

Lucifer did not swipe at the wisp. He barely seemed to notice them at all. He gripped the ends of the armrests, eyes locked upon the man. His expression was not one Pitch recognised as common to the king. Fear lay there, bold and unapologetic, with barely a hint of royal daemonflame to see. He was dull, Pitch thought. Too dull. But he spent little time observing his sire. Edward, wretched with unnatural twists and jerks of his body, was negotiating the platform, Charlie and Jacquetta helping him ever closer to the prone man.

To whatever play this was, in Seraphiel's end game.

Pitch watched it all, the world around him moving in a languid way, his ears stuffed with cotton, voices muffled and distant.

Silas reached him. And did not seek to drag Pitch from his place, but joined him there. Stood beside him, his back to the wall, his hand just touching Pitch's own. Not a word said, nor question asked, only offering the comfort of silence and presence. And Pitch wondered, as he did so often, if love was what he felt for this man. Because these odd feelings were intangible and indescribable, and made him troubled and euphoric at once.

Silas ran his smallest finger over the back of Pitch's hand, and together they watched as Edward sat himself beside the sleeping beauty. The lieutenant laid a hand upon the other man's chest. One that did not rise nor fall, so far as Pitch could tell.

The moment that contact was made, Pitch could see the tension drain from Edward's beleaguered body, his muscles relaxing, his head settling straight upon his shoulders. Edward was free now, to look over, and find Pitch.

Something passed between them, in that pause between now and what was to come. And Pitch feared it was regret, there upon his friend's face. Edward Charters understood it was he who must strike the flint to start this fire, that it was he who would bring a daemon prince to the altar of his fate. And it pained him.

Pitch smiled, and poured all his regard for the man into the gesture. 'It's all right,' he mouthed.

Perhaps he spoke the words aloud, he could hear nothing to tell him it was so. His blood ran too fast, made too much noise beneath his skull.

Silas's hand engulfed his, and their fingers found place among one another, as readily as petals closing over at night. The scythe was a resolute firmness in the tangle, and Pitch swore a tiny pulse came from the ring where it rested against his skin.

Edward drew back his shoulders, and nodded. He said something to Charlie, who shook his head, ever the resistant spirit. Jacquetta took hold of the lad and pulled him back, down off the platform, whispering in his ear.

Taking him out of harm's way.

Out of Seraphiel's way.

As Jacquetta continued to whisper, Charlie's fight left him. He was grim faced but compliant. He stood by. Waiting, as all the rest.

Edward leaned down, and opened his mouth. Light spilled from him. A haze as yellow as the down on a newborn chick.

Silas held on tighter, but asked nothing of Pitch. Simply reminded him it was as Silas had always promised. He was not alone.

Edward drew closer, the light spilling over the slumbering stranger's face. Another inch closer.

He brought their lips together.

The powder keg was lit.

The explosion was brilliance; sheer and blinding brilliance.

Silas's cry tore through Pitch's muffled existence, ripping away the shroud that had kept him strangely distant from the world in this room. The simurgh fluttered deeper, seeking refuge.

Silas shielded Pitch with his body, as though fearing the light had arrow tips.

As well it might. But none had a hope of seeing them coming. The glow was cataclysmic, sweeping like a wave to fill the room entirely, utterly blinding. Pitch cowered, eyes stinging, and pressed his cheek against Silas's chest, desperate for somewhere darkness could thrive.

The ankou roared, his ribs humming against Pitch's skin. Beneath the bone and flesh, his heart thundered, pounding against Pitch's ear.

He clutched at Silas's coat, terrified suddenly that the light had nasty tips after all. 'Are you hurt?' he cried. 'What is it?'

The ankou bowed his head, spreading himself over Pitch like a dark swan over its cygnet.

'Life...' he gasped. 'It is life.'

He roared again, and the light roared back, like the torrent of a mountainside waterfall. Cascading, pummelling, seeking to fill every crack and gap. Pitch clung to Silas, held on as though the torrent might sweep them both away. Because it was doing its level best to do so. The luminance brought static with it, lifting the strands on Pitch's head, prickling every fine hair on his body. Fuck. If this was life, it was unstoppable.

Pitch listened to the momentum of Silas's heart, each beat a thunderous boom. And feared what it meant for a messenger of death to bow to life.

The radiance extinguished. No warning. No waning.

Just there one moment, and vanished the next.

Thrusting them back into a world scorched with white shadows, the burning at the back of the eyes that brought tears forth.

Silas and Pitch had been floored, and neither seemed to have realised it. Pitch gazed up at Silas who braced his hands to the wall either side of Pitch's head. He was on his knees, and Pitch flat on his arse. Both blinked at one another, cheeks wet.

Pitch touched a hand to Silas's cheek. 'Are you all right?'

He was gasping, but nodded. 'You?'

'Shaken but mostly in one piece.'

That brought a welcome, tremulous smile.

'Bring him to me.'

The smile vanished. Silas's eyes narrowed. He moved to turn and follow the voice, but Pitch grabbed at his shirt. 'One more moment. Just give me one more moment.'

He didn't need to look.

The simurgh scratched at Pitch's insides. But he could not say if it was to run to or from its maker.

Silas cupped his face. 'Breathe, my darling.' He did so, gently, shifting the hairs that had fallen into Pitch's eyes. 'Breathe.'

Not so easy, not here, in this old cell, with an old master. But Pitch indulged his lover, and played at an inhale and exhale. Drinking in the heart-aching smile it drew.

'I said, bring him to me.' The angel was demanding. He'd never been anything less. Death, or whatever had befallen him, had not changed that.

Pitch abandoned his breathing lesson. 'I'm ready.'

Silas nodded grimly. 'And I'm here.'

He lifted Pitch to his feet, and stepped back, just enough to allow Pitch view of the room, but not so far that they did not still touch.

Edward was slumped by the side of the bed, groaning. Charlie crouched with him, sobbing, and indifferent to the enormity of all else. Jacquetta was on her knees at the foot of the bed, in a deep bow, one shift of the knees from prostrating herself.

That angel was now seated bolt upright. His linen nightshirt had slipped from one shoulder; his hair, ridiculously long, splayed like a golden web around him. Pitch noticed at once that this creature held no aura. No magnificence of design that screamed, *Seraphim*.

What aura should encompass the body–hugged it like a second skin–existed entirely in the angel's eyes. They glowed with an intensity that had, a short time ago, nearly sent everyone in the room blind. And those eyes were fixed upon one person.

Silas glanced at Pitch, his puzzlement obvious.

Neither of them attracted the angel's gaze.

Lucifer rose to his feet, shaking where he stood. His bruising and battery never more obvious; and barely a hint of flame survived in his gaze.

He had but one word to say. But one word was enough.

'Seraphiel.'

CHAPTER 26

Seraphiel. But how in the Celestial's name was such a resurrection possible?

Lucifer's mind rioted as he held the gaze of the angel he was so certain he'd lost. He searched, for sign of foul play, deception...anything that might explain the strangeness, the utter improbability of what was happening.

'Bring him to me, Lucifer. Am I not heard?'

'You are very much heard.' Lucifer forced the words clear. 'But that does not mean I understand what is happening here.'

Seraphiel stared unblinking, unwavering. And instantly recognisable. This golden-haired reiteration of his form was one Lucifer knew well. The angel had worn this suit of flesh on the occasions he'd lured Lucifer to the human realm with promises of new-found libraries to explore. He'd worn it as they sat beside fierce hearth fires, with aperitifs in hand; perhaps Seraphiel's head upon his shoulder, the angel exhausted by his driving obsession with Blood Lake's legacy.

The pair of them close, but never intimate; as Lucifer preferred, and Seraphiel tolerated.

But this could not be his Antinous. Lucifer had been there when Enoch delivered the killing blow, one delivered at Seraphiel's begged behest.

The angel had died. Lucifer had tasted grief ever since.

But there in the dazzling glow of his white eyes was the aura Lucifer mourned.

'One last chance. That is what this is. What you have given me.' Seraphiel did not sound as ethereal as he recalled; there was a plaintive note where none had existed before. The angel finally shifted his gaze, watching as the purebred grasped the prophet beneath the arms, seeking to drag the unconscious man away. The tiny miscreant levelled Seraphiel with a most impressive look of defiance, as though daring the angel to make any attempt to stop him. Impressive, considering how diminutive the puny creature was.

'Charlie, careful now.' The ankou of course; ever careful with his purebreds. But more so with his daemon. Silas did not leave Vassago's side, shielding the Dominion prince with his great bulk. The ankou's devotion to the daemon was as mysterious as the presence of a living, breathing angel in the bed.

'I will not leave him just lying on the floor.' Charlie hefted the prophet's arm about his shoulders, using his curious strength to lift the man, as though he were only an empty hessian sack. 'He needs help, Silas.'

Seraphiel watched, his spine stiff, his hands slack in his lap. He'd only moved to turn his head so far, like a beautiful automaton.

'Take him, Jacquetta,' Seraphiel said, and the Child fairly flew to her feet. 'The prophet has served me well. Perhaps use the east wing, there's a decent view of the loch there. And that hearth doesn't smoke so badly as the rest.'

Lucifer frowned, trying still to make sense of all that was happening.

'Yes, your grace. At once.'

'Food, if you have some. The purebreds require much of it. Some quail perhaps? With roasted potatoes? Do we still have that Rhenish wine in the cellar? Decent drop, that one.'

'Yes, your grace.' Jacquetta bobbed. 'I'll see to it.'

But Lucifer noted the subtle consternation on her face. As builder of the Sanctuary, Jacquetta knew the instability of the Seraph. She likely knew her master, as well as Lucifer himself.

'Right then, off you go.' Now Seraphiel lifted his hand. But the wave he gave was limp, his fingers hanging, the shift of his wrist floppy. 'I have things to do.'

Lucifer frowned, a lick of alarm finding him. In this ill-placed conversation he recognised something of the angel he'd known at the end, the creature whose mind had been slipping towards madness. Seraphiel would go from godly and fearsome, to speaking of the fineness of the weather, and his yearning for a plate of decent oysters, in the tick of a clock. As though he believed himself truly human, forgetting his divinity.

Lucifer acknowledged the glance the Child sent his way, as she shepherded Charlie and the prophet from the room.

'Do you need the chair?' The boy with cornflower blue eyes asked of his companion.

'No, not now. I can walk. But Christ, I'm hungry,' the one named Edward moaned. Which seemed to please the other one no end. He laughed and grasped him in one of the infernal hugs the purebreds favoured.

'Then you shall eat till you burst, sweetheart.'

'Where are they being taken?' Silas was not so keen about their exit, of course he was not. His propensity for trepidation must have been what killed him in the first place, Lucifer decided.

'It's alright, Silas. I don't think we are important enough to concern them anymore.' The small purebred was vastly intelligent. 'Keep each other safe, boys. And if you call, I'll come running.' An odd look crossed his face, as though struck by sudden revelation. 'We always do, don't we? The loch binds us...my family...to you. I was always meant to help you.'

'You never let me down. You shall always hear my call.' The big man had a way of softening that turned him from formidable to marshmallow in a heartbeat. He was all mush now. 'Scarlet, go with them, will you? It would ease our worries.'

The damned fellow couldn't even find it in himself to order about a paltry wisp. Silas was insipid, considerate and moderate, a blunderer who had managed to turn a wretched daemon blithe. Vassago was no longer mindless with violence. The Cultivation was not his master, and he was not its jailer. There would be no repeat of that day upon the cliff, over the Lethe River. Not while the ankou survived.

For the first time since the Dominion Prince's creation, Lucifer considered him worthy of the throne of Daemonkind.

The wisp nearly startled the wits out of Lucifer. It hovered in front of him, those ghastly stationery eyes even more disconcerting than the Seraph's. It bobbed in a curious curtsy, blew him an unwelcome kiss, and darted away.

He would not watch the blasted thing leave. It mattered not a jot if he saw it again.

Not a jot.

'Seraphiel.' Lucifer returned to the angel, who studied his own hands, eyes still shining like full moons. The Seraph had barely even glanced at Vassago.

At the prince who held the simurgh. The entire reason for all of this.

'Will you explain what I am seeing here? You are dead. I watched you die. I held your corpse.' The reflection scalded his tongue; the pain of that day had never subsided. Lucifer swallowed hard. Gods, he needed to sit down before he fell down, but he'd be damned if he'd show signs of weakness here. 'But I know this to be you. How has the prophet's kiss brought you back?'

'It merely released what had not yet gone.' Seraphiel peered at him, the same drilling way he'd always done. 'Are you well, Lucifer?'

'Answer my question reasonably.' He'd never feared the Seraph the way many in White Mountain had, and he'd be damned if he'd fear this spectre. 'What was in that pendant watch I delivered?'

'You are not well,' Seraphiel said, not quite a question, but not a statement either. And his staring was infernally annoying.

Of course Lucifer was not well. He'd sustained deep wounds from a Seraphim, among other injuries, but what importance did that hold now? Lucifer had Seraphiel's eyes upon him, but he knew the ankou watched carefully, too. He only hoped Death's Messenger would keep his damned bearded mouth shut about what he likely knew of a king's condition.

'Seraphiel!' Lucifer lost his thin patience. 'Answer me. How are you here?'

The angel's stare returned to him, this time with a familiar twitch of impatience at his jaw.

'Because of you. You delivered the watch and preserved the vessel that held my Cultivation.'

'Mind what you say, angel.' Silas's admonishment would have seen him imprisoned in Arcadia. 'Address the prince by his name. He is far more than your vessel.'

'Silas, it's all right. Leave it be.' Vassago played peacekeeper. A role he'd not worn once in four hundred years.

'I'll not have them speak of you in such a way.'

But Lucifer did not have time for their pitiful defence of one another. He was interested in the angel alone. 'You are explaining nothing, Seraphiel. If I did not hold your corpse in my arms that day, then what the bloody hell was it?'

'Our Lord Enoch did what had to be done, but I had foreseen such a day arriving.'

'A day you would die?'

'Yes. The Seraph are not immortal, you know that.' The angel's gaze finally found the prince, but there seemed no great recognition, no acknowledgement of all he had worked for, standing before him. 'I knew myself tainted. Samyaza's curse upon the waters of Blood Lake makes it deadly for any of the Seraph. But I had worked so long on my Cultivations and knew none of them strong enough to withstand the lake. I needed something extraordinary to fortify my work. I needed a drop...just a drop of those waters, Luci, that was all.' He spoke to Lucifer, but he looked only to Vassago. Silas glared, one arm thrown to shield the prince's body. 'And then I would finally have what I needed to bring that traitor down.'

Lucifer dared to stand, tested his trembling legs, and found them wanting. 'But that was not all you needed, was it, Raph? You stole the Primordial Flame, you great fool, and Michael knows of it. He searches for this place. Why would you do such a thing? Little wonder, you are...' he hesitated. 'You are not what you once were.'

Lucifer looked away, determined none would see any hint of his pain. He felt the flame's poison eating at him. He felt every one of his wounds, even down to the infinitesimal bruise on the tip of his nose from the wisp. He felt bloody awful. Lucifer was no god; Michael was right in that. But he was no lesser daemon either. His fight would be to the last.

He lifted his head to find himself once again scrutinised by the angel. Seraphiel had not moved, nor made an attempt to do so, sitting like a bed-bound invalid, but he could pin a man down, nonetheless.

'You know of the Primordial Flame?'

Lucifer cursed himself for the furtive glance he directed at Silas, but Vassago mistook the look as meant for him.

'I am aware the simurgh holds the flame.' He was sharp, vigilant. 'Now I am to believe the water of Blood Lake in me also?'

'Not believe, but know.' Seraphiel addressed the prince for the first time. 'For it is so. The adversaries of water and flame, forced into allegiance.'

'And it killed you.' Lucifer gave in to the need to brace himself against the chair. He'd thought to move to the bed, but just the notion of lifting his violated leg up to the platform had him sickened.

Seraphiel bunched the linen in his hand, frowning down at it. As though he could not recall the next step necessary to get out of bed. 'Much of me, yes. That which was rotted, and wasted away. But I had thought myself clever. I thought this piece I saved, to be pure. But now...I fear you and I are as broken as each other, Luci.' He lifted the covers, pushing them clear. Seraphiel moved with wooden slowness, making his way slowly to where he could slip his legs over the edge of the bed, and touch his feet to the floor. The angel sat there, back straight as though a corset lay below his simple linen nightgown, but still clutched at the hanging, as though he might deflate at any moment. Lucifer desired to go to him, to aid him, but to let go of the armchair was to fall flat on his face.

What a miserable pair they were. Antinous and Hadrian would be appalled to know their names adopted by such dismal creatures.

'What do you mean, piece?' Vassago, in contrast, was robust. Demanding. 'What did you do to Edward, you bastard?'

Seraphiel concentrated on his feet, as though trying to understand what next to do with them. It made Lucifer's chest ache all the more. 'The prophet received a blessing from me, Prince of Arcadia. One spark of my Creation Flame existing and thriving inside him, should all else start to wither and die. As it did. The watch held the spellwork I would use to set the wheels in motion, should there come a time when all that remained of my presence lay in that purebred man.'

'You placed Angelic creation fire in Edward?' Vassago fumed. 'You thought a simple man, a purebred, could withstand the likes of you?'

Seraphiel turned his head. His scrutiny was intense, the vibrancy of his eyes intensifying. 'He'd weathered my possession often enough. I knew him strong, and capable of surviving. In the short term at least, albeit the end would be grisly –'

'You drove him fucking mad.' Vassago pushed free of Silas's wary protection. 'But you let me believe it was my doing. I cannot count the number of ways I despise you.'

Seraphiel found his feet. He stood and the wood cracked beneath him. The room shook. Lucifer dug his nails into the leather, the ghost-feel of his lost finger there to taunt him.

'I do not need, nor desire, your devotion, Dominion.' The angel stepped down onto the tiles, and a long, winding crack ran across the room, stopping where Vassago stood with fists clenched and his revulsion unconcealed. 'Your hatred is even less of a concern to me. What I have done here is far greater than you, or your purebred, or this cretinous ankou.' His gaze shifted to Silas. 'There is something peculiar in you. Go. There is no need of you, anymore.'

Lucifer winced. And not solely from the pain. If he'd needed any convincing this was truly Seraphiel, it was gone now. The Seraph were blunt, arrogant creatures. Focused servants of the Lord who stood just one step below the Celestials. Seraphiel would truly believe he could dismiss Silas Mercer with a simple word.

'He will not leave me,' Vassago said, cool with certainty. No hint of his flame. 'And you are not his master.'

'But I am yours. Step forward. Let me see the Cultivation.'

The prince's smile held no warmth, and lifted only one corner of his mouth. 'You are the simurgh's master, not mine. I have done as you designed. I have carried your freakish child, and now I deliver it to you. So take your fucking bird, and then piss off and die, completely this time.'

Seraphiel stood so rigidly, so without hint of whether his ire was raised. Lucifer had been able to read the Seraph well, but this was not the whole creature he had known.

'Death is a certainty for all, save the gods,' Seraphiel said. 'Or does the ankou promise you otherwise, so you shall warm his bed, just as I promised you pleasures that no other incubus had known, so you would fall into mine?' He tossed his head, sending the gold shimmering in his hair. 'You were so very easy to manipulate.'

Lucifer shifted the weight on his feet, wishing this throwing of insults over, so he could sit down and nurse his pains. He braced, thinking that even Vassago's newfound discipline would not withstand these insults. But no unfurling of daemonic flame came.

The prince tilted his head, biting at absurdly plump, pink lips. 'I was, yes. But you have been an ugly sleeping beauty for a while now. You shall find me much changed.'

'Then all is lost, if you are not still wild.'

Seraphiel slumped, all the stiffness going from him. He collapsed and Lucifer found himself moving. Reaching. Catching at the angel before he toppled. Fighting his way through a flare of golden-hair to ease him onto the bed once more. There was no gratitude to be found.

'Leave me,' Seraphiel said, petulant and utterly like himself. Trying to rise again. 'I am not broken. If you'd done as I asked sooner, I'd not be like a mummy just unwrapped from their sarcophagus. Too much time has passed.'

Lucifer would have flung insult right back at the angel, in distant times, and they would have parried back and forth. But he had little strength for such things now. 'We are here now. Vassago brings you the simurgh.'

'Did I call it that, Luci?' The angel pressed at his temple, his demeanour shifting swiftly as a wind-change. Gone was the imperious Seraph, returned was the simpler creature. 'Is that what I have made? A simurgh?'

Lucifer saw the look that passed between Silas and Vassago. One laced with more than a little desperation.

'What the fuck is wrong with him?' Vassago demanded. 'Why did he say all is lost?'

'Just give him a moment,' Lucifer replied.

'We keep being told we don't have any left to give.'

Seraphiel's head jerked, and he turned to find Vassago. 'The prince. You are here.' He looked back at Lucifer, eyes like starpoints. 'Do you see, Luci? I told you he was strong. That he was the one. Your spawn. The vessel could only ever come from one of your bloodline, for that is where might lies. Do you remember I said so?'

'I do.' Lucifer's very tired heart sank a little further. 'But you have seen Prince Vassago already this day.'

The angel's features shifted with their first semblance of emotion. 'I have, haven't I? I recall now. He has the Cultivation with him. He has an ankou with him. Strange fellow.'

'He brings the Cultivation, yes. Though I fear it has been damaged. There was an incident...with an Archangel, and the Exarch, and...' He went no further. So he would tell no lies. His decision to bring Wrath upon the cockaigne had nearly prevented this moment existing at all.

'Was it they who hurt you, Luci? You are dying.' Ever blunt. Empathy barely a smear.

Vassago swore, but the ankou quietened him.

'No, no, it was not them. And I shall heal.' Even as he spoke, Lucifer's body rotted, but now more than ever there was need to keep his wits. For the angel was barely holding onto his. 'Do not focus on that. The simurgh, the Cultivation, is what is important. And you will need to see to it, before you send it into the lake.'

'With the prince who is no longer a Berserker, there may be no point.'

'Tell me what you mean,' Vassago said. He and Silas moved closer, cautious, and with the ankou's tension seeping from him. His shadow held court upon the floor, darkening the cracks that Seraphiel had made.

'You said you have changed.' The angel still held his rigid pose. As though he could not shift from the laid out position they'd found him in. Perhaps it truly had been too long. 'If he is no longer wild–the mad prince–if he has lost his lust for blood and violence, then he is not enough for a lake that holds little else. The Cultivation's power comes from the strength he provides, and he is made stronger for its power. A symbiosis I sought to perfect.'

Seraphiel had found coherence, but how long it would last this time, Lucifer could only guess.

'So I am not just your vessel.' Vassago's voice cracked the silence. 'I am your entire monster, after all.'

Resignation underscored his words, and Lucifer knew from the downcast look on Silas's face that both these fools had believed this was a simple case of delivering the simurgh, and being done.

'Did you care to be anything else?' Seraphiel's eyes cast a glow over the bed linen as he found the prince. 'It never seemed so to me. You were voracious in all appetites, and made no apology for it.'

The ankou was utterly predictable in his interference. 'He has always been more than what you assumed of him.'

'He shall need to be.'

'Is there no other way?' Silas pressed. 'He must enter the lake?'

Seraphiel shifted his shoulders, there was no flexibility there for him, so he moved like one stuck in a strait-jacket. 'Of course he must enter Blood Lake, there was never any other way. How else shall he destroy the halo? What fool question is that?'

Vassago chewed at his bottom lip, his arms crossed at his belly. The ankou looked evermore like a dark thundercloud, though he gathered the prince into his arms with a butterfly's delicacy.

Neither of the fools said a word.

No one did, until Seraphiel turned to Lucifer, his mouth twisted with indignation.

'Why am I in bedclothes, Luci?' His hair moved like spiderweb in a breeze. 'I have no need for sleep. Get me up at once.'

Lucifer's exhaustion swept him anew. His own injuries drained him, but it was the ruin of the angel that made his knees weakest of all. Seraphiel hung by a delicate thread to the life he had reclaimed; his mind as damaged as it had ever been.

He could not look at Vassago. For he knew what he'd see there. Doubt, prickly as a rash from the sun. What hope did this Cultivation have, in light of its creators failing state?

Lucifer said nothing, merely nodded, when the ankou brought the vacant wheelchair to the side of the bed, and lifted the curt and exacting angel onto its seat, saying nothing as Seraphiel ordered him as if he were a valet, and not a lord of death.

Lucifer stood, teeth ground against his revolting pains, grateful for the handles against which he could brace himself. He refused an offer from Silas to wheel the snappish angel to the north wing; where a dressing room he preferred was located. The journey sounded torturous, but what was a few more arduous steps?

'No. I have him.'

After all, Seraphiel had said it plainly enough. He was only here, *because of you.*

Lucifer had begun this; now he must survive until the game played out to its end.

CHAPTER 27

Pitch straddled Silas's lap, where the ankou lay across a window seat marvelling at the array of blooms in the courtyard below. The bay window was diamond latticed–much like the one Pitch had awoken next to, after the Fulbourn–and afforded a fine view. Milky water spilled from another grand fountain. This centrepiece was a depiction of a creature, part horse, part mermaid; teeth bared, its mane a luxurious flow of carved marble, its lower half all sea creature, with a wide fluted tail.

Pitch could not bear to look at it. He was unsteady enough after the meeting with the angel. To remember Lalassu now was too much.

'Look at all those musk orchids,' Silas said, his back propped against silk damask cushions. 'They are lovely though, don't you think?'

Pitch hummed in the same noncommittal way he'd been using for the past twenty minutes, tracing his fingers over the smooth velvet of Silas's vest. A jerkin, in keeping with the odd affinity for clothes of eras past that Jacquetta seemed to relish. But by the gods, how the style suited the ankou.

By strange coincidence, or simply because the colour suited him so well, the jerkin laid out for Silas was royal blue, the same shade exactly as the ankou's beloved Inverness coat. Black trim around the embellishments at the shoulders and waist made the jerkin even more reminiscent of that coat.

Pitch ran his finger over the trim. The tightness of the fit accentuated the broadness of his ankou's shoulders, the solidness of his girth.

'You like this outfit?' Silas asked, deep and soothing.

Pitch nodded and tapped his nail against each of the gun-metal grey buttons that ran down the jerkin's front; worn over a black satin doublet which was fastened tight at the wrists. Black leather trousers completed the ensemble, trousers that were far tighter than Silas liked, and he had said so a dozen times already. But they were exactly tight enough, as far as Pitch was concerned. He sighed and curled his fingers into his fist. His thoughts kept straying to the damage done to Lucifer's hand. His vestige gone. Torn free by Michael.

The Seraph was not known for complacency. He'd hardly scurry back to his rooms at White Mountain because of one fire-lashing from a couple of errant daemons.

Michael would hunt.

Pitch leaned back, resting against Silas's raised thighs. The ankou lay with his knees raised to accommodate the shortness of the seat and his considerable length. Pitch's fingers followed each line of the criss-cross laces on Silas's trouser front.

Jacquetta had directed them to a dressing room–deep within the meandering halls of the massive palace–where hose had been set out for them to wear. The Child had seemed surprised at Pitch's refusal.

'You enjoyed the frivolity of fashion in the past. These were among your favourite.'

All the more reason to refuse them now.

'Trousers,' he'd replied, and Silas's relief had been tangible.

She'd returned with simple linen for Pitch, and these sublimely cut black leather trousers for Silas. Pitch moved from the laces–where Silas's cock was nicely pronounced beneath the material–and cupped his hand to the bulge. But he did not hunger. Instead, he sought to take each part of Silas and carve it into his memory, setting every curve in stone.

'Are we going to sit here just discussing flowers, Silas?'

The ankou set his hand to Pitch's cheek, his fingers touching the dampness of the hair framing Pitch's face. It had been a welcome relief to see washbasins full of warm water, and thick washcloths. Pitch had scrubbed hard at the dirt on his cheeks and the scent of Lalassu on his hands.

'Are you in the mood for firmer things?' Silas said, his fingers splayed against Pitch's thigh. 'I am not sure how well I can oblige you, darling. My stomach is in knots.'

'I don't want us to fuck.' Pitch tilted his head back, and his hair slipped in beneath the flat collar of his shirt, tickling at his skin. 'I should be hung, drawn and quartered for such blasphemy, but desire is not upon me either.'

Silas chuckled. 'Not now, perhaps. But what a fine day we'll have when this is done.'

Pitch's head snapped forward, and heat spread through his eyes. 'That is what I wish to talk about. You should stay here, and I should go on alone.'

He'd hardly expected peaceful acquiescence, nor did he get it. Silas grabbed his waist, and swung them both about, setting his feet on the floor, holding Pitch firm against his knees, glaring at him.

'There is no discussion to be had here,' Silas said.

'You've seen the state of Seraphiel. He's fit for residency in an asylum, but if what he says is so, I will need to be just as mindless to see this done. The lake was already too dangerous for you, and now it is intolerably so.'

'Utter rot. Don't test me on this, Pitch. I am no weakling.'

'No, but you are a handsome dead man, and I don't fancy seeing you otherwise.' Pitch put on his very best coy smile, whilst his ribs felt ready to shatter with rising desperation.

'I will be there with you. You are wasting your breath.'

Pitch wriggled against the impudent fellow. 'Let me go, Silas.'

'You're not going in there alone. End of discussion.'

Silas was more than handsome; with his belligerence brightening his cheeks, and the tight clench of his jaw causing muscles in his neck to work. Defiance made Silas breathtaking.

'I meant, let me off your lap. Don't hold so tight.'

The release was instant and the apology ready. 'Sorry.'

'Forgiven.'

'Then this discussion is done with.'

Oh, good gods, the sternness was prick-stiffening. On any other occasion, Pitch would strip Silas's trousers off and impale himself at once.

But this occasion did not lend itself to carnality.

'Fine.'

Pitch turned away and walked to the sideboard, where a pottery pitcher and matching cups sat. The tang of cider was evident. He poured himself a serve of the warm liquid, another for Silas. All the while, his mind worked furiously, searching for a clear path to follow; anywhere the Berserker Prince must be was not a place he'd allow Silas Mercer to set foot.

They sat quietly, sipping on the cider. It was warm and sweet, and Pitch would have devoured the entire pitcher; again, on any other occasion.

The Sanctuary had stolen every appetite from him; overwhelming in its grandeur, its memories, and the threshold it signified.

After a time, the soft pad of footsteps came from beyond the double doors with their gold motifs and wheat-field handles glowing. Jacquetta appeared, changed as well, into an ankle-length tunic, belted at the waist, with long draping sleeves. It was one-tone silver, a clear flouting of the obvious palace theme of gold.

'Your Highness, they are ready for you. I will show you the way.'

When Silas rose with Pitch, she shook her head. 'Just the prince, my lord. That is my instruction.'

'Absolutely not.' Silas set down his cup in a way that made his already obvious displeasure plainer still.

But here was a chance for Pitch to make sense of his tangled thoughts. A moment away from Silas to think straight.

'If that has been instructed, then that is what will be done.' Pitch picked at loose cotton on his long white shirt. Its billowed sleeves felt like blasted wings, the clothing so damned oversized. 'The Seraph wishes to know the state of the simurgh. You heard the message earlier. I'm not about to go running off into the lake, considering we know there is damage done to the bird. But it is sensible that you are not present when a delusional angel is playing with divine magick.'

'That is *exactly* when I should be present.'

Jacquetta's bluntness proved useful as she said, "You are not invited, my lord."

'I don't need a bloody invitation.' Silas fumed, his neck reddening.

Sensing that this argument could go on until the next turning of the tide, Pitch ruled with an iron, somewhat cruel fist.

'I don't want you there.' He tilted his chin, determined not to let the hurt in Silas's eyes affect him. 'It shall be bad enough being poked and prodded yet again, without knowing that you stand there as witness. The simurgh was taken from me once already, and it was not a pretty scene. I know it will not make you happy, which will make the experience far worse for me than it has ever been.' He looked to Jacquetta to escape the ankou's visible distress and forthcoming protest. 'Jacquetta, after I am delivered, take Mr Mercer to Charlie and Edward, and Scarlet.'

'Of course, my lord. They are resting currently. The prophet is much revived.'

'It would be best if we judged that for ourselves. That is why you will take Lord Death there whilst I see to the simurgh.'

Silas muttered against the title, but otherwise stayed agreeable; as Pitch had known he would. The rare thing that could separate Silas from Pitch's side was his love for those he called friends.

And it was not as though Pitch himself held no concerns for the purebreds and the wisp; he'd find comfort too, knowing they were safe.

Silas insisted on a kiss, and Pitch did not deny him. Brief but deep, it held a comfortable intimacy, though was spliced with a violent longing that threatened to engulf Pitch. He pulled from the kiss first; and stepped away without another word.

He followed Jacquetta with the ankou's wetness on his lips, and a lovely pain on the tip of his tongue from Silas's teeth. He'd been forceful, more so than normal; as though leaving Pitch with a reminder that he was here; or irritated at being left behind.

But if Silas had known the thoughts that jostled for position in Pitch's mind, the growing plan, he would have never have just stood there and watched him go.

Pitch was guided through long hallways and down several flights of stairs, using spiral staircases that left him dizzy. More halls followed, some expansive, lined with mirrors that reflected the white air, giving the impression of walking outside, beneath rows of heavy crystal chandeliers. The floors were so polished in places it was like mirrors lay there, too. All of it combined to give the place a sense of vastness that was unsettling.

He paused at one point, a dark corridor catching his eye. It was the only hint of gloom he'd seen since they stepped foot inside a palace that glowed.

'Not that way.' Jacquetta had been terse, immediately bobbing her head in apology. 'Sorry, your highness. But that is not the way.'

Pitch briefly considered telling her what she could do with her way, and heading down there regardless. But the simurgh stirred: hidden deep, making its presence known.

He kept on.

They travelled down another set of stairs, then another, until they were in the cellar, a domed room with a low ceiling and rack after rack of wine bottles, many with cobwebs and thick dust coating them. No wonder Seraphiel had been so adept at keeping Pitch inebriated here. This supply would take a decade to work through.

The simurgh brushed along the bottom of his ribs, slipping around his spine. The first definitive movement from the Cultivation since Seraphiel's awakening. There was no pain, but the sensation itself was ghoulish; as though the creature was trying on his skin for size or perhaps looking for an escape route. Who was not?

'Will this travel never end? I'll be another hundred years old before I see Seraphiel, at this rate.'

Jacquetta produced a ridiculously huge key from the equally large drop of her sleeve. 'We are here, your highness.'

'My name is Pitch.'

She said nothing, and kept on to where there was a simple wooden door, thick panels, with black iron reinforcing it; Pitch noted the surplus of subtle runework on the wood.

'This is as far as I go, your highness. They are waiting on you.'

The Child inserted the key into a lock whose large opening Pitch could have slipped four fingers into. Sparks jumped at the key's touch, and the waft of orange blossom briefly filled the air. Faerie magick always tended on the pretty side; even the UnSeelie cockaigne had not been without beauty.

Leaving the door closed, Jacquetta hurried away, promising to head straight back to Silas.

'Come in, hurry up,' Seraphiel called. 'Why are you just standing there?'

Patience was not a virtue of Higher Angels, nor of a princely daemon for that matter. The door swung open, perfectly silent.

Pitch bent to accommodate the low roof of the doorway, and stepped into what appeared to be little more than an extension of the cellar–minus the plentiful supply wine–but with the uncomfortable addition of a rectangular metal table, one that would fit nicely in a mortuary.

He looked away. Lucifer was in the invalid chair. The poor bastard still looked dreadful, but both he and Seraphiel wore outrageously elaborate coats.

Seraphiel had his long golden hair now tousled with curls, and looked ridiculous in a white satin justaucorps; with thick gold embroidery upon its deep pockets and enormous cuffs, and heavy braid work at the flare of its knee-length hem. White stockings defined a pair of muscular legs and accentuated his red heels.

'Are you preparing to whisk back in time and join the Sun King in his court at Versailles?' Pitch made no pretence of enjoying the angel's elaborate look, not only was it gaudy, but it made him feel near naked for how under-dressed he was; and vulnerable. 'What on Earth are you wearing?'

'Clothes hardly matter, Vassago.' Lucifer's coat was a deep crimson, with the requisite gold trim. He wore breeches, and plain black shoes, so polished Pitch could have shaved with them as his mirror. Perhaps the king had done that, for his own moustache was gone. He was clean shaven, but still looked like he needed a decent wash; thanks to the patchwork of bruises, which seemed worse, not better.

'Are you not healing?' Pitch frowned. 'Or was the angel far too rough with you in his bed?'

Lucifer smoothed at his already slicked hair, glaring his very best glare. No hint of daemonflame in his irises, though. Another anomaly, considering how readily he usually flared with temper when Pitch was around.

'Get on the bench.' Seraphiel drew on a pair of gloves. Surprisingly, not gold, but the duller grey of chain mail; *actual* chain-mail.

'I prefer to stand.'

Pitch shot up into the air, a pressure throwing him onto his back, lifting him up and over the metal bench.

'Fuck, set me down. Now!' He flailed his arms, and kicked his legs, like a child in the throes of a tantrum. He was dumped onto the table; a surface cold and hard.

The simurgh fed on his distress, losing its feathery mind: pressing at his stomach, stabbing at his hips, causing a scream to slip through grinding teeth.

'Let me be.' Pitch reached for his flame, trying to find its brilliance in the calamity. Only the merest warmth rose to find him. He was being suppressed. 'You cunt, let me fucking go.'

What moron was he, to have left Silas behind?

'Calm down, Vassago.' Lucifer offered unwelcome advice.

'Fuck off.' Pitch bucked his arse off the table, groaning with the effort of fighting off a pressure that urged his legs to part.

A futile effort, evidently. Each leg moved, a heel to each corner of the table. The resounding crack of restraints came; at the same time their coldness met the bare skin at his ankles. Memories were pounding at the back of his head, trying to force their way through bone.

'Don't tie me down, fuck...don't do this.'

Seraphiel stood by, still adjusting the fit of his gloves. 'As always, the sooner you calm, the sooner this shall be over. I need to examine the simurgh.'

Pitch's arms were thrust over his head, and restraints slipped around his wrist. He cried out. The pounding in his skull was excruciating.

As always: those two words shifted the stones weighing down his memories.

He'd been held here before; laid out and tied down, many, many times by this angel.

Panic was a wild stallion, stealing his breath, making his vision red and blurry with the crush of his trapped flame. He thrashed his head back and forth, trying to roll his shoulders, his hips, anything that would at least let him pretend he could escape this.

This is where he had been manipulated, and made a freak in Seraphiel's show. How could he forget?

His thoughts screamed, and barriers came crashing down.

This room was where he'd truly been trapped. Not that other; where he recalled lounging between silk sheets, or taking long, hot baths with a whisky in one hand and sweet cake in the other after he'd laid with the angel. That other room was illusion, or distorted reality at best; a dumping ground for when Seraphiel was done with him.

Here was where Pitch had actually suffered; worked upon and weaponised without agency, his freedom stolen.

'I said fucking let me go.' If he roared loud enough, would Silas hear? Fuck, fuck. No. Stupid idea. Seraphiel would destroy him.

Pitch's chest heaved. The simurgh was a colt to his panic's stallion, kicking its silvered heels against his organs, thrashing itself mindless as Pitch's fear caught like kindling and burned them both.

'Will this go on much longer?' Seraphiel was cold, clinical as he'd been every other time.

'I don't need your chains, you arsehole. It is by my own free will I am here.' Pitch was screeching, sounding every inch the maniac he felt; and with the way the simurgh flew like a mad hawk within him, he'd be bleeding out of his orifices before long.

'Stop. There is no need to restrain him.'

Lucifer wheeled his chair closer and touched a hand to Pitch's shin, just above one of the cruel shackles. Pitch stilled, gasping.

'There has always been a need in the past.' Seraphiel frowned.

'But that time is over, Raph. Just as you are not the angel you were, nor is Vassago the same daemon you worked upon. Let him be. He does not seek to escape his fate.'

Even the simurgh seemed lulled by the daemon's speech; reducing its chaotic scrambling to a quieter restlessness. Pitch hissed his breath, trying to gather himself; wrench back from the precipice.

He let his head rest against the metal; nekhri he'd assume, for how powerfully it bound him. Pitch waited for the two powerful lords of Arcadia as they duelled in a silent battle of wills. He had thought he and Silas the strangest of lovers, but here were the true champions of that title: a sexless king and a mad angel.

Seraphiel's lips twitched, his eyes ever radiant, but the creases at their sides hinted at a frown. With a tight nod, he turned away.

'Fine. I have no time to argue with two stubborn creatures. But if you cannot keep perfectly still, daemon, it will be unpleasant.'

'I am well aware of how much it hurts,' Pitch said.

Seraphiel's surprise was farcical. 'You remember?'

'That you tortured me? And that your supposed prowess in the bedchamber was all imaginary? Yes. But I know too because the simurgh was taken from me by the Morrigan.'

Shadows rippled over the angel's face, and he looked beyond Pitch, beyond where Lucifer worked at the restraint around his ankle.

'Do not gloat, you fiend.' Seraphiel's grin was poorly shaped. 'Do not listen to this and think you have won. You'll not take it from him again, Samyaza. Do you hear me?'

Seraphiel spoke to the wall; where runes flourished, crawling over the stonework like pretty serpents, covering every inch of the cellar. But nothing else, and no one else, was there.

'Raph, keep your focus upon the prince,' Lucifer said, still working at Pitch's restraint. 'The Watcher King does not hear you.'

The cuff came free from one of Pitch's ankles, and the next followed quickly.

'Oh, he taunts me, Luci.' Seraphiel's laugh was part hiccup. 'You do not hear what he whispers. He challenges me to fail.'

Lucifer's shoulder's lifted with a silent sigh. 'Very well, then best you meet his challenge.'

He unlocked the restraints at Pitch's wrists and moved away. The king pushed at the rounded metal of the chair's wheels, moving himself to where the roof curved low and would likely have brushed the top of his head were Lucifer not sitting with shoulders so hunched, and head lowered. Pitch had never seen the daemon so boneless, in all the years of studying his arrogance.

Seraphiel appeared, sudden and bright-eyed, standing over Pitch, who barely had time to lower his arms, and rub at the abrasions there.

The angel handed him a short length of wood, not much larger than a clothes peg, and about as round.

'Take this. Bite into it.' Seraphiel's eyes grew shockingly white and bright. 'If you truly remember as you say, then you will know that what I am about to do makes you wish your life was already over.'

245

CHAPTER 28

Silas embraced Charlie, holding on tight while the lad regaled him with talk of the tastiness of the cockle soup Jacquetta had arranged.

'Astonishing, Silas you must have some. The saltiness is heaven-sent.' Charlie laughed, giving Silas another squeeze before letting go. 'Oh, I am so glad Tobias wasn't here to hear that said. You know he'd make something vile of it. Where is he?'

The lad wore fresh clothes, as did Edward: simple fare of white linen shirts with unbuttoned, dark green and burgundy vests respectively, and with loose-fitting, chestnut brown trousers tied at the waist. They looked enviably comfortable.

Charlie peered around Silas to the doors which had shut firmly behind him once he entered the wood-panelled parlour; a warm and inviting room with its plentiful settee and armchairs, heavy curtains of a sunlight gold, a modest rounded dining table that held a multitude of platters and covered bowls.

'He's with you, is he not, Silas?' Edward had a forkful of mashed potatoes halfway to his mouth, his plate already scraped half clean by a pleasing return of appetite.

'No. Not yet. He will join us eventually.' Silas adjusted his collar, finding it too tight suddenly. He'd agreed to this separation with an ill-feeling. 'He wished time with Seraphiel alone. They must investigate the soundness of the simurgh.'

He kept his reply measured, but something in Pitch's manner bothered him, and he certainly wasn't happy with him being alone in the company of the angel and daemon: one of whom seemed barely sane, the other in a shockingly poor state. Silas would never fully trust Lucifer–he'd not be so foolish–but even if the king had fully sided with Pitch and sought to keep him from harm, he barely had the strength to lift his own eyelashes; let alone fend off a Seraph.

Edward swallowed his mouthful. 'Simurgh? Ah, you mean the fire he carries.' He nodded. 'I felt something of it when I touched him as I recovered after the Fulbourn. If I recall, I ended up being thrown out of bed with the force. And nearly punched in the mouth by Tobias, because of it.'

'Do you remember much of the Fulbourn, of all that followed?' Silas asked. 'You were so very unwell.'

Edward's smile was grim. 'Indeed, I was. I remember small things. Just fragments, really. Mostly there was light, just light. Golden, and not so terrible. But what struck me most was the loneliness.' He glanced at Charlie. 'I knew you all to be so close. I could hear you speaking to me, tending me, caring for me... but I was...well, I was truly a world away.' He smiled, but it was rather downcast. He set down his fork. 'Will he be all right, Silas? I know he is strong, but do they place too much upon his shoulders?'

Silas let his hand fall from his collar. He adjusted the set of the jerkin. 'They have always done that, and he has always met their challenge. He will see this through. And I, with him.'

Charlie took Silas's hand. 'And what a formidable union it is. Now come, have something to eat with us. Whatever lays ahead, best it's not done on an empty stomach.'

'I'm not much hungry.' He frowned. 'Where is Scarlet?'

'They insisted I open the window, and promptly flew off. I think they rather enjoy hiding in those enormous roses.'

Silas eyed the window, but they were several levels up, and there was no sign of the bountiful gardens. An odd irritation found him at Scarlet's frivolity. This was hardly time for play. 'Mr Mercer, will you stop with all that frowning?' Charlie adopted the curt admonishment a nanny might give a protesting child. 'Come on, quickly now and have some food before it cools further. I won't hear another word said. Look at you, you are fairly fading away, skin and bone.' He winked, letting it be known he thought his own words utter nonsense.

Edward joined in the charade of lightheartedness. 'Trust me, my dear fellow, you are best to do as you're told here. Charlie will make a frighteningly stern father one day.'

Silas had barely taken his seat when the door opened and Jacquetta entered, pushing a large trolley where something lay covered beneath a white cloth.

'Everything to your liking?' she asked.

'Very much so,' Charlie replied. 'But I don't suppose there shall be any dessert? Not for me, mind, but I have a friend who would cheer to see a strawberry tart or sponge cake with all the cream you can whip.'

'The prince, you mean? Already underway. He's always had a penchant for sweeter things.' Jacquetta sent a sidelong look Silas's way. 'They'll be ready for him as soon as he's able.'

As soon as he's able.

What a sour feeling those words pushed through Silas. He was one breath away from demanding to be taken to Pitch that instant, when Jacquetta pulled away the cloth, revealing an ornate dressing-table mirror beneath. It was triple-panelled, with the centrepiece largest, and smaller at the wings.

'I thought this may help you while away the time, distract you, perhaps.' She lifted it, and it was evident the piece was heavy, with its thick plasterwork edges that scrolled like faded gold parchment, and curled feet at the base of each panel. The glass was onyx black. Silas's thoughts went immediately to the obsidian in the ashmen's eyes.

'This is a scrying mirror?' He abandoned the serving of food Charlie had just delivered and moved to assist.

'Out of my way now.' Jacquetta scowled until he stepped back. 'Don't think I'd be as levelheaded as I am, if I hadn't been able to take a peek at how the world was living.' She set the mirror down with a grunt, fussing at it until it was set to her satisfaction upon a sideboard of whitewashed wood and sparkling crystal handles.

The blackness of the glass seemed viscous. As though to touch it was to dip your finger into tar. Silas stared at his reflection. His beard needed trimming, and he looked as troubled as he felt.

'Why have you brought it here? Has the angel found us?' His stomach turned, the rich smells of the food now nauseating.

'The one who killed your horse?'

Charlie let loose a brief cry. 'Is there a need to be so blunt?'

But Silas gave the Child a steely glare. He could not afford the ache that came with thinking of Lalassu. The hurt was bottled up tight, for now. 'Yes. That one.'

'No. The Ferryman brings no word of his return. But we are watching.' Jacquetta adjusted the side panel of the mirror, bringing the angle in sharper, so the display sat curved like a fire screen. 'And your mare was a fine djinn. Her defence of the cave continues, even if she does not. The Red Horse grows herself strong from the White Horse's roots. Noble steeds.'

It was a peace offering for her bluntness. 'They are the noblest,' he said, clearing the thickness from his throat. 'Now what of this mirror?'

'A distraction. Charlie tells me you both share a connection to the loch, and the residence on its shores. I thought perhaps you may like to study them more closely.' She kissed the tips of her fingers, then touched them to each of the panes of glass.

The surfaces swirled; like colours produced by the hint of oil in water.

Rossdhu House appeared in the distance, from a viewpoint out upon the loch. Charlie let out a choked cry.

'Edward, come and see.' But the scrape of chair legs was already underway, the quick thump of feet on floorboards as Edward joined them.

'It shall not last long.' Jacquetta stepped back. 'And you can go no further or wider than the house. It takes too much of my magick for that, and I'll be needing to reinforce the Sanctuary boundaries now you're all in. Just touch the glass to show it where you want to go, and two taps to draw you in closer. Think of it like a flat out telescope. Alright then?'

Silas mumbled a reply, fixated on the mirrors. Charlie pulled Edward in closer. And Jacquetta left them with a subtle rattling of the trolley.

'I haven't used a telescope,' Charlie said. 'What does it do?'

'Makes the world smaller and closer.' Edward nudged Charlie. 'Go on then. Show me your favourite place in that wonderful garden. Your gardener is truly talented.'

Charlie lifted his hand, hovering his finger above the glass. But did not move to touch it.

'Is something wrong?' Edward asked.

'The garden is lovely, our family's pride and joy...and I know I said I'd like you to visit...but...' Charlie's throat bobbed as he swallowed.

'You fled your home for good reason,' Silas said, softly. 'You were not happy there. If it troubles you, we need not look at all.'

He did not know which way he hoped the lad's choice would go. Silas himself was torn about what a closer study of the estate would do to his own state of mind; already punched full of holes of worry and trepidation. And this was, as Jacquetta had said, a mere distraction. But he wasn't sure he wished to be distracted from the thought of what Pitch endured in that moment.

Charlie shook his shoulders, a firmly exaggerated motion, and blew out a breath. 'Bloody hell, I'm being ridiculous. After all we've been through, and I'm frightened I might lay eyes upon my father?'

Edward settled a hand on Charlie's shoulder. 'I'm not sure it's foolish at all. If this were my mother's home, I'd have this mirror turned to the wall in a heartbeat.' He shook his head. 'She'd have a row of potential brides lined up for my return, and my trunks packed for the blasted honeymoon.'

Charlie laughed, and Silas smiled, but he'd never felt less amused. He'd spotted the long length of the jetty in the mirror's right-hand pane, reaching like a long grey finger to point towards him. As though it sensed him there. Of all he had forgotten, he wished the memory of his death at that jetty–his last, he presumed–was not among them.

'Well, she shall have to keep waiting, and you do not have need of a bride,' Charlie said, firmly, returned to his more robust self. 'Perhaps if we flatter her cooking enough, Jacquetta will let us stay here.' He glanced up at the lieutenant. 'How does that sound?'

Their shared glance felt a very private thing, and Silas looked away. Back to where the loch and all its hidden history taunted.

'That sounds bloody marvellous,' Edward said. 'I'm not sure how I feel about that world out there anymore. Or where my place in it is.'

Not an unreasonable statement, but Silas shook his head.

'You have a place there, Edward. You too, Charlie,' he said. 'And as soon as I am able, I'll see that you find it. Once you do, relish every moment that life affords you.'

He touched the mirror and ran his finger over the jetty; where his moments had once ended.

The focus drew in. Like they watched from the back of a seabird gliding over the water; soaring over the slight turbulence in the waves and stretching up and over the jetty.

Such a simple thing. A coat of white paint was evidenced only by the patchwork of flakes that remained. There was some rot along the edges at the end, and a pile of fishing nets, tangled and long past their days of being used. Peeking from beneath them was the flattened end of an oar.

Silas drew in his breath, the horrific memory striking like a hot poker. When Nemain had held him down in the greensward, much had been forced to the surface; none of it pleasant.

He'd met one of his ends here. Upon this very jetty: struck with an oar, his brother screaming at him. Cain. That had been brother's name, in the beginning at least. Perhaps endless lives had seen it changed, but Cain's rage never altered.

You've ruined us all, you bastard. He had been livid, drunk beyond measure, beating Silas until he could barely stand. Accusing him of causing their family's undoing. An affair. With a son of Rossdhu House. *I told you it would ruin our family to bend for the likes of him. Too busy thinking with your prick. Now the lord's son is dead, and he has lost his mind with the grief. You've made our family homeless, you selfish cunt. We are to be cast out.*

Terrible accusations made all the worse for Silas not being able to remember a single moment. Had he loved the lord's son as he loved Pitch? Had his grief at the man's loss brought wails of anguish and unending rage that terrified even the most vile monsters of the world, as it would if he lost Pitch?

On that jetty, Silas had faced yet another demise at the hands of his sibling, and another hopeless attempt by a young man to save him. He'd not seen the lad's eyes, but he knew them blue; another from the long line of would-be saviours and guardians of the bandalore, from whence Charlie came.

'Silas?' Charlie stirred him from his deepness of thought. 'You look terribly sad. Is there something you recall from your time at Rossdhu?'

Silas scratched at his beard, bringing himself back to the most important of places. Here and now.

'I don't suppose you ever heard tell of a death...a drowning, perhaps...by that jetty?'

Silas readied for a rejection.

'Yes. But not just a simple drowning. There have always been whispers of a murder.'

His pulses skipped faster. 'Is that so?' The woman's lavender dress held a firm place in Silas's mind; as if its bright colour secured the memory, whilst all else about that horrid evening was blurred and dark. But the design of the dress was not entirely foreign to the fashion of his current day; the memory was not terribly old. 'How long ago was this terrible event?'

'Early in the century, at least fifty years past, I'd say. A long time ago, but murder takes hold of people's imaginations and sticks there. They make for fascinating gossip. The kitchen staff enjoy a tattle.' Charlie shrugged. 'And I enjoy listening to all their tales. Far better than being berated for refusing to wear a gown.'

Silas gave him a sympathetic smile, but his heart was still racing. 'I dare say. Who was murdered?'

'The gardener, I believe he was.'

Silas nodded, his gaze once more upon the grounds of the estate. 'Yes,' he whispered. ' I believe he was.'

One piece of the enormous puzzle of his life slipped quietly into place; he was certainly a man of the earth.

'What was that?' Charlie asked.

'Nothing. Do you know what his name was, this unfortunate fellow?'

'I don't. Sorry.'

More of the puzzle seemed set to elude him. But it did not bother Silas too greatly. He preferred the name Pitch knew him by.

'But,' Charlie continued. 'I know he likely died because of a scandalous affair he had with my grandfather's older brother, Gilbert.'

'Gilbert?' Silas held the name, turned it over in his mind, searched for some hint of recognition; emotion that might bring forth deeper memory.

There was nothing.

'That's positively awful.' Edward winced. 'Did they catch the culprit?'

Charlie shook his head. 'No, though can you believe there is some talk it was a member of his own family?' Silas stayed silent, and waited for him to go on. 'They lived in a cottage on the estate grounds. It's been torn down now, but they were forced out after Gilbert died at sea.'

'At sea?'

'He ran off to war when he was forced to forgo his lover. He'd rather have faced Napoleon's army than wed.' Charlie's face shone with marvel. 'From the moment Kirsty, my lady's maid, told me the story, I knew I would leave Rossdhu, whether or not I had permission. I intended to be just as brave as he, and run as far as I could from my father, and the shackles of that place.' His defiant mood subdued. 'Rather strange to have come full circle, and be just a loch away from the one place I was running from. But I suspect you are feeling the same, Silas?'

'Quite.' Silas ran his finger over the crystal handle on the sideboard drawer. 'But you have been very brave indeed, Charlie. Being alone is not easy.'

Charlie kept watching him. 'No. It's not.'

'I wonder if you know who found the body?'

'I heard it was my grandaunt, and her son. Elizabeth tended to be remembered, as she had a passion for the colour lavender. Not a day went by when she did not wear it, much to her family's annoyance.' Charlie grinned.

'Lavender?' Another, smaller piece of Silas's puzzle finally found its place. 'I imagine she looked quite lovely.'

'So do I. And all the more because it clearly made her happy to wear it.'

'And her son was with her, you say?' Silas prompted.

'Yes. Phillip. He was just a young child, it must have been awful for him. I was always told how much I looked like him. Our eyes. The exact same blue apparently.'

Silas's finger stilled against the crystal. 'It is a striking colour.'

'And rarely shows, apparently. Phillip had died a year before I was born, found dead in his bed at a ripe old age, after a life well lived, by all accounts. There was quite the fuss over me when it was clear my blue eyes would not change after my newborn days were done. Some even said I was Phillip come back to life. But I know I am my own person. Silas, what did you say you did at Rossdhu House, when you worked there?'

'I didn't.'

'Let me guess? You were a gardener.' Charlie made the leap with great confidence. 'You were the gardener that they found. Weren't you my friend? That is why you are so terrified of the water.'

'Hang on there,' Edward laughed, a nervous twinge to it. 'Did you not just say the chap was murdered, and in the early years of this century?'

'I did. But that does not mean it was not Silas.'

Silas's laughter was not much more sure than Edward's. 'Come now, I know you have seen some strange things, but that's quite a deduction.'

'Are you seriously going to try to convince me I'm being unreasonable? After I've seen Edward possessed by an angel who has been resurrected before my very eyes, and is now chin-wagging with Tobias, who is a daemon himself, and Lucifer,' Charlie flinched at that, 'who is the King of all daemons. Do you truly think I've put my own miraculous strength down to a decent few meals and fresh air? And if you think I could wipe the event of the Fulbourn from my mind, you are not so sensible as I imagined. I saw you command...' he searched for the words, 'Ghosts...the undead, spectres or ghouls. Whatever I name them, it is not human. But above all else, I cannot ignore the deep sense of connection I have with you, Silas. The feeling that our meeting was inevitable.' The red flecks in his hair were prominent in the gold-stained light of the Sanctuary. It had grown long, tangled at its ends, giving Charlie something of a wild-man's look. It suited him. 'I'm not certain what you are, Silas, and it doesn't really matter, because I know who you are. I've known since the moment I came across you, trying to fish so terribly in Wyre Forest. I know *you*,

Silas. The moment I stepped into your company, it was like...' He bit his lip, clamping back the words.

'Home,' Edward whispered. 'You told me, while we waited in that cave, that Silas felt like the home you wished for.'

Charlie nodded, his cheeks flushing pink as he looked to Silas. 'It's terribly sentimental, but you are strong, and constant and so terribly kind. Who would not find sanctuary with you? I understand perfectly why even Tobias could not help but fall for you, and am glad that with him, you do not seem so lonely anymore.'

Silas opened his arms, and the lad did not hesitate to move in to embrace him; the brave young boy whose ancestor had always sought to save Silas. No, who *had* saved Silas; rescued him from believing the world entirely cruel and ugly.

'Thank you, Charlie.'

'For a hug? Happy to oblige anytime, so long as you keep Tobias from glaring me into oblivion.'

Silas grew serious, relaxing his hold. 'I need to go to him.'

Charlie was grim-faced, but nodded. 'I'm surprised you lasted this long, to be honest. Go, Silas. We are fine, as you can see, and will take care of one another. It is not us who need you most right now, no matter how Tobias tries to convince you otherwise.'

'Good luck to you, Silas.' Edward offered his hand. 'You're a damned good chap. A hearty thanks for all you've done for me, and for Tobias. I'm bloody glad he's got you on his side.'

Silas gripped the lieutenant's hand. They shook with a warm and painful finality. 'You're a fine fellow, Edward.'

The lieutenant ducked his head. 'Go on now, so it's all the sooner we see you both again.'

Silas took a last look at the mirror, at the distant shore where his past lay. Lives long since lived. All of them were untouchable, unchangeable.

But not so the present.

He turned, and walked away.

CHAPTER 29

Seraphiel dragged Pitch's shirt high, exposing his belly. He pressed the palms of his cold metal covered hands to warm flesh, words of nefarious magick falling from his lips.

Pitch threw back his head, his hips bucking uncontrollably. His teeth dug into the wood, and his scream bulged in his throat. It was like being struck by the angel's gods-damned halo all over again; Iblis and Gabriel had been gentle compared to this maltreatment.

Pitch's hands sought purchase upon anything that might ground him in this cage of torment. He flailed, wondering if he shouldn't have just succumbed to being restrained, after all. His fingers touched at firmness, and he dug them in; into the roundness of a body, the hint of bone at his fingertips. He gripped a shoulder, the collarbone unyielding.

White specks marked Pitch's vision, and the roll of his head back and forth was barely under his control, but he glimpsed Lucifer. Sitting by the table; his head bowed so low his eyes were hidden. Pitch did not know if he'd intended to place himself within reach, but he did not shift away now; despite how cruel a grip Pitch had on him.

The world shrank down to a terrible, bone-deep ache; hot pain radiating through his hips and up his spine. All that kept him anchored was the king's silent, solid presence.

Seraphiel dragged the Cultivation from where it sought to barricade itself in Pitch's depths, brought it up through his skin, tugged it from his veins. The simurgh fought the fresh assault. Pitch spat the wood and cursed the angel to a thousand miserable ends. The simurgh's fight was vicious.

But futile, when it was its creator who summoned.

There was no holding back an anguished cry. Pitch's back bowed, his shoulders lifting, and the Cultivation was torn from him once more.

The simurgh appeared above Pitch's belly; big as a peacock, but all shades of sunrise and sunset and lavender fields. Delicately, and deceptively, beautiful; save for the blackened claw, and spots of ruin upon its neck and wing. Damage wrought by its perilous encounter with Azazel. Damage that made Pitch's sweat run, his eyes water with the pain.

Seraphiel kept on with his hymnal speech, the unknowable words of the Higher Angels, weaving their way around the simurgh. Pitch felt a subtle prodding at the wildness, like the brush of a moth's wings at his core, as the angel assessed the Cultivation.

The simurgh settled. Its talons landing upon Pitch's belly, resting on sensitive skin like cooling firebrands; the flap of its wings laboured.

Seraphiel's displeasure did ugly things to his features. 'If those angels had not already paid for this, I would make them do so a thousand times over. How dare they lay filthy hands upon my work?' The simurgh's topaz eyes were riveted on the angel, their brightness pulsing like the beat of a heart. 'If the Lord had given me what I wanted sooner, I could have rid us of Samyaza's legacy long ago.'

Pitch floated in the aftermath, his heartbeat loud in his ears, his breath heavy and reluctant to leave his lungs. He loosened his grip from the king's shoulder, let his hand fall to drape over the bench's edge. He had no strength to do anymore.

'You mean if Lord Enoch had given you access to the Primordial Flame?' Lucifer raised his head, watching the simurgh that moved its wings like a drunkard, as knocked about by the experience as Pitch.

'Yes, yes, of course. Without it, any Cultivation was doomed to fail. I had done so enough times to know there was only one path to take.'

'And you were forbidden to take it.'

Seraphiel turned on the king, his temper like a weighty cloak. 'The Lord would not listen to me. To me! His truest servant, the Celestials' greatest angel.'

'Modest, too,' Pitch mumbled...or dribbled...or did not speak aloud at all. His head spun, delirious from the onslaught.

'Without the Primordial Flame,' Seraphiel continued, 'no Cultivation could be enough. I told him.'

He stripped off the chain-mail gloves, casting them aside.

'And *with* that flame, any Cultivation you made was extraordinarily dangerous.' Lucifer was measured, far calmer than Pitch had known. 'You are the Celestial's supreme angel, Seraphiel. None would deny that. Your Cultivations are mighty. But the Primordial Flame is an immense power, one fit only for the gods. Azazel almost got hold of it. The results...well, they don't bear thinking about.'

'But the Exarch did not obtain it, did he? You were there.'

Pitch wondered, as the heat and sharp random pains quieted, if Seraphiel yet knew of Lucifer's summoning of Wrath; of the part his uncertainty had played in allowing the simurgh so close to Azazel to begin with.

If the king was smart, he'd say nothing at all to an angel already teetering.

'But I will not be there in Blood Lake.' Lucifer was astute. 'Nor you. And now the simurgh is damaged. Perhaps this is not –'

'Don't say another word, Lucifer.' Seraphiel's command was the cracking of mountain ice. 'Don't you dare. You have defied the Lord of Arcadia with all you've done, you've struck at the Seraph Michael, you are mortally wounded, and yet you stand here and tell me you have lost faith? Do you see what creature's form I had this Cultivation take? Do you see it?' His voice strayed back into those tight rises of hysteria. 'The simurgh was a favourite of yours, is it not? From those purebred tales of which you are so enraptured? Do you see it, Lucifer?'

'I do.' The fatigue in his voice was like stone. 'I see it. And it is remarkable.'

The simurgh's cry moved up its long throat, a low cackle against the weighty atmosphere. Pitch blinked, trying to think clearly. Lucifer mortally wounded? A preposterous notion for a King of Daemonkind. Seraphiel's madness made him exaggerate, clearly.

'I do not turn on you.' Lucifer took Seraphiel's hand, and it seemed the angel might snatch himself away, but the king had gumption yet.

'Look at me, Raph. Never have I, or will I, lose faith. I am here with you, am I not? At the end. And I shall not move from your side until this is done. But you must be honest with me. Can the simurgh's damage be undone?'

Pitch watched them, the blood pounding in his ears, the room strangely distant, bathed in the charming hues of the simurgh.

Seraphiel pulled his hand free, rubbing at it as if the daemon's touch burned. 'I can do a modicum amount, but complete repair would require drawing on the magick of the Sanctuary.'

'Then why not do that?' Lucifer asked. 'If it will see us through.'

The angel resumed his pacing, his red heels clacking whilst he pulled the lengths of his hair over his shoulder, fingering them restlessly.

'Because if the Sanctuary weakens, Michael will see what lies at its heart.'

Pitch lay there, like a sole audience member to a play. His jaw hurt too much to add to the dialogue, but if able, he'd have shouted at the angel to get to the fucking point.

'And what is that?' Lucifer showed none of the impatience he was renowned for.

'My Seal upon Blood Lake,' Seraphiel sighed.

'It is here?'

'Did I not just say that?' the angel hissed. 'Yes, yes, yes! I used my portion of Samyaza's bones to seal him away. Is it not sublime irony?'

Seraphiel paced faster. And Pitch counted his footsteps, trying to drag himself more forcefully into the world. He needed to clear his fuzzy mind.

All in Arcadia knew the lore.

The Watcher King's corpse: torn into three parts, given to each of the Seraphim who destroyed him, the angelic bones immeasurably powerful in Cultivation.

Many a drink had been raised to the awesome power of the Seraphim. Blood Lake itself was no secret: the burial ground created by the Flood on the Day of Ruination was a monument to the power of Arcadia. A rare few knew it far more than simply Lord Enoch's warning to all traitors to beware.

It was Pitch's own vile mouth that had told the wrong people of the lake's true purpose.

Pitch had not expected the desperation that gripped him. After all they had gone through there was to be no resolution? Silas would be left with this world in the stranglehold of the Blight. Pitch had bled, over and over, for absolutely fucking nothing?

'Surely there is something else you can do?' he slurred. 'You're a fucking Seraph.'

'Vassago,' Lucifer's voice was low with warning.

'What? Is he powerful enough to destroy the Devil's fucking halo, or not?'

'If you'd been more careful, daemon,' Seraphiel glowered, 'then your enemies would not have bested you, and the simurgh would not be compromised. I thought you were strong enough for this. Perhaps I was wrong.'

'Prick.'

'Enough. Both of you. We have no time for this.' How strange to have Lucifer the most reasonable in the room. 'And if you wish to lay blame, Seraphiel, then look to me. I faltered in my resolve at a time most critical.' Not only reasonable, but self-deprecating. Strange times, indeed. 'If you cannot draw on the Sanctuary's magick, is there anywhere else that might serve you? Fae magick from the Child, perhaps?'

Seraphiel's eyelids fluttered, as though he'd been miles away in thought. 'No, no Jacquetta must spend all her magick upon the Sanctuary, and besides, it is divine magick I need.' Seraphiel turned sharply, still pacing, his hair like gossamer flares around him. 'Gods, I should have kept part of my halo here. Fool, I am.'

'Did Enoch truly cast it back into the Creation Flame?' Lucifer wheeled his chair out of Seraphiel's erratic path. 'Or was that as half-true as your continued existence?'

The angel eyed him. 'Don't be petulant, Luci. I left myself in your hands. Was that not enough to show your importance to me?'

'You could have told me.'

Seraphiel stopped, freezing with his hands stretched before him, like he was about to start a piano recital. 'A vestige...it is angel bone...will you give me a piece of your vestige, Luci?'

Lucifer's silence held the pressure of a storm cloud. He stared down at his hand where it lay in his lap. But still Seraphiel seemed to have utterly forgotten the king's grievous injury, and looked him with a frown.

'What's come over you? Are you sleeping, Luci?'

'Michael took his vestige, you rotten bastard,' Pitch snarled at the angel. 'Are you blind as well as mad?'

He expected Seraphiel to swell with pomposity and indignation. Pitch did not expect the angel to fall to his knees beside Lucifer's chair.

'Gods, forgive me. My mind...is...well, you understand. I told you I am not what I had hoped.' Seraphiel's sudden tameness vanished again, and his mood shifted. 'You, Dominion. Your vestige? Where is it? I've used shavings from it for Cultivations in the past. It may be enough.' He rose, fussing at a mark on the white satin near his wrist. 'Do you have it with you?'

Pitch's utter astonishment gave him the impetus to push to his elbows. The simurgh tucked in its wings, giving him room, its eyes heavy-lidded as it roosted upon his belly still.

'No, Seraphiel. I do not have my vestige. It was taken from me when I was accused of murdering a Seraph, if you recall.' With each passing moment, Pitch grew less convinced of going a step further in this fool-hardly quest. Even if the repairs could be made, was the angel in any state to make them?

Lucifer rubbed at his fresh-shaven chin. 'Enoch did not even deign to return the prince's vestige to the Flame. He destroyed it, so that it would not taint the fire.' He inhaled sharply. 'The ankou. Perhaps he can –'

'No.' Pitch and Seraphiel spoke in unison, though with very different motives.

The angel clicked his tongue in irritation. 'Ankou have no divine magick, and he'd be dangerously susceptible to the Blight.'

'He is no ordinary ankou,' Lucifer said. 'He is the Pale Horseman.'

'Lucifer, stop.' Pitch was sharp; his chest tight.

They paid him no heed.

'He is still death,' Seraphiel replied.

'He is Nephilim.'

'Gods, shut your fucking mouth!' Pitch cried.

Seraphiel wheeled about, eyes ablaze. 'He is what?'

'Nothing,' Pitch shouted.

And was once again ignored.

'Nephilim,' Lucifer said. 'At least...he was, but has been in Izanami's employ a long while. Who is to say what he is now, but it was strong enough to bring down –'

'A Nephilim dares step foot inside this Sanctuary?' The angel clacked his heels to where Lucifer sat and grabbed at his collar. 'You brought a child of Samyaza here, to the very shore of Blood Lake, where their sire's halo holds the power?'

Lucifer glowered and pulled his collar free before he answered. 'If not for him, then you would have no simurgh. Besides, I did not know of Silas's truth until he and Vassago were too infatuated to dare try to separate them.'

'Dare to try? You are the King of Daemonkind,' Seraphiel shouted in disbelief. 'Lucifer does not try. He *does*. You should have forced the separation.'

Pitch made the mistake of laughing. Every muscle protested, and the simurgh hissed a thin sliver of tongue from its golden beak.

'That did not work out for me as I had intended. Luckily so,' Lucifer replied. 'Silas found his way to Vassago regardless, and is all the stronger for it.'

'All the more reason he must be removed from here.' The angel returned to his rough twisting of his hair. 'If he were to fall under the influence of the Blight –'

Lucifer shook his head. 'He has withstood it thus far –'

'That foul creature has never been so close to the halo, that which belonged to his sire!' Seraphiel's shout had the simurgh flexing its talons. Pitch swore at the creature, trying to shift from beneath it. 'Do you know what a danger he could become, if the halo rules him? He must go, Luci. He must be banished from here.'

Pitch stilled. Seraphiel was right. How had he been so fucking thoughtless? *Blood Lake is a graveyard*, Silas had once said, claiming that good enough reason he should join Pitch on the quest. But it was not just any graveyard; it was his sire's final resting place; where a remnant of the power of the Watcher King remained.

Silas was strong, Pitch knew that better than Lucifer. But strong was not invincible.

Pitch's doubts about ending the ankou's journey here, evaporated.

'Alright,' Lucifer continued. 'So, you would risk opening the entrance to the Sanctuary once more to banish him? What if Michael waits for just such a moment?'

Pitch felt his lips part, felt the knife-tips of the words in his throat. He heard himself speak as though watching from the lofty peaks of Arcadia.

'You are right, Seraphiel,' he said. 'Silas Mercer is a danger to us. We should never have brought him here.' He refused to look at Lucifer, in case it made him falter. 'If you cannot banish him, then restrain him. But do what you have to, to keep him from the lake.'

The simurgh twisted its long neck to regard him, raising the crest atop its crown. A blink, a flash of topaz, feathers ruffling.

'You wish the ankou gone?' Lucifer spoke.

'Far away preferably, or at least very much hindered.'

'Are you sure of this? Do you not need him?'

'Yes. I fucking need him. Which is why I cannot be distracted by him in the lake.' Pitch dropped back onto the metal, eyes fixed on the swirls of the runes overhead. He lifted his arm to point; it was like moving through syrup. 'Can you seal him into a room with some of those? Drug him with pixie dust? Perhaps the Child has fae magick for that, if she cannot aid you with the simurgh.'

He despised the sound of his own voice, the air he used to make his lungs work the words free, but Pitch had never been so clear-headed. Silas must stay.

What a horror it would be to see him taken over by Samyaza; a nightmare Pitch could never forgive himself for. And who better than Silas to be here and deal with the teratisms, when Pitch's attempts at destroying the halo likely failed?

'Yes, yes.' Seraphiel moved up beside the table, and presented his arm to the simurgh. 'Go, speak with Jacquetta. I am busy here.'

The simurgh moved its gem-shone gaze between Seraphiel and Pitch. It lowered its head, touching the tip of its beak to Pitch's chest.

'I said, come to me. Now.' Seraphiel bristled with impatience.

Pitch tilted his hand, letting his fingers brush at the underside of a wing. 'Go on then. Let him fix you the best he can, so we won't be the laughingstock of this blasted lake.'

The simurgh, the wildness, the beast who'd never listened to a damned command in all the time it had coveted his depths, now listened to Pitch well; stepping onto the angel's arm, like a hawk ready for the hunt. Its wings flared as Seraphiel turned abruptly and moved away.

Lucifer offered Pitch a hand as he struggled to rise. After a momentary pause, he accepted the aid of the king, and dragged himself off the bench. His feet pained with pins and needles.

'You made a deal with the bluecaps queen, did you not?' Lucifer lowered his voice, leaning forward in his chair. 'In the Forest of Dean? Satine told me she learned of it through the horses. You promised yourself to them, in exchange for allowing the ankou to go free.'

Pitch scowled, rubbing at the back of his neck, loathing talk of the horses. 'So what if I did?'

'Then you can renege.'

Pitch shook his head, regretting it for the rattling of his brain. 'Speak your mind, Lucifer. I do not know what you are talking about.'

'You should read more in that case as I do. I have some rather magnificent old tomes from the Seelie Court –'

'I swear, Lucifer, I shall pluck out your eyes if you do not get to the point.'

'You can renege on your deal with the Bluecap Queen. There is an ancient law of reversal that can be enacted, so long as there is still a boon to be had for the fae. Here, you would give them Silas.' He paused, perhaps letting the magnitude of what he suggested sink in. 'The law results from a long-buried agreement between a king of humankind and a love-struck fae prince. Speak with Jacquetta. She will claim she doesn't know of it. The fae, half-blood or not, dislike reminders that they too can be tricked into deals they don't desire.'

Pitch stared up at the King of Daemonkind, pulses quickening. 'Very well. I'll ask. You speak so generously to me. It is not like you. Is there something I should know of your injuries? I'd hate to suddenly become King of Daemonkind on top of all else.'

'Who in their right mind would name you as my successor?' Lucifer turned his chair. 'Get away, before Seraphiel peels you open for his remedy.'

'What if there is not one? A remedy, I mean?'

'I have an idea I shall share with him. A source of some magick. Perhaps it will work.'

Pitch nodded, resettling his shirt, tucking it into his trousers. 'And what if I am not enough? You have wagered much on this, dear pappa.'

The expected growl did not come.

'You are stronger now than you ever were upon the Hellfield. The angel was never mad in choosing you. Now go.'

Lucifer pushed at the thin metal wheels, straining in his effort to move himself to where Seraphiel muttered over the simurgh. Pitch stood there a long while, watching the king, before he moved away, leaving the angel and daemon to their urgent deliberations.

CHAPTER 30

Silas despised Sanctuaries. They were intent on making his life difficult. He was being led astray, he knew: sent up stairs and down, along corridors that kept their ends from him until he was seething with impatience, only to find a doorway that led to yet another fanciful parlour, or empty dining room, bedroom or library. There was a potent number of libraries in the place. As though the Sanctuary sought to taunt him with endless words he could not read.

Every one of those rooms was empty, nary a sign of a fly, let alone Jacquetta or the prince.

'Pitch?' he called, yet again.

And yet again, no answer came.

He was foolish for thinking this would be a simple task, to reunite, but Silas had liked to imagine their connection transcended name-calling now. That Pitch would simply know that Silas looked for him.

He huffed at his sentimental folly.

'Jacquetta, I've had quite enough of this. Come out, at once.'

The palace was thick with utter silence.

Silas paused in the middle of a music room, piano gleaming, sheet music waiting for a musician to strike up a chord.

Silence. He ran his thumb over the ring, the double scythe every bit as quiet as the rooms of this enormous dwelling. The moment he found Pitch, he'd separate the scythes again, and give him the second ring. Then he'd never have to run about senseless again; they'd have the constant connection he craved.

A tiny thrill came over him. He spread his fingers, staring down at the ring.

Pitch had worn Balthazar Crane's scythe.

'You know him.' His voice was loud in the quiet space. The ring hummed against his finger, a tickling vibration. The first hint of its voice in a long while. 'Find him.'

The humming continued, but nothing more. He wasn't sure what he was expecting. He'd not sought to use the scythe as a hunting dog before. And there was the small matter of Pitch being very much alive. These were tools of death.

But the idea had ignited, and Silas would not let it burn out.

He left the music room and stepped out into another impressively wide corridor. Every inch decorative, elaborate, and, of course, golden. He surveyed either end of the way and found it endless once more. But he'd been in just such a predicament before. At The Atlas, and more significantly at Harvington Hall where the spectre had taught him special lessons in how to find his prince.

Do not believe the illusions. Strike out where the way is most denied. But too many ways lay open here to choose from.

'Wake, and aid me.' Silas clenched his fist, squeezing the ring between his fingers. 'Do you know his melody?' For Silas did not. Pitch had always been a quietness to his ear. Perhaps the prince had been too meddled with by the Seraph for his naming melody to hold readable notes; who knew? But the scythe had laid upon Pitch's skin. Izanami herself had held Pitch back, as Silas battled her sister Morrigan. Death knew the daemon.

The certainty swelled like a rose blooming in Silas's chest.

'You know him. Find him.' His command made the sconces' candles flutter, the chandelier sway against their fittings. The ring hummed harder, the vibration travelling along all the tiny bones in his hand, moving up his arm.

Silas unfurled his fingers. The shifting light glanced off the ring, catching it in a way that reminded him of the glint of Crane's spectacles.

His hand jerked forward, a sudden tug that had Silas taking a stumbling step forward. Towards the wall. The pull at his fingers led him to the smooth surface, the plaster like silk beneath his palm.

'Of course it's through the bloody wall,' he muttered.

With an exhale, he shook his shoulders, readying to strike at something that did such a good job of seeming solid. But he'd not be played with any longer.

Silas moved a few steps back, giving himself a chance for a slight run up, then leaned into his conviction and ran at the wall; shoulder lowered to take the brunt of the impact that seemed certain.

The illusion evaporated, as though fearing his touch, and Silas went racing into a new room, nearly coming off his feet after putting far too much effort into his barge.

His hand lifted, the tug of the scythe now undeniable, and he kept on, straight through a buffet filled with an assortment of figurines and dust-gathering trinkets, through another wall, and onwards into a room gripped with confusion. The place did not seem to know what it was. His headlong path had the Sanctuary working frantically, it seemed, for this room shivered between designs: a half-tester canopy bed with gold tasselled cushions and damask covers sat at one side, whilst on the far side of the room an enormous cast-iron stove glowed with heat in its furnace, and pots bubbling on its surface.

Silas was driven towards the stove. Dragged forward by the scythe that now followed his command with the eagerness of a hunt hound scenting a downed pheasant.

Silas did not hesitate. The heat reached him when he was still several feet away from the stove, the fire that burned warmer than he'd expected of illusion.

But he'd not doubt the scythe. He'd not doubt himself. Silas felt free, strange as it was, after seeing Rossdhu House and the jetty. The past had been such an anchor, the good and the bad of it. He'd hungered to know of it, but looking at the remnants of his past, in the shape of that mansion and its gardens, and its loch, it was as though his desire sank into those waters. His period of mourning was over.

What was done was done.

More important was what remained to *be* done.

He ran on.

Heat bit at his knees, and he swore he felt the sting of boiling liquid sear his front as he passed through the pots.

Silas emerged into a small room, a chapel, perhaps, though who knew what gods were worshipped here. The altar was plain, marble cut, with only two gold candleholders for decoration. There were mats upon the floor where pews might be in a church, lined up for a handful of worshippers. The floor itself was a marvel, a mosaic of opalescent tiles, with gold pieces strewn seemingly at random among them. But most glorious of all was the window, an arch of glass so pristine in clarity he thought for a moment the room to be open to the elements.

Beyond the glass, an incredible array of wildflowers grew upon a slope in the ground, with the jut of moss-covered stones visible through their colourful display. They were in something of a circle, the stones, and Silas wasted no time lingering here as memories of the greenswards' faerie circle disturbed him.

He was led out of the door, this time, into a white-tiled corridor. The ferocity of the scythe's guidance abated, softening from the near-painful prickling in his arm, to only a feathering at the tips of his fingers. A door, with half its body made of frosted glass, lay ahead. Silas opened it and stepped inside.

The conservatory was modest, with its glass ceiling set within a thick white wooden frame, and filled to near overflowing with many wondrous ferns and orchids, plus an untold number of blooms he did not recognise. Everything was bathed in that gold-hued light the Sanctuary so favoured. As was that which lay beyond the glass, where the wild flowers he'd seen from the chapel continued, interspersed with adders's tongue ferns, and some astonishingly strange plants, one with leaves of onyx and blooms as colourful as Scarlet in their full rainbow array.

Silas made his way through the unseasonal orchids, their spectacular flowers as large as his palms, and the fronds of ferns that had grown far beyond their natural size: moonwort and maidenhair and holly-fern large enough to rise over him and hang in his way, giving him the sense of being lost in some exotic jungle.

The tingling at his fingertips vanished. And voices reached him. Soft murmurs. One stood out.

'Pitch?'

Silas swept back the drape of an enormous Harts-tongue leaf.

Pitch stood with Jacquetta. Very close. The Child of Melusine had one hand upon Pitch's cheek, whilst she rubbed her thumb over his lips.

They jumped at Silas's voice. Jacquetta stepped back, thrusting her hands into hidden pockets upon her silver tunic.

'Mr Mercer, where did you come from?'

Never had a pair looked so guilt ridden, but Silas cast aside any notion that this was some intimate indiscretion.

'What's wrong? Are you all right?' Christ, he longed for a time when there would be no need to ask that of Pitch constantly. 'Are you hurt? What did they do? I knew I should not have left you.' He reached the prince, and was stopped from saying more by a press of slender fingers to his mouth.

Pitch was warm, his eyes not exactly bright but gleaming enough, and he managed a small, wry smile.

'Silas, stop. I am fine.'

Admittedly, he looked so. His lips were full pillows of pink flesh, shining and damp.

'What has she given you?' Silas spoke against the fingers that pressed at him gently. 'Are you in pain?'

To his great surprise, Pitch nodded. 'Some, but nothing worrisome. Jacquetta's balm will set me right.' He withdrew his fingers, and Silas leaned into the loss, following the closeness he coveted.

'Were they able to repair the Cultivation?' He touched his hand to Pitch's belly, and with the thinness of his shirt, the tensing of muscle was evident.

'I do not have it. Seraphiel took the simurgh, to see what can be done.'

Silas planted his hands on Pitch's shoulders, bending his knees so he could bring them eye to eye. 'And was he unkind with it? That can not have been easy for you.'

Pitch's smile looked like it came easily. But Silas suspected he was working hard to make it rise. He glanced at Jacquetta, who was watching them from where she stood by an odd plant, one with garish spikes up its short trunk, and tiny white flowers clustered at its peak. For a moment he thought her about to speak, her focus firmly upon him.

'Thank you, Jacquetta, that will be all. I'd like some time alone with Silas while we wait. If you don't mind?' Pitch said, catching at Silas's trouser waistline, hooking his fingers there, urging Silas closer.

'Are you sure, your highness? That being alone is what you wish for?'

'Quite sure, thank you, Jacquetta.' Pitch was precise, sharpened to a point.

Silas wore a bemused frown, glancing between the Child and Pitch. 'What is this about?'

'Lack of privacy,' Pitch said, airy, intent on pressing in against Silas.

'As you wish,' Jacquetta agreed, though to what Silas could not say. 'I wish you all the best, my lords.'

Silas turned from his study of Pitch's features to look at her, but he was waylaid by another press of warm fingers.

'Don't mind her, my dear,' Pitch whispered. 'We won't have long to be alone.'

He raised his eyes, and something in their shock of emerald gave Silas pause.

'Are you sure everything is alright?'

Needlepoints of laughter followed. 'Of course not. Nothing is *right* about this, silly oaf. But I'm hoping you can at least make it feel better.'

The prince rose onto his tip-toes and pressed in, covering Silas's mouth in a feverish kiss. One which Silas opened for, and welcomed.

Pitch did not taste of his usual, particular bitter-sweetness. There was another floral hint there. The balm, he supposed, but Silas was not about to spend a fortune in time wondering. The kiss took a rather desperate turn. Silas wrapped his arm beneath Pitch's arse and lifted him off his feet. The daemon folded his legs around Silas's waist, hooking his ankles at his back.

Pitch's teeth found the tip of Silas's tongue, nipping, forceful, and Silas groaned into his mouth. He dug the fingers of his free hand into Pitch's hair, shaping around the back of his slender neck, the ring catching a fine strand of hair. With a soft, tantalising whimper, Pitch pulled away.

'Let's go outside,' he said, hoarse and warm. 'I want you to fuck me in the garden.'

Silas answered with a grunt more worthy of a beast than a decent man, but Pitch hardly needed an answer. He could feel Silas's eagerness well enough.

Silas sized up the location of the doorway before returning his attention to the feverish man in his arms. He knew Pitch was passionate, and hungry for ravishment, but he'd never known him so...needy; whimpering when Silas had lifted his head to eye his way, and pressing in as though he were trying to bury beneath Silas's skin.

It was glorious to know he was making this creature come apart in his arms, but terrifying, too. For Silas felt the desperation in Pitch's want; and understood it well.

Silas kicked at the door, caring little if he cracked panes or broke latches. He was not about to let go long enough to twist a handle. The door gave way easily, as though it had already been opening when he raised his leg.

Two stone steps weren't easy to negotiate blind. Silas stumbled, and their teeth clacked. He was light-headed from the lengthy press of mouths, but neither moved to surrender. Pitch's moan hummed against Silas's lips.

A narrow stone landing gave way to a pathway of moss–shining moss–that seemed oddly familiar, but Silas was too preoccupied to place it. His arms brushed against the curtains of delicate wildflowers and ferns that surrounded him. Orchids, of all the colours imaginable, bobbed as he carried the prince down the path.

It was a short distance to where the path opened wide, and the wildflowers gave way to a spread of moss; a deep natural cradle as round as Silas was high. The perfect place to lay the prince down. Beneath the verdant, vibrant layers, tiny fronds shimmered with gold like morning dew. There must have been larger things buried at the edges of the circle, for the moss jutted higher at regular intervals around the circumference; affording privacy, if such a thing were possible in a place like this.

But Silas could not have cared less if the entire population of Scotland watched on. He wanted Pitch, with a potency that choked him. A desire that carved him hollow.

Silas went to his knees, lowering the prince carefully, when he was suddenly overcome with dizziness.

He gasped, touching one hand to the moss.

'Sickle?'

'It is nothing...I'm fine.' As though to prove him wrong, the world tilted. 'Oh, my.' Silas sat back on his heels, but that too had him reeling. His hand went wide, searching for a hold, landing on one of the peaks beneath the moss: a tree stump perhaps, a stone, overridden by the wild growth of the garden.

'Here, lie down, quickly.'

Pitch guided him softly, gently, but with purpose. Too calmly. The first stirrings of alarm gripped Silas. He ran his tongue over his lips; lips still heated from their kiss. 'Pitch...'

'Hush now, you don't seem well. Lay your head down, Silas.'

'But I want to –'

'And you will. I am yours to take however you please. But perhaps just a brief rest first?'

The shrills of alarm rang louder. Silas knew things were amiss, but he could find no strength to protest. And the world was losing its substance. The colours about him seemed to drip. The vision of loveliness that was the daemon would not quite be drawn into focus.

Silas clenched his eyes shut, laying back with a grunt. 'Just give me a moment.' Of all the confounded moments to become unwell.

Softness brushed over his legs, covering them with a pleasant heat, at his waist too, a soft slithering, but he couldn't open his eyes just yet. He just needed another moment.

The faint crackling of moss came as Pitch shifted closer, taking up Silas's hand and wrapping both of his around it. His warmth was sublime.

'You will be fine,' he said. 'This shall pass. Just rest.'

Those alarm bells were clanging now. Since when was Pitch so ready to forgo intimacy? Silas opened his eyes, and his heart seemed to freeze mid-beat.

Pitch was ethereal, utterly exquisite with the frame of golden light about his head. His hair was all but spun gold now, not far removed from that of the Seraph. And his eyes glistened. Not with any mirth or devilry, not with a hint of flame or vibrancy, but with unshed tears.

Silas's world seemed to fall from beneath him, leaving him in a terrible abyss of realisation.

'Pitch...what have you done?' He fought to keep his eyes open, to keep them fixed upon the daemon, who should have been indignant with denial just then; protesting against the accusation.

Pitch raised Silas's hand to his mouth and pressed his lips near the ring. He whispered, 'I renege on my deal made. I return thee to the fae who made claim upon thee.'

Silas rolled his head. He was hearing things, surely? Those words must be part of a fever, its suddenness felling him. He tried to pull away, but he'd lost control of his limbs, and nothing at all happened, despite his best efforts.

He moaned, though he'd intended to call Pitch by name.

The prince bowed his head, the glare of him nearly too much for Silas to gaze upon. 'I will not give you up, Sickle.'

Silas fought to keep his eyes open, cursing every fae he'd ever known for the magick that was rendering him so utterly useless. Pixie dust perhaps, though this was far crueller, for he was not asleep at once. He just lay there, his body insensible as the moss covered him over.

Silas could do nothing but watch, whilst Pitch made a terrible mistake.

'No...no.' Silas's lips tingled. 'Pitch...'

'Hush. It is what I want, and I will have my way in this.'

Silas's moan was borne of desolation. Realisation settled on him like the Morrigan's ravens. 'Don't...leave me.'

Pitch shook his head, a blur of golden brilliance, with a hint of green gems and fire at their midst. 'They cannot take everything from me, Sickle. Do you understand? They will not have you.'

'Stop...stop it.' Silas worked at forming the words, but he could not tell if they actually made it from his mouth. 'Let me...go.'

'You don't belong in Blood Lake, you fool. Can you imagine the suffering you would shoulder there? You must live, however much time you have. I want you to live. And I shall ensure it is without the Blight to plague you. Think of how wonderful it will be, spending your remaining days tripping over your own feet and fussing over your dead with your pretty little sickle. You will drive your ghosts mad with all your intolerable gentleness and patience –'

'No.' Silas felt the world cracking open; readying to swallow him.

'It must be this way. You'll see it soon enough.' A childish fervour clung to Pitch's words, a plea to be believed. 'They'll not make monsters of both of us, Silas. Do you hear me? One is enough. And I am used to being vile. I was made ugly, but you were born in defiance of your maker. If you were to succumb to Samyaza...I fear what my rage would make of me in that place. I would be beyond the Berserker Prince, beyond an angel's Cultivation. I would bring down an apocalypse upon us all, if you were taken from me.'

Silas stared up at him. His vision was hazy with a crushing need to sleep, and the boil of tears. Anger simmered, too.

'Bastard.'

He was sinking, drifting down where the air and light could not reach him. The moss made a steady creep over his body, and the scythes were useless about his finger, ignoring his unspoken commands for help.

'I tried to tell you what I was,' Pitch said. 'But you would not listen, my stubborn, remarkable oaf.'

Pitch was all but a blur; a setting sun delivering its last rays of warmth and promise.

The moss tucked him up like a body in a shroud. The plant life he had always felt such an affinity for betrayed him in the worst of ways: aiding Pitch in abandoning him.

He struggled against it, but Christ, he wished to sleep; to close his eyes to this nightmare.

Pitch leaned over him; leaned down and leaned close.

'Goodbye, Silas Mercer. What a wonder it was to have known you. You have carved a heart in this chest of stone. Now sleep for me.'

His kiss was serene and impossibly unfair.

The caress of daemonic enchantment swept over Silas, and he knew the battle lost. The prince's incubus charms fed on feelings that already existed; inflated them and rendered their owners insensible.

Silas would already do anything for him, without manipulation. Now, he was Pitch's slave.

He gave in. He closed his eyes and slept.

CHAPTER 31

The moment Pitch knew Silas deeply asleep, every rasp of breath familiar, he stepped from the faerie circle. He knew what he'd done was right, but that Silas would view it as an act of cruelty.

But Silas was at rest now; as he deserved.

Pitch had kept him safe. In one piece for his goddess. Time would wipe away his sorrow, and Silas would find another on whom to bestow his affections. Of course he would; if he could love Pitch, then he loved too easily.

Pitch's feet sank into the spongy depths of the moss, and his heel found the edge of one of the faerie circle's stones. Jacquetta had told him that the island on which she'd built Seraphiel's Sanctuary held many ancient circles; some so old, she doubted the most long-lived of the fae could speak of their origin. This one, where Silas slept, was primordial. Pitch had nearly choked on the irony.

Pitch stepped back onto the path. He ran a rough hand across his mouth, trying to wipe clean not only Jacquetta's potion, but the memory of Silas's face when realisation had dawned. For all Pitch's talk of wishing to save him, he had drowned Silas anew; done nothing, whilst the greenery smothered him, and enchantment overwhelmed.

But he had kept the ankou safe.

Was that not selfless? And weren't those who loved supposed to be selfless?

He rubbed at his stomach, all the more hollow for the absence of the simurgh. He needed that wildness returned, so he could get lost in its stolen power.

'He sleeps deeply.' Jacquetta appeared at his side, falling into step.

'I will not speak of the ankou.' He could not do so if his mind were to keep its pieces intact. 'Take me back to Seraphiel. I go now, or I do not go at all.'

'This way, your highness.'

She moved ahead, and he followed. Seeing nothing, hearing little. His pulse was like a drum in his chest, measuring out the paces, a foul nausea sitting with him as Silas's heartache replayed itself in his mind's eye.

They traversed a long corridor, moving back into the depths of the palace. He almost called a halt at one point, thinking he was going to be ill. He took hold of himself, shouting down the clamouring instinct to run back to the circle, and tear its prison apart.

He forced himself to recall his days as the Berserker Prince; when he'd cared for little but destruction and chaos: nothing so pretty and fragile and confounding, as that which plagued him now. *That* prince was the creature he protected Silas from, every bit as much as the Watcher King and his halo.

Jacquetta drew them to a halt at the foot of an imperial staircase. Two sets of wide stone steps, curving in opposing directions and winding back towards one another up at the landing. Jacquetta looked to the left, eyes narrowed, head cocked as though listening. Which indeed she must have been, for she nodded, and turned to face him, silver gown whispering.

'You will be met at the ballroom. We will not return to the cellar.'

Jacquetta took the set of stairs on the right and made her way up.

Pitch trailed behind. 'So long as this leads to an end, I hardly care.'

'You'll be pleased, then. The ballroom is where you shall enter the lake. That is where the Seal lies.'

'Here? In one of the rooms?'

'Yes. What did you suppose?'

He wasn't sure what he'd expected; a long walk through a dark forest, or another trip with the Ferryman perhaps, to reach the entrance to Blood Lake?

Seraphiel's talk of using the lake waters in his Cultivations seemed far less of a mad fantasy now. Not only had the angel stolen a piece of the Primordial Flame, he'd entered a place that had been made deadly to Seraphim; defying Samyaza's curse that barred Michael and Ariel and Seraphiel from the lake.

Pitch did not doubt now that Lord Enoch had extinguished his favoured angel; an unstable Seraph with Blood Lake in his veins, was a catastrophe waiting to happen.

Pitch lowered his head: watching his knees bend as he took the stairs, his slippers set upon smooth stone, his hand grip at the carved balustrade.

Now, *he* was that godsdamned catastrophe that awaited; the keg to the simurgh's powder, with Blood Lake the fuse.

He grinned, crooked and thin. A good thing he'd betrayed the ankou, then. Kept him safe.

The lake could go ahead and swallow Pitch whole.

'But you cannot have him,' he whispered.

They reached the top of the stairs, where there was but one way forward, with no sign of the landing that should have existed between the staircases.

Here there awaited only elaborate white double doors, with their gleaming crystal handles, and ornamented golden scrolls carved into the woodwork.

'His Grace is inside. He shall show you the way, for he is the only one who knows it.' Jacquetta lifted her hand, fingers positioned as though she were a conductor readying an orchestra to begin. 'Shall I open the doors?'

'What else will you fucking do with them? Get on with it.'

'Is there anything you'd like me to tell him...when the time comes, and it is safe for the Seelie Court to retrieve him?'

He wanted to slap the pitying look from her face. Instead, he let his flames dance at his fingertips, raising his hand towards her until she flinched.

'There is nothing to be said. Silas will understand.'

'Very well, your highness,' Jacquetta said, wincing. 'Forgive me. I intrude.'

A twist of her wrist had the doors flinging open.

A ballroom lay beyond, just as she'd said, but it was no empty room, like all the others.

This one brimmed with a crowd that seemed poised to begin the next dance.

Jacquetta stepped aside, bowing low, muttering about tending to things. Perhaps wishing him good luck, it did not matter. Pitch was already moving on.

Crossing the threshold into the ballroom. The door clicking shut behind him.

Crowded as it was the grand room was perfectly silent.

All stood as though ready for the orchestra to strike at any moment.

The costuming was an astonishing mis-match of attire. Evening wear from every era of humankind that Pitch could recall: hose and bloomers were plentiful, as were high waistlines on sleeveless, flowing gowns, which contrasted those with enormous puffed sleeves and skirts wide enough to cause a black eye or two. Some men wore stockings; while others wore trousers, others still combined both, with shortened trousers to the knees, and stockings for the lower legs. Doublets and jerkins abounded, and intensely beautiful embroidered coats, with lace spilling at the cuffs. Cleavages were on display, pale white bosoms bursting the banks of square-cut necklines on rigid corsets, while others covered their tits entirely in lace, up to high necklines where frilled collars brushed beneath the chin. Pitch eyed them all with ill-placed jealousy. The assortment, hotchpotch as it may be, was utterly divine.

He glanced down at his own simple clothing, a loose shirt, looser trousers and slippers now stained from the moss.

He deserved no finery.

'So what is this, then?' He called into the silence. 'A dance before destruction?'

No one answered, much less moved.

Men and women were paired for the most part, but the gathering was not restricted to such partnerships: there were women together, and men in couples. Each pair stood ready to begin, arms lifted and hands clasped, frozen in a silent moment.

At the far end of the considerable room, a balcony housed a quartet: two violin players, a cellist and a harpist. Only the tops of their heads and the necks of their instruments were visible to Pitch, but they were as still and silent as the rest of the crowd. There was no conversation to be had, not a hint of life at all.

A panel along the far wall opened, and the colours of dusk and dawn emerged. The simurgh bobbed through the crowd, its elegant neck craned, peering over the heads of the parting dancers. Pitch frowned, trying to fathom how it moved so without its wings extended in flight.

'Dominion, it is done,' Seraphiel spoke from amongst the throng.

The crowd parted, and the angel walked the length of the dancefloor.

The simurgh rode upon his shoulder, its colours contrasting the singular hue that the angel wore. Seraphiel was ludicrously resplendent in gold, head to toe; even his knee-high boots shone as though cut from the precious metal. His waistcoat relied on the purity of the fabric for splendour, rather than embellishment, with only the snow white lace at the cuffs breaking the dominance of gold satin. His hair was loose, like a veil of sunlight moving with him.

The simurgh's eyes of topaz were all of the creature that even came close to matching the angel for golden glow. And one of those eyes did not leave Pitch as they drew nearer. The bird's head tilted to watch him, its turquoise crown of feathers raised. One claw was still curled and useless, talons charred black.

'It is not fully recovered?' Pitch said.

'What could be done has been done. Lucifer could give no more.'

'Lucifer?' Pitch studied the creature, frowning. Noting that the colourlessness at the neck was filled in now, returned to the spectrum of violet. 'What has he to do with this?'

'Everything.' Seraphiel raised his arm outstretched, and the simurgh stretched its wings just enough to jump its way along his arm, and settle near the flow of lace at his wrist. The blemish of grey at its wings was gone now too. 'But I can take no more of his blood without killing him now. And though he told me to do what I must, I could not do it.'

He sounded so very surprised at himself.

'What could his blood do for the Cultivation?'

'Fix it, as you can see.' Seraphiel cocked his head, as the simurgh had done. 'He is poisoned with many a vile thing, not least of which was divine magick. Now, brace yourself. I will make the return brief.'

'Return?'

The simurgh alighted from its master's shoulder and swept down at him, coming in like the mist rolling in from a restless sea.

Instinct pushed Pitch back a step, his pulse quickening. Wings spread wide; casting the bruised purples of evening across the room.

A gleaming beak widened, a forked tongue darting forth, its length obscene. And mesmerising. He watched the odd dance of the tongue, felt his body loosening. His eyelids growing heavy.

'Wait.'

Pitch was allowed that single word before he was struck.

His world went black. There was nothingness, and then the hardness of the floor at his back. The subtle stirring of the simurgh within his belly.

The Cultivation was returned, and he'd not felt so much as a pinch.

He blinked, staring up at an enormous chandelier, one with a forest of candles gleaming over its complicated array of crystal teardrop prisms.

'Get up, Vassago.' Seraphiel moved nearer, an upside down vision as he stood at Pitch's head. 'We do not have time for you to lie about.'

'I feel fine. Thank you for your concern.'

'Get up.'

He took Seraphiel's proffered hand, noting the golden colour of the angel's nails: painted or perhaps even gold itself. There was no give in the Seraph's flesh. He was hard, his skin tepid.

'Follow my lead,' he said. As though Pitch had any other choice. 'I will unlock the Seal, and you shall move to Blood Lake.'

He spoke with a child's enthusiasm, as though they were about to step into a parlour full of sweets and lollies. Pitch had never desired sweet things less.

Seraphiel led Pitch through the throng of waiting dancers. None turned their heads, nor flickered a glance. It was as though they were truly frozen. The angel did not lead him far, and stopped where the parquetry circled an intensely beautiful crest formed by differing shades of wood. Seraphiel's own crest; carved above his door in White Mountain, and in his throne which now sat vacant alongside Lord Enoch's in Gimli Hall.

The design replicated the eternal wheels of guardianship that circled the Creation Flame. A thousand eyes watched from those wheels, and all were of the same size, same hue: red as cherries. But on Seraphiel's crest one eye was made much larger, and clear as a diamond; declaring him more watchful, more focused than all those who claimed to protect Arcadia.

Pitch moved with dull co-operation as the angel positioned him, edging him this way and that, urging his feet apart, raising his arm, like a too-studious dance partner seeking to ensure perfection. Pitch was distant to all the man-handling, with the simurgh a pressure on his bowels; making it feel as though he'd left it too late to relieve himself.

They stood beneath another chandelier, far simpler than all the rest, with only one tier. An assembly of white glass flowers, shaped with the wide petals of Easter lilies, on long curving stems of chalk white. The flames at the flowers' centres were the only hint of colour; rebelling against the golden standard with a blue flame.

'Pay the bones no mind. Concentrate, Vassago.'

Pitch stared at Seraphiel. 'Bones?'

'Of the Watcher King, of course.' Seraphiel urged Pitch's elbow higher, frowning when he did not follow the instruction at once.

'Stop that. Those are Samyaza's bones?'

'Not all of them, great gods. You know the legend well enough. His body was cut up, and each Seraph has their piece. Mine anchors my Seal. I think Ariel has his embedded in his throne in Gimli Hall, so he might be seated on the traitor's face. Now, just tilt your chin higher.'

'Touch me again, and I'll bite off your finger.'

But if Pitch had hoped to truly threaten the angel, he failed. Seraphiel's face was split by a rare and unwelcome smile. 'You have fire in you yet. Good. Now, fix your hair.'

The angel tucked a finger beneath the strands near Pitch's ear.

'Piss off, Seraphiel.' He jerked his head away. 'I swear to you, you will lose that finger.'

But that only amused the moonstruck angel ever more. 'Then I shall match Luci. Do you think he would like that? It seems the least I could do. I've rather made things difficult for him, don't you think?'

How did one answer such lunacy? Pitch grunted, the only reply he'd offer. His chest was tight. His fledgling hope that this journey into the lake might be a success was fading.

Pitch turned away from the glaring divinity that held him like a master with their string puppet.

Instead, he looked to the beauty of the woman's gown on his right. Magnificent folds of lemon silk, with creme ribbons dangling from her wrists and wound through her brunette hair. Her corset was cinched tight, an hourglass with the narrowest of waists. His thoughts insisted on returning to when he'd last been clad in rustling layers and tightened stays. The Crimson Bow remained a tiny island of paradise within his memories, his own sanctuary in which to hide from the horrors of his world.

'You might have at least given me decent clothes to wear to my doom,' Pitch said.

'What nonsense.' Seraphiel stopped nudging at Pitch's slipper, fussing still with position. 'It hardly matters what you wear. You were always too preoccupied with such trivial things.'

'How would you know? It seems you had me rendered mindless whenever I was here.'

The angel scowled. 'Set your feet wider. This is a dance, not a presenting of arms.'

'I might feel more like dancing if I were dressed for such things.' Pitch decided on churlish for his mood. 'I am all but covered in rags.'

'I care little if you are naked.'

'No, apparently not.' Pitch widened his stance, assuming the position as directed. His taste for churlishness was done quickly. 'Did we ever fuck at all? Or were those instances I recall just a conjuring of your making? Did I ever find any pleasure in your company?'

'You are stalling.'

Well, he'd not argue with that. This room held a dank energy, as though all the dancers had been in throes of movement the second before he stepped through the doors. The air was faint with a hint of exertion, sweat, and, oddly, the ripe odour of the sea. Not entirely pleasant, and yet bracing at the same time. Base and...he struggled to find the word in his mind...primitive.

The quartet struck their first notes, tuning their instruments. The coarse notes had Pitch wincing. He licked at his lips, nerves jangling. The hint of Jacquetta's potion remained on his skin, and his downturn in mood plummeted further. Gods, let this be done with.

'Your pleasure was not, nor is now, my concern.' Seraphiel answered a question Pitch no longer cared about. 'Your strength is what occupies me. Now, rid yourself of this ridiculous melancholy, Vassago. Focus on the task at hand.'

Well, the angel could fuck himself very briskly. Pitch would make his pleasure Seraphiel's concern whether he liked it or not; just for old time's sake, and because he'd like to make the Seraph's life difficult, even if in the smallest of ways.

'I'll focus as soon as you find me something decent to wear.'

'What by the all the Celestials are you on about?'

'You heard me. Or is your hearing as far gone as your mind?'

Twin moons, brighter than all the dazzling lights and jewels in the room, fixed on Pitch, a serious mouth tight. 'Your appetite for the vanities of this world has not changed then.'

'I'm surprised you noticed any of my appetites at all.'

To his great surprise, Seraphiel's gaze shifted away from him. 'I noticed everything about you, Vassago. Why else would I have chosen you? You were not hard done by here.'

Pitch scoffed at that. 'You Seraph have a strange idea of excellent treatment.'

'You believed yourself endlessly fornicating, pleasured until your incubus blood was brimming –'

'But I wasn't, was it? I was being worked upon in harsher ways. I was kept chained in a lie.'

'I serviced you when necessary for your needs. You were sated, I assure you. It was simply not so often as you recall. And I have given you a power that the Lord Enoch himself would envy.'

'Oh, so now you favour blasphemy? Enoch would be proud.'

The dancers shifted, fine materials rustling, polished shoes creaking. A thud came from the orchestral balcony. Seraphiel tightened his grip, and for a brief moment, Pitch wondered if he'd be traipsing into Blood

Lake with Angelic injury on his person. Though really, what more could Seraphiel do to damage him?

'What colour?'

Pitch frowned. 'Colour of what?'

'Clothes. Shall you be happy with gold?'

'Dare it and I'll scream.' His mind went to a time of great pleasure, and what he'd worn in those stolen moments at the Crimson Bow. 'Grey. I want grey taffeta, and its corset must be lined with diamond buttons. There should be lace at the collar and cuffs.'

'I'm not partial to lace. But the rest can be worked with.'

The angel's hand slipped from the small of Pitch's back to the nape of his neck, and a soft hush of air moved against Pitch's cheek as the angel whispered a summons of his divine magick.

Warmth ran over Pitch's skin, and a tug came at his clothing, down at his shirt's hem. He glanced down. Half expecting to see Scarlet there.

But there was no rainbow light.

Nor, though, was there a plain linen shirt and oversized trousers covering his body.

His clothing was transformed. Not quite the same shade of grey as his gown at the Crimson Bow: this was lighter in hue, French grey as opposed to the cloud-grey he coveted, but lovely just the same.

A sudden tightening came at his waist, a cinching of unseen laces to force his figure into the lines of the hourglass. The simurgh nudged against the intrusion into its space.

'Tighter,' Pitch said, breathing in to raise his ribs and lengthen his torso. 'Tight as you can.'

Seraphiel obliged. The great and terrible Seraph, the Lord's favourite angel and Arcadia's mightiest since Samyaza, played couturier to a daemon's whim.

The assembly continued a moment longer until all was complete.

The gown was glorious, no doubt, its petticoat layers soft against Pitch's legs, its long sleeves snug as gloves. The taffeta had a velvet trim of viridian, and a jewelled brooch sat at the decolletage. He tilted it against its pin, trying to examine it from such a close angle. A portrait brooch, with emerald accents in yellow gold.

He tried to make sense of the image painted at the centre. Sickness swept him as he realised who the tiny bearded man with dark hair was in the portrait.

'What the fuck are you playing at?' He demanded, snatching his other hand free, so he might tear the brooch away.

Seraphiel stared at him as though it were Pitch who was losing his mind. 'I did not pay the ankou much mind, have I remembered him wrongly?'

'Are you trying to torture me, even now?' Fabric tore with the rough removal of the brooch. 'I am not carrying this pathetic trinket with me. I want no reminder of him.'

'Lucifer said you had an unreasonable affection for the ankou.' Seraphiel shrugged. 'The king has such sentiments for me. And as he was particularly enraptured by the brooch I made for him, I assumed you'd be pleased too –'

'Stop talking, for the love of all gods and their Celestial arseholes. Stop.' Pitch drew back his arm and cast the brooch deep into the assembly of dancers. 'Open the Seal, Seraphiel. Now.'

The angel had followed the path of the flying brooch, and continued to stare into the crowd. 'Was there something I was supposed to recall about that ankou?'

Pitch's flame shuddered. 'About Silas?'

'Yes, yes. If that's the large man's name.' He drew his gaze back to Pitch sharply. 'I'm sure there was something of him that was memorable. Was he anything more than ankou?'

Pitch delayed the answer by reaching for the angel's hands. By the gods, this creature was falling apart. Not a bad thing, in this case, forgetting that Silas was Nephilim; but what if Seraphiel also forgot how to open the fucking Seal?

He entwined their fingers and set his position once more.

'I'm ready,' Pitch said.

'Whatever for? Wait...yes...you're right. We are preparing...' A moment of unconcealed distress whispered across the angel's face, his eyes' light dimming. 'For something important, are we not?'

Pitch's heart struck up a violent rhythm.

'Opening the Seal…sending me into Blood Lake.' He worked dutifully at keeping his voice even, the panic at the angel's frailty hidden. 'Have your musicians begin. Perhaps that will help you recall?'

Another wave swept the angel's expression, and this one carried the confusion away; brightened his eyes and raised his cleft chin. 'Music, yes. The dance. We are here for the dance.'

The quartet struck their first true chords. Seraphiel adjusted his pose, stepping back so his feet were not hidden beneath the length of Pitch's gown. His skin warmed and the glow of his eyes made Pitch blink.

'Begin.'

One word, with a resonance that worked past the fabric, and through the whalebone, through Pitch's own skin and bones, to where the simurgh waited. The cultivation swept up, nudging at the base of his ribs. Making shallow breaths even shallower.

The harp joined the violins; the cello coming in last of all with the robustness of its notes.

Seraphiel drew Pitch into the first step of the dance, and it began.

CHAPTER 32

Pitch followed Seraphiel's lead, his slippered feet moving with a life of their own. He should have asked for better footwear. But then, if he were expected to swim after this, he'd be casting off these flimsy shoes quickly.

'When I arrive in the lake, what must I know?' he asked, ignoring how the sea's waft grew stronger.

Seraphiel twirled them about–proficient in his dance skills at least–as they moved from beneath Samyaza's bone chandelier.

'You know what you must.'

Pitch ground his teeth, but was not surprised by the vagueness of the answer. He was just grateful Seraphiel knew what lake he spoke of at all.

'But are there no hints of what to expect?'

Seraphiel released his hold on Pitch's waist and spun him out to arm's length. Taffeta formed a cloud of soft grey about Pitch's legs, before Seraphiel drew him back in, right up close, so they stood body to body. The angel was tall, not so tall as the ankou, but that did not stop a painful comparison.

'I expect that your way will be clear,' Seraphiel said. 'And what is needed to be obvious. Listen to the instinct that guides you, follow the Cultivation's desire, for it shall crave nothing else but to serve my will.'

Pitch opened his mouth, a torrent of questions ready, and Seraphiel threw him into another spin. This time, the angel let him go.

Pitch floundered only briefly, before his hand was taken by another. A fellow in a dapper black tailcoat and velvet collar, with shoes that tapped out every step he took. The fellow was adept. Moving Pitch in three clockwise turns this way, then four in the other. A dip had Pitch bent backwards before he was raised with a firm hand between his shoulder blades. The man did not look at Pitch as he held him, staring over his shoulder all the while. Never blinking, not speaking a word.

Every dancer was the same. This was a crowd of automatons, everyone an able mover but rigid in their approach, like soldiers tasked with simply getting the job done. The air grew heavy with strenuous movement, and the pungent scent of the ocean was dampened somewhat.

Pitch was handed over to another, a woman in garb not unlike Jacquetta's, though this tunic was scarlet in collar. Pitch glanced about the room. On the fanciful chance he might see the absent wisp returned. Waving its chubby hands to farewell him.

Pitch sighed. Was he any less mad than the angel?

After a few more turns, and three more partners, Pitch saw a pattern emerge. His exchange moved in something of an hourglass shape, taking in a corner, moving into the middle, then back out to the adjacent corner and across the top of the floor, or bottom, depending on the stage of the dance.

The longest pause was beneath the floral chandelier of bone, where the irritating dips occurred, and Pitch was bent back, grateful for the corset which braced him.

With each replay of the pattern, the music quickened.

Pitch searched for Seraphiel amongst the dull-eyed crowd. He was not far, one pair over, performing all the steps required but with his eyes never leaving Pitch.

'How long shall this go on?' Pitch called, already a little breathless.

'Until it is done.'

Gods, he despised the evasive nature of the Higher Angels. All their holier-than-thou espouses were so fucking patronising.

'Am I to enter the lake with bleeding feet and exhaustion?' He gasped as the woman who led him pushed him into another back-bending movement. 'Fuck...must you be so rough?' She said nothing, her eyes fixed beyond him, their whites a little bloodshot. Her ringlets barely shifted, despite the increasingly frantic pace.

'Do not disturb the dance,' Seraphiel shouted. 'Don't resist, daemon.'

Pitch growled a curse as the woman tilted him back upright, her fuchsia gown tangling with the folds of his own, creating the look of sunrise fighting an oncoming storm. She drew him in close. So close, he smelled the stench of her breath. Pitch turned his head, gagging.

What a stench it was. Of rot, and last week's roast.

Gods, she might be human, after all. The woman cast him off to the next dancer. He was flung up against a burly man whose light brown beard brushed Pitch's cheek as the momentum brought them together. A swathe of unwanted thoughts emerged, of another man's beard, how it felt against his skin when they kissed.

Pitch clenched his eyes shut. But that only made it worse. He saw Silas as he'd left him; buried beneath the beauty of the fae circle.

'Faster,' he hissed, stepping back, adjusting his position. 'Get on with this.'

Of course, there was no word from the chap who led him about. His eyes were as bloodshot as the woman before. The dance dictated a raise of the man's arm, to spin Pitch around beneath. The fabric at his armpit was darkened by sweat, and the odour smacked Pitch in the face as he completed the turn. It made for a sickening companion to the already briny lacing of the air.

'These people are alive?' he called out. 'Or do you excel in your illusions?'

He swore he saw a flicker of the dancer's eyelids.

'No illusion.' Seraphiel stepped back from his partner, leaning into a brief bow, before the pairings changed yet again.

'You have trapped them here?' Pitch looked to the bearded man with fresh, horrified eyes.

'When you seek to bind a Seal to the purebred world and strengthen it, then purebreds must be used in the Cultivation. I thought that much would be obvious, even to you.'

Arsehole. 'And do they consent to being used this way?' Pitch was certain the bearded man's fingers tightened at his waist.

'Theirs is a noble sacrifice.'

'That's not a fucking answer to my question.'

'It was a foolish question.'

'You're right,' Pitch laughed, high and unhappy. 'Of course you have not sought consent. You never do. I know that well.'

As Pitch was passed to the next dancer, he did so without fuss; not wishing to make life even more miserable for the unfortunates who held him. He was dancing through an appalling prison, a crowd whose abuse exceeded his own. At least he'd been allowed a life of sorts.

'Complete this task, and these shall be the very last purebreds needed to anchor the Seal.'

'Don't!' Pitch shouted. 'Don't you dare burden me with their fate.'

'Dance, Vassago. You shall find the Lady of the Lake soon.'

Pitch searched again for the angel, who, for a tall, glowing man, was remarkably adept at hiding in the blasted crowd.

'Lady of the...you mean Satine?'

'The djinn has gone by many names.'

The scent of the ocean–of the seaweed and carcasses within–grew stronger. Coming in waves, in an olfactory mimic of the sea's currents.

A young man embraced Pitch next, and the cello took over the symphony, its baser notes dominating. The man was barely out of boyhood.

Where had the unlucky bastard been plucked from, to end up here, in this cursed ballroom? He appeared to be of the upper classes; clean shaven, his shoulders held with that haughty air that the wealthy performed so well. Family would be searching, and worrying; perhaps already grieving.

Amidst the horror of an angel's disregard, Pitch allowed himself to think of the ankou, to be thankful Silas had not witnessed this. If he'd been here, they'd likely never have made it through to Blood Lake. Silas would have refused to turn his back on these miserable souls.

The tinkling of glass drew Pitch from his thoughts. A shudder ran through the floor, and overhead the chandeliers jiggled, their flames flickering.

'Faster,' Seraphiel roared.

The dance moved from quick to manic, in the matter of a heartbeat. And the volume of the music rose until he could no longer hear the padding of feet on the floorboards. The rich smell of the sea rose over and above the sweaty odour of the human workhorses.

Pitch was hurled from the young man to a bare slip of a girl who held no hint of aristocracy beneath her fine evening clothes. Her lips were cracked, and there was a scar upon her chin. Dirt beneath her fingernails, too.

'What is wrong?' Pitch shouted. 'Are we close?'

Another shudder hit the ballroom. Another pungent wave of fetid water moved through the room.

Pitch struggled to find sign of the angel through the gathering, and then, with a suddenness that made Pitch recoil, Seraphiel was right alongside him. His dance partner was a wide-eyed, stiff-backed man with a monocle that had cut into his skin, blood trailing down his cheek.

'The boundaries are tested,' Seraphiel spoke at a hiss. 'Show me, now.'

For a moment, confusion gripped Pitch, thinking the angel spoke to him. His misinterpretation was quickly amended, with the emergence of a hand-mirror from the crowd; a yellow-gold frame with diamonds set in its back. It flew, unaided, at deft speed, and settled its long handle into Seraphiel's outstretched palm.

The glass panel held no reflection of the angel's golden hue, nor the sunny brightness of the ballroom. The glass was dark as tar. Obsidian, whose blackness swallowed all the light.

'Show me,' Seraphiel shouted, whilst the dance continued unabated.

The blackened surface rippled and brought forth a reflection. Not one of this ballroom, but that of the loch that held the Sanctuary secret. Charlie's home was a blur in the distance.

But nearer, much clearer, something, or rather someone, travelled in a boat across the loch. Two figures were in the vessel; one seated, the other clad in a suit of armour that dazzled with the clearness of the day.

'Is that your Ferryman?' Pitch asked. Only to be whirled away again before an answer came. He was shifted to the centre of the room to perform the dreaded dip beneath Samyaza's bone. 'Damn it, Raph. What the fuck is happening? Who is with them?'

'Michael has found the Sanctuary.'

It was the answer Pitch dreaded, but it came with little surprise.

'But he cannot enter, surely? Wasn't that why you had to meddle with Edward to begin with? You alone can unlock this Sanctuary.'

His partner turned them at a maddened pace. Pitch's neck jarred with trying to keep his eyes on Seraphiel and the mirror, who moved in an opposing direction.

'I don't need my Sanctuary explained to me,' Seraphiel bellowed. 'Let me think, you damned daemon. Shut up.'

But the angel had not given Pitch the answer he needed. 'Tell me this Sanctuary cannot be compromised, Seraphiel. Tell me Michael cannot enter.'

His pulse already beat faster for all the movement, but now it did so unsteadily. Silas and the others stood between Michael and this maniac angel.

'He'd not dare.' Seraphiel's laughter was strained. 'He'd not dare.'

'That's no answer, you fool. He nearly killed a king of daemonkind to prevent us from entering here. He'd dare to knock on your godsforsaken golden door. Fucking gods, let go of me.' He shouted at the dancer who held him, but he might as well have shouted at a rock. 'Stop this dance.'

'Focus on your task, daemon.'

Pitch grunted as he was man-handled onto the next dancer. He tried to pull free, but the young man, with the merest of fuzz upon his chin and a startled look etched on his face, held a magickal strength, one that would require Pitch to use a brute force that would not serve the man well.

'Seraphiel, let me stay until we have dealt with Michael. Lucifer cannot do it. I've left the ankou vulnerable.' Gods, what had he done? 'You must protect –'

'The Nephilim.' Seraphiel was suddenly, and violently, at Pitch's side again, his partner's shoulder jutting at an unseemly angle: a dislocation most likely. 'The Nephilim is to blame for this. That must be how Michael found my Ferryman.'

A fresh horror took hold of Pitch. 'No...no, don't...he had nothing to do with it...' He gave in to his panic. 'Don't touch him. Do you hear me? You're wrong, you mad, fucking bastard! Leave him be. Promise me, you shall not harm Silas, nor any who are with me.' Pitch snatched his hand from the young man's hold, and there was definitely a grunt of pain. 'Seraphiel, listen to me.'

'Ready yourself. There are but two chords that remain.'

'Fuck you, Seraphiel. I'll not go another step further.'

He punched at the man who sought to take hold of his hand once more and cursed himself for the dull whimper the blow brought.

'You will go where you have been built to go.'

'Tell me that Michael cannot enter this Sanctuary. My friends are innocent in this. You must protect them.' His tongue caught on the foreignness of naming others as friends.

'I must do nothing you command, Dominion. You endanger them by lingering.' Seraphiel's glow lit the ballroom so intensely, Pitch could barely keep his eyes open. 'It is my Cultivation Michael seeks to destroy. He was always jealous of my work. Of my favour with our lord.'

Pitch drew his flame forth before thinking through the danger of it. The young gent let out a scream, the first true sound from any in the room.

He stifled the flame at once, but the damage had been done.

'Shit, I'm sorry...I'm so sorry.' Cruel red burns marked the man's hands, but his servitude to the angel did not allow him to release their hold. His expression remained blank and unreadable, but the tears that fell were horribly clear in the room's brightness. 'Oh gods, forgive me.'

'Inevitably, the innocent shall suffer when the mighty play their games,' Seraphiel said, in a sing-song delivery, like a priest reciting a well-worn prayer. 'You know this, Vassago, you have been an instrument of their suffering yourself. Ready yourself. There is but one chord that remains.'

Pitch drew in a breath, the reek of the sea searing his nostrils, the glare stinging his eyes. 'Seraphiel...please...tell me you will not harm the ankou.'

'If you truly wish to free that creature, then see the Death Wish undone.'

'His name is Silas, curse you –'

'His name does not matter.'

Pitch knew himself back at the centre of the room, beneath the bone chandelier, but the glare lay like a haze his vision could barely penetrate.

The simurgh slithered within, twisting about the knots he was made of now; his efforts to save Silas had only brought him certain harm. He sagged into the wounded dancer.

'Give him your promise, Raph. All he seeks is reassurance.' Lucifer's voice moved through the brightness.

'Luci, you should not be here. This is a dangerous place for you, after what you gave for the Cultivation.'

'I was weak well before you used my blood, Seraphiel. But I did it willingly, to enable you to repair your work. I asked for nothing in return, but I do so now. Give him your word, Raph.'

Their voices floated from the brilliant haze, only slightly louder than the fading music, which was all but a faint few notes dissolving in the air. Pitch could barely open his eyes wide enough to look on the young man who still held him in a dancer's pose.

'It is too late,' Seraphiel said. 'He shall not hear us now. He is deep into the Seal.'

'I can hear you!' Pitch bellowed. 'I can fucking hear you.'

'Gods, would it kill you to offer solace?' Lucifer said, anger lifting his voice. 'To give reassurance at the end? You failed to do so for me. You will do so for him.'

'Luci, you must leave this room. Do not take another step.'

Pitch coughed, choking against the stifling waft of brine and salt, and the loathsome sense of failure that consumed him. Could he not do a decent fucking thing in his miserable life? Now he'd only succeeded in laying Silas in his grave before time.

His partner drew him in, wrapping their arms to prepare for yet another spin. Pitch did not protest, nor struggle.

A single, far-off note penetrated the illumination. A violin, reaching high, its note hanging up in the radiance.

The young man spun Pitch out, holding his hand firm, until both their arms were outstretched. He let go.

The ground gave way beneath Pitch, and his skirts billowed with air as he descended in a tranquil fall.

'I give you my word, in honour of your sacrifice.' The voice resonated all around him, as though he fell into a deep well and its curved surface held the sound. 'So far as it is in my power, Vassago, no harm will come to those who carried you through your journey. I will do as you've done and keep Silas safe.'

Not Seraphiel, but Lucifer.

Pitch closed his eyes. Letting the king's vow flow over him. The sire he had never truly known, giving Pitch what he most desired.

'Thank you,' he whispered, knowing himself too far gone for the words to reach any ears but his own.

Pitch pressed his hand to his belly, letting flames play there. The simurgh lifted from its domain, sending a surge of something vaguely uncomfortable, but immensely powerful, through his bones.

The fall was brief and gentle. He drifted down like an enormous grey leaf upon the wind. An icy breeze that plummeted as he moved further down.

His slippers touched on solid ground, his skirts whispering as they swept over the new surface. The brilliance of the angel and his ballroom was gone. The light here was a contrasting shade of grey to his dress.

A chilling breeze toyed with his hair, brushing icicle fingers against the back of his neck. Pitch surveyed his quiet place.

A vast, flat field of ice.

He was utterly alone.

The ice field stretched for miles, barren and flat. Emptiness, going on forever, in every direction.

'Is this it?' he said loudly, for the silence was awful. Despite the simurgh's restless distraction, the dank beast of fear found a footing in Pitch's gut.

The tundra beneath his feet groaned, and from its depths there came a riotous crack. Pitch glanced down, gathering in the insensible lengths of his gown–the fineness so wildly out of place–to peer beneath his feet.

Something vast and restless slithered there beneath the ice.

'Satine?'

But this was no form he'd ever seen the lady take.

Cracks sprawled out from beneath his feet. 'Shit...shit.' The spider-web of faults spread rapidly, etching themselves upon every inch of the surface. There again, the groaning and splintering of thicker ice. Far less pleasing a sound than when it came from the whisky glass.

Beneath him, a vast shadow beneath the ice moved. Shockingly fast. Growing frighteningly large before he could even think of moving an inch.

The ice shattered. Black peaks rose either side of him, the stench of fish and sea overwhelming.

Pitch cried out, flailing and falling. Down into the reaching, cavernous maw of a fathomless beast, to be swallowed whole.

CHAPTER 33

Pitch's bellow held fear and anger entwined. He passed through a strange assembly of fine fillets, like the gills beneath a mushroom, and tumbled head over heels, his dress an appalling companion as he struggled to keep its copious layers under control. He slid down into a gullet so wide, his hands could not reach the sides.

The smell was atrocious on entry, but as he moved deeper, with his gown dampened and a slipper missing from his foot, the stench abated.

Darkness prevailed, and Pitch summoned his flame to hand.

'Don't you dare burn us. Hold your fire, daemon.'

The unexpected, but familiar, voice sent shock hurtling through him. Pitch drew the flame back beneath his skin.

'Satine? Where the bloody blazes are you?'

He landed on his arse, in a tangle of petticoats and taffeta, upon a surface that had him thinking of marshmallow. When a pinkish light cracked open the oppressive darkness, he saw it was far from a sweet treat he'd landed upon. He was in the beast's belly, amid bulges of innards and unpleasant scatterings of bones.

'Oh, shit...gods.' He jumped to his feet, his wet hair falling into his eyes and forgetting he'd lost a shoe until the squelching between his toes reminded him. 'Fuck, that is disgusting. Satine, is it truly you?'

Or had he just been eaten, by the very first fucking predator he encountered in the lake?

'Truly me.'

He was gripped by the arm. Pitch dragged the hair from his eyes, revolted by the syrupy wetness there. 'Shit!'

'Don't be afraid, Tobias.'

It was no hand upon his arm, rather something tubular and white, like the tentacle of an octopus. He whirled about, straining against the tight hold. Not an octopus, but a massive serpent lay behind him, curled around a pile of bones. The monster was white as the bodily remains; save for a faint rose gold patterning upon the scales which were each the size of saucers. Huge eyes of faceted, clear quartz regarded him.

'Satine...you are a...I didn't expect...'

'My true form to be so beautiful?' A long tongue, forked at its tip, shot forth from between lips of pearl white. 'No, I don't suppose you did.' Her voice was perfectly clear, no hissing, no slithering, as one might imagine from a snake, as though her long tongue wrote the words in the air and they took life from there.

'You are beautiful, it has to be said. And I never imagined describing a serpent so.'

Satine's diamond head lowered, acknowledging the compliment. 'And how do you wish to be known, prince of many names? Who stands before me now?'

The Lady Satine had always been rather decent to him. Standing by silently, as he acted out to deal with his pains. Protective, too, though he'd failed to notice it as he struggled. And now, here in the guts of this mammoth creature, the lady offered him what he craved. A choice. However small.

'Vassago.' He stumbled with the roiling motion of the sea creature. 'Those other pitiful sods, Tobias and Pitch, could only ever exist in the world I have left behind.'

'You are wiser for having known that world, restless prince.' Satine's coils twisted and shifted around her mound of bones. Curious bones they were, of shapes and angles he was unfamiliar with. 'You understand the need to shed those gentler skins and return to your given form. So that this might, at last, be done.'

The beast tilted wildly to the right. Pitch had no hope of keeping his footing and was saved by Satine's tail at his waist; keeping him mostly vertical, while all else was adrift. The lady could not, though, stop all the loose bones from moving. One glanced against his head, earning it a cursing cry of protest.

'What damned creature holds us? It shall kill me before I even set eyes upon the halo.'

'Leviathan. She is the djinn, and the djinn is she.'

'Whatever it is, it cannot seem to swim in a direct line.'

'Nor would you, if the waters of Blood Lake boiled with cretins who sought to bring you harm.'

Pitch lowered his hand from his bruised head. 'This is it, then? I am here...in the lake.'

'You are here...in the lake. Does the Cultivation not tell you so?'

The beast, the Leviathan, now tilted in the opposite direction, even more drastically this time. Pitch was left dangling in Satine's hold, like bait at the end of a hook.

'It tells me,' he grunted, 'that it prefers not to be hurled about like this. I'd like to face the halo with my intestines where they ought to be, if you don't fucking mind.' His struggle stilled with a thought. 'I thought you claimed to have no idea of the lake's location, nor the Sanctuary? Yet, here you are. Have you made this journey far more arduous than it needed to be?'

As if in contempt the Leviathan bucked, a movement that had every-thing loose in its belly rolling like cargo on a storm-blasted ship. Satine stayed even, which meant, thankfully, Pitch did too.

'Do you not think I wouldn't have had Sanu carry you here at the first moment if I had known such things?' Satine's disdain filled her hiss. 'Besides, we did not know what the Seraph intended for you in the beginning. All Lucifer understood was that you had to be protected. He held onto the watch for a long time, before deciding to pass it to you. Then we learned along with you what must be done.' The lady's coils flashed as she adjusted her position. 'But even if I had known sooner, I could not have shown you to the lake, for its position is not stagnant, and the Seraph alone maps its place in the world.'

'They move the lake?'

'Rarely, but yes. Its weight upon the world is great, even if it is only the Seals that connect it now to the purebreds' domain. In moving the lake, they seek to maintain a balance that will not rend the world apart.' Her massive head lowered. 'But even if the lake remained where it was grown, I still could not have shown you here. I was not privy to where the events of the Day of Reckoning took place. The djinn were chosen by the Lord Enoch on that dark day to harness their nature-given power in this single, magnificent creature. A great guardian of the lake. I was the djinn chosen to tend to her, to bring her the sustenance of the natural world that would sustain her. But I was born within the Leviathan, and this is as far into Blood Lake as I have ever been, or may go.'

The beast dived at a gentle angle, then returned to level, its fleshy sides flexing and contracting as it swum. Pitch stared at the serpent, at the djinn who lay like a parasite in the belly of a beast.

'You have been like this since that day?'

Pitch was a mere four hundred years old, and he already felt haggard with what it was to be a servant of the Lord Enoch. Satine knew thousands of years chained to his will.

'I have. Of course I can enter the purebred world to feed, so there is some respite, but always I must return.' Her tongue darted more slowly, her scales lifted and lowered like huge thickly woven fans. 'I am tired of this place, Vassago.'

The Leviathan stole Pitch's chance to reply. The beast rolled, and all the world turned upside down. Pitch's gown, a terrible choice in hindsight, flipped like an umbrella thrown inside out in a violent wind, covering his face entirely. As he was averse to drawers, and Seraphiel must have remembered it, he was also giving Satine an almighty show of his arse and cock and balls. 'Fucking Malik's taint. This is ridiculous.'

'I see the ankou did not cure you of your foul mouth.'

Despite the gentleness of the jest, and the flush of sympathy he'd felt on hearing the lady's story, her comment grew hot fury behind Pitch's eyes.

'Don't you dare speak of him.' He knew very well how threatening he sounded. That was entirely the point. 'Say nothing of him again, unless you wish to see your fish baked to a crisp.'

Quartz eyes watched him, wide and without blinking, just like the wisp. At least that was one goodbye he'd not had to endure.

'Has Silas fallen? Have I lost my rider and my steed? I see nothing else keeping him from being at your side.'

The Leviathan drew back onto an even keel, and the moment Satine set him down, Pitch lunged for her. He wrapped his hands about her neck: thick as a drainpipe, smoother than the taffeta of his stained gown, and hard as rock. Even with his formidable strength, he barely made an impression.

'Silas is safe.' The hurt was physical, the ankou's name a razor to his tongue. 'I left him behind so he would not be harmed. Do not mention him again. I warn you.'

Coils shifted. 'I understand.'

'Make sure you do.' He loosened his hands, stepping back, the wretched softness of the beast's belly making him unsteady. Pitch exhaled, calming the fire that had risen. Seeing how grossly he'd overlooked another pain. One Satine would know well. 'I overstep...my apologies, my lady. I must...I am...' But truly there was no time for hesitancy. He considered going to a knee, but the thin, slimy covering on the leviathan's innards decided him otherwise. 'I ask your forgiveness for Lalassu's death.'

The words scoured his throat, but gods, their release was blissful.

Satine's tail tip shook, standing bolt upright. 'My Pale Horse knew your importance. She made her choice accordingly. It was not you who struck her.'

'But if I had not been so reckless –'

The hiss blew the sodden hairs from his face and made the damp lengths of his skirt rustle. 'Enough. You cannot be like this.'

'Like what?'

'Sorrowful, repentant.' Her solid head weaved back and forth. 'Frightened for those you love. You said you were Vassago. Then be him. Not Tobias or Pitch, or a man broken by the loss of his lover, and the downfall of a mare. Leave them behind. Be the prince the angel chose. And if you truly wish for my absolution, then become the single-minded beast that is needed here.'

If you are not the mad prince, you are not enough.

Seraphiel had said it.

They needed the Berserker Prince. He who knew no allies, certainly no friends, and absolutely no lover who might distract him from his purpose. He who could be a destructive maniac, precisely because he desired to be nothing else.

That prince was exactly why Seraphiel had chosen him.

The simurgh seemed to swell inside him, reach up between his ribs and into the crevices at his joints. Shaking loose the pieces of himself that Pitch had tried to hide. Rattling at them, desiring them free.

He did not protest.

'I assume your fish takes us to the halo?' He smoothed his voice clear of sentiment.

'As close as can be. I have made her as large and layered as the centuries would allow, but the heart of Blood Lake is treacherous. We shall take you as close as the Leviathan's strength, and my own, can abide. The rest is for you to endure.'

She still held him with a coil at his waist, for the unpredictable passage of the Leviathan had not abated. But Pitch had agency enough to reach for the cracked bone he'd spied. A shard that held the point of a knife. He tugged against Satine's hold until it slackened enough that he could drop to his arse on the creature's soft innards. He set to hacking at the fine taffeta, cutting himself a shorter skirt; bringing it roughly in line with his knees. If he'd known he was to be dropped straight from the ballroom to the lake, he might have chosen his clothing more carefully. But never had he been more grateful for the cinch of the corset, the pressure reminding him to temper his breath; the rigidness adding steel to his spine.

The Leviathan nosedived. Pitch let out a cry, barely avoiding slicing his leg when the bone knife slipped. Shock morphed to anger, and he took hold of his rage, as firmly as Satine wrapped him in her coils. Her beast thrashed and twisted in the slow, laboured way of giant animals.

'Let me go, damn it!' Pitch shouted. 'Do not restrain me. If I cannot stay on my feet in here, then I shall be fucking useless outside.' His flame shivered from his fingertips, rising along with his temper, and he glanced his hand against the lady's rose-gold tinged scales.

A serpentine hiss erupted. Satine let him go at the exact moment the Leviathan righted, and water rushed into their fleshy cavern. Carrying with it a fresh corpse. Pitch threw himself out of the way of the grotesque, bloated figure. He'd never seen such a creature: one solitary leg and one arm on a torso filleted with bleeding cuts, green blood flowing from the wounds. The head was like an enormous egg, and had only one lone eye, dull and yellowed like an old newspaper.

'What the fuck is that?'

'The purebred legends call it a fachan.' Satine lowered her triangular mouth near to the corpse, tongue flicking over skin that was covered with thick, saturated feathers. 'But it has no true name. It is one of Blood Lake's spawn. The halo continues to make monsters, even in the absence of Samyaza, and gives life to aberrations such as this.'

The Leviathan's killing work was ongoing. The creature's flesh bubbled, peeling away to expose bone, black as an apple seed.

Pitch stared in revulsion at both the messy deconstruction and the deformity itself. 'But if this is Blood Lake's creature, how do the purebreds know of it?'

He braced against the marshmallow pinkness of the Leviathan's side, too irritated to mind the damp, doughy feel beneath his hand. Satine drew her tail in, keeping it clear of where the fachan dissolved.

'The halo's potency did not create only the Blight, it bred these creatures, too. The Order names them the Fuath, those born of Blood Lake. And though the Leviathan does well with her hunts to keep their numbers low, they are too quick to multiply. Their existence creates a pressure beneath the Seals, and at rare times that pressure is vented through the angels' protective veil. The number of Fuath they allow to enter the purebred world is tightly controlled, and only the weakest among them are ever freed; the fachan is one, the selkie and the nucklevee, among many others, though I have argued since the first purge that last one is too dangerous, considering a nucklevee's appetite for flesh of any kind.' Her tail vibrated, shook like a rattle. 'Mr Ahari and I always loathed those times, when word reached the Order of their presence.'

'Gods.' Pitch breathed, ever more grateful that Silas's journey into the lake had not come to pass. To hear that not only were lost human souls haunted by the lake, but their living were cursed with its predators, too, would have given him great pains. 'So, the Blight...those bastards are venting it also, aren't they? The angels allow that menace into the world.'

He did not need to ask the question. The answer was so starkly, horribly obvious. Satin's bulging quartz eye could not seem to find him. 'Yes. The Blight is difficult to control, as it is not so easy to see as these monsters. There is a propensity for it to escape in high measures at a venting. And that is when –'

'That is when the Pale Horseman is summoned to deal with it.' Pitch balled his fists and stepped up to the rapidly decaying fachan. Much of the flesh was eroded from the skull, with only the enormous bulge of the eye remaining. 'You are fucking cunts, the damned lot of you. Arcadia treats this world as nothing more than a drain in which to dump its sewage.'

His blood was heated, his eyes searing with flame.

'Do not include my cunt in your assessment, Vassago.' The Lady Satine writhed, her coils flexing and tightening. 'We djinn are nature's children, born of her might and balance. For two thousand years, I've had to watch over this place, a birthplace of chaos, and try in vain to prevent it from ruining the perfection of the natural world. And now I must watch, as they send you to stir this cauldron of strife once more. It is your arrival that has unsettled all things. Now, should you fail, and this turmoil bubbles over, it will be I and the Order left to deal with the maelstrom. I am tired of being Lady of the Lake. Do not fail.'

'Your motivational skills are fucking appalling.' His throat thickened with anger; at the unfairness of the comment, the weight of expectations, and the sharp bite that fear of failure brought. 'And do not speak to me of maelstroms. I have known nothing but chaos.'

Save for a precious few moments–unexpected and unlikely–journeying at a dead man's side.

Pitch pressed his bare heel into the jellied mass of the fachan's eye, and the dull pop and slow flow of bodily fluid brought a sickening release. A sense of falling back into his old skin; atrocious daemonic skin, of flint and rock and molten heat, and utter distaste for all other living beings. The simurgh came alive, creeping into his sinews, into the fine hairs upon his body, his return to himself encouraging it, coaxing it deeper. Pitch ran his tongue over his lips, re-tasting all the blood he'd spilled over the centuries, re-breathing forgotten air: that of a mad warrior upon the Hellfield.

'Do you know what you must do?'

Satine's question drew him back to dull existence. His smile was lifted by bitterness and loss.

'Forget and remember.' Pitch pushed at the hem of velvet and taffeta at his wrist, tracing a fingertip over fine skin; where veins were stark and bulged like worms. 'Forget this suit of flesh and all its memories. And recall the truth of my nature.'

He should be eager to do so. For humankind was crude and pitiful. Readily built to break down. It would not be so terrible to shrug off the mantle he wore. It was an illusion, anyway. He'd been designed differently; and no layer of silk or skin that bloomed under a lover's touch could change what the Creation Flame had made him. What imbecile had he been to imagine otherwise?

'Then make haste, Prince of Arcadia.' Satine's hiss lifted the hairs on the back of his neck. 'For you cannot take this creature to face the halo. It shall be your downfall.'

'The simurgh? It is the reason we are here at all.'

A terrible vibration moved through the Leviathan. It was, Pitch suspected, a watery roar as it negotiated its sea of hellions.

'I speak of you, daemon.' Satine's body moved like a ribbon of silk falling from a table's edge. 'There is no place for Tobias Astaroth here, and yet he stands before me, hesitant and unhappy. You have softened, and it will make you vulnerable. You are not the daemon Seraphiel chose, and you must be, to see this done.'

'Softened?' he spat, welcoming the molten fury that filled him, sucking upon it like marrow from a bone. Feeding his monster. 'I remember all too well what it is to hate, I assure you.'

'Do you? You are so careful with your hatred now. You hold it in check too well. That is not how you lived before. You had no regard for its collaring, you were careless with its distribution. Quick to a fury that left you mindless and almighty. Your time here has reshaped you. I should have put an end to your partnership sooner.'

'Partnership?' he asked, though he knew her meaning well.

'You and the ankou. I had not expected the alliance to bear anything but tolerance and strength. Instead, this closeness you have formed weakens you both.'

'I am here in your fish's gut because of that alliance.' The realisation formed even as he spoke. 'If not for the ankou, for all those along the way who helped us, I'd not be here.'

The lady hissed, her scales clacking with her annoyance, and he was glad to see he had pissed her off. 'You should be here because you hunger to destroy, as you did upon the Hellfield. I do not see the mad prince before me. I see one possessed of a broken heart at leaving behind his dead lover. I see grief, not rage.'

'Keep talking this way and you'll see enough of the latter to satisfy you.'

'But that is my point entirely. You are in control. You hold your temper, your nature, in check, despite what I know to be a great turbulence inside you, a turbulence that needs your ferocity to feed on. Let him return, Vassago. Stop denying yourself. Allow the Berserker Prince to take hold. Remove this disguise you wear, for you know as well as I, it is false. You play a game here, as surely as the angel does with his simurgh.'

Pitch's skin glowed with barely suppressed flame as the lady chipped away at him, breaking down his charade piece by piece. Seeking to expose the beast at its core.

Satine's head swayed low, quartz eyes shifting away from him. 'Let go the false belief there was ever a place for you in this world. You ride the Red Horse. And she will accept none but those who carry the flames of strife and carnage. You are my Horseman of War, Vassago. That is the nature of you. The ankou may love Pitch or Tobias–he has fallen for the illusion you made for him–but he could never love that which lies behind the mask. And you know it.'

He'd lied earlier when he said he knew what it was to hate. He'd forgotten, somewhere in the gardens of Holly Village, and the hold of a dead man; what it was to hate so fiercely his blood caught fire.

But he recalled now.

He despised her, because every word that left Satine's mouth was true.

Even his fucking horse had known it. He was corporeal chaos.

Had he not told Silas from the beginning that he was a terrible creature? That he was one of those harbingers of death the ankou fought against.

Pitch could change his appearance but this pretty body had only ever hid a savage core.

The ache in his chest splintered.

The simurgh stretched itself, its wingtips caressing the bones in his arms, its tail moving through the columns of his legs, making his marrow itch.

An inferno ignited at the tips of his toes, eating its way upwards, urging the simurgh ever higher, ever closer to the surface. The Cultivation wrapped itself around every vein.

'Let me out.'

'We're not close enough.'

'Command your leviathan to release me. Now, Satine.'

It was not the voice of Tobias Astaroth that left him. It was not even that of Vassago.

Pitch heard himself as though listening to a stranger. A stranger who could command a thousand legions.

The serpent, the Lady of the Lake, retreated from him. Sliding back to create a distance. One she bowed low into.

'Your Highness,' she said in a small voice. He'd never thought of her as small. Satine had always been a force to be reckoned with. 'May the gods go with you.'

'I need no gods.'

His insides swelled, and the simurgh grew ever larger. His flame lit up the insides of the Leviathan, as if every gas lamp from the London streets was planted in its flesh.

The beast tilted at a sharp angle upward, and Pitch allowed threads of his flame to release from his back and splay out like tentacles to brace him. The roar from the beast reverberated through Pitch's body. His feeble body, dressed in all the whimsy and ineptitude of the purebreds. He was a child's fable; the wolf dressed in sheep's clothing. And he could barely wait to shed its layers. He relished the damage the flames did to the delicate garb now; the first of much destruction to come.

Shifting bones and half-digested corpses were cremated in his fire, their fine ash coating the leviathan's innards like cruel bruises. The creature levelled out, and Pitch straightened, setting his shoulders back. He made his way forward, and Satine slithered ahead, clearing the detritus, removing all obstruction from his path.

Vassago paid her no mind.

She mattered not.

Very little mattered but reaching the mouth of the beast, finding those hanging folds of fibrous mass that acted as strange teeth.

With each step he took on spongy flesh, the simurgh beat its wings, a powerful brush that seemed to inflate Vassago larger. Returning him to his true vastness.

The Cultivation readied to play its part. Now the Berserker Prince would do the same.

CHAPTER 34

For a frail creature Seraphiel held significant weight. Lucifer struggled as he moved him from the ballroom, where he had collapsed beneath the chandelier of bone flowers, with an obsidian mirror clutched tight in his grip. Lucifer could not loosen it when he gathered up the angel; Seraphiel snarling like a rapid dog until he desisted. The ground and walls trembled, as though a great storm churned beyond the windows. One blow had been violent enough to rattle all the chandeliers in the ballroom. But he knew it was no natural storm.

Lucifer leaned heavily upon his walking cane, whilst trying to keep the angel upright and moving, in a palace that seemed set to shake itself apart.

'Jacquetta!' Lucifer bellowed, not for the first time. 'Blast you. Come and guide me.'

Seraphiel was a muttering imbecile, and Michael held the Sanctuary's Ferryman hostage.

This was not a fortuitous day.

And this damned labyrinth of a palace bamboozled him. He wished to return Seraphiel to the bedroom he'd been found in, the same bed Lucifer had been relegated to–at the angel's insistence–after his blood was taken for the Cultivation. But he was damned if he could recall which hallway led there. So far he'd only discovered sitting rooms with no settees, a dining room with lavishly cushioned chairs, and another bloody music room; the piano covered in a sheet of delicate golden lace. None of the rooms, save perhaps for the dining room where he might have laid the angel out on the table, had anything remotely suitable for reclining the failing Seraph.

Glassware rattled in buffets and ever-present ferns shivered in their pots, as yet another blow struck.

'Coming, your majesty!'

At long last, Jacquetta appeared, running down the length of yet another corridor that seemed to have no end. Lucifer longed for his simpler confines in the Arcadian Siltron Ranges, his tower of retreat, with a handful of rooms, beautiful for their plainness. Seraphiel had always pushed for elaborate redecoration, but grandeur made Lucifer's head ache.

'Where have you been?' Lucifer glowered. 'Where are his grace's rooms? He must be in his bed.'

'This way, your majesty.'

He did not like the haunted look on the Child's face; she knew things he was not going to enjoy hearing.

'Quickly,' he hissed.

The angel found some strength and tried to wriggle from Lucifer's gathered embrace. 'No time...Luci...he will ruin it all.'

'Stay still, blast you, or you'll put us both on our arses.'

Lucifer was dizzy, among many other things. The blood Seraphiel had taken from him to repair and fortify the Cultivation was not regenerating. He was drained and was not filling. He'd hardly expected to feel sprightly after such a taxing undertaking being performed upon his beleaguered, dying body, but he'd never had a day in his long life where he did not feel strong.

This was the first.

Still, there had been no alternative. The angel had needed divine magick for the repair. Lucifer was the perfect poisoned chalice; struck by Michael's halo, and diseased with the Primordial Flame.

Jacquetta moved them down the corridor, throwing many harried glances over her shoulder. Lucifer suspected she wished to tell them to hurry the blazes up, but would never dare.

His stomach churned, and if not for the cane, he doubted he'd be on his feet, but he could hardly have draped Seraphiel across his knees and wheeled about in that confounded chair. The cane had been a hurried and fortuitous find in Seraphiel's bedchamber. One very unlike the angel to own. But then, the Seraph had not been himself for a long time.

'This one. It is closer than his chambers, and he favours this room. There is no bed, but a settee to lie his grace upon.'

Lucifer glared at her back, but chose not to admonish her for suggesting Lord Enoch's Highest Angel should be settled on a mere settee.

Lucifer dragged the still-protesting angel into the room.

A library. Bookshelves covered all the walls, save for the one where a well-set fire crackled in the hearth of a dark wood mantle. Books everywhere he looked, floor to high ceiling. Lucifer relaxed in his struggle with the angel, staring open-mouthed. Jacquetta moved in to take the weight of Seraphiel from him.

Lucifer drank the room in; embellished spines, thick tomes with glorious calligraphy naming them, a gilded ladder on wheels to move about and reach the top of those impossibly tall shelves, overstuffed armchairs one could sink into for days.

'This is my library.' He drew his gaze from the familiar setting to find Seraphiel wincing as he sat. 'You built a replica here?'

Another tremor struck, and the closed shutters banged against their clasps. Shutters covered both of the two windows, just as Lucifer enjoyed in an identical library in his Siltron Ranges' tower: a place he'd designed so as to hide from the trials and tribulations of Arcadia, and lose himself in other worlds.

'It's not quite right, those decanters need work. Yours are finer, if I recall.' Seraphiel flipped his hand toward the side-table, with its assortment of glass, and scowled at Jacquetta as she lifted his legs to drape them on the settee: deep blue damask against Cherrywood. Lucifer had been torn between blue and red at the time he'd created his library, so he'd simply made another settee and used them both. 'I thought of bringing you here one day. I thought perhaps it would please you.' Seraphiel shook his head, his golden strands falling over one shoulder. 'But that day never came. Stop bothering me, fae.'

His snappish tone had Jacquetta stepping away, her jaw tight, but her decorum unruffled. 'Of course, your grace.'

'It pleases me.' Lucifer cleared his throat. 'Very much.'

'What does?' Seraphiel gave him a narrowed stare. 'What are you on about?'

Lucifer sank down onto one of the armchairs, tired beyond words. 'This library. You said you made it for me...and it is beautiful.'

'Hardly matters now.' Seraphiel lifted his mirror. 'This bastard seeks to ruin it all.' He frowned into the black glass.

'This instability, the tremors, they are Michael's work?' Lucifer asked, knowing the answer well, but hoping to bring the angel's thoughts onto an evener keel.

Seraphiel grunted, focused on his obsidian.

'They are, your majesty.' Jacquetta nodded. 'The Ferryman resists him for now, and refuses to dock,' she glanced at Seraphiel. 'But the Sanctuary's magick suffers with Lord Michael's assault.'

'Can you not add fortification? I could assist, perhaps?' Lucifer had his flames, though how long before they too dwindled, he could not guess.

Seraphiel sniffed. 'What could you do? You're mostly dead, Luci.'

The Child looked appalled, but Lucifer gave her a small shake of the head. 'What else might be done?' He spoke calmly, but his fingers dug into the yellow-gold head of the cane.

'Your offer is gracious, your majesty, but...' Again, the fae glanced at the angel. 'This shall take great magick, to withstand him much longer.'

'Unless that's what you want, Luci?' Seraphiel lifted his head, a sharp motion, his white eyes narrowed. 'Perhaps you wish to see this Sanctuary fall.'

Lucifer sighed inwardly.

'Whatever do you mean?' He braced for the fresh wave of madness he knew would come. 'Why would I wish that?'

'Enoch has sent you, hasn't he? He always held you in high esteem. You had his favour, much as I.' His eyes brightened. He nodded at his own faulty reasoning. 'Do you work for the lord, and seek to kill me, again? Have you betrayed me, Hadrian?'

The angel grew stiff with his frenzy, dropping the mirror in his lap and pressing himself upright, arms rigid.

'Settle down, you fool. I am no traitor to you, and you know it, Raph.' Lucifer scowled, but his pulses beat fast. Seraphiel did not know he'd taken Wrath to the cockaigne, but he feared what insanity it would stoke, should the unstable Seraph find out. 'I saw that the prince was delivered to you, at a cost I cannot pay. You know me dying. You have seen what Michael's halo did to me when I fought him –'

'Trickery. Illusion. You were in the Erlking's court. Perhaps he too aids you in my downfall.'

'What utter rot. Listen to yourself.'

Seraphiel's hair swayed as he shook his head. 'Don't try to disillusion me.'

'You are doing a fine job of that on your own.'

The angel stabbed a finger towards Lucifer. 'Your vestige! You claim Michael tore it from you, but who is to say you did not hand it over? And that enables his vice grip upon the Ferryman.'

Anger pushed aside Lucifer's pains. 'Careful. You go too far, Raph.' His fingers danced with feeble flame, but there *was* guilt there. The idea he'd handed his vestige over was preposterous, of course. Michael had stolen it, in an act of cruelty, along with the piece of Lucifer's daemon-stone. But those thefts had certainly led the Seraph to the prince at the cave.

Lucifer's inability to fend off Michael, was the very reason the Sanctuary now groaned in its joints.

'Do I really go too far, though?' Seraphiel grunted as he shifted, setting his feet back on the floor, though looking in danger of toppling over at any moment. Jacquetta hovered nearby, at the ready. 'What of the flame? The Primordial Flame that eats at you...you sought to steal it from me...' His eyes widened, his hands white-knuckled where they clutched at the settee, as he danced onto another wild theory. '*You* damaged the simurgh, not the Archangel, nor that infantile Iblis. You are working with that Nephilim, aren't you, Lucifer?' Spittle flew from his mouth, the veins in his neck bulging. 'You both seek to stop me. I will kill you, Lucifer.' He pushed to his feet, the radiant light from his eyes near blinding. The mirror landed on the rug with a thump. 'I will kill you here and now.'

Lucifer lunged, grabbing at Seraphiel's shoulders. He shook him fiercely. 'Stop this, do you hear me? How many times must I tell you? I am no enemy. I never have been, nor ever will be.'

The angel's eyes dimmed. Seraphiel did not fight back, moaning softly. The sound brought Lucifer to a sudden halt, his breath ragged. His body trembling.

'Gods, Raph...I didn't mean to –'

'Forgive me,' Seraphiel whispered.

'There is nothing to forgive. I know your true mind.'

'But I fear it grows more and more foreign to me.' He pressed his forehead against Lucifer's chest. 'Luci, it is not your death needed here. It is mine. Once and for all.'

Lucifer felt the rare brush of a chill. 'Don't speak that way.'

'Why not? It is the truth. I thought I had outwitted the waters, their poisoning of me, but the lord was right. It cannot be done. Even this part of me I hoped to keep pure is succumbing again.'

'Not yet, it isn't. Now sit down,' he said sternly, to cover any fear that escaped him. 'Catch your breath and let us think this through.' Lucifer assisted the angel as he sat back down, far gentler with him now. 'Vassago has gone through the Seal. Has the lady found him? Can we know?'

The palace shook upon its foundations, the room rattled, and somewhere behind them a book fell from its shelf. This time, the far distant roll of thunder accompanied the shaking.

Jacquetta handed Seraphiel the mirror. Her hand trembled. 'Your Grace, will the mirror show you?'

Seraphiel shook his head, his shoulders slumped. Lucifer bit his lip, glancing away. His was not the only life ebbing away. He hoped his end would arrive before he was forced to watch Seraphiel slip from him a second time.

'The mirror cannot scry into the lake.' The angel lay his hand over the glass, nearly covering the small, rounded piece entirely. 'But the lady can reach me in her own way.'

He closed his eyes, dulling the room, and whispered a few words. He went still. Jacquetta wrung her hands, glancing at the clock on the mantle. It had been barely twenty minutes since Vassago had disappeared from the ballroom; whilst he stood beneath the chandelier of bone lillies and blue flame, begging for the ankou to be protected. Lucifer had never heard the prince beg for a thing in his four hundred years.

'Your Grace,' Jacquetta whispered. 'You are bleeding.'

Lucifer had seen it already. A thin trail of black ran from the corner of Seraphiel's mouth. Lucifer wiped it away with his thumb and received a ready slap.

'Never mind that.' Seraphiel said, flashing teeth stained pale black. 'I told you I had little time to survive in this body.' He paused. Lucifer found himself studied. 'Vassago has taken his first step into the lake.'

Lucifer blew out a breath, a great weight lifting from his chest. 'He has?'

'Of course he has,' Seraphiel wiped at the corner of his mouth, with a hint of a bittersweet smile. 'He was sired by the greatest King of Daemonkind Arcadia has known.'

Lucifer stared at him. What did one say to such gross exaggeration? 'Well, I hardly think –'

Whatever he thought didn't matter. Another tremor struck the Sanctuary. A violent rocking of the foundations, one that sent books tumbling from the highest rows, and sending the decanters Seraphiel had been so dissatisfied with shattering against the woodwork. Jacquetta swore, the curses befitting a fishwife, as she grabbed hold of the settee.

'Your Grace, if that angel brings down the Sanctuary, the Seal goes with it.' She was brusque, forgoing all flattery. 'And I have nothing left to give to reinforce this place. These walls will not hold if he continues.'

Lucifer frowned. 'What do you mean the Seal goes with it?'

'Never mind all that.' Seraphiel said, glaring down at the mirror. 'The Sanctuary will not fall.'

Jacquetta huffed in frustration, her seemingly endless patience with the delicate Seraph clearly at an end. 'Begging your pardon, but you are wrong. I have built you a formidable stronghold, and followed your orders to feed the Cultivation and fortify the Seal, but that has compromised my structure, and now we have lost this Sanctuary's greatest weapon which was concealment.' She drew in a hurried breath, continuing. 'They could not destroy what they could not find. But now Michael knows he is on the right path.' She looked to Lucifer, her anxiety hardening her features. 'Has he told you that the Seraph rides in the

Ferryman's boat?' She gave him no chance to answer. 'That boat and its guide are a buttress that strengthen the Sanctuary, and Michael knows it. He seeks to break the Ferryman's will, as he would break a lock, and peel away a layer of protection from my build. These tremors mark his attempts, and they grow stronger each time.'

'And the Seal?' Lucifer adopted his poise of command, his face empty of expression, his demeanour equally so; as he'd done a thousand times before on the Hellfield.

Jacquetta eyed Seraphiel, hesitating. The angel stared down into his mirror; Michael and the Ferryman were visible now in the glass.

To look at them there seemed nothing untoward. The boatman stood in their suit of armour at the bow, whilst Michael, in his human guise, sat in the middle; that great bruiser of a man who had made the people in the tea-house in Slaidburn tremble, a rival to the ankou in his solidness and breadth, the sort of fellow best avoided in a dark alley.

Michael wished to frighten. Well, he had the King of Daemonkind fearful now.

'Tell me how this affects the Seal. Now,' Lucifer demanded.

Seraphiel spoke, his eyes casting a glow against the obsidian. 'Simple really. I knew my death might have dire consequences for my Seal, and that if Michael or Ariel took it over, there was no chance I could return. No chance the vessel would ever be allowed through. So I created a Cultivation that would, in the event of my demise, anchor the Seal to the Sanctuary, and feed from it, to maintain its strength. They would have no reason to claim it, for it would hold.'

'And this Cultivation has something to do with the ballroom? Where Samyaza's bones lie?' Lucifer tried to overlook how certain Seraphiel had been in his death.

'The bones are the lynchpin, yes.'

'So the dancers...they are a part of the Cultivation, too?'

The angel watched Michael, who sat like a statue of stone in the boat. His gaze was such that it seemed he looked straight at the mirror.

'What greater thing to counter death than life?' Seraphiel spoke like a poet over his cups, a whimsical note to his words.

But Lucifer understood the darkness that truly lay there. 'The purebreds...they are what feed the Seal in your absence.'

'They keep insisting on dying though...' Seraphiel's laughter was short. 'I cannot seem to make life bend to my will. She refuses to offer the eternity that her sister Death provides.' He poked his finger at Michael's head, twisting it, as though he sought to grind the image of the angel from the glass.

Lucifer turned to Jacquetta as thunder strode like giants' footsteps across the sky. 'Do you have more? Purebreds, I mean?' Perhaps Seraphiel had thought to stock up a dungeon before he went and got himself killed.

'No.' Jacquetta answered as Seraphiel sang a vicious song of hatred beneath his breath, counting all the ways Michael was flawed. 'I have used all those we had, as I didn't dare to send the Ferryman to collect more, knowing of the great unrest in the Blight, and of maleficium's return.'

Lucifer felt the weight of his own blood in his veins, the snapped beat of his burdened heart. 'So those who dance there now are the last, and when they are no longer there to sustain the Seal, it shall turn to the Sanctuary to feed.'

'Yes, your majesty. And if Michael keeps up his assault, the Sanctuary will fall –'

'And Blood Lake may flood this world once more.' Seraphiel did not raise his head from the mirror, letting gold strands hide him away.

'Then we must feed the bloody Sanctuary.' Lucifer paced away, his fingers going instinctively to his moustache. Or at least, where it had once been; with half scorched away by the interlude with Michael he'd decided on being clean shaven. Not his preference, for he found the endless running of fingers over oil-slicked hair strangely soothing, and was pleased to feel the hint of coarse hair growing back already. He needed some refuge from this nightmare he'd landed in.

'Could you reason with Michael?' Jacquetta offered, though she sounded doubtful.

'He has always been one to exterminate a threat before he learns anything of it. And he is set on destroying Vassago,' Lucifer said. 'Plus, he knows of the simurgh.'

'He will be determined to see this Sanctuary razed.' Seraphiel paused in his derogatory tune, returning to sensibility. 'And he does not know my Seal is here. I've always kept its location hidden, and moved it on occasion, as all my brothers have done with theirs. Michael would come in, halo blazing, and not pay us a whit of attention. By the time we could convince him my Seal was here –'

'It would be too late.' Lucifer nodded, his fingers still working over his bare lip.

'Time.' Seraphiel rose to his feet, warding off Jacquetta's step forward to help. 'Time is the only weapon we have against him now. Vassago needs time. He will see this done. Look how far he has come.' He shifted his hair back behind his shoulders, and Lucifer saw the steadiness in his hands. His Antinous had returned, however short the visit. 'Knowing how long he has endured my Cultivation, even I am taken aback by his tenacity. Perhaps you were right to make that vow, to keep the ankou and those purebreds safe, Luci. Vassago deserves that much.'

Lucifer's fingers ceased their tracing. The thudding blow that struck the Sanctuary might as well have landed against his chest.

He *had* vowed to see them safe; Silas and Charlie, Edward, and the wisp.

But the stakes had grown exponentially higher than that odd gaggle; if the Seal were to break, it was not just those within the Sanctuary, but every single creature who had aided Vassago in reaching this place, who now lay in harm's way. Worse still, every writer of Lucifer's beloved tomes, every storyteller who had built wondrous tales in which he could escape–all those who still lived–now faced a monumental threat.

Lucifer's fingers moved again; and ran along the scratch of coarse hair forming above his lip. He was not gone yet. There was life in his weary bones.

'My blood. Can you take more of it? Perhaps give it to the purebreds who still dance?'

'That was enough for the simurgh, but not for the Seal.' Seraphiel shook his head.

An idea sparked in the grim depths of Lucifer's innards, and bloomed bright; defying the poisons that broke him down. 'You need more.'

'Far more, yes.' Seraphiel said, carefully. He moved closer, head tilted. 'Share your thoughts, Luci.'

But Lucifer had shared enough years with the angel, spent enough time in quiet contemplation with him to know he already understood.

'We are enough, aren't we, Raph?' The idea was like ivy now, wrapping itself around him, beautiful, and suffocating. 'We could revive the dance.'

Jacquetta drew in a breath, but knew better than to intervene.

'We could.' The angel pressed his hand to Lucifer's shoulder. A rare moment of contact between them. 'Are you sure, Luci?'

The tremor shook one shutter free of its clasp, swinging it open; flooding the room with light. Lucifer waited, barely feeling the rumble at his feet, for he was unshakeable now. 'Vassago needs time, and you and I have used all but the last minute the gods have granted us. I am sure, Raph.'

CHAPTER 35

Silas lay on his back, in sunshine that beat down with a perfectly lovely heat. The air was dank with the waft of honeysuckle and roses, utterly charming and rich enough to make him a little light-headed. His hands rested beneath his head, his chin tilted to take in the warmth, his eyes closed against the glare. There was grass beneath him, he smelled its pungent, spring-fed scent, felt its soft padding beneath his back. His bare back.

That caused the flicker of a frown. Why did he not wear a shirt? But almost at once he had the answer, and his smile could not be wider. He chuckled to himself and touched at his lips. There was still the hint of the daemon upon them, that bitter-sweetness that was such a part of Pitch: kisses like lemon pie, when the chef had been too heavy-handed with the lemon and cinnamon.

Pie. Is that where Pitch had gone? To get them something to indulge in, now they had finished indulging in one another.

Silas smiled, blinking into the brightness of the day, stretching his arm to play at the grass there. Pitch was definitely not with him. A tiny whisper of discontent came with that, but then the waft of honeysuckle and roses rushed in, and Silas decided it was not discontentment after all, but hunger.

Pie. Tarts. That was where the daemon was, rustling up a picnic, to fuel them so they could indulge in intimacy with returned vigour.

Silas exhaled, imagining what he would next do to Pitch, how he would make him whimper in that blissful way of his, watch as he threw back his head and moaned, spreading his legs wider for Silas.

With such thoughts, Silas's concerns slipped away.

He was content.

Insects moved about him, the buzz of a bee there, the click of a cricket to his right. At his arm, an ant tickled his skin as it made its way over the mountainous range of his limb.

Silas breathed in, letting his eyes flutter open, and exhaled once more. He rolled his head, taking in his surrounds. Grass, as he'd suspected, verdant, short-cropped. A greensward.

The thought snagged, and the pitter-patter of the ant grew more ticklish. More irritating. Silas shifted his arms from beneath his head, shaking the tiny critter free. The wash of honeysuckle came in stronger, almost to the point of sickening. Almost. The roses tempered the strength of the scent perfectly, and Silas abandoned the thought of sitting up.

It was perfectly lovely here. An exquisite greensward.

A pain bothered at the back of his eyes, and he rubbed at them.

Another sweep of floral magnificence came, and the pain slipped away.

He glimpsed a stone. A block of granite peaking through the grass. Another stood not far away, and something in their rough cut and tilted stance caused his thoughts to snag yet again. A butterfly appeared, a pretty thing of speckled blue and black, which decided his nose was a proper landing place. Silas waved it off, and it danced in the air above him. The movements were mesmerising, the fluttering hard to look away from as it repeated the same pattern over and over and over. Perhaps he'd doze a while longer, whilst he waited.

His eyelids grew leaden, eager to close.

Silas rolled his head in the opposite direction, all but ready to give in to the urge to sleep, when his gaze fell upon more stones. Just like the others, they were half consumed by the grass.

He was surrounded. In a circle of stones.

And all at once, he was afraid. The butterfly sought his nose once more.

'No.' Silas sat up, swiping more vigorously at the insect. His hand swept through its flimsy mass and the butterfly burst, small blue petals fluttering. 'Where am I?'

His contentment was slipping, like a blanket falling free when one woke from a nightmare.

Silas squeezed his eyes shut, his thoughts snagging once more. They dangled, half-shaped, refusing to form. He touched his hand to his bare chest, suddenly awash with confusion. He could not recall undressing, and was certain he'd remember if Pitch had undone his buttons. Where was his coat? And his boots?

Damn it, this was not right. A thought tingled, like the blasted ant returned, then wriggled down more like a worm, deep into his mind to hide.

'Pitch, where are you?' His voice had no reverberation, no hint of echo. 'Are you there?'

'Hush now, Lord Death, is this not a wonderful enough haven for you?'

Silas jumped at the figure, a man, lying right beside him on the grass. Silas's first thought; *it is not Pitch*.

'Byleist?' Silas's thoughts were pickled with confusion. 'This is an illusion. You cannot be.'

'And yet I am.'

The ants crawled through Silas's mind and their tickle drew his thoughts away from where he sought to lead them. 'But you died...when you aided us in escaping the cockaigne. I saw you entombed in the glass.'

Some forgotten gleam of information dangled itself just out of reach. Something he should recall.

Perhaps this was the crazed landscape of a dream, Silas reasoned with himself. And he'd wake, yelping like a fool, Pitch dozing at his side, ready to make a right mockery of him for it.

'Did you hear my death notes, my lovely fellow?' The Dullahan, or rather the fae he'd once been, lay with his elbow crooked, resting his head upon one raised hand, working a fine sliver of grass between his lips. His bone hand. A skeletal remnant of Silas and his scythe, freeing a headless horseman from servitude. Byleist grinned. 'If you say I am dead, then it must be so, Lord Death.'

'I...well, I suppose I didn't...' Silas pressed at his forehead, wishing the damned ants would stop buggering about. 'No...I heard no death note...but you were entombed in the glass.'

'Entombed, yes. Dead, not quite so.' The fae grinned, his teeth too sharp to be called pleasant. Even in York, as Byleist showed more evidence of his true self, there could be no doubt he'd been a striking elf in life. He was glorious here, the array of gold earrings on his pointed ears catching the sunlight on crystal prisms, the purple hues of his long hair distinct and bright, and his eyes like black cherries in syrup, glistening and inviting. And distractedly alluring. 'Though I did wonder, when that angel was so rough about it, whether I'd end up dead at his hands.'

'Michael.' Silas said, for no particular reason, with no particular emotion behind it. Just a name. Just an angel. No bother.

The butterfly settled upon Byleist's shoulder, upon a shirt of the finest, thinnest silken silver, his nipples like tight rose buds beneath. Silas stared at the blue wings on the insect, their slow sweep back and forth was soothing.

'That is the one, yes. He searched for you, but I gave him nothing.'

'Thank you,' Silas sighed, contentment warming him once more. 'You are brave. And I am much relieved to know for certain you are well. It pained me to leave you that way, especially without a chance to tell you of my deep gratitude for all you did for us.'

Byleist's sultry grin vanished, replaced with something much more sombre. 'You could tell me now, my lord. It shall help us pass the time.'

Silas smiled and settled onto his back. 'Very well, then. I thank you, Byleist. For your Duty-bind, and your persistence in honouring it. Without you, my friend...' he shook his head. 'I don't like to imagine how bad things might have gone.'

'My friend,' Byleist whispered. 'Do you truly see me as such, my lord?'

'I do. But I'd see it more clearly if you'd stop addressing me that way.'

He wondered how long it would take for Pitch to return. Silas wished to see how delighted he'd be to find Byleist well. The daemon and fae were firm friends. Were they not?

The ants were getting bothersome again.

'You are not fond of a title, are you?' Byleist's smile returned, along with his pointed teeth and his stare. 'I think titles are quite fetching. I certainly shall command no one to cease addressing me as Regent.'

Silas scratched in behind his ear, searching for what tickled at his thoughts there. 'Regent?' The grass was warm as a rug lying before the fire. He ran his hand out over it, eager for it to be covered once more by Pitch's body. 'That is quite a grand title, indeed.'

'Isn't it just?' Byleist mirrored Silas's move onto his back, tucking his bone hand behind his head. 'But fortune favours those who survive long enough. The Erlking is no longer, and, it turns out, was a dreadful king, with barely a subject who could stand him. Myself included, of course. The UnSeelie Throne sits empty, and I have been chosen to keep it warm for now. I suppose they assume I despised Lokke most of all, with being his Dullahan so long as I was, so I am least likely to follow in his tradition of making appalling alliances with angels and sorcerers.'

'Angels and sorcerers?' The butterfly's wings were not so brilliant blue as Silas recalled. 'I don't think I like either of those...' But he really wasn't sure. All that was certain was that ants were making a maze of his mind.

He brushed at his hair, trying to shake them free.

'There, there. Don't fuss with those superb curls.' Byleist took him by the wrist, urging his hand down. 'All is well now. You are very safe now. That is what we both wanted. At least he and I have that in common.'

Silas lowered his hand, letting the fae entwine their fingers. 'The Erlking wished to see me safe?' He may be addled, but that made no sense whatsoever.

'No, no, my charming ankou.' Byleist settled their hands upon Silas's bare chest. 'The daemon. He reneged on his promise, and as Regent I was in the fortunate position of being able to accept your bequeathing to the fae, and claim you as my own. You are perfectly safe now. He knew there was really only one place for you.' Byleist sighed and laid his head against Silas's shoulder. 'And that is with me.'

Silas frowned up at the pretty sky, with its perfect clouds and sublime temperature. He'd not noticed any clouds before. 'The daemon? You speak of Pitch?' Why did that simple question seem weighed down and difficult to put into words? 'He reneged on a promise?'

Thoughts were forming amongst the ants, and Silas resisted the urge to brush them aside, get rid of their prickly pieces.

'Yes, yes. He promised himself to the bluecaps queen, in exchange for your freedom. Even though that queen is dead, the promise is not. Clever boy, that daemon, to discover the clause of reneging. It is long buried in the annals of the Courts' histories. Of course, as soon as I knew you were being returned, I claimed you for the UnSeelie Court. So here we are, just two chaps enjoying the illusion of a fine summer's day. Though I'm pleased, that the daemon cannot see I've made you shirtless. He's a far more affable fellow than I'd imagined, but he gets rather heated over you.' Byleist squeezed Silas's hand. 'But perhaps I worry too much, and he'll just be pleased to know you are admired and desired.'

Suddenly the warmth was cloying, the grass like hedgehog quills against Silas's back. And the ants, the blasted, bloody ants, were still insistent. Silas shook off Byleist's hold and sat up.

The fae made a noise of irritated surprise.

'He is not here.' A pickaxe of certainty drove itself into Silas's thoughts. 'He is not here. What have you done to him?'

Byleist sighed, flopping onto his back, draping his arm across his eyes. 'Gracious, I told Jacquetta to have him sign a blood agreement before he toddled off. I told her you'd not believe it.'

Silas whirled onto his knees, no easy task when his skull felt heavy as a cannonball, his limbs weighted like they were turning to stone. 'Toddled off? Where the blasted hell has Pitch gone?'

Oh, the ants were scattering now from his thoughts. Fleeing for their bloody lives, as they should.

'Off to the lake, of course.' Byleist was infuriatingly matter of fact about it. 'I'll be honest. Both Jacquetta and I were shocked at his self-lessness.'

Shock squeezed Silas's lungs. He could barely speak for the rage. 'He left me?'

'Good of him, don't you think?' Byleist withdrew his arm from his eyes, smiling up at Silas like a lover ready for his due. 'Never thought he had it in him. You are quite safe now, Lord Death.'

'Fuck, I don't wish to be safe, Byleist,' Silas shouted, but this strange twilight held him deadened in all ways, stuffed with cotton and stones.

'It is not selflessness, it is utter stupidity. Let me out of this place. I have to go to him.'

The damned ants weren't done yet, nibbling at his remembrance of how to get to his feet. Hard as he thought on it, he could not recall which limb moved first.

'Of course you think you need to go to him, my lord, but the daemon was quite right. It is best you stay here, Jacquetta has you quite safe, trust me. And I'll be there the moment I'm given the go-ahead to retrieve you.'

'No one will bloody well *retrieve* me. And not a one of you may determine what is best for me.' Silas had never been more furious at Pitch. It made his blood thunder in his ears. 'Release me. Now.'

Byleist's seductive smile melted like heated wax, and his gaze shifted to the sky. The clouds were dark smears now, where they had been white puff balls before. He sat up. 'My lord, calm yourself. It is not that simple to walk away from a royal claim of the UnSeelie Court.'

'Make it simple. Release me.' The voice rose from the bottom of Silas's chest, that guttural depth of voice he'd discovered in the cockaigne. The one that gathered all his years in its wake and used their mass to propel it from his lungs.

The sunshine wilted. Byleist tilted his head, his hair sweeping at the grass that was now turned brown and crisp beneath him. He appeared as close to worry as Silas knew him capable. 'You must understand, it was your prince's choice to renege –'

Silas grabbed at Byleist's shirt and dragged the elf in close. 'I promised him he would not see this through alone, do you hear me? He may renege on his promise, but I will never, ever go back on mine. Never. My vow is as certain as death.'

Byleist smoothed the alarm from his face. 'The lake is the daemon's burden. His fate lies in those waters. He fears you seeing what he will become, and was sickened by the thought you'd be there, watching as he fell. Stay here, Silas. It is what your mighty prince wished for you.'

'Wished for me?'

'To save you from any suffering.'

Silas's heart truly ached, not just a pinch of muscle at his ribs, but the pumping, frantic vessel itself.

'This does not save me, Byleist. It curses me.' He loosened his grip on the fae's shirt, his hands shaking. 'Pitch is a fool if he thinks this death wish shall spare me any suffering. You say you are my protector, and my friend?' Byleist nodded. 'Then help me. My days, my hours perhaps, are numbered, and every breath will be an agony if you do not let me go to him.'

Byleist rocked onto his knees, bringing them almost face to face, for the fae was a tall, lithe creature. The brittle grass crackled with his weight. He cupped his bone hand to Silas's cheek. He allowed the intimacy, too busy searching the fae's face for a sign he would agree.

'My Lord, my friend...this is for the best. You are the only one who cannot see it. I cannot let you go.'

Silas's fury sat like dark, smouldering coals in his belly. The earth rumbled beneath his knees. Byleist shot a look of unconcealed fright at the shaking ground.

'My lord, I beg you, calm yourself. You are in neither one world nor the other, and I fear what shall become of you if you damage this place.'

'Then let me out.'

'I cannot.' Byleist sounded truly anguished. 'I don't want to.'

Silas dragged in a deep breath, finally clearing his head. The scent of the soil found him; loam and iron and coppery depths. Rich and teeming, the giver of life.

The scythe hummed against his finger, waking along with him. Sending a surge of clarity.

The soil; giver of life, but formed by death. The result of living things returned to the earth, and broken down hungrily. Made immortal.

Silas edged away from the fae and leaned down to plant his hands upon the ground. He dug his fingers into the dying moss, and it dissolved like sand between his fingers. The moss that had swallowed most of the faerie circle stones now fell away, making naked the granite stones; dull with their rounded tops and mediocre size, their uninteresting parched surfaces, smoothed by time.

'My lord, I beg you, take care.'

'Tell me what must be done.' Silas dug his hands into the dirt; felt it drive beneath his fingernails. The rumbling grew more intense, enough that Byleist braced his fingers against the ground to steady himself. A dusky light held court now, the sky clouded over.

'Silas –'

'Tell me what must be done.'

'It cannot be done. That is what I'm trying to tell you. The fae circle is held closed by the reneging of his promise.'

Silas drew in deep lungfuls of air, letting the waft of decay seep into him, spread through his body like a welcome disease. 'If it can be closed, it can be opened. Tell me what must be done.'

A bird dropped from the sky. Landing dead between them. Byleist's cry was one of horror and awe. 'My lord –'

'I'm losing patience.'

An anguished sound came from the fae. 'You will be harmed –'

'Byleist.' Silas's roar brought with it the fall of another sparrow, another fluttering of butterflies. And a sharp crack.

A fine break in one of the stones.

The fae's black eyes widened, his pretty lips parting in astonishment. 'You have found it.'

'Found what?' Silas growled, another booming reverberation moving through the ground, as though all the long ago-dead raged with him. No matter the world or realm, no matter the longevity of the life within it, there was no place that death did not know.

'Your way.' Byleist spent a moment in a clear struggle with himself. Then he muttered what could only be curses. 'The stones, they are what hold you. Break the stones. It will not sever your allegiance to the UnSeelie Court, but it will free you from this purgatory. I cannot, I will not, aid you in this. And I do not know how it might harm you, but I dare say that does not worry you much.' He rose to his feet, an imperious bearing to the way he stood over Silas. 'I shall not stay to watch, though. I do not trust that the urge to save you from yourself will not overwhelm me. Perhaps then I would become another bird to fall from the sky.'

Silas had been focused upon the ground, upon the shift of every grain of soil that might aid him. He raised his head. 'I would not harm you.'

Byleist's sly smile returned. 'Oh, my dear, that is a lie. There is nothing you will not do for him. None are safe whilst the lord of death seeks his lover. Perhaps he should have known that not even the entire UnSeelie

Court would be enough to keep you away.' He raised his bone hand to his lips, kissed his white fingers, and blew the kiss to Silas.

'Thank you, Byleist. For all.'

He did not speak of seeing the fae again one day. What point in any more promises to be broken?

'Good luck, Silas Mercer. If you free yourself, I hope you find him well enough to know you, and glad enough of your arrival. You chose a troubled creature to love.'

Silas turned his attention to the circle. 'And he in return.'

When he glanced up again, the Dullahan was gone.

Silas dug his feet deeper into the soil, and slipped the scythe from his finger, forming the weapon he'd take to the stones; a war hammer. A slender weapon with a silver twined handle, and a ridged hammerhead with an opposing sharp spike.

He stood over the nearest stone, the one already hindered by a crack. Silas settled his grip and raised his arms over his head. Lightning flashed but the thunder did not dare to rumble. Silas closed his eyes, picturing Pitch as he led Silas down to this circle, with dark betrayal on his mind.

The anger needed little kindling to spark again. He opened his eyes. Took aim.

And whistled for all the deadness in the ground to heed him. His note was as sharp as the spike on his hammer. And he drove them both down.

The earth rose at his summons, pushing the stones forth like unwanted children from its womb. Sending them up against the driving force of the hammer.

The scythe struck the stone, lacing it with cracks. Silas spun the hammer, turned the spike downwards now, and completed the blow.

The tip met stone and shattered it.

The first of the faerie circle stones succumbed to him beneath a flash of silent lightning.

Silas breathed in the victory, its scent making him heady, craving the next dose. He licked his lips, readying them for another note. This one was higher than the last, drawing upon all the thousands of years of death that were packed into the earth, dragging it up from the darkness where the deathnotes of those creatures great and small were long since broken down.

The faerie circle's magick was attacked on two fronts.

And it did not have the strength to defend against him.

Seven stones. Each had shattered like eggshells left in the sun. Another flash of quiet lightning with each. A silent protest at the ruin.

A useless protest.

Silas saw his way out and lunged for it like a starving wolf on a carcass.

He broke the last stone, sweat running down the back of his neck, soaking his underarms. The white light flashed once, then was replaced by a colour like the first peaches of the season; the dawn's hint at the edge of a sky, with a touch of violet tinging its depths.

'Silas.'

Panting, he turned around; the hammer held loose in his hand. Edward stood with Scarlet upon his shoulder. The wisp waved with both hands, fingers bloated, but Silas was in no mood for simple things. 'Where is he?'

'He has gone into the lake. How did you end up here, Silas?'

'Through good intentions that were ill-thought through.' The thump of Silas's heart felt dulled, still buried beneath all the dirt and decay. The scythe reshaped, finding its place upon his finger once more. 'Edward, I must follow him.'

'Of course.' The lieutenant stretched out his hand. Silas had not yet stepped from the death-scorched ground with its shattered stone. 'Scarlet woke me...and brought me here. I see now why, but what happened here, Silas?'

'Pitch wishes to take his trials alone. I disapprove.' Silas took the lieutenant's hand, a tiny crackling came with their contact.

He stepped from the remnants of the faerie circle, struck by how truly quiet it had been within them. Now the sounds of the Sanctuary were many, the wind stronger than he recalled; causing distant trees to tilt and groan, a window shutter somewhere to slam, and far off birds to call out warnings.

'Is Charlie safe?'

'Yes. Sleeping, thanks to Scarlet.' Edward tilted his head at the wisp, who had risen to its stubby feet. 'They bid me come alone. Do you know what they intend?'

'It had best be to show me where Pitch entered the lake,' Silas said. 'Scarlet? Why have you brought Edward to me?'

The odd little creature performed a twirl, turquoise arms spread as though they embraced an invisible partner in a waltz.

A deep rumble moved through the ground. Different to the sound Silas's interference had made. This was like the rattling of a steam engine as it barrelled past a humble dwelling, causing all to shake. Edward's arms lifted, searching for something to brace on. Silas stepped forward, steadying him.

'It has happened a few times now.' Edward said, with nervous glances about. 'But this is by far the strongest. What do you suppose it is?'

The sound passed, softening, running beneath the earth, like a fox fleeing deeper into its den.

'I don't know,' Silas said. 'But if Pitch has just set foot in the lake I fear the unrest stems from there. I must find a way in.'

Scarlet darted from Edward's shoulder, and moved right up close to Silas's face, planting chubby mandarin orange hands against the tip of his nose, reminding him of the bothersome butterfly. But Silas had no doubt of this creature's loyalty, nor intentions.

'How do I find him, Scarlet?' he whispered.

The wisp grabbed at the scraggy lengths of his beard and pulled him forward. Back towards the palace, whose elaborate peaks were never out of sight.

'Back in the palace?'

A squeak, as clear an answer as any. Yes.

'Let's go, Edward.'

The lieutenant gave Silas a tight nod, his face furrowed with his concerns, but he did not hesitate to fall into step.

Silas rushed away from the shattered faerie prison; from the place where Pitch had dared to bestow a kiss he'd intended to be their last.

CHAPTER 36

The Leviathan's maw parted, and a thin seam of light peaked through the curtain of bristles at its mouth.

Red light. The colour of a fresh cut.

Vassago took another step, kicking at the skull of some unfortunate creature that had snagged in a fold of spongy flesh. He breathed into the restlessness of the simurgh, the yearning to be set free.

The Leviathan opened wider, allowing more light to filter in, and reveal this place that had stolen so much from him.

Blood Lake did not live up to its name.

The water was clear. Crystalline to the point of barely being visible at all. There was certainly no hiding place for the dense layer of bones upon the lake bed, some of which were piled till they pierced the surface. But those piles were not large. The lake here was barely a foot deep.

'It is shallow?' he said, taken aback.

'This close to the halo, yes,' Satine replied. 'Elsewhere, the fathoms are great. This shoal is the first of many, then you shall find a more treacherous reef. The halo stands there at its centre.'

Vassago turned to ask another question when the howls came.

The morose, anguished cries took him straight back to Goodrich Castle. An age ago it seemed, since he'd shattered the Blight-filled prism and freed the Spirit of the Forest. But he'd not forget the cries of tormented dead.

'The lake does not welcome us,' said the lady.

'You don't fucking say?'

The cacophony told of endless sorrow, of grief-spiked rage, of all things lost and unknowable. Vassago wavered on his feet, bent over by the wretched. But as he braced himself upon the thick baleen hairs at the Leviathan's mouth, he smiled.

'You will never know him,' he whispered. 'You will not take him from me.'

A small, but important victory.

Leaving Silas had pained Pitch, like no torture he'd ever known. But this moment was a sweet justification for his betrayal. If he was so hammered by the despair of all the long, lost dead here, how much torment would they have brought Silas?

'Your Highness, do you hesitate?'

The question stirred up his anger nicely, and he let it ripple through him, feeding it to the simurgh who took it up greedily.

'Of course I do not hesitate.' Flame stoked in Vassago's eyes, and warmth filled his skull.

'The cries are terrible.' That much was obvious. Even the Hellfield had not sounded so rotten at its fiercest battles. Vassago said nothing. 'What blessed relief it will be when you silence them for the angel, at last.'

'There is no surety in this.' He glanced back at the serpent, where only her head was visible, the rest of her long length extending into the Leviathan's gullet as she stretched to follow him. 'And I don't do this for Seraphiel.'

'Your reason is far greater. And it is why are you are best placed to succeed. Now go, Vassago. We can draw off the creatures of the lake only so long, but they will return in greater number.'

She stretched her body long, slipping her head between the corner of the Leviathan's lips. With a forked tongue taking place of the wave of a hand, she drew Vassago's attention out to the deeper waters on their right. Enormous swells disturbed the surface, froth lifting from their tips; the triangular fin of an gigantic creature cut a path through the pandemonium. Another identical point of calamity lay just west of the first; another fin moving like a knife through sponge cake.

'There are more Leviathan?' he asked.

'No. Only one. She creates illusion to draw the dwellers of Blood Lake away from here.'

Vassago clenched his fists and looked away. He'd seen such a talent for replication in other djinn before: in the Red Horse, and Pale Horse.

Vassago pressed thoughts of Lalassu aside. The Berserker Prince did not mourn.

He stepped up to the lip of the massive creature who bore him, gripping the baleen hairs, coarse as a dead man's beard.

The Berserker Prince did not suffer heartache, either.

Vassago took all thought of the ankou and set his flames to them. Burning them upon a pyre of rage that was ever-growing. A curl of hunger gripped him, the bloodlust of old stirring.

Here he was free to be nothing but the lady's Horseman of War.

The simurgh let out a cry, one that made his blood bubble and spit.

With his pulses maddened, and his skin heated through, Vassago jumped from the pliant folds of the Leviathan's lip, and landed in the shallow, utterly clear waters of Blood Lake. The water was tepid.

Lady Satine and her monster had delivered him to a sandbank, one of firm, though coarse, sand. He kicked off his one remaining slipper, and his heels sank only a little as he gathered his bearings.

There was little to see but endless stretches of water. Sparkling, like he'd been dumped in an empty paradise. The light was red, but neither the water nor the sky took on the tinge. Both were clear. And so similar to one another with their white hues, above and below reflected like mirror images of one another. It added an oppressive feel to the place; despite its vastness.

Vassago grimaced at the pummelling of deplorable cries. He despised this place. The simurgh's wings shifted, dancing across his bones, whilst the Seraph-made wound at his back pounded with dull pain. He despised the angels, too.

'Do you doubt yourself?' Lady Satine stood framed by the rounded mouth of her beast. Its huge bulk was more evident now through the clarity of the water. Shaped not unlike a whale, but with a fin that reached skyward, tipped with a strange gathering upon its point; as though a great eagle had made its nest there. The Leviathan's mass was such that no tail end was visible; its green-grey flesh disappearing in the depths. That flesh held an astonishing array of barnacles; some large as anvils, peaked like tiny volcanoes, others smaller, and layered like cold hard roses.

'No, I do not doubt.' The Berserker Prince had never dwelt on failure.

'Good. Then this is the last time we meet. I shall go with the lake into oblivion, when the halo is no more. The djinn will finally be free of this oath.' She did not hide the swell of longing, of exhausted happiness beneath her words.

'You and I were not so dissimilar, Satty. The chains that bind us to this lake are only slightly different.'

'Arrogant youngster.' Snakes could smile, though not well. Bare gums, dark grey, glistened around sharpened fangs. 'My chain held many more centuries in its links than yours, but I am glad were are not so similar there. The waiting would not have suited you at all. Goodbye, Vassago. May your fire burn true.'

The serpent withdrew into her beast, the red light tinging her quartz eyes crimson, visible until the very last, when the Leviathan's slowly closing mouth finally shut the Lady of the Lake away.

He did not say goodbye, he was tired of farewells.

Bones cracked and snapped as the beast sunk back into deeper waters. Vassago was alone.

The simurgh shifted, its tail battering his leg bones, suddenly, painfully and rather aptly.

He was not truly alone.

'All right. Show me the way.'

He took another step, the shoal of bone crushed fine as sand, a natural pumice upon his soles. The water seemed thicker than when he'd taken his first step, dragging harder against his ankle. And the forlorn cries were louder, as though the Leviathan's massive presence had kept them at bay.

Vassago followed the weight in his legs, the alternating pressure that urged him forward, one step at a time. He followed the simurgh's instruction, walking on. The water rose slightly, never higher than his knees, lapping at the jagged cuts of his shortened gown. He tore open the bodice, the diamond buttons spilling into the water like stardust, and pulled it off, letting it drift away on the current less liquid. Seraphiel had not bothered with undergarments when he clothed Vassago. There was no underbodice, nor a chemise under his corset. And the corset itself was plain ivory satin with no trimmings, no lace.

All the better to be ruined.

Vassago moved on, his foot catching at larger pieces of bone, his ears reverberating with the calamity of sound that lay upon him, heavy as a drenched shawl. Now that he stood in the Blight's birthplace, he did not wonder at how such a force had come to be, but how the sheer pressure of the lake's dolorous air had not shattered the Seals, and spread its anguish further and wider.

He leaned into the oppression, his breath coming in short bursts, his back aching as Seraphiel's wound pin-pricked with pain beneath the growing load of Blood Lake's raucous agonies.

They touched at him like bees testing their stingers, glancing at his skin, seeking the soft places to impale.

Seeking a way in.

Not into his flesh…but into his thoughts.

The onslaught was quick. Stealthy.

And he doubted himself before the next breath.

He dragged his feet, the enormity of the lake all around him, reducing him.

Dampening his rage, raining upon the fire he sought to burn.

'Fuck off, fuck off.' He hunched his shoulders, searching for his strength. Finding only misery. Cracking fortitude. Vassago kicked out at the water and its impossible clarity; his own reflection barely flickering on the surface. The water was warmer now; like a bathtub.

That thought slipped in like an assassin, quiet and dark. Landing its knife upon him, digging up the ashes of times spent with the ankou.

The Blight sensed his falter, like it was truly blood in the water, and rounded on him. Pummelling him all the harder with its gloom and woe.

Bringing forth a surge of lament.

What if Lucifer double-crossed him once more and reneged–just as Pitch had done–on his promise to protect Silas?

The ankou was left vulnerable. Open to hurt.

Pitch gasped, tripping over a bone large as a stovepipe. Water splashed up into his eyes, stinging like vinegar.

'I have to go back.'

The certainty overwhelmed him. Sickened him to the very depths of his soul.

He was not Vassago, not Dominion, not the Berserker Prince. He was simply a fool, who had made a terrible mistake to believe in the lies of a mad angel.

The simurgh rose up and scratched at him, right at his heart.

Pitch cried out, stumbling where a dip in the terrain marked a shift from coarse sand to rough chunks of coral the size of loaves of bread. He lost his footing, and his shin found a sharp edge.

A thin trail of dawn-pink fluid stained the pristine water. He stared down at it, dazed, uncertain why he was crouched in warm waters.

'I have to go back.'

That was all he knew for certain, though the *where* eluded him.

Another jolt came from the simurgh. A vicious slam against his senses, a boiling of his marrow.

'Fuck.' He clutched at his belly, trying to calm his scattered thoughts. Trying to move beneath the drenching press of sadness. He was miserable.

Go back.

Go back. Save him from this.

For this was Silas's lot, this utter despair. Day in, day out.

He shook his head. 'No...no, that is not it. That's not how it will be done.'

The cut on his leg stung like a branding iron. His blood ran freely, fanning into the water. He swept his fingers through the mixture, making the blood swirl in pretty patterns that defied the ugliness of this place.

The desperation of this place.

That single word stirred something...a memory, a thought, a message forgotten?

Whichever it was, he knew it. He was desperate.

Desperate for what? Pitch's hand flew to his belly, where a sharp pain bit at him. A misstep followed, and he was going down again; onto both knees where the reef of bones was ready to stab at his flesh. He sent his hands before him, a terrible mistake for the shards of whittled bone impaled his palms. Pitch stared at the white stalks that protruded from the back of his hands: revulsion, anguish and agony mixing a terrible cocktail inside his head. A cry of woe echoed around him.

But it was not a sound he'd made.

Tearing his hands free released two macabre dribbles of blood, further marring the clarity of the water.

Blood Lake. The single thought pushed itself forward, and he grasped at it, tried to hold it long enough to make sense of what that meant. The stab in his belly repeated. He was shackled by despair. Fuck, he felt atrocious.

He sent a bloodied hand to his back, a point near his hipbone where his flesh seemed to throb with a discomfort even greater than that at his belly.

The angel's mark.

An angel had hurt him. Manipulated and deceived.

The thoughts flashed and died quickly. Too much so to do anything but cause confusion.

Pitch dragged himself to his feet, feeling the tug of his flesh as his knees came away from the bony reef. He stood in a spreading film of his own blood. The water nearest him now matched the pale red hue of the light.

He searched the landscape. For someone? Perhaps. There was an endless stretch of the water and reef.

He took another step and found it akin to walking through treacle. Treacle laced with pins and razor blades. The skin on the underside of his feet tore open. Another step and the blanket of blood around him darkened.

But he should move on. He should continue to suffer. He must...why the fuck could he not recall what he must do?

'What am I doing here?' he asked of the mournful cries that accompanied him.

Their loud and debilitating wails were beneath his skin, behind his eyelids, tying his veins in knots. They soared around him, a flock of ravens setting eyes upon its prey.

Pitch clutched at his head, a dazzling pain behind his eyes. A flashing image of birds aloft: feathers drifting, feathers upon a mask, cloaks of black, horns of onyx. Chocolate eclairs. A man with silver glasses. Hot cups of tea. A cloven foot. A dagger that flashed as it came for him. Pitch cried out and threw himself beyond reach of the attack.

Only to find the unyielding hardness of the reef. Another cut of skin. Another bloodletting. And the near overwhelming desire to give in to a torrent of tears.

Pitch blinked, his eyes stinging. Tears were not familiar to him. This was not right.

Heat filled his belly. Not scalding, but comforting. He drew in a breath and cradled his bleeding, punctured hands against his stomach. He found satin and stays; damp and hard and familiar. Pitch looked down at himself, his fingers tracing a bloody line over the simple corset he wore.

'Blood Lake,' he whispered.

Something fluttered beneath his skin, fanning the fire that despondent sorrow sought to destroy.

Destroy.

Destroy the halo. He was here for the halo. The Blight faltered in its song of dread and loss.

'Where the fuck is it?' Pitch shouted. 'Where are you, Samyaza? It is pointless to hide from me.'

Pitch ran. The bones slashing at his feet, his blood leaving a cape of crimson spreading out behind.

He ran. Trying to outpace the gathering storm of the Blight. Trying to bring Vassago to the fore once more.

The toes on his right foot were all but bone, and his lungs were wracked with painful spasms by the time he finally saw a shift in the landscape. A singular rise amongst an endless flatness. All the hue and cry of the lake's woeful inhabitants suddenly dulled, his blood thundering in his ears. A dizziness sweeping over him.

The hilt of a sword protruded from a jagged assembly of bones piled high in the shallow waters, as though swept up by an enormous broom, left for a cleanup that had never come.

The halo.

Pitch let out a wild laugh and rushed forward, lamentations rising around him, surrounding him. He stepped over the countless dead, the many who had fought and lost and fouled these waters with their regret and sorrow, and whose remains took the flesh from his own bones. They bled him until he was woozy with the pain.

But he was so close.

The simurgh spread itself into his fingertips, into his badly damaged toes, and right down the lengths of his hair. Urging him to lift his feet higher, even as the flesh there dangled and the white of his bones shone through. Misery scratched at his back, and grief tangled itself in his thoughts. His face was streaked with tears that would not stop falling.

But he was so close.

The hilt of the sword was plain, the pommel a bulge of dull iron-grey, the grip black as tar and its leather fraying, the blade blunt where it was not buried in the stone.

The water grew shallower. Barely covering his bleeding feet.

Just another few strides and he'd be there. At the source of so much suffering.

A sob left him. A searing wretchedness that burned his nostrils. And by the gods, it was agony to take every step. He faltered, and the Blight came at him again, with a hammer strike of abject wretchedness. His cries joined the chorus.

'Bleed, little prince.' The voice emerged from the cacophony of forlorn regret. Or, rather, the voice *was* that cacophony. 'Feed the lake. You are in good company, amongst those whose only greatness lies in the magnitude of their failures.'

'Failure...' Pitch coughed, spraying yet more blood into the water. Crying more tears he did not fully own. 'No, I'm not a fail–'

The suffering crashed down upon him, an enormous wave, invisible to the eye but all too well-known to the soul.

Pitch was lifted first, cast upon his back, and then thrown down. He struck a reef of destitution, impaled on the lost armies of the Day of Ruination. Fingers of bone pierced him, striking through between the ribs, at his collarbone and his groin, there too, upon his thigh. Another spear of stark white pushed through his belly, emerging drenched in specks of flesh, blood cascading.

A terrible, dislocating ache began.

'No,' he gasped, understanding, despite all else, the devastation of that blow.

Another wave crashed upon him, driving him down into the crevices. The bone reef reddened with the terrible flow of his blood.

A coral born of corpses.

The regretful choir struck up again. Blood Lake drank of him. Took its fill of his sorrows and regrets, and grew fat-bellied upon them.

The fire in his belly waned. The buffeting of the simurgh grew weaker. They slipped from him, those wilder parts of himself, draining away in bright red rivulets: Vassago, the Berserker Prince, the Dominion daemon, and the wildness, flowed from his veins and into the lake.

The inferno that Satine had stoked was all but dying embers now.

The waters lapped at him, caressing his emptying body. His tears added to the flow; failure was salty and hot and stinging. He struggled still, worked his ruined body against the bones, but only sunk himself deeper into their pinching clutches. The halo lay within arms' reach, but his guise of skin and bone was too fragile to reach that far.

Pitch had hesitated to shed his skin, to destroy Tobias Astaroth, and return to the wild prince Seraphiel had chosen him for. Now, at the worst possible time, he learned the cost of being human.

To be ruled by more than mindless rage or lust for battle.

To be crippled by a power that went unseen. That of self-doubt and lost chances, laments and, most destructive of all, grief.

Now, the dead armies of Blood Lake claimed him. And the halo lay hauntingly out of reach.

CHAPTER 37

T he wisp seemed to forget that not everyone could fly. Scarlet set a cracking pace through the gardens, taking them in through a large paned-glass door that slid open, rather than swung. They were so far down the corridor by the time Silas and Edward reached the opening; they were barely more than a smudge of colour, the size of a dandelion head.

'Scarlet wait!' Silas shouted, standing in the doorway whilst waiting for Edward to catch up. The lieutenant reached him, puffing, discarding his burgundy vest into the shrubbery.

'Bloody hell, they are fast.'

'Are you alright?' Silas led him inside, into a stunning sitting room with its ever-present gold embellishments. This one was different for its highlights of onyx, and the assembly of colourful paintings on one of the wall panels.

'Fine, fine. Clearly in need of more decent exercise.'

Silas urged Edward ahead, pleased to see the return of a glint in the man's grey eyes. His new freedom had put pink in his cheeks.

Scarlet tittered at them from way down the hall, where a junction was evident, and circled about in mad whirls that made their impatience clear.

'We're coming,' Edward called.

The palace shuddered. A deep vibration that had both Silas and the lieutenant bracing, ready for a movement that might knock them off their feet. In the rooms along the way, anything that was loose rattled loudly; china and glasses and heavier sounds. Like the shift of furniture on wood.

Silas and Edward exchanged a glance, neither of them saying what was vastly obvious; that was the worst of the tremors so far.

'Go quickly,' Silas urged.

They broke into another run. Down the hall, a turn left, another long corridor laid out with a rug as white as the peaks of the Highlands they'd glimpsed from the boat. More shaking occurred, vehement enough to make Silas glance at the ceiling, half-expecting to see cracks there. The pristine plasterwork was unblemished. For now.

Edward halted; a standstill so sudden Silas nearly ran him over.

They were at the base of an imposing imperial staircase. With two directions to choose from. Scarlet hovered at the top of the stairs on the right, jumping about like a colourful flea in irritation at their pause, chittering loudly enough to outdo the distant roll of thunder that menaced overhead.

'What is it, Edward?'

'Do you not hear it?'

He was staring up towards where Scarlet waited. Silas frowned. 'The wisp? Or the thunder? Neither are very pleasant to listen to, if I'm honest.'

'No, not either of those...the music.' He closed his eyes, and his head tilted back. 'Oh, Silas. It is magnificent.'

'Edward, are you sure you're alright?'

His eyes opened; their grey deepened to match the storm that gathered. 'This way. I understand now.'

He raced off, taking the stairs two at a time; leaving Silas the one to catch up now. Whatever Edward understood, Silas was still at a loss. But so long as it enabled him to reach Pitch, all the strangeness in the world could descend upon them.

Edward did not pause as he approached a pair of embellished white doors, very similar to a hundred others in this multi-roomed palace: gold lock sets and escutcheon, rounded crystal levers, and yet more gold in the detailed scrolling patterns, carved into the wood.

He stepped right up to the doors, planted his hands upon the knobs of gleaming crystal, and whispered something Silas did not catch.

The door latches' clicked, and Edward pushed forward.

The doors swung inwards. Blinking light burst from within, bringing with it a wash of prickling air that raised the gooseflesh on Silas's arms. He shaded his eyes, searching for the source of the glare. A myriad of chandeliers hung from a high ceiling.

And the ballroom was full of silent dancers. Everyone stock still, in the pose of one beginning a dance. The colours of the gowns were brilliant, jewels sparkled on ladies necks', in their hair and upon their wrists. Gems there too, for some men, brooches pinned to dress coats, and earrings that dazzled at their lobes. Silas searched for Pitch; holding his breath as he looked for that fine figure amongst the crowd. The fashions worn were wide-ranging, all manner of clothing that Silas did not recognise; or did not remember. Gowns with skirts of varying widths, and waistlines that sat at all manner of places upon torsos.

But he searched for only one costumed body of note. Barely noting how the scythe tightened on his finger; how his chest was heavy with a discomfort he could not name.

Scarlet startled him by settling on his shoulder, crooning quietly, stroking at his hair.

'Is he here?' Silas swallowed against the thickness of the air. The scythe held close, with a distant hum that spoke of caution.

The wisp flew off his shoulder, facing him head on. The emphatic shaking of that bulbous little head was answer enough. Scarlet poked a sea-green finger towards Edward.

The lieutenant moved through the dancers, humming to himself.

Silas scratched absently at his arm, for the room's strange atmosphere bothered his skin. It was there in his head too, scratching like a cat eager to be let indoors.

'Edward, where are you going?' he called.

The lieutenant stopped and looked up.

'Here.'

He'd placed himself right beneath the strangest and simplest of all the chandeliers; the only one not made of crystal like all the others. White glass flowers formed the arms of the chandelier; Easter lilies with long curving stems, and blue flames where the yellow of their pollen should be. Silas stared harder, and knew he'd assessed the design wrongly.

'That is bone, not glass,' he whispered.

Bones with no death note to tell him who hung here in the ballroom. But he suspected. And he was thankful he did not have to hear Samyaza's melody.

He hurried through the dancers, nose twitching at the heavy waft of bodily odour. He glanced at the assembly as he moved between them. No one looked to him, though eyes were wide, and chests heaved with recent effort. Sweat shone upon most faces, staining clothing, too.

Silas was almost with the lieutenant when he spied the first body. A woman of middle age, laid upon her back, hands still raised to embrace her partner. Her cheeks were hollow, blood trailed from her parted lips, and her eyes were already filmy with the creep of death. A death Silas could not hear, nor feel. He curled his fingers against the reassuring firmness of the scythe.

This room was dreadful, in ways he could not fathom.

'Keep going, Silas,' Edward said. 'That is how you can best help them.'

The fallen woman's partner stood over her, arms raised as though she was with him still. A full-faced man, with a beard that touched his chest, his long grey hair held up in a ponytail, and his knuckles thick with gout. He too was sweat-soaked, but Silas thought the larger bead, rolling down his cheek, may be a tear.

Shudders moved through the palace, rocking the chandeliers, making their candles flutter.

'What is this place?' He could barely speak for how raw the room made him.

'The way in,' Edward said, a dreamy quality to his voice. He had one hand raised, swaying it back and forth, hearing some silent song. 'You truly don't see it?'

'I see a room of horrors.'

'And of mastery.' His smile was grim as he surveyed the dancers, who held perfectly still. Waiting. 'I see the lines we must follow. The angel is a true craftsman.'

'Lines? Edward, speak plainly. Will this lead me to Pitch?'

He needed to escape the barbs of this room before they rubbed him raw. The wrongness of it, the unnatural construction, the defiance of death's laws, made his teeth grind. The thunder rolled, as though in dire alliance.

'It will. There is a dance here. One I will lead.' Edward inhaled deeply. 'And we must hope that what I see is the true path. That I'm prophet enough still to know the heart of the angel who claimed me.'

'I need more than hope, Edward.' Silas shrugged his shoulder, trying to ease the itching there. This place was driving him out of his skin. The scythe swirled like a viper around his finger, straining to hear his call to arms. 'Bloody hell, I cannot just leave these poor bastards this way.' He clutched at his head, the hammering of wrongful death agonising. No notes, no death cries. The silence was appalling; this was neither life nor death, but a monstrosity in between.

'Silas, look at me.' Edward placed his hands against Silas's chest. 'Even you, the wonderment that you are, cannot save them all. They must stay. We need them for this dance. Even if I do not understand how, I know their part must be played. There is no escape for those we stand with here. But you can prevent any more going the way of these people. Find Tobias. Find the halo. And it is all over. Do you hear me?'

Silas clenched his fist, the sharp point of a partly formed blade piercing his skin, as the scythe fought against his command. He inhaled deeply, taking in the scent of this deformed life, letting it filter down into his lungs, where it would be remembered. Each reasoned word of the lieutenant sobered him. And curtailed the sickened rage that bade him strike down every poor soul in the room; releasing them from this vile chamber.

'Silas?'

'I hear you.'

'Then let's give this a try.' Edward raised his arms, and his calm demeanour was betrayed by the tremble at his fingertips. 'May I have this dance, Mr Mercer?'

Silas could not offer the smile Edward might have hoped for. There was too much loss here for that. And perhaps far more waiting ahead.

'Hurry, Edward.'

He nodded, his own smile too weak to survive long. 'Alright, follow my lead as best you can.' His left hand touched at Silas's hip, while his right arm raised and stretched to their side. Silas's large hand engulfed Edward's reasonably sized palm.

Scarlet, mostly silent until then, launched into a stream of urgent tweets, making a headlong path through the crowd, back towards the open doors of the ballroom.

They were a foot from the door when a figure stepped into the frame; just as a truly violent shudder gripped the palace.

'What the bloody hell do you think you are doing?' Lucifer braced against the doorway with one hand, his other upon a walking stick. 'Silas, good gods man, will you not stay down?'

'Lucifer, stay back. I warn you.' The candles flickered madly, threatening to blink out, and some of the stony dancers shifted on their feet. 'You should have stopped him.'

Lucifer's laugh was brittle beneath a growl of thunder. 'I know you are no fool, ankou. Lord Enoch himself could hardly stop that blasted daemon when his mind was set. Vassago wanted you to stay behind, to be kept safe.'

'Well, Pitch,' Silas bit down on the name, 'does not always get what he wants from me.'

Two sharp tremors, each following the other quickly. From out in the halls, glass shattered, and wood behind the plaster groaned. Silas caught the look of horror that crossed the daemon's face. It looked so out of place on him. And gravely worrying.

'Get away from the fucking seal,' Lucifer sounded little different to a wolf, growling at those who trespassed its territory. 'Michael is determined to bring this entire place down upon us. Don't make it bloody easier for him.'

Edward tugged Silas back into the pose. 'Don't listen to him. You must go.'

That took Silas aback; to hear the affable, very-human man so forthright. 'Why are you so certain?' Silas asked.

Edward's frown was tugged with confusion. 'I'm not sure I under-stand half of what I feel anymore...only that I'm certain of it. As I was with the Ferryman. The right thing to do was very apparent –'

'And this is the right thing to do?' Silas had not lost his desperation to follow Pitch, but leaving both Edward and Charlie in a place that was rattling its foundations was hardly appealing.

'You can't do it all, Silas.' Edward said, as though reading his mind.

'Mercer,' Lucifer hissed, limping his way deeper into the ballroom, both hands braced to the head of his cane. 'Seraphiel speaks with Jacquetta now on reinforcing the outer boundaries, but he will be on his way here soon. If he sees you, I cannot say where his madness will take him. Leave, now. He and I shall deal with this.'

'I do not fear that angel.'

'But he fears you, and that is far worse.' Lucifer glanced back at the doorway. 'I'll not give you another chance. Leave.'

Silas bristled with protest, and knew his shadow crept larger, more threatening than before. But before a word left his mouth, Scarlet moved between them.

Their rainbow hues shone brighter, a spectacular prettiness that ate at the malformation in the room.

They brightened until Silas was blinking, and Lucifer was lost from view. Edward grunted, protesting the glare.

But it was over quickly.

The spectacular brilliance faded.

The daemon had not moved, but something in him had changed. The line-etching fear had softened. He was still troubled–still frail–but a weight had left him.

He looked to Silas. 'Good luck, Mr Mercer. Be quick. You won't have long. Make sure you are not here when I return.' Lucifer turned, but paused, the move half-done. 'If you reach him, if you should survive...tell him...tell him I truly intended to do as he asked. I'd like to think his opinion of me goes no lower, when all is said and done, and I am not there to protest otherwise.'

The King of Daemonkind did not wait for an answer. He turned away, nodding at the wisp that fluttered in close, and chittered sweetly. Each step seemed pained, but he was soon out the doors.

They closed behind him; vanishing both the daemon and the wisp from view.

What the bloody hell had just happened? How did a tiny creature–sputtering nonsense–cajole a great daemon into walking away?

'Silas...he's giving us time. Don't waste it,' Edward said. 'Put your hand on my shoulder, and let's begin.'

In something of a daze, Silas did as he was bid, and he assumed the position. Ready for the dance. He winced; thinking of the Crimson Bow when he'd last danced. Pitch had sought to teach him. The longing was near overwhelming.

Edward spoke one word. Strange, but with an elegance that made it float in the air. Angelic.

The quartet struck up. The harpist playing the first notes, the violins joining, the cellist last of all.

Edward lifted Silas's hands up and down, working into a rhythm. Then he took his first step. The first few were hesitant, and Silas had to work not to stand on his toes. But as the melody flowed, so too did their dance. Edward grew surer, the tension in his face softening, and he lead Silas firmly. Once they had to step over a body, a jarring experience that roiled Silas's gut. The dance used all the floor, and after a time it became clear that it was a pattern repeating over and over; out to each of the corners, crossing at the centre, then out to the remaining corners. An hourglass.

Edward's grip on his hand tightened, painfully so for one who'd been so frail not so long ago. Silas breathed in sharply at the blood that ran from the lieutenant's nose and one of his eyes.

'Christ, Edward.'

'Never mind me,' he said through clenched teeth. 'It is almost done.'

A dull reverberation ran beneath their feet, the angel's attack unrelenting. Silas could only hope that purebreds would escape his wrath; his ferocity focused on the daemons and angels alone.

Edward took his hand from Silas's hip and shifted in behind him with a grace and ease that Silas could only dream of. Wrapping about Silas's waist, the lieutenant whispered, 'Good luck, friend.'

He cast Silas, a man easily double his size, into a spin, sending him out to arm's length. Letting him go.

The pace of the spin was whirlwind fast; the room blurred, the melody distorted, as though strings broke on the players' instruments. Silas threw out his arms, seeking something to hold, right before the world fell away beneath his feet.

Silas plunged.

Into watery depths.

And he sank like the proverbial stone.

Into misery.

He kicked out, spreading his arms in wide strokes, fighting against the dragging down of his body.

He knew exactly where he was.

The utter chaos of deathnotes made it impossible not to know this for Blood Lake. The sullen drag of the Blight was formidable. The weight of centuries spent mourning loss and despising failure, made this an unpleasant place to be. But Silas had been to so many unpleasant places before, and survived them all.

And Blood Lake had his daemon. He'd never been so fucking happy to be in such a terrible place.

Silas laughed, the sound bubbling the water; he felt a little delirious, a little wild, with a raging hunger to reach his lover. He kicked out, challenging the waters to stop him, until he recalled the scythe's transformation in the cockaigne. The place where he'd taken on a goddess and won. He set about reshaping the ring, intending to create the kite that had lifted him out of the mud, and flown both Pitch and him out of the tower.

The current beneath him shifted. Turning from dragging anchor to forceful uplifting pressure in the blink of an eye. A great force was rising.

Silas abandoned the kite for the spear, as a movement from below displaced the water. A mammoth disturbance. Rushing up at him from the abyss.

His arm was drawn back, the tip of the spear pointed down, and all but ready to throw, when Lady Satine's melody drifted up from the darkness.

Leviathan. Lady of the Lake.

Impact came a moment later; a breathtaking slam into his midriff. His cry was engulfed by the waters, and he was rapidly ascending at a speed that gave him little option but to grip tightly; hold on to a great bulk that had him clasped between gentle, vast lips. He scrambled for a handhold, and found the roughness of barnacles, cutting his hands as he clung onto them. He'd take what he was given. It felt like he was being shipped along by an island. The force pressed him flat against smooth, cool skin.

'You took your time, my Horseman.'

Satine's voice was more vibration than sound, coming through the beast that lifted him.

'How does he fare?' Speaking underwater, when moving at a rate of knots, was like talking into a gale. Silas did not ask if Pitch lived. He knew that answer.

'He is lost. The halo leads him astray, and he has forgotten himself. But you are here now, he will remember.'

'I hope so.' Silas's cheek was pressed so hard against the Leviathan he could barely open his mouth to speak.

'You shall need more than hope here, my Horseman. Now go. Show your sire Samyaza that he could not make monsters of all men.'

CHAPTER 38

They broke the surface, soaring into a world that hummed with the lament of the dead. The Leviathan lifted him high, high above the water, through air tinged red, as though somewhere a great fire burned. Silas blinked through watery eyes, seeing a lake far more beautiful than he'd imagined. Crystal clear, mostly, save for another hint of red, this one far distant, upon the surface; like a lone rose which sought to bloom.

He wiped at his eyes, as the Leviathan's arc reached its zenith and the downward plunge began. The creature had a slow movement, like the dragging shift of a great ship. Silas took in the spread of stark white coral that lay beneath the water like fine lace.

He saw it for what it was and felt its enormity grab at him.

These were bones. An astonishing numbers of bones. Ringing out their notes in one impossibly wretched song of the dead. Most lay beneath the surface, with mere tips poking forth–like perilous caps of icebergs–save for one huge pyre, far in the distance. Beyond the spread of red.

His pulse raced. The scythe grew tight and fixed.

He could see no sign of a golden-haired daemon.

The Leviathan spat him out. Sending him like a man shot from a cannon, soaring him towards the shallows. Silas landed amongst the bones, crashing through them with such speed he feared he would sink right back down to the depths. He sank into the haphazard assembly and was buried in a hard sea of white. Covered by Blood Lake's long-dead. Caught beneath the bitter, tepid waters.

But Silas was exacting; purposeful and unafraid. He'd spent enough years being fearful of the water. Now he shrugged it off, like an uncomfortable coat that pinched at the neckline.

The ring worked fast, eager for the command, shaping itself into a familiar, and unexpectedly calming, bandalore. Silas punched his hand skyward, crashing through bone, the cracking amplified beneath the water. The boxwood flew from his palm, humming along the long, long length of its string; unsullied now by their arduous journey with a thin thread of silver replacing the stained white string. Shooting up through the surface. Finding an anchor point.

Silas pulled at the silver string, testing the steadiness of the bone. Finding it strong, he hauled himself upright. His head cleared the shallow water. He spat out the liquid and shook his head, spraying it from his hair.

The water buffeted him as the Leviathan's wake reached him. There was no sign of the creature, but out where the waters were a deeper shade with depth, where white peaks sat atop turbulent waves, a thrashing in the water indicated a distant turmoil.

Silas pocketed the bandalore and kept on, towards the largest of the protrusions of white bone, seeking some height to view this world. The bones shattered beneath his feet. It was like walking through a field of sharp mud, each footfall needing to be dragged from the depression it made. He frowned at the strange conglomeration of tangled bones. So many were shaped in confounding ways, as though fused together, or from a creature so foreign to him, it was unrecognisable. Silas climbed atop a massive piece, thick as an oak, but puckered with holes. These were not creatures of the purebred world. That much was plain. And he did not know what lay beneath the sublime skins that the angels and daemons wore.

Perhaps Pitch lay here.

Silas reeled at the vicious doubt. And the cries of the lake lunged at him, hammering at him harder, seeing a fault in his resolve. But he was no stranger to the devastation of their laments. He knew far better how to deafen himself to them.

'Pitch!' His bellow rang out like a war cry; as cool and consuming rage settled on him.

Only the dead whispered back. Circling him, like wolves frightened of a campfire, but ready to lunge should the light fade.

'Pitch, are you there?'

Despite the openness of his surroundings his voice echoed against the reddened sky, and bounced off the endless sea of bones. What he'd not expected of this place was its quietude. The souls were there, of course, with their endless downtrodden sorrow, but the lake itself held a stillness, an utter absence of life that unsettled him far more.

Silas spied a greater viewpoint, and made his way there, unrepentant as he stepped upon the bones. He found a rounded piece, a perfect dome to stand upon. And undeniably a skull. He sent the scythe back to its ring form, seeing the easy footholds, there upon a massive jaw, and another in an eye socket so large he could have huddled in it. Grand dimensions he did not linger upon, for he knew this was no angel nor daemon; he knew giants well enough. Silas pulled himself onto the dimpled crown of the skull. He stood at full height, hiding from none.

'Pitch!'

The rattle of bones was his only reply. Silas glanced down. Rattle of bones, indeed. Where he had trod, breaking a path through the bone bed, depressions of shattered bone had marked his path.

There were none now. No trace of his foot path. The bones had re-knit, mending the damage made. Silas narrowed his gaze. Here were his wolves, showing a hint of themselves in this unnaturally sterile world. A rattling began, like the shaking of coins in the poor box.

The bones moved beneath the water, as though buffeted by a current. But the surface of the shallow waters was utterly still. The rattling came from behind and to his side. The reef was shifting. Gathering in.

Surrounding his lookout upon the skull.

The Watcher King's legions were on the move once more.

'Shit.' Silas fingered the scythe, mind racing. To use the scythe as a kite once more was impossible. For all the movement in the water, there was none in the air. Blood Lake held a dead calm.

He braced, searching for sign of where the first attack would come from.

The bones gathered thickest behind him, pushing themselves up into a rough wall, a crescent shape around the skull, their pieces grinding and snapping as they rose. Blocking his path.

'You fool, Silas.' He hissed at himself.

Beyond the rapidly rising wall was the tall pyre he'd spied earlier, and that bloom of red; quenching the thirst of a lake parched dry of blood.

Realisation was brutal.

Bile pressed at the back of Silas's throat.

He was a fool. An oaf. A dolt.

He'd stood here, shouting at the sky, while the lake bled Pitch dry.

Silas's rage was instant. Consuming. Twisting him up inside till the pain was unbearable. The sky darkened with his fury. And the ache behind his eyes flecked his vision with white. He took a step, intending to jump. The skull shattered beneath him. Fragile as a bird's egg. He barely stumbled before his feet found the thicker bed of bones that formed the reef.

Silas glowered down at his buried boots. They seemed oddly distant. The sharpness of his pain could not blind him to the strangeness here. The bones that covered his feet were not so sturdy as he recalled, and smaller; dwarfed by his shadow.

A shadow that stretched far out across the bones.

A brittle laugh hiccoughed from him.

The bones were not smaller. Silas was larger. More aligned with the fallen giant whose skull he'd just crushed; a Nephilim who had not escaped the Flood. Whose disadvantage came with not having a brother who despised them, feared them, and killed them; before the Lord's Wrath could do so.

Silas's laughter was askew, as broken as the pieces that fractured and rattled and gathered around him. They stacked their pieces, one atop one another, rising in a wave that sought to bury him.

Him! The Pale Horseman, Death's Messenger. Child of Samyaza.

These miserable minions of failure thought burial would stop him from reaching the prince?

They were ignorant, then. Wishful. Silas may be part angel, but he was all too human; a race who were weak and pitiful, capable of great cruelty and vice, but uncontested in their propensity for deep, unreasonable, insensible love.

The shift within him was like the buckling links on a train carriage cranking into place. With a roar worthy of the greatest of giants, Silas let go the mortal coils that bound him; opened himself to the shadows that made him.

He stepped into the darkness willingly, so long as it might draw Pitch into the light.

The suppression of lifetimes fell away. The fissures that had appeared when he brought down the goddess Morrigan, now cracked wide open. Silas rose. High. Higher still. Not merely with a hint of great shadow, but growing with substance. Stretching high above the death bed that surrounded him. Their tiny peaks and troughs were pitiful against his emergence.

The past tore away from him, the ties that shackled Silas to his goddess snapped free with the titanic release of thousands of years of restraint.

His time drew ever nearer to its close. Let it end with the greatest deathnote he could summon.

'Pitch, I promised you.' Silas need not shout anymore. His voice could carry across worlds. 'And I am here. It is not over.'

The scythe formed itself once more. A mace emerged; wooden handle thick as a yew, a spiked metal ball, big as a carriage wheel and a thousand times heavier, hanging from a fat chain. A perfect fit, no matter how monstrous his hands had grown.

He drew back his arm, his long shadow stretching further, the move stirring the deadened air. Silas landed the mace with all his fury behind the blow, his ears closed to the onslaught of dejection and penetrating grief the lake threw at him. He was too furious to be forlorn.

The impact wrought a crater in the reef and lifted a storm of white shards as the scythes pummelled the anguished bones to grit.

But the lake was not cowed by him. Not yet. No sooner had he forged a way, than the unending bones moved to fill the void, building the reef anew, this time tinged red. Great waves of crimson rose. The howl of the destitute, the regretful, the enraged, filled the air as Blood Lake sought to claim him as one of their own.

Let them try.

With great swipes of the mace and adding his own kicks in for good measure, Silas ploughed his way across the massive cemetery. The Blight played its forlorn notes for him. At him.

But he'd learned to listen and be unafraid. Untouched.

He strode through the shallows, through the piles of bones that whispered their misery, and clamoured for him to succumb. He'd done so when the Herlequin found him clueless and vulnerable. It had nearly cost him the prince then.

Nothing could fool Silas into making that mistake again.

He moved on, towering, impossible, dark and raging, the twisted melodies of the Blight's birthplace glancing off him. It was a graveyard, and a terrible one at that, but Death had long ago fled this place. Silas understood, being in its midst, what the Blight's true power was. How it drove those who fell to it, mad and twisted with grief. It was not fear of death it goaded them with, but fear of being the one left behind. Caught in the agony of endless bereavement.

Silas's long strides ate up the distance that kept him from his daemon. The quake of his footfalls shattered bones to mere dust, but no sooner had he lifted his feet than the shallows were renewed. The hint of red was everywhere now. And the only source of colour lay with Pitch.

Bloodshed had given rise to this place, but it had been starved of carnage for centuries. The lake had drunk itself dry; now blood flowed from a fallen prince, sating a timeless thirst.

'Pitch.' Silas's breath stirred whirlwinds in the stagnant air. 'Hold on. Do not dare let go.'

He'd sought no answer, and it shocked him when it came.

The weak glow of embers. The hint of flame amongst the stain of flowing blood; a precious, gut-wrenching glimpse of life.

The lake saw it when Silas did. The bones were raucous, their mad dance growing more manic. They came for him.

But Silas went blind to all else. Barely feeling the clamour of the dead upon him, their skeletons seeking to burden him; clawing up his legs, digging their broken pieces into his body. A body thick and large and solid enough to endure their assault.

He quickened his step, and the barriers rose. Small mountains standing in his way. Hastily assembled walls that echoed back at him; a symphony of despair. Silas shouldered his way through every one, struck out with the scythe, time and time again, and using his body as a battering ram. The bones moved like sand-hills buffeted by desert winds, shifting their position, appearing in front of him before he'd had a chance to catch his enormous breath.

Fatigue was raising her unwelcome head. Silas over-extended himself. He knew it, felt it in the ache that came to his arm with each raise of the mace. He was stealing from his Nephilim origins, drawing on his angelic blood; all lost long ago. This transformation could not last.

Silas was neither man nor monster: not as weak as a purebred, but not so strong as a living giant, either. That could cost him dearly here.

He wore a cloak of bones now, piled upon his shoulders, dragging at him, encumbering him with their ancient sorrow. Seeking to drag him back, and down, into a grave that Silas would not escape this time.

He growled his defiance, and the sky rumbled.

Just a few more steps. A few more behemoth strides and he would take Mr Ahari's place; rescuing another from their grave.

Silas burst through a cliff face of bones, and into a wall of heat and fragile orange flame.

Pitch was a terrible vision, and yet beauty personified. He lay impaled in too many dreadful places, held aloft like a macabre trophy. His golden curls were darkened where his head hung low and touched them to the bloodied water.

Silas's heart clenched, and his own blood fired, seeing the state of this creature he loved. So still and terribly wounded, and so desperately close to the halo.

The pile of bones, the pyre Silas had seen from afar, was but an altar. And now, as he loomed over the lake and all those imprisoned in it, Silas saw the halo.

Its hilt jutted from the stacked and melded remains of the slain. So close, Silas might have reached out and touched it. But the halo was not for his hand. It was not his to take.

Silas went to his knees carefully, for fear of causing more pain with the shift of water. He leaned towards the one whose fate it was to end Blood Lake's painful legacy.

The bones came for Silas, swallowing his lower legs as he knelt, climbing the heights of his body, marching ever upward, ever determined.

But none were so determined as Silas to tip the balance. And steal this goodbye.

Pitch lay in a shadow of Silas's making. The prince was more terribly petite and fragile than he'd ever seemed before. But Silas fixed his gaze on the strong glow of fire at his fingertips, turning the water gold, hiding the seep of blood from so many wounds.

Silas reached for him. The maelstrom of mournful cries reduced to a whisper. Pitch's slender fingers twitched, movement stirred behind translucent lids.

Silas took his hand, ignoring the flames, careless of their burn. It would not be long before Silas felt nothing of this world's pains, and he would weather far worse for this last touch.

Pitch was warm. Not cold and lifeless. A subtle clench of muscle came; a frail clutch of the hand. Pitch knew he was here.

Silas smiled, his heart twisting and his soul lifting. 'Rise now, my love. Show them how magnificent you truly are.'

CHAPTER 39

Vassago was lifted from the bones; extricated from his cruel prison with strange gentleness.

The simurgh had shaped itself around the bones that invaded him, and now the Cultivation filled him with a comforting lightness.

'I am no failure.' The words blurted from him, straining free from where Blood Lake's morbid heart had trapped them earlier.

'Never.'

The tone sent a rapturous thrill through his ravaged body. Vassago opened his eyes. He was overshadowed by an enormity that was unmistakable. He was cradled in the palm of a great hand, an island of refuge in this groundless place.

'Silas.'

Although perhaps only in name. There was a hint of the man amongst the shadows and greatness, but Vassago suspected his own imagination placed them there.

'Do not fear me.'

Silas's voice held the distant rumble of thunder and disturbed the very waters of the lake. Waters that still held the thinnest trace of Vassago's blood. But these ancient flood waters would find no more sustenance from him. They could not reach the safe place where his ankou kept him.

'Never.' He repeated Silas's words back to him. 'And I ask the same of you.'

How raw his voice sounded; hanging onto its humanity by the last thread.

'You know you do not need to ask that of me. We shall always know each other.'

Silas had always been wiser than he.

Vassago could not even contemplate fearing this creature. This giant. Silas was written all over the greatness; there beneath the thick mess of black hair, wild as a jungle and just as vast. He was there in the darkness of a beard that hung like a cliff. He was there in brown eyes large as ponds, and there in lips that stretched like banks of sunset clouds.

Vassago–no, it was Pitch, for just a moment more–braced himself against the astonishing girth of Silas's fingers, and pulled himself onto his knees. Every hole in his body sent a chorus of biting protest, but the simurgh swept into the cavities and the pain grew dull.

'Careful now, my darling.'

And there Silas was again, unchangeable and unabashed.

Pitch leaned over the ankou's thumb, one thick as a shot tower, and watched as his giant carried him closer to the pyre where the halo stood embedded. He glimpsed movement far below, a shifting of white, and his flames lashed beneath his skin. Silas's body, the hillside that it had become, was being overrun by the bones. They covered him like barnacles, sharp as oysters and climbing ever higher over the shadowy vagueness of his lower body.

'Silas, do they harm –'

'Do what you must, Pitch.' The thunder rolled. 'And leave them to me. I will hold them back.' Silas lifted his other hand, rattling the chain of an enormous mace; its spikes glinting silver.

Pitch's grin was vicious, a flicker of bloodlust rising. The simurgh brushed a wing against the back of his eyes. What a sweet fucking irony this was. A child of Samyaza would deliver his destroyer to the halo.

His eyes blazed, his skin stretched with the strain of a rising inferno. His mind was as crystalline clear as the lake. All the bitter, soul-eating destitution of earlier was vanished. He was washed clean of doubt. And there was no entrance for it to return.

Pitch looked up at his favourite monster.

'Oh, I do love you, Mr Mercer.'

Silas smiled, and the merest rise of his lips cast a breeze in the stagnant air. Thunder prowled. 'Then I need no death wish. All that I desire, I have already.'

Pitch rose to his feet, teeth sharp at his bottom lip. He would give Silas one last gift, if such a thing could be said of standing naked with all ugliness exposed. But he knew the ankou wanted all of him. So he would give it.

'I am ready.'

Silas's pond-wide eyes glittered, and the slow nod of his head was like the felling of an oak. Slow and steady and irreversible.

Pitch reached his fingers to his own cheek and dug his fingernails into his beautiful disguise. Silas's eyes never left him, as all of Blood Lake screamed. The clatter of the bones grew frantic, manic; there was chaos below. But not above.

Pitch shed his skin.

Tore strips from the facade he had built, and let go the delicate beauty he so coveted. He laid himself bare beneath the unwavering gaze of the Nephilim. Showing Silas his true self, wanting him to know every layer that existed, before all was said and done.

The Dominion emerged; his true daemonic form. Black and hard as basalt, with rivulets of fire running like magma through a spiderweb of veins. Rough-hewn, and impenetrable. And though he bore the same limbs as purebreds, his were harsher in their lines; cut carelessly, with need only for bestial strength.

Little trace of beauty was found in the brutish assembly of a daemon.

His flesh fell away, his bloodless skin gathering in Silas's palm.

Vassago grew, swelling so large his lithic physique dangled over the edges of the ankou's colossal hand. But still their eyes did not leave one another; Vassago's burned like the belly of a volcano, while Silas's were warm and brown as tilled earth.

The ankou's fingers splayed, giving a daemon space to grow. Unafraid of touching what so many feared.

No words moved between them as they drank in all of each other. They hid nothing from one another. No more secrets existed.

Silas delivered Vassago to the very top of the pyre, gentle to the last. A look passed between them, volumes said in the glance.

And it was Pitch who turned, ready.

He leapt.

The journey from haven to cursed halo was a short one.

And the final game play began.

The screams that came from the lake matched those of the fiercest battle on the Hellfield, but Pitch did not utter a sound as he lunged. He wrapped daemonic hands around the black leather hilt, dug his feet into the pitiful dead, and welcomed the surge of the simurgh within.

The wildness poured from his natural seams, unifying his fire with the Cultivation's subtler hues, casting a spotlight upon all that remained of the traitor king.

Pitch hauled on the hilt, while the calamitous crunch of bone grew louder. He knew Silas held back the tide that threatened. Vassago relied on it.

There was no shift in the sword from its bedrock of bone.

Once more, Pitch heaved on the ancient weapon. Again, there was nothing. The simurgh pressed beneath his hardened skin, billowing, eager to be set free. Pitch ground teeth of rock, his fury cracking open new fissures in his form.

A ripple ran along his spine, tracing the lines where the amuletum had laid, pooling around the great gash in his exterior made by Seraphiel's halo. There was no hint of his molten flame in that place, extinguished eternally, an abyss he would always carry.

But he had survived. Not only the Seraph's blast, but the mess it had made of him after, and before.

He would not succumb here.

He resettled his hands. The cacophony of the lake's protest rose, the cries of a thousand deaths and two thousand years of resentment, drove at him, made razor-sharp by desperation.

He tried to pull the blade from the bone another time. Then another.

With each try his fury bubbled; with each failure rage ate greedily at his patience.

On the sixth try, he was livid, driving his foot into the shattered remains, screaming his foul discontent. Cursing all manner of man and god. His flames billowed; his desperation to see this done was hollowing him out.

Something turned his head. An impulse that struck him firm and fast. And changed everything.

The ankou was down, smothered by the bones, a few trails of his hair like long black rivers cutting through the clear waters. He was buried yet again, and in water, no less.

The Berserker Prince's roar resonated through the pyre, setting the halo vibrating with a ferocity that fed his insatiable hunger to destroy. Sweltering mindlessness took hold. Lust, the most savage and blood-thirsty of its kind, tangled through his flames, setting him ablaze.

The simurgh screamed. The halo groaned. The bones cried for mercy.

On the seventh attempt, Samyaza's halo slid free of its bony sheath.

The prince held the halo aloft, his entire body aflame, bones turning to ash around him. The simurgh crashed against his basalt walls, cracking them open; the wildness was intoxicating. Vassago dived into the intoxicating bedlam of fury. He rivalled a hundred suns. Never had he burned so.

But it was not only he who must burn.

Guided by instinct, he aimed the tip of the halo towards the black crags of his chest and drove the blade into his ill-beating heart.

The simurgh was there, the Primordial Flame at its own heart. Positioned perfectly. Waiting for this longed-for spark.

Seraphiel's work was complete.

The stupendous collision of ancient Death Wish and divine Cultivation shifted the world beneath Pitch's feet. Stealing the ground from beneath him.

But he did not fall.

He soared.

CHAPTER 40

Lucifer stood in the ballroom, surrounded by fallen bodies. Jacquetta hurried Edward, away. The purebred prophet had been found gasping for breath and bleeding beneath the bone chandelier.

In reply to Seraphiel's sharp command for an answer, the man muttered something about having stumbled across all the purebreds, and wishing to guide them somewhere safe. The Sanctuary's near-constant trembling added some weight to his explanation.

Lucifer did not look at him as the Child hurried him by. He had the answer he sought well enough. The ankou was not here. And as Silas would not have left Edward in that state–nor those few survivors who remained on their feet–for anything but a matter of the gravest importance, he knew Silas Mercer had entered Blood Lake.

'Is there something you wish to tell me, Luci?'

Seraphiel stood at his side, vibrant, and yet drained. He had discarded the luxurious layer of his coat, and was clad plainly in a white shirt and gold breeches that gathered at the knee where black boots rose to meet the material.

'No. I simply await your instruction.'

'You do nothing simply.'

Lucifer frowned, but did so lightly. There could be no darkening of the Seraph's mood here. The ruin that lay around them was evidence enough. Barely a handful of couples survived. 'I don't understand what you are asking.'

He did. Seraphiel knew Edward had not been here for the dancers.

'You were searching for someone when we entered.' The angel had always been difficult to hide from.

But Lucifer knew himself equally difficult to read when he set his mind to it. Such were the games they played with one another.

'No, I was merely taken aback by the state of the dancers.'

'Are we to end things on a lie, Luci?'

Lucifer sighed, mostly at himself for not knowing when games should come to a close. 'No. We are not. The ankou has –'

'Gone into the lake.' Seraphiel bore hint of a sly smile.

'You sod, you knew.'

'Only when I entered the room.' His smile slipped. 'How weak I must be, if I did not realise sooner. The prophet? He unlocked the way?'

Lucifer nodded, bracing for the expected tirade; the feverish ramblings of retribution that seemed to overtake Seraphiel at random. The angel simply looped his arm through Lucifer's, leading him towards the centre of the room. Picking a path through the dead.

'He is not a man to be easily stopped.' Lucifer spoke into the uncomfortable silence. He did not wish to end this on a lie, nor disagreement. 'I overstepped, I know but –'

'It is done now,' Seraphiel sighed, which made Lucifer more unhappy than if he'd started raging. The angel was slipping from him. 'And you told me often enough of their connection. I did not listen. I have never listened to you often enough, Luci.'

Lucifer's reply was to do something he'd not done often enough. He pulled his arm from the casual hold and embraced the angel's waist. A rarefied hold, on which Seraphiel made no comment, but Lucifer felt the way he tensed, heard the faint inhale of breath. The embrace, though barely intimate, took Lucifer far from where he was comfortable. But he would push himself; before all things were lost and irretrievable.

'I did not intend to deceive you...' His thoughts drifted to the strange interaction with the wisp, of the certainty that had overcome him as their colours engulfed him. That he should allow Silas to go had not been in doubt. 'But it felt to me he had proved himself capable of withstanding the most significant of challenges. And his blindness when it comes to Vassago cannot be equalled.'

'I trust you, Luci.' Seraphiel stepped over a man in a doublet and hose whose dead eyes were marbled with unpleasant black veins. 'More so than I do myself.'

Thunder struck. The chandeliers shivered like trees in a storm. Lucifer glanced up. In time to see one tear from its base.

'Move!' he shouted, throwing aside his cane and lifting Seraphiel off his feet to pull him clear. Crystal prisms smashed against the floor, crushing the body of a young woman, and slipping like ice across the polished wood.

Without the cane, Lucifer doubted he'd stay on his feet long. Every inch of him ached, his chest heavy, and throat tight, as though he drowned, simply standing here.

'Luci?'

'Best get on with this.'

The faint trickle of water could be heard, its direction unclear. Seraphiel used the finest of Arcadia's archaic curses.

'Beneath the bones, quickly.' Seraphiel was the one carrying Lucifer now, acting as the cane he'd lost, manoeuvring him the short distance to the room's centre. A hint of his angelfire shone beneath his skin. 'Play, now!'

The quartet struck up, the deep notes of the cello beginning the tune. Lucifer dragged in a breath, and the coppery hint of blood hit his nostrils.

'Raph, do you –'

'I smell it.' Seraphiel was composed as he brought them face to face. He winced, lowering his head. A moment later, his wings bloomed, carvings of golden light as wide as Lucifer recalled, but lacking their usual brilliant lustre. Seraphiel tried to stifle it, but his soft moan pained Lucifer's ears.

'What does the blood mean?'

'That we must hurry, but aside from that...I'm uncertain. I've never known the scent of blood to come from the lake before.' He wrung his hands, light sparking. 'What have I done? I was so certain of my path here. So sure I could undo what I had created.'

Lucifer took Seraphiel's hands, the pulse of Angelic power rocking him on his feet. The angel was still strong so now he must retrieve his own waning fortitude. 'Do you have any word from the lady?'

He shook his head, in that wilder way of before, when he was set for another fit of madness. 'Luci, why did you not stop me before now? Why did Enoch take so long to strike me down?' His eyes glowed dangerously bright, and he tried to pull free of Lucifer's hold.

'Raph, calm down,' Lucifer demanded, deciding careful handling would not help here. 'Listen to me...look at me.'

But Seraphiel was sinking, mumbling words that slipped between recognisable and not. His wings swayed in haphazard motions, sweeping high and dipping low, cutting across the surrounding bodies, as surely as the ankou's scythe. Slicing terrible wounds wide open, letting more blood flow.

'Raph, don't do this. I know you hear me.' Lucifer winced beneath the growing strength of the angel's light; it came from his wings and eyes, and now through rivulets tracing through his skin. The body he wore would not hold even this weaker, lesser piece of the Seraph much longer.

The harp joined the cello; the quartet following instruction still, whilst their master shook as much as his Sanctuary. Lucifer tried once more to gain his attention. And failed.

Lucifer gathered himself, prepared for the driving pain he knew would come, and ignited. Letting his flames mimic the glorious wings of the angel. Only their hues differed; Seraphiel white as stars, and Lucifer the heart of the sun.

He had the angel's attention now. Seraphiel stared, lips parted, at the daemonflame that danced in courtship with his own. His wings lost their calamity, slowing their beating, finding the rhythm of the dance Lucifer laid out for them. For the first time in their long association, Lucifer found himself with the greater wingspan, and the more radiant.

His wings were bright as the lava that churned in the River Lethe. Their light played against Seraphiel's face, lined and cracked as it was, as the angel's essence shone its last.

But he had his Antinous back.

'Now, take what you need.' Lucifer heard the groan of timbers, the shattering of a window pane, the fall of another chandelier, all as if they were a world away. 'I give it freely.'

Seraphiel nodded, and touched his hand to Lucifer's cheek, calmed once more. 'Do you find regret here, my king?'

His touch rocked Lucifer on his feet, but the Seraph was there to keep him steady.

'Only that I could not save you from your burden.'

The quartet played–a harp amongst its number now–with delicate notes, whilst a brutal siphoning of power began.

'I was the master of my demise, Lucifer, never you. And I know that you warned me countless times. Now here is your reward. I take more from you than the gods should allow.'

Seraphiel drew them both into his Cultivation, his magick like the nicks of a knife and the sear of a furnace. Their wings curved about one another, taking them into a place where no other could follow. Lucifer fought the urge to close his eyes. He wanted to watch the angel until the last.

'The gods would not dare. I have the stain of free will in my veins. And I have grown a taste for making my own choices.' The pain was ebbing, a numbness growing in its place. He felt wonderfully light. Free of all burden. 'I dare hope, though, that they see fit to find us a place near one another, in the world that comes after death.'

'I defy the Celestials to try otherwise when I take my place in their ranks.'

The Seraph surrounded him, coveting him; seeping into every crack and crevice that had formed over Lucifer's seemingly never-ending years. His eyes were narrowed to cracks, his legs had given way, but still the Seraphiel held him. Took from him, whilst Lucifer gave. Emptying him until nothing remained but all he had to give. His creation flame; the last spark of a daemonking's soul.

A fragile gasp brushed his ear. And the angel's hold tightened. 'I see him, Luci. The prince...the halo is his.'

Seraphiel sobbed into his magick, his tears vanishing with the molten heat.

'You are free.' Lucifer's words were fire, the last dance of his creation flame. 'We are free.'

They fell into one another and merged. Coming together in an explosion of angelfire and daemonflame. A herculean force that neither the legions of Arcadia nor Samyaza had hope of thwarting.

Lucifer had laid down his crown.

And left the way open for a new King of Daemonkind to emerge.

CHAPTER 41

Silas held back Blood Lake's angst-ridden tide, arms spread against the surge of almighty resistance. The mace swung, shredding the boney onslaught, but more gathered at his back and climbed atop his shoulders; an invading horde seeking to spill over a mountain range. The water sought entry between his feet, trying to find a path through the shadows he cast.

It would find none.

He would allow nothing to steal sight of the culmination of all things.

His beautiful, terrifying view of what was always meant to pass.

The halo was remarkably plain, its hilt leather-bound, its blade dull. But there was nothing insipid about the daemon who pulled it from its bedrock of bones.

A daemon incapable of ugliness, despite what he may believe.

Silas took in every inch of the Berserker Prince, every river of liquid flame that ran through an exterior as rough and jagged as a barren mountaintop, and black as night. Atop his head, a rough cut of basalt curved like a diadem, the great ember at its centre, an indescribable gem.

Pitch had chosen a delicate visage in his human form, and Silas understood now how the contrast must have pleased him, for his true form was all stony brawn and powerful dominance. Immovable solidity.

The daemon was not so large as Silas's Nephilim, but was far more formidable. The bones crumbled to ash beneath him. Samyaza's pyre was reduced to grains of sand with the twist of an onyx heel.

Pitch...Vassago...stood triumphant and raised the halo high, a sight fit for the heavens. The lake surged, the currents buffeting Silas anew as the Watcher King's legacy saw its fate sealed.

He did not sway, nor shift, or stumble. He would not look away.

Even as the prince raised the halo.

Even as he drove it into himself in one swift strike.

Silas did not cower at the glare that came. Pitch vanished beneath the explosion of light, his silhouette like a ghostly imprint within the brightness. The clamour of the bones and their interminable weight lessened. Silas drew himself up and threw off the weight of the lake's misery. Raised himself to full height, the bones raining off him.

The mace shivered in his grasp and returned to a simpler form; the two-toned metal ring, now tarnished and scored with fine cuts.

A single note rose above all others. A call for Silas's ears alone.

Child of mine.

A last, desperate cry from an angel whose cause was well and truly lost. An attempt at final manipulation.

Samyaza's hail would go unanswered.

There, within the brilliance of Seraphiel's divine magick and Pitch's unyielding resolve, Silas glimpsed the Watcher King. His sire. The spectre whose refusal to hand himself over entirely to death had wrought so much misery upon those who had once thought his cause noble.

Perhaps, once, that cause had been so. Silas was far removed from the wars of the Angelics; further still from the court of Lord Enoch and its machinations.

But he cared little for past grievances; more concerned with those of the here and now.

Samyaza's desecration of this graveyard–his torturing of the souls it contained–negated any righteousness.

And in any case, those were not the worst of the Seraph's sins.

The Watcher King was taking Pitch away from him. That was unforgivable.

Silas shrugged off the whispering of his sire. The pleading.

'I am no child. And you were no father.'

The easy denial infuriated the flimsy ghost of the once-potent angel.

A shockwave struck at Silas, and he spread his arms, letting it wash over him. His blood screamed in his veins as Samyaza's final deathnote rang out. Tolling its last.

Thinning to nothingness.

As Silas, too, thinned.

His tremendous weight took him to his knees. His greatness draining from him, as a form emerged from the brilliance where Pitch had last stood.

An inferno that rose skyward.

Dwarfing Silas where he knelt and bled away his past.

The fire held neither daemon nor simurgh, but an almighty convergence of the two.

The firebird rose, its wingspan stretching over great swathes of Blood Lake's crimson sky. A daemon prince at its heart.

Silas knew Pitch's flames as he knew his own truth. He spied his prince; there in the blazing expanse of tail and wing and claw.

His great love, hidden away, but never lost.

Silas reduced, whilst Seraphiel's Cultivation distended to engulf all the tragedy and perdition that festered here. His eyes stung, his throat thickened as his humanity rushed in to fill the void left by the drying of his Nephilim blood; he had been birthed a child of Samyaza, but would not die one.

The firebird's shadow rippled over the still waters as it soared higher. Silas had thought himself behemoth when he'd opened his Nephilim heart. He had thought the Lady's Leviathan a great and daunting creature, but they were, all of them, mere specks beneath the firebird's shadow.

The creature born of primordial fire and daemon flame was vast as the heavens themselves.

And surely far more beautiful.

Silas craned his neck, watched the epic sweep of infernal wings, felt the furious blast of their movement upon his cheeks, and cursed his tears for how they blurred his vision. He did not wish to miss a moment of Pitch's last spectacular display.

Silas prayed the prince knew himself wondrous. Let Seraphiel have given him that, at least: a chance to realise the magnificence Silas had always known.

The firebird opened its mouth, a beak curled like a massive ocean wave, and sent forth a holocaust of flame. The touchdown against the lake was the eruption of a volcano, the brilliance making Silas wince. He raised his arm, shielding himself from the heat. He was far from where the firebird struck, a half mile at least, and yet his hair singed.

Again and again, a devastation of fire worked at evaporating Blood Lake. The firebird made no sound, save for the rasp of wings and hiss of the torrents as they jettisoned.

And Silas had much else to listen to, as the lake was turned to ash.

The exhale of breaths long held.

The shackles of the Watcher King's regrets and furies coming loose, falling away.

Those who had languished here, drowning in their own laments, now pierced the surface and opened themselves to the cleansing fire.

The water grew lower and lower around him.

Silas watched, his neck aching with the weight of his own bones. His spine fractured as he refused to look away, his fingers snapping when pressed to the thick ash to bolster him. Silas crumbled along with all the bones.

'Not yet, please, I beg of you,' he implored his goddess. 'Let me be the one to bring him to you. Let us go together.'

But if she listened, he heard no reply. The scythe did not whisper, nor tighten in assurance. Perhaps he was voiceless; now that his ride was done.

Ash floated from the fiery sky; thousands of years of turmoil now insubstantial as dust.

Silas bent to the whim of time, naked and breaking, finally kneeling at mortality's feet.

The firebird circled around, the shifting light betraying the movement. Silas felt his bones grind as he forced his head to raise. The pyre was gone, but the mound of bones Silas had created still stood tall. Those he had cast off whilst he was giant, now overshadowed him. The last collection the firebird needed to decimate.

Silas sought to rise to his feet, but death had her gentle hands upon him now, coaxing him to lie down his head a final time.

But not here, not this way.

He did not know if Pitch watched on from behind the firebird's eyes, and understood the blissful havoc they wreaked. But Silas would take no chance with his love's last moments.

Prince Vassago had been haunted by the strike that had downed Seraphiel. The guilt and remorse had eaten at him. He had not loved that angel, and yet he suffered. How much greater the suffering if Pitch struck down the oaf he had finally, so wonderfully, found cause to love?

Silas ground his teeth and fought death once more. Not with the scythe, as he'd done with Sybilla, but with all the resistance his purebred blood could muster. Humanity held an innate desire to fight against the goddess. For time immemorial, they had sought to elude and outrun Death. He knew that better than anyone alive.

Their evasion was pointless, but there was something to be said for their tenacious belief in its possibility.

He joined their ranks; and clung to wistful hope. He dug his fingers into the shifting ground, seeking to drag himself clear of the last bastion of bones. The water was a thin film that had turned the ash to grey mud; adding further duress upon his feeble body. But he tried. An inch here, another there. Trying to outpace death on two fronts.

The air brightened, and his skin burned from the proximity of the firebird. He was barely a foot away from the pile. Hope was one thing, but stupidity was another. It was ludicrous to imagine himself far enough away to escape the oncoming blast, and plain insanity not to notice his broken wrists and splintered knee bones. He was done for.

The soft whoosh of sweeping wings grew louder. Silas sank into the sludge. His heart slowed. His end song rose, while the Seraph's magick descended.

He dragged his gaze upwards. Taking a breath that must number amongst his last.

The firebird's cavernous mouth opened, the inferno luminous at the back of its throat.

A tilt of the head. A topaz eye set on Silas.

A pinpoint of emerald at its centre, glowing. The firebird's head twisted sharply, redirecting the flame, but the beast had already breathed its fire. A cry rushed forth; the first sound the creature had made.

'It's alright,' Silas whispered.

The bloom of catastrophic flame descended.

His tears were vanquished by the heat, his lips cracked by its rush.

He was smothered. Pressed down into the sediment which took him readily. The wildfire raced over him. Leaving him untouched.

Go well, Silas. My thanks to you both, for this freedom.

The weight upon him did not belong to ash or bone. Silas tried to form her name upon his lips, but found them too ruined to speak.

The air cooled, and the weight slipped away. Silas lay, half buried in the ashen mud, blinking slowly at the petrified corpse by his side; a massive serpent he did not recognise. But her shape did not matter. Silas knew the touch of Satine against his mind.

The Lady of the Lake had burned in his place.

Silas breathed in slow rasping drags. With the striking heat gone, a chill seeped up through the mud. He heard his deathnote now: solitary, and lonely. He had no strength to raise his head, but his eyes lifted just enough to see the firebird circling above. Low and close, and spectacular, giving off only the mildest warmth. Barely enough to stop Silas from shivering.

Lower, closer.

Still, Silas was not scorched.

The firebird descended. Touched its claws of dying ember to the dampness, evaporating the last drops of Blood Lake. Turning the mud to warm sand.

Silas sighed into the softness and heat.

The great destroyer of Blood Lake settled near him.

A sob escaped him, drawn from his tired body by the sheer perfection of what he heard. He smiled through hopeless tears, copper upon his tongue as his lips split wider. Silas listened as the firebird's remarkable flames flickered and dimmed.

Pitch's song played itself out. Not just his death note, though that lay there too, but his whole medley, shattering the silence that had always surrounded him.

Daemon. Dominion. Saviour.

Silas inched his hand through the calming warmth of the sand. Finding the tip of a velvet wing, sighing at how it mimicked the familiar press of the daemon's hand.

They shaped together perfectly.

'You are here at the end.'

Pitch's voice found a way through his sublime melody.

'I promised you...' Silas's lips stung, but he still smiled.

'You oaf.'

'A fool for you alone.'

Verdant light shone through Silas's fading vision. He blinked, barely daring to believe what he saw. But death need not always be cruel. She could be a rescuer, a granter of wishes.

Pitch lay amongst smouldering embers, the ruins of the simurgh spread beneath him like sunset fallen from the sky. He was caught between his two worlds; the exquisite, delicate human just visible within the great, smouldering fortress that was the daemon. Pitch lay within Vassago; and there was no telling where the seams that joined them had been sewn.

His eyes, those gems that shone duller now, never left Silas.

Their melodies played them ever closer to the goddess.

Her tempo was relentless, but Silas was eternally grateful for her mercy. She had stayed her hand until all things were said, all things were done, and his soul mate found. Few had such blessings.

The notes quietened. Silas's heavy heart slowed its beat.

Pitch smiled at him. He'd never seemed so unafraid.

The gleam in his eyes vanished. His hold on Silas's hand slackened.

He exhaled.

His melody died.

The silence was endless.

Silas would breathe no air without him. He let go, setting himself adrift. There was nothing to tie him here anymore.

One shallow breath later, he followed his daemon.

The humans had been right, after all.

There was a light that still shone when life extinguished; a bright beacon to guide Death's children home.

Izanami waited there in the glow, arms outstretched; a slender figure with eyes of viridian by her side.

CHAPTER 42

Pitch was not in the mood for being woken. Least of all by a ceaseless, irritating slap against his earlobe.

'Get away,' he mumbled. 'Or I'll turn you to cinder.'

He dug himself further beneath the bedcovers, drawing Silas's arm over him more tightly, pressing back against the ankou who snored lightly behind him. 'I told him he snores,' he muttered. 'Never believed me.'

He knew the ankou was too deeply asleep to have heard. Silas only snored when he was utterly exhausted, or had had too many ales.

Pitch frowned into the feather pillow, eyes firmly closed. Had they drunk last night? If so, it might account for why he could not recall a single moment of the evening. But his head was groggy with sleep, not a hangover. Aside from being fully unprepared to open his eyes just yet, Pitch felt rather good. Not a single ache to be had. Actually, that wasn't so good.

His arsehole didn't ache, which meant he'd not been ridden into the mattress by the amply endowed ankou any time recently. A terrible shame; to be rectified at once.

He shifted, pressing his arse against Silas's groin, sighing contentedly to find a firm pillar of morning glory there. The ankou muttered, his hand drifting down Pitch's front until it found another upstanding greeter of the morning. His fingers played at Pitch's cock, teasing him for only a few moments before stilling. A short heartbeat later, Silas returned to snoring.

Pitch sighed, and something of the exhale gave him pause. His hand drifted up from beneath the bedclothes, a divine layering of satin and silk, to touch his fingers to the base of his throat.

He recalled a sense of breathlessness, a vague memory that refused to hold still long enough for him to grab onto.

Another pat, this time on the top of his head. One he tried to swipe at, only to find his hand plunged into a swathe of soft pillows.

He still hadn't found the impetus to open his eyes, and realised then just how fucking tired he was.

'Scarlet, do you not wish to live any longer?' There was no reply. Which was odd for the wisp who always had far too much to say. 'Frightened you off then, did I?'

Pitch resettled beneath the covers, deciding that perhaps he'd imagined the bloody thing after all.

Silas stirred at the sound of Pitch's voice and nuzzled into his neck. His hand took up its caress once more, and Pitch tilted his head back with a soft groan.

'Do you have trouble sleeping?' Silas mumbled, leaving gentle kisses along the length of Pitch's neck. 'Shall I make you tired?'

'I can't imagine how you could do that.'

'I'm fairly sure you can imagine, but I shall give you an example.' The tempo of his caress quickened, his broad hand engulfing Pitch's cock. There was the hush of satin as Silas moved himself about so that his own prick slid between Pitch's cheeks. Not seeking entrance, but rubbing between the flesh in a slow back and forth. His groan against the back of Pitch's neck made the hair on daemonic arms stand up, and ready balls lift. Pitch grabbed at the blanket, pulling it over their heads, hiding them away; capturing them in a world with a population of only two.

Pitch kept his eyes shut, and the darkness behind his eyelids deepened. He rocked with the ankou's rhythm, craving their intimacy with a ferocious lust. Pitch was not hungry. This was not incubus desire that drove him. Just a deep want for this man.

'Silas.' Pitch arched his back, arse shifting as he sought to guide the ankou's prick into deeper territory. 'I need you.'

'And you shall have me.' Silas's chuckle was dark, sending vibrations through Pitch's body that made every nerve jangle harder. But the ankou didn't understand, not truly, for if he knew how frantic Pitch's desire was he'd not move his hand so languidly, nor explore so patiently the tight curl of muscle so eager to bloom.

'Now, quickly,' Pitch panted.

Silas moaned against him. 'But I've not prepared you.'

'I don't care. It doesn't matter.' Pitch cast back his hand, searching for Silas's hip under the covers. Digging his fingers in to skin, bare and warm. He urged the ankou in closer. His chest pained him, the urgency stifling. 'Now, Silas. Fuck me.'

Before the chance was stolen away. Before whatever nirvana this was ended.

Pitch opened his eyes. It was not entirely dark. There was light finding its way through the bedclothes; bedclothes impossibly soft, a fabric that caressed the curves of his body. Familiarity niggled at him, but his growing panic dominated. His frantic need for the ankou only growing.

'Pitch.' Silas's voice found a way through the thunder of blood in Pitch's head. 'My darling, calm yourself. I'm here. I'm not going anywhere. We can take our time.' Silas slid his hand from Pitch's cock and drifted higher, a caress that brushed over nipples and went higher still. Silas ran his thumb over that spot upon Pitch's collarbone that never failed to make him shiver.

It did not fail now.

He moaned, slowing his manic attempts to force Silas inside him.

'There we are, good boy.' The murmur at his ear made his blood heat, and his hips buck. 'Let's get you ready.'

Having seduced his prey into compliance, Silas set about opening Pitch to greater things. He used Pitch's readiness; the wetness at the head of his cock, slicking his fingers. Silas eased his damp fingers between Pitch's cheeks. Considerate, as always; seeking to make things pleasant.

But Pitch didn't want pleasant.

'No, this isn't right.'

He wriggled away.

'What are you doing?'

'I want to see you. I have to see you.'

Pitch rolled onto his back, and there was a great shifting of covers and blankets as the ankou found his new place between Pitch's spread legs.

They stared at one another. Stared, as though they had not seen each other in decades. Again Pitch was caught by breathlessness, by the tug at a corner of his mind. Silas licked his lips, his gaze shifting to Pitch's own mouth. Studying it intently.

Pitch knew he felt it, too. That the world was off-kilter.

Silas traced a finger over Pitch's cheekbone, quiet and contemplative. He bore more grey threads in his dark hair, at his beard too, with new wrinkles there at the edge of his eyes.

'Does it hurt you, my love?'

Pitch dragged his gaze from the ankou's changes. 'You are not inside me yet. What could hurt?'

A wistful smile. 'I speak of your face. There is some damage here.' His fingers went again to Pitch's cheekbone, and so he raised his hand to the same place. The skin was rough. As though burned.

Great weights pushed at the back of his mind.

But he repelled them. He didn't want to think. He wanted Silas.

'No. No it does not hurt at all.'

A tear slipped down Silas's cheek. 'Pitch...what has –'

He pressed his finger against the ankou's lips. Attempting to hold back all that threatened to overwhelm them.

Pitch was not ready. 'Don't speak of it, not yet.'

If this were fantasy, an illusion or dream, then let it stay so. If this were the delusion of a dying daemon, then so it should remain.

Silas leaned in to kiss him and enter him. The desperate urgency melted away as Pitch was opened wide; the ankou's thickness blissfully painful.

The fantasy held.

Thank the gods. What lay beyond this bed was large and terrifying, and no place Pitch wished to visit until he must.

Theirs was a slow union, a deliberate drive of body against body. The hurt was there; the ankou was large and Pitch not nearly readied enough. But the pain was exquisite and raw, and so very welcome. Bringing him to life.

Silas covered him, took him slowly, deeply and with his usual cascade of beautiful whispers.

Neither spoke of the differences to be found in one another; the bruises and marks and stains that had come from that world beyond the sheets.

All that mattered right now was the familiar.

The synchronicity of their bodies. The touch of tongues and fumble of fingers as they sought to know each other everywhere, all at once.

Pitch bit at Silas's lip, and his ankou obliged with a deeper thrust of his hips; a quickening of the pace.

They fucked in their own little world. Their haven of silk and satin, and each other. He pressed his hands to Silas's cheeks, holding his gaze as they moved in gasping unison towards that highest, most glorious place of all. Pitch tried hard not to close his eyes as his climax threatened. He wanted to watch Silas come, and the ankou was close.

They grunted and hissed, snarling into their pleasure; no less bestial than animals in the forest. Silas's steady thrusts broke Pitch apart in all the best ways. He was overwhelmed by his release; an avalanche of ecstasy that tore frantic cries from the bottom of his lungs.

Silas praised Pitch as he spilled, the ankou's voice strangled by the thundering approach of his own climax. Pitch blinked his eyes open, panting, his body jerking, his prick still spitting the remnants of his load.

'Now, let me see you,' he gasped.

He tightened himself around Silas's cock, and watched as the ankou toppled over the precipice.

Silas came; his bellow primeval and covetous. His last thrust seemed sure to split Pitch in half. He grabbed Pitch's shoulders, using the leverage to bury himself deeper still, his body shuddering. His release was a torrent; filling his vessel to overflowing. His hips thrust one more time; driving his cock through the mess he'd made, the sounds of sopping flesh disgraceful.

Spent, Silas collapsed his weight upon Pitch. He growled as he ran his tongue over Pitch's collarbone, licking at the sweat there, one final delicious torment. They both twitched and shivered, and groaned curses. They reeked of spill and exertion. Silas's powerful thrusts had driven Pitch up the mattress; his head glanced at the headboard. At some point during the rut he was fairly certain he'd heard one of the mattress slats break.

The fuck was rough and vulgar; it was utter perfection.

'Well, that was nice,' Pitch said.

'Fucking hell, wasn't it?'

Silas drew Pitch with him as he rolled onto his side. He sought to keep them joined, but he was limp, and Pitch's arse cheeks too flooded to prevent his cock sliding free with a slick whisper.

'Leaving me so soon?'

Silas burst out laughing. 'Fear not, I shall return.' He ran his hand along Pitch's side, chuckling as the touch made him shiver. 'Just give me a moment.'

Someone cleared their throat. Someone not in their haven. 'I'm afraid you don't have a moment, my lords.'

Gods, Pitch knew that voice. But it was impossible.

He pushed back the covers, blinking into the sudden brightness. 'Fuck. You?'

'Yes, I, your highness.'

Silas sat up, hair every which way, throwing his arm in front of Pitch. 'Stay back. Good god...what are you?'

The hydra inclined each of his three heads, his smoothed foreheads speckled with yellow spots. 'My Lord, I am Forneus. His Royal Highness, Prince Vassago's valet.' He smoothed at the matching yellow cords on his coat.

Silas was a comical delight, struck dumb with astonishment, his mouth open wide enough to catch flies. Sweat framed his widened eyes.

'What the fuck are you doing here, Forneus?' Pitch pressed Silas's arm down.

The hydra shifted in obvious discomfort, his multitude of spindly legs tapping at the floor. He continued to preen himself, a habit Pitch knew hid his irritation; he'd always been preening when in Vassago's presence. But he seemed to have another master now. The tassels of his uniform, the chest plate emblem, were those of Lucifer.

'Oh dear, I thought you'd already been informed.' Forneus spoke from his central head, his favourite. 'The explanation is not for me to give. I am sent here to attend to your needs. Should I have the linen changed? And will you and his lordship be requiring any sustenance? What does a purebred prefer to eat? I'll have the cooks arrange something immediately. I suspect you are both quite famished after all of that.'

Silas gaped, a tiny sound of mortification.

'How long have you been standing there?' Pitch growled.

'Well...a little while.' Forneus bobbed his bald heads in succession. 'Apologies, but I'm unfamiliar with the extent of humankind's' breeding behaviours, so I was unsure when was an appropriate time to enter.'

'Never. Never is an appropriate time, you silly bastard.' Pitch took in the room. It was rounded, like the blasted tower in the cockaigne, the stonework unpainted, and the exposed beams overhead the rich hue of mahogany. 'Oh, gods...'

'What?' Silas touched his shoulder. 'What is it?'

He slipped from the ankou's touch and drew his legs from beneath the covers. 'Fuck, fuck. This cannot be.'

Pitch left the bed, rather wet between the legs, and very naked, but he didn't give a damn. He strode across the room; past a chest of drawers, with a water pitcher and wash basin atop, past a wing-back chair with carved trim and silk upholstery, past a side-table with a stack of books and a small ceramic clock. His pace moved a tapestry that hung upon the wall; an embroidery of an English summer garden. But this was not England. And that sun had never shone into this room.

'Pitch, tell me what is going on,' Silas said.

Something in his tenor, something fragile, had Pitch glancing back. Silas sat with his fingers pressed to his temples, wincing. The euphoria of fucking was gone, and their unified decision to ignore reality now crashed down around them.

Pitch stared harder at the ankou.

Or rather, the purebred.

Silas's aura was the barely there grey of humankind; none of the silver ribbons and movement the ankou's had held.

'Well?' Silas pulled a blanket to cover himself and stood up.

'I don't know yet.' Pitch moved to the window, covered over by a velvet blue curtain.

'Your Highness, is something not to your liking? I can have it changed. I'm sure his majesty would have wanted you to be comfortable here in the tower. May the Celestials bless his divine soul.' Forneus was solemn and pious, just as he usually was. 'Strange furnishings here though, I'll give you that.'

Pitch took hold of the curtain, the hydra's words like the toll of an unwanted bell. His stomach was tight with nerves. And nothing else.

No stirrings. No wildness.

But then, he'd known that from the moment he awoke. The simurgh was gone.

'Whose room is this?' Silas said. 'Will someone bloody well tell me where we are?'

Pitch pulled back the curtain, revealing clear glass filling an arched and narrow window behind. The view was breathtaking. And it was certainly not Scotland.

'Oh fuck,' he breathed. 'We did not die.'

The bleeding godsdamned obvious was finally said.

Silas came to stand at his side, and he too took in the view; a land of colours and contours he would find utterly foreign. He was the palest Pitch had ever known him. 'Perhaps...this is the afterlife?' Silas clearly didn't believe his own shaky words.

'No, my dearest. Not even close.'

Silas opened the blanket and drew Pitch into its fold. 'You know this place.' Wisely, he did not make it a question.

'I do. Those are the Siltron Ranges.'

'I see. And where do those ranges lie?'

Silas guessed it, Pitch knew from the waver in his voice, but he was waiting for Pitch to say it aloud. To speak more impossible truths.

But a new and altogether too cheery voice interrupted their stunned reverie.

'They lie in Arcadia, my fine fellow. Welcome to Arcadia.'

CHAPTER 43

Ayoung man, with an astonishing tangle of golden-orange curls,
stood just inside the doorway. He was plain faced, neither stunning nor unattractive, with several large dark freckles on his sun-kissed
face. He held a bunch of flowers, of a type Silas was not even going to
guess at, after what he'd seen beyond that window.

Silas stepped between the new arrival and the prince. Realising as he
did so that the scythe was gone.

There was little time to fret.

'Oh, shit,' Pitch gasped. For a moment Silas thought him about to
faint, but the daemon was doing something equally strange.

He went to one knee and bowed low at the waist.

The hydra–the remarkable creature with three heads and legs as knob-
bly as a giraffe's, though half as long–seemed to lose all of his minds.
He threw himself to the flagstone floor, covering his central head with a
clawed hand.

'My Lord Enoch.'

Silas's own knees went rubbery. 'What? He's the...that's the...'

Pitch grabbed at Silas's blanket, no doubt trying to urge him down,
but with Silas's shock came a loosened grip. The blanket slipped away,
and both Pitch and Silas met the Lord of Arcadia utterly naked.

A strangled cry left Silas, but the prince kept his head bowed, and was no bloody help at all with the retrieval of the blanket, slapping at Silas's hand as he reached for it.

'Kneel, damn you. You're embarrassing me.'

Silas glared at the top of his head. 'We have our bloody balls out.'

'He's seen such things before. Get down.'

It took a moment to register the laughter. Another moment for Silas to wade through his cheek-burning mortification, to realise the young man, the ruler of daemons and angels, laughed.

Rather heartily.

Enoch clutched at his chest through the white smock he wore. Both it and his knee-length breeches were smudged with a dark substance Silas hoped was dirt and not blood. Considering the lord's feet were also bare, and also dirty—with darkness between the toes—soil seemed the more fortunate option.

'If there were any doubt of your humanity, Silas Mercer, it is eased now. What a specimen you are. The goddess has a fine eye all round.'

Lord Enoch smiled, and the breath left Silas's lungs. He forgot he wore not a jot of clothing; forgot the horrors he had just endured, and the land beyond the window that he did not recognise. There was nothing in the world but that smile; it bathed the entire room with radiance, an ethereal lightness beyond comprehension.

A jab at his leg startled him.

'You are staring,' Pitch hissed, shoving the blanket at him.

Silas took it absently, holding it so just enough covered his most private parts. What point was there in hiding from this being? His presence must filter into every crack and crevice in the world.

'My Lord, forgive us.' Pitch was flustered. 'We didn't know…it has been very…I truly don't –'

'Don't understand. I know Vassago. But I assure you, we meet again under very different circumstances to the last. All of Arcadia gives thanks for what the pair of you have achieved.' Arcadia's master, in the guise of a farm boy barely free of his childhood, extended the bouquet. 'Welcome, Silas Mercer. I hope these flowers please you.'

Silas nearly tripped over the dragging blanket as he rushed forward to accept the blooms. Roses, perhaps? They were tied with a simple blue string, and must have been picked some time ago, for they drooped a little.

'Yes, I know. They are a little wilted,' Enoch said, brown eyes warm as hot chocolate. Silas blinked. Christ, he could read minds? 'And no, I cannot read your mind. You have your privacy here. I am just very good at deciphering expressions.'

Silas kept his gaze fixed on the flowers. Not roses, but vaguely rose-like, with their pink petals contrasting with hearts of yellow pollen bobbing on long, black stems.

'They are...' he didn't mean to hesitate, but it was all a bit too much.

'Beautiful. They are beautiful, Silas,' Pitch said firmly.

'Of course, yes, yes. Superb.'

Enoch laughed, right from deep in his belly, and there again was that smile. Silas relaxed, if only a little, and made his way back to Pitch's side.

'I'm told you adore the garden, so I thought flowers a suitable welcome gift.'

Just as soon as the lord had put him at ease, he shifted Silas off-balance again. Who would have told him such things? And why the blazes would Enoch remember such a triviality?

'Yes, my lord. I do love the garden. Well, nature in general, I think.' Silas's tongue was like a spooked horse, racing away from him. 'I certainly feel most at ease amongst the foliage, with the ground beneath my feet. I can see you share my affinity for the soil. Nothing like dirt under the nails, wouldn't you say? I think perhaps, at some point, I was a gardener.' Pitch elbowed his leg. And it was only then that Silas took a breath. 'Forgive me, I am quite nervous, and talking far too much. I didn't mean to insult you...about the dirt...if it's dirt...it could be anything, I suppose.'

Pitch groaned. 'Silas...stop.'

'Sorry.' Silas clutched the bouquet so hard, it was a wonder the stems did not snap.

'You apologise a lot, don't you? They said that of you, too. But they also said you usually had nothing to apologise for, and were a decent, affable man. I quite agree.' Enoch turned his head. 'Why don't you come out, little one? I truly doubt Vassago will be angry with you for waking him. Both he and Mr Mercer shall have plenty of time to rest and recover. We won't keep them too much longer.'

For a moment, it seemed he'd spoken to thin air. Then a small sunrise peeked through the wild curls of his hair; apricots and strawberry hues, and a rounded pair of black, unblinking eyes.

'Scarlet.' Silas's voice cracked. 'Oh my god, look, Pitch.'

The wisp darted out of their hairy hiding place, whipping towards Silas with a speed that blew Lord Enoch's hair wide. Scarlet filled the air with their wondrous, happy colours, chittering madly, with arms outstretched, as though the tiny creature thought to hug him. Instead, they flattened themselves against his cheek, nuzzling and cheeping. Silas laughed against the vibrations of the wisp.

Scarlet buzzed away, a spectrum of colours radiating now as they focused on Pitch. He was still kneeling, staring wide-eyed at the wisp.

'Off your knees, Vassago,' Enoch said. 'And tell your friend they are quite forgiven for waking you. They've been most concerned about you both. It was no simple task keeping them out of here, and in the end, I just gave up.'

Silas watched Scarlet as they bobbed towards Pitch; the tiny critter whom the Lord of Arcadia had given in to. What in all the great confounding blazes was going on here?

Pitch rose to his feet and was bombarded. Scarlet went utterly mad with excitement around him: darting around his head, dashing into his hair and wriggling about like a chick caught in its nest.

'Will you sit still, you bloody lunatic?' Pitch shrugged his shoulder, screwing up his face, as Scarlet played in his hair. But his eyes glittered, his smile a quirk at the edge of his lips. 'My lord, how did they come to be here?'

'They chose Arcadia as their reward for assisting me.'

'Assisting you?' Pitch bowed his head. 'I beg your pardon, my lord, but how did a wisp assist you?'

Silas was bemused by Pitch's unfamiliar formality. This was such an unexpected day in so many ways. And likely not done with its surprises.

'In the way small things often do. Scarlet has been most gracious in allowing me to use them, so I might have my eyes and ears upon you.'

'You watched us?' Pitch's reply was far less acquiescent than the last. 'Through the wisp?'

'Yes.'

Silas's pleasant mood slipped.

'For how long?' Pitch did not quite demand an answer. He was close, though.

'How long have you known the wisp?'

Pitch took a step back, his hands clenched. 'You watched us all this time?'

'Well, not all of it,' Enoch said, as though the idea was simply preposterous. 'I have a world to command, and a war to see to, and the Celestials are most demanding on my time. But I dipped my toe when I could. Am I using that phrase as intended, Silas?'

The sudden swing of the conversation had Silas stuttering. 'I suppose it could...maybe. Yes, my lord. That's it exactly.' He bobbed his head, completely at a loss as to proper etiquette. Scarlet left Pitch's hair to plant themselves against Silas's bare chest, where the hair made for easy handholds. It pinched, but he was more concerned with how still Pitch had become.

'Scarlet was with me in the cockaigne.' The prince spoke too carefully. It made his stifled anger more obvious. 'So, you were there when I was held in that coffin?'

The boy, the lord, nodded, rocking on his feet, hands behind his back. 'For some of it, yes. Like I said, eyes and ears. I was an observer only. It is not for me to interfere in the design of the fates.'

Silas counted his breaths, feeling his own ire rise. The Lord of Arcadia was close to godliness then; for the gods spent their time simply watching, rarely interceding.

'You just stood by,' Pitch said quietly. 'You stood by when so many suffered.'

Scarlet pressed against Silas's chest, as still as the prince.

'Pitch...' he warned softly.

'I know you suffered, yes, Vassago.'

Pitch shook his head, knuckles pale. 'As Silas did, and Sybilla, and all those creatures who had no hope of challenging the horrors that befell them.'

'But they had a hope,' Enoch said. 'In you. And Silas. And Sybilla. Or they had hope in themselves, as did Charlie, or in their purpose, as it was for Edward. You did not need me, not a single one of you. And that is how it had to be. Or all hope was lost, anyway. Seraphiel chose his path, as did Samyaza. It is not for me to deny any creature their freedom by interfering. The chance to forge one's own destiny *is* my will. That is what I told Lucifer, and he understood.'

Silas stared down at the wisp, whose rainbow coloured his skin. 'Lucifer's free will nearly destroyed our chances, but in the end, he was the one who stood aside and allowed me to enter the lake. I'd like to thank him for that.'

'That won't be possible, I'm afraid,' Enoch said.

Silas glanced at Pitch, who frowned. 'What do you mean?'

'He has gone to the gods. Lucifer, and Seraphiel, gave of themselves to prevent the breakdown of the Seal. And to give you time, Vassago. Time you used in a manner that does their sacrifices honour.'

'May the gods seat King Lucifer at their right hand,' Forneus said, with reverence. He had shifted from prone to kneeling, his lanky legs curled up beneath him. All heads bowed.

Silas's blood chilled as the truth sunk in. 'Lucifer did not survive?'

'He did not.' Enoch's tone was like his features, neither here nor there; not unkind, but no hint of empathy, either. 'He made his choice, many of them, in fact. And they led him to the end of his road. It was his fate, and he set course towards it willingly.'

'Oh my god.' Silas's heart sought to pound out of his chest. 'Did all at the Sanctuary succumb?'

If one so powerful as Lucifer was lost, what hope for Charlie and Edward?

'No,' Enoch said. 'Because Lucifer ensured your friends would be safe. As he promised.'

Scarlet lifted from Silas's chest and flew to Pitch as he stumbled to the bedside, sitting heavily on the mattress. He stared ahead, fingers tight on the bedclothes.

Silas crouched down in front of him, placing his hands on his thighs, caring little when his own blanket slipped dangerously. 'Pitch, I am so sorry.' The relationship between prince and king had been complex, to say the very least, but Silas thought at the last it had softened. 'He did so much for us in the end. We have much to be grateful to him for.'

If Pitch heard him, there was no telling. He kept staring at something beyond Silas's shoulder. Beyond his reach.

'Was this his doing, then?' Pitch said, his tone dull. He did not look at Silas, but he shifted his hand so they touched. 'Did Lucifer make this Death Wish? Is it he who brought us back?'

Silas's legs shook with holding his weight in such a crouch, but he could not move. 'He was powerful enough for such things?'

'Perhaps,' Enoch said. 'If he had died as strong as he'd been made. But Lucifer was much ravaged by all that has come to pass. He was dying, as was the last remaining shred of Seraphiel's soul. Together, the angel and daemon were enough to prevent Michael, and the lake, from putting a premature end to your endeavour. But Lucifer had nothing left to give to a death wish.'

Pitch stood, and the suddenness would have cast Silas onto his arse if not for Scarlet. The wisp burrowed at his back, just strong enough to prevent a fall.

'Then who fucking did, my lord?' Pitch chewed on the title. 'We have had a fucking rotten day, so forgive me if my patience wears thin.'

Silas scrambled to his feet, reaching for Pitch. A wave of light-headedness struck. His outstretched arm blurred through speckled vision. A strike of memory dazzled him; an image of light and silhouettes. A goddess reaching for him.

'Shit.'

'Silas?' Pitch slipped beneath his outstretched arm, bolstering him. 'What's happening? Talk to me.'

Those words drew Silas back. He'd worn them thin during their time together, but this was the first time they had come from Pitch.

Silas blinked, his mouth desert-dry. 'Izanami. The goddess did this.'

He felt Pitch tense, felt his warmth grow. 'This? Us? Brought us back?'

'Yes. She did.' Enoch's appearance merely mimicked human; Silas saw it now. The lord was too still, too constantly poised. He did not understand that mortality made for restlessness. Humanity did not have the luxury of standing still; there was not time. 'You were Her favoured child, Silas Mercer. As Seraphiel was for me. My Seraph was over zealous in his bid to please me and if he were not already dead I would have no choice but to make it so...again.' Silas swallowed, and Pitch pressed in closer. 'But his sacrifice purified him, thankfully. Both he and Lucifer shall not be judged too harshly by the Celestials. But judgement is not something you need worry about, Mr Mercer. You have pleased your goddess very much. She rewards you greatly. It is Death's wish that you be granted what you were deprived of for so long.'

'And what was that?' Silas asked. That commanding, fathomless voice he'd held now barely an echo. 'What was I deprived of?'

Truly, he felt blessed already. Having this precious time with Pitch; pleasure after such pain.

The lord did not blink, nor shift at all; hands behind his back, bare feet upon cold stone. 'Life, Silas. You were deprived of your life.'

Silas stayed quiet, thoughtful, as he lifted the blanket and once more drew the all-too-quiet daemon into its folds. They pressed close, and Scarlet nestled between their shoulders. 'And did she grant Pitch such a miracle, too?'

'She is a goddess, Silas, she is no fool. What point in making you mortal, giving you years in which to live freely and perhaps grow old, if you spend them in deep and bitter mourning? But Izanami is not a Celestial of Arcadia. Under normal circumstances, the prince's fate would be beyond her control. But the death of her sister Morrigan, at your hands, Silas, has lifted her ranking among the gods. Combined with my full support of her endeavour to relight Vassago's Creation Flame, Her Death Wish has been honoured in its entirety.'

'You are truly benevolent, your grace,' Forneus muttered.

'Well, we know that is not true,' Enoch said with a shrug. 'I had a vested interest in Vassago's return.'

Pitch inhaled, his release long and controlled. 'And what is that interest, my lord?'

'I want something from you.'

'Bloody hell,' Silas muttered, pulling the blanket tighter.

'Go on,' Pitch said.

'You both shall remain here in Lucifer's Tower. Recovering and enjoying the start of your new lives. Silas will need time to adjust to our world, of course. I'm sure you shall be adept in teaching him its ways.'

'I shall be very thorough,' Pitch said, giving Silas a nudge. But Silas was far too shocked to do more than stare dumbly. 'Is that it, then? You want me to play schoolmaster? I agree to your terms in that case.'

'Those are not my terms, but they are reward. I want something else of you.'

Silas could feel Pitch's mood darken. 'Have I not done enough, my lord?'

'You have done far more than enough. Even I could not determine the likelihood of the Seraph's Cultivation working.'

'You knew of the simurgh, of Seraphiel's plans, right from the start,' Pitch said, no question in it.

'Of course. I am the Lord of Arcadia,' he said, as though that explained it all, which it did. 'Lucifer thought he stole you from the abaddon through his expertise alone. I never told him such a feat was impossible without my hand in it. But even once it was done, and the die cast, I placed no bets on your success. I tended towards a nugatory outcome.' Pitch huffed beneath his breath. 'And you surprised me. I like that. So, here is why I implored Arcadia's gods to grant Izanami's wish. When the time comes, and I ask it of you, you shall take your sire's place.'

Pitch dug his nails into Silas's waist. 'You wish me to become a King of Daemonkind?'

'Yes. And I'm sure those in my council at White Mountain can be made agreeable to you taking a purebred as your consort. Your union would have my blessing, so it will be done.'

Silas pressed his lips tight, frightened the thoughts in his head might burst out. His language would be quite appalling.

Pitch laughed. A very inelegant sound. He pressed his fingers to his lips. 'I see. What longevity did the goddess grant us? A week? A few days? If I am to be king for a day, then I agree wholeheartedly. How about you, Silas? Are you happy with being a royal bed mate for a day or two?'

Silas just stared. And Scarlet tittered, far too amused for his liking.

Enoch smiled. A weapon, Silas decided, for it disarmed and beguiled, and made a man think perhaps everything would be perfectly fine. 'The goddess does not give her secrets away,' the lord said. 'You shall live as all others do, not knowing when your last day has arrived.' His warm gaze shifted to Silas, who felt it like a strike of gentle lightning. 'You are human, Silas, with all their vulnerabilities. You will die one day. But not this one, nor the next. So take your pleasures as you will.' He looked to Pitch. 'Both of you. Now, Forneus will stay in your service, to see to all your needs.'

The hydra, a consummate professional so far as being seen and not heard was concerned, nodded emphatically. 'Anything you wish for, your highness, my lord, ask and you shall receive. I am here for your every whim. Ever loyal, ever efficient, ever –'

Enoch held up his hand. 'Thank you, Forneus. Let us leave these gentlemen to enjoy one another in whichever regard they see fit.'

'Oh, they have very vigorous regard for each other, my lord,' Forneus said, rather unnecessarily.

'Purebreds are fond of vigorous regard, Forneus. Hence why I allow Vassago to retain his human form here.'

Three heads nodded. 'Yes, my lord. I see the fortuitousness of that now. There could be no vigorous regard if his highness took his true form, could there?'

'Well, there could be, but I doubt Mr Mercer would survive it.' The Lord of Arcadia turned on his dirty heels. 'Come along Scarlet, you promised to draw me a picture of that coat you say Mr Mercer is fond of, so it can be replicated.'

'And the coblet, for his highness.' Forneus's multiple feet, or rather small black hooves, clicked against the stone.

'I think you'll find it's called a corset, Forneus.'

'Yes, my lord. Sounds dreadful, if I'm honest.'

'Best not to be then, for your master has a taste for them, so Scarlet says.'

The wisp lifted from Pitch's shoulder and executed a loop in the air, the streaks of their colours streaming out behind them. They darted straight at Enoch, slipping in under his smock, emerging a moment later.

Tottering with the load they carried.

Silas stared in astonishment at the wooden disks; a dirty white string dangling from between them. 'The bandalore.'

'And only that now, I'm afraid.' Enoch settled his smock where Scarlet's invasion caught it on the waist of his breeches. 'I forgot I had it.

Immortality is troublesome that way. Izanami wanted it passed to you. A memento.'

The wisp darted back to Silas, dropping it onto his outstretched hand. Scarlet gave them an imperious salute, and then zipped away, squeaking at Enoch's ear as he walked them both out the door, humming with interest at whatever it was the wisp had to say. The lord left dirty footprints as he went.

Pitch and Silas stared down at the bandalore. Neither moved to touch it.

Forneus cleared his throat. 'Right, well, is there anything that I can –'

'Leave us,' Pitch said. 'Leave now.'

'Excellent. Just pull on this chain here, if you need something, and I'll –'

'Forneus, go.' Pitch was firm. 'Thank you for your service, but do not disturb us the rest of this day. I wish to show my human some vigorous regard.'

Silas's cheeks burned. Forneus rushed from the room, doing so at a backwards trot whilst bowing; impressive, considering all the limbs.

When he was gone, Silas said quietly, 'You are not disappointed?'

'About what?'

'That I am only human.' In truth, it did not feel so bad.

Pitch lifted the bandalore from Silas's hand. 'And that I don't have to share you with Death any longer? That I'll never again have to watch the anguish of lost souls consume you? Yes, terribly disappointed.' He toyed with the bandalore's thin silver string. 'What of you? Are you disappointed, my dearest? Your goddess has been very gracious. But she wanted to gift you a life you have been denied...in your world, with your gardens to wander, and your kind to live amongst. Perhaps you imagine having a family, taking strolls in the sunshine, going to dinner parties and simply being mundane. You deserve as much. But you are trapped here in this tower, with me, and all this ridiculous talk of kingship. Arcadia is not simple, nor would a life here be. I understand if you wish to be returned to your world. To Charlie, and Edward, and all who loved you there. I will not resent you for it.'

He had begun flippantly, but by the end Pitch was so earnest, so obviously afraid, Silas's heart ached. 'Pitch...'

'Yes?'

'You are a dolt.'

Brows lifted, and that perfect cupid-bow mouth parted. He wriggled free of the blanket trappings. 'That's no way to speak to a King of Daemonkind.'

'Lucky you are only a prince then.'

'Bastard! I shall have to punish you.'

'I should hope so.' Silas cast the bandalore away, tossing it onto the wing-back chair with its stacked books, waiting for a reader who would never return. Perhaps Silas would begin his new life by learning to read; in honour of Lucifer. 'I have just the punishment in mind. Though I suspect I won't hate it very much.'

Pitch laughed, turning away. Silas could have bathed in the sound of his happiness.

Which gave him a marvellous idea. He stared unashamedly at Pitch's glorious arse as he leaned over the bed to rearrange the pillows. 'Would you mind if we called Forneus back first? I have a request.'

Pitch gave him a quizzical look. 'He does not have a cock, if you're hoping for a threesome.'

'I am not hoping that. I am not sharing you. But I'd like him to draw a bath. Hot as he can make it, and deep.'

He relished the sharp lift of Pitch's chest. 'So you might watch me bathe? We know you enjoy a good peep.'

Silas loomed over the prince, for he could still do that well, and pressed him back gently onto the bed. The prince went willingly. Silas braced his hands on either side of Pitch's head, hungry for him once more. 'So I might bathe *with* you. Lie with you in the water until it is filthy with all we do to each other. This is my new life, after all. I shall start it unafraid.'

'Dare we believe it?' Pitch gazed up at him. His eyes had never held such a verdant gleam. 'That all this is real for us? I'm frightened that if I step outside those doors, there shall be only emptiness, or a cruel illusion.'

Silas kissed his forehead, then drew back so they could both clamber beneath the covers, and find their well-worn places against one another. They lay face to face, legs tangled. 'Then we don't step outside. Not until we are both ready. We don't leave this bed until you are so sick of me making love to you that you beg for escape.'

Pitch laughed. 'I have remarkable endurance.'

'I don't doubt it.' Silas drew the bedclothes over their heads, so they were both lost beneath warm layers. Into the dimness, he said, 'But I mean what I say. It is just you and I. For however long we need.'

'Just you and I.' Pitch pressed his lips to Silas's chest. 'I adore that idea, Mr Mercer.'

'As do I, Mr Astaroth.' He traced his fingers through his lover's hair, and dared to believe what Pitch could not; that this was no illusion. Silas's heart beat hard and true. 'Tell me, how should we begin, my love?'

Pitch's smile was bewitching. He leaned in close and whispered his desire; and Silas learnt at long last, what it was to be truly alive.

The End

ABOUT THE AUTHOR

Danielle K Girl is an Aussie living in stunning Tasmania with her three furkids, cats Luffy, Sweetie and Ren; and feathered fowl ladies, hens, Calliope and Hyacinth. She's continuing a lifelong fascination with all creatures that go bump in the night; and the dark and spooky and macabre tales of folklore and legend. She'd never call herself a history buff, but thinks history is pretty damn buff nonetheless, and loves searching for new story ideas amongst the lives of all the folk who have come before us.

Check out my online store!
Find Ebooks, Paperbacks and Exclusive Bundles.

And come say Hello on the socials!
https://www.instagram.com/daniellekgirl/
https://www.facebook.com/DKGirlbooks

Bonus 'Alternate' Chapters

Thank you for reading the series.
To soften the blow of saying goodbye to the boys, scan the QR Code to receive your bonus 'alternate' chapters from The Death Wish.
(Via StoryOrigin app. Ebook file only. Includes option for PDF and EPub)